A STRAND of GOLD

Elizabeth Connor

A STRAND of GOLD

Elisabeth Conway

atmosphere press

For Christopher, with love

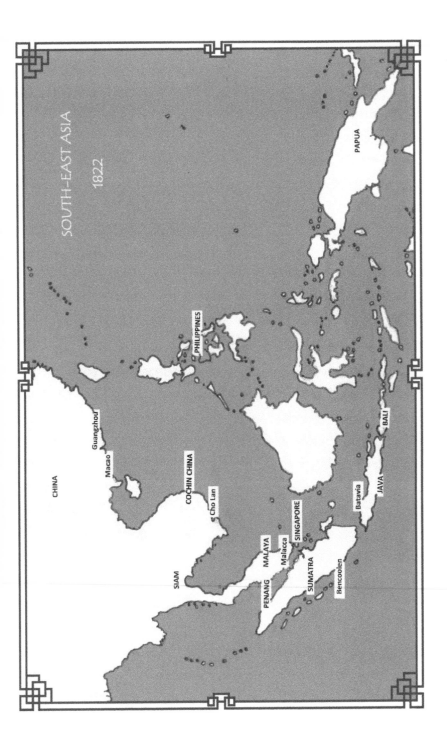

PROLOGUE
23ʳᵈ January, 1822, Guangzhou

'Hurry, Papa, we'll miss the Lion Dance.'

'Patience, daughter.' Li Soong Heng smiles as he guides her ahead of the crowd. The procession will move in their direction soon enough. But now he needs her to focus on the entertainment whilst he scrutinises each face for any sign of recognition.

He lifts Chin Ming onto an old abandoned wooden crate and is amused when she protests. He realises that at eighteen, she wants to be treated as an adult, but he knows she will enjoy the spectacle more from this vantage point. He wants her to relish every moment, knowing the dangers they are about to embark upon.

A moment later the first creature, mimicking a yellow lion, leaps into the air and begins to prance towards them. Chin Ming claps her hands together; she beams at her father as flashes of yellow and white sway before her in time to the music. He feigns interest, but his main concern is to find the man he's arranged to meet here today - when will he make himself known?

'What's wrong, Papa?' he hears his daughter ask, but is saved from answering by the arrival of a band of drummers. Two men, who strike their cymbals loud and strong, join in to demand her attention. There is still no sign of the man who has promised to meet him. How much longer will they have to wait? They must leave Guangzhou behind and start a new life. Today, amidst the turmoil of the spring festival celebration, is the perfect opportunity.

The cymbals accompanying the yellow lion are now muted in the distance. They will be joined shortly by the red lion. Soong Heng's heart misses a beat as a small group, anxious to follow, bumps into Chin Ming's platform. He helps her regain her balance and is relieved to hear more drums, heralding the appearance of the third lion. Gongs begin to sound as it comes into view.

'Oh look, Papa,' she says. 'It's the one who loves to fight - the black lion. His ears are tiny, and his beard is as black as his face. Can you see?'

'I can indeed daughter,' Soong Heng says as the vibrating bells on the creature's body reach a deafening crescendo. He is pleased that Chin Ming is so delighted with the spectacle; happy also that she is unaware it may be the last time she sees such a performance. When the time comes, how will he explain everything to her? How will he persuade her to move quickly and not ask any questions?

He keeps looking over his shoulder, searching the crowd for a clue. How much longer? he asks himself.

All of a sudden, a new group begins to bear down on them; they wave banners and shout in a dialect with which he is unfamiliar. The other spectators become agitated. They know instinctively that these people are nothing to do with the celebrations.

Soong Heng sees Chin Ming look towards him for reassurance. He smiles, but beyond her, he recognises one of the men he has accused of being involved with the opium trade. It is not the man he is expecting, his blood runs cold. He steps closer to Chin Ming.

'Take this,' he whispers, sliding a tiny scroll tied together with fine gold thread into her hand. 'Keep it safe for me,' he says quietly. 'You must get it to the man called Raffles in Singapore.'

'What is it, Papa? Why are you looking so troubled?'

A foul-smelling cloth is held against his mouth. There is no escape from the man his enemies have sent to silence him. The crowd surges forward like a great tsunami. People begin to scream, the sound of gongs and cymbals assaulting their eardrums.

As he is dragged along, Soong Heng sees Chin Ming through a blur, fear on her face. Her arm is raised up above her head as if she is reaching out to him. The last image he has is seeing her fall; she is being carried along in a sea of bodies. Helpless now, he hears her scream, 'Papa, where are you Papa?'

CHAPTER 1
22nd September 1822, Guangzhou

Chin Ming knew Papa would not deliberately abandon her, but the memory of him being dragged away haunted her every single night. Maybe he was being held somewhere as Father John suggested. Maybe he was sick, but she refused to believe that he was dead. All she could remember now, after the arrival of the black lion, was the crush of bodies, losing sight of Papa, the noise, the shouting and ... falling. They said she's been trampled on, but she had little memory of anything after hiding the scroll Papa had pressed into her hand; that, and his last words.

She needed to find out what had happened and deliver Papa's scroll to the man in Singapore. If she stood any hope of seeing him again, that's the place he would begin to look for her.

She had clothes and books, but very little money. There was no way that she could purchase a passage on any of the ships in the harbour. If only she could get aboard one of the vessels without anyone noticing.

Unable to get this thought out of her head, Chin Ming made her way down to the quay. It was, as usual, a clandestine visit, because she wasn't supposed to go there on her own. She was careful to choose a place where she could survey all the activity, whilst keeping herself well-hidden. She squeezed between two carts - one was piled high with vegetables, the other had chickens in bamboo cages balanced precariously one on top of the other. An elderly farmer wandered towards her, intent on leading his pig through the crowd with a rope hung around its neck. She ducked down further to make sure that he didn't see her, but when he swerved away and headed in the direction of the rough and ready buildings in the centre of the square, she eased herself forward to a place which afforded a better view. She scrutinised everything very carefully and continued to watch the multitude of activities involved in preparing the ships for their next voyage. She quickly became aware of the methodical manner of loading the junks, how the crew dressed, the type of cargo taken on board and where each ship was bound. Today was the first time she'd taken any notice of all the young boys who constantly scurried up and down the gangplanks. They looked like the ants that made their determined way across the kitchen whenever someone spilled the sugar. She decided, on her way back to the Mission, that if she could change her appearance so she looked like one of those boys, then she may have a chance. It would be easy enough to plait her hair, and she could borrow one of the coolie hats that lay around the Mission, but it would be more difficult to find any clothes similar to those worn by these young workers. If she was to blend in with the frenzy of people loading supplies for the voyage, that would be essential.

She was still agonising with this idea when Father John came looking for her. She followed him to a room towards the back of the building, where he pointed to a vast collection of clothes folded away in a cupboard. It was an assortment accumulated over many months, and given out to unfortunate poverty-stricken souls, of whom there were many around the docks.

'Could you sort through the whole pile?' he said. 'Decide what's useful and what's too old and needs to be thrown away.'

Chin Ming began by pulling everything out of the cupboard onto the floor. Some of the things she came across turned out to be only fit for rags, but she decided she could salvage most of the items. She began to make a list, grouping them into three piles - trousers, shirts, plus miscellaneous odds and ends. She secretly hoped there might be something that she could take for herself, but the majority appeared to be European in style with only an occasional pair of peasant trousers. She was beginning to think that she'd never find anything suitable, when she picked up one pair of trousers, much smaller than the rest - exactly what she needed. The next pair was almost identical and ordinary enough; she was sure that they wouldn't be missed. She felt slightly nauseous and light-headed; it was almost too good to be true. She took a few deep breaths and then returned to the task with renewed energy; a plan was beginning to take shape in her head.

She examined the remaining garments carefully; so far, she had been unable to find a shirt that would fit. Her inventory was growing long, but there was nothing else that she could take for herself. Nearly every week, someone handed in a bundle of clothes to the Mission - she would just have to be patient. She was reading through the list that she'd prepared for Father John when she discovered one last bag that had been missed earlier. About halfway through the package she found a plain grey shift - it was perfect. She folded up all three garments, left the inventory in a place where Father John would easily find it, and tiptoed back to her room. There, she hid her treasures under the mattress.

*****

One week later.

It was almost two months now since Father John had last tried to caution Chin Ming about the perils of going out alone. She always responded by reminding him that she could easily find her way around the city. It was true, she had accompanied her father everywhere, even along the back alleys and the short-cuts. They had eventually reached a compromise; she could venture out for a short time each morning, provided she agreed to wear one of the cloaks belonging to a novice monk over her brightly coloured tunic. Today, she had seized the opportunity to deliver a message to the harbourmaster.

Once the errand was accomplished, she found herself drawn further along the quay towards her usual hiding place, but this time she stayed only a few minutes. Her attention was immediately captured by one particular ship, it was the largest and most magnificent junk she had ever seen. She edged nearer, hoping to remain unnoticed, wanting to discover its name; it was called the *Golden Phoenix*. She thought that was perfect and suited the vessel completely. Could it perhaps be an omen? Towards the stern, she noticed two deckhands who stood idly chatting to each other, maybe they would be able to tell her where the ship was heading. She strolled towards them.

'When is the *Golden Phoenix* due to leave?' she said, hoping that they understood Cantonese.

'Tomorrow,' the shorter man said.

'Where is it going?'

'None of your business,' the other man barked at her.

'No harm in telling her we're off to Singapore,' his mate said. 'It's not as if she's going to be coming with us, is it?'

The men both laughed; Chin Ming turned away before the tall man said anything else. She didn't want anyone to ask what she was doing there. Her excitement mounted as she hurried back along the quay. She noticed some other members of the crew loading bales of silk - all the colours of the rainbow, large wicker baskets packed tightly with porcelain, and other packages whose content was not obvious. None of that mattered to her, the important thing was that this fine-looking vessel was bound for Singapore. Papa had often talked about the small island and how they would make a new home there;

but of greater significance now was the fact that it was where he'd said she would find the man called Raffles. As she made her way back to the Mission there was only one thought in her mind.

She tried to hurry, but local merchants going about their business packed the narrow lanes. Groups of men huddled together in conversation and processions of Chinese servants ran past taking jars of water to the factories belonging to foreign traders. She zigzagged between them, trying not to draw too much attention to herself, but it was difficult. Eventually, she managed to squeeze passed some of them and slip into the British compound. She stopped for a moment, to let her eyes travel upwards to the triangular gable on top of the elegant, white stone columns that sparkled in the sunlight. She loved the circle of sculptured leaves, its detail as neat and tidy as the well-tended gardens that lay between the complex and the river.

She was only a short way across the peaceful courtyard, when Father John hurried towards her and her heart sank. A tall, slim man, his gentle face was now crumpled into an anxious frown.

'Chin Ming, where have you been? It's well over two hours since you left to take my note to the harbourmaster, I was getting worried.'

'I'm sorry Father. I delivered the message, but the streets are really busy today. When she'd caught sight of the *Golden Phoenix*, everything else had gone out of her head and she'd simply lost count of the time.

Father John knew, of course, that whenever she left the confines of the Mission, she often spent her time talking to various people, listening to others, or simply strolling through the market. It was natural that such an intelligent young woman would not want to be confined within these walls. Nevertheless, he felt responsible for her care and worried constantly until he knew of her safe return.

'Well, at least you're back before everyone takes their afternoon nap,' the priest said, not unkindly. He studied her for a moment.

'People criticise me for letting you go out unchaperoned in the morning, but to see a young lady alone on the streets in the afternoon would be unforgivable.'

'But Father,' she began.

'I know what you're going to say, Chin Ming. Your Papa encouraged you to do all sorts of things, but now you don't have him to look out for you, I'm afraid you need to behave differently. I don't want to be told that you too have disappeared or that your body has been found in the ditch.' She flinched when she heard the word *disappeared* and closed her eyes, blocking out the bad memories.

'You must be careful,' the priest continued. 'There are people who condemn the way your father brought you up. Many of them are the same people who do not approve of the Mission. I've always thought that it might have been such a person who betrayed your Papa.'

She was uneasy. 'I'm sorry to upset you, Father, but I do try to behave like a grown-up, just like Papa taught me. He wanted me to learn to be independent.'

'But you have led such a sheltered life, Chin Ming. You do not have enough experience of the world to survive on your own. There are wicked people around, always looking for an opportunity to do bad things. I think it might be wise if we try to find a suitable family with whom you can settle down.'

'But Father,' she said, 'Papa would not like that.' She needed to think of an excuse quickly; all her plans would be thwarted if Father John went ahead with such a proposal.

'Papa always said I was not the same as other daughters. I think I would not fit in. Neither Mama nor Papa believed in foot-binding, it is not a Hakka custom; most people think my feet are ugly and too large.' She took a deep breath before continuing. 'I was not brought up in a village, expecting to have a marriage arranged for me, and have no experience of all those traditions. I have no Elder Sister or Elder Brother to guide me - and, until I can find Papa, I have no family now.'

'I am aware of all of these things, Chin Ming,' sighed the priest, 'and that is the problem. Your father believed you should be educated, as a son might be educated. Now he is not here, I'm afraid your upbringing may cause a great many problems.'

She knew, deep down, that the priest was only concerned for her welfare. Perhaps taking on the responsibility for someone like herself was beginning to take its toll. Chin Ming hung her head but said nothing. She knew Father John believed that her father was probably dead.

'I'm sorry to remind you of something so upsetting,' he continued. 'It is only because your father was my great friend and I care about you that I worry. Let's not discuss it any further now. They've kept some food for you in the kitchen,' he said, changing the subject. 'You'd better go there quickly and make your peace with cook.'

She was just scraping the last spoonful from her bowl when Father John put his head around the kitchen door. She thought he looked apprehensive. He was always busy with never enough time to fit everything in. So, why was he looking for her again, what did he want to talk to her about? Was it because she'd reacted badly to his earlier idea? She hadn't meant to upset him.

He walked across to where she was sitting and sat on the bench opposite. Chin Ming put down her spoon and looked across at him. He wore a simple brown hooded robe, drawn together at the waist by a corded rope belt.

'Father, may I ask you something?'

'What is troubling you, my child?' he replied.

'Why are you so sure that Papa is dead?'

The event that had taken place back in the spring was the last thing on his mind. As often happened though, he was completely taken aback by her candour. He paused for a moment before attempting to reply.

'Your father was an intellectual, Chin Ming, he was always wanting to engage in discussion and explore new ideas, but I'm afraid there are many people - those with of lot of influence - who did not approve of his attitude or the opinions he held. You see, most people just want an easy life, they don't like change and some of the things your father talked about made them feel uneasy. They thought he was criticising them. He once told me that he suspected some of the other *Shenshi* had become corrupted - do you understand what I'm saying?'

'Papa said he felt sad because some of his fellow scholars took bribes from the secret societies, is that what you mean?'

'Exactly. They also said he should be more resolute in his Confucian beliefs and show less interest in Christianity. You may not know this, but your father reported an unscrupulous Dutchman to the authorities. I suspect someone found out it was he and decided to punish him.'

'How would they do that?'

'I do not know, Chin Ming, I have no evidence. Maybe he was kidnapped, maybe he was seized and is being held prisoner somewhere? Maybe he did indeed escape, then something went wrong, and he was unable to come back for you. I fear we may never really know the truth. I'm not even sure that these bad men know that you are still alive. The couple who brought you here after the incident at the docks just pulled the bell and left you on the doorstep. I have no idea whether anyone was paid to bring you here or, whether they brought you here by chance.'

'Will you get into trouble, Father, for letting me stay? I know Chinese aren't supposed to come to the foreign factories unless they are the servants who bring the water.'

'We may be based in the British factory, Chin Ming, but we are not engaged in foreign trade so there is nothing for you to worry about. Now you're fully recovered, I'd like to engage your help. More and more children are being sent to us all the time. I thought you might like to show them how to write their name? You see, I suspect you may have inherited your father's talent for teaching. May I ask you to think about it?'

Chin Ming smiled at the priest and thanked him. He rose from his seat and nodded to her, indicating that their conversation, for the moment, was at an end.

When he had gone, Chin Ming left the kitchen. She climbed the two flights of stairs to her room to think about what she needed to do; it was time to put her plans into practice. The junk she'd seen in the harbour today might be the only opportunity she would get.

She knew Cook worked non-stop from the time that he woke up until the last person had eaten; he would now be taking a well-deserved nap. She crept back down the stairs and checked carefully before entering the kitchen, making sure there was no one else around.

All was quiet apart from the soft, rhythmic snoring coming from the adjacent room. Cook was in the habit of making extra food, in the form of steamed dumplings, so that they could be offered to any unexpected guests. They would be ideal for her journey, but she needed to choose wisely, taking some containing red bean paste; they would remain fresh much longer than those with pork or egg. She looked at a bowl filled with dried fish but dismissed the idea because of their distinctive odour; it might give away any hiding place she managed to find. Instead, she chose some dried fruit - peaches, plums, and kumquats. Without a sound, she wrapped it all into a piece of muslin cloth.

Her main problem would be a supply of water. On a shelf, under the bowls of food and storage containers, she recognised a row of flasks. The missionaries used these vessels when they went travelling. Just as she was about to lift one up there was an enormous grunt, followed by a series of wheezing noises from the room next door. She stood perfectly still and held her breath. A few seconds later there was another noisy inhalation of air from the exhausted cook before he sank back into a heavy slumber.

Chin Ming listened and waited until she was absolutely sure that it was safe to move. Then, she quietly took the largest flask she could find and tiptoed over to a storage jar in the far corner of the kitchen. She filled it right up to the brim. Even as she replaced the stopper, she knew, no matter how careful she was, the precious liquid would not last long.

Back in her room, she put together her few precious possessions - a change of clothes, the small collection of food, and her water flask. She looked sadly at the collection of books she'd brought from her home, but knew they had to be left behind. Instead, she opened one of the volumes and took out a single sheet of paper. It was the scroll that Papa had given to her for safe-keeping and charged her to deliver to the man he'd named in Singapore. She marvelled at the fact that she had managed to keep the letter hidden for the last eight months. Now, she rolled it into a tiny scroll again and tied it with the gold ribbon; then she unpicked the stitches in the hem of her shirt, slipped the precious document into its new hiding place and carefully - very carefully - began to sew.

CHAPTER 2
30th September 1822, Guangzhou

On one of the small upper decks of the *Golden Phoenix* stood another Chinese woman, some ten or so years older than Chin Ming. Before today, Wing Yee had never been on any type of vessel other than a sampan and knew nothing about the preparations needed for a long voyage. She'd come aboard with her charge last night, just after dusk. The captain had given her a perfunctory welcome before escorting them to the small cabin that had been set aside for their use. She'd expected him to summon her later in the evening, but no word had come, and they had been left entirely alone. Now it was already light, and she needed to get away from the tight confines of the cabin. She wanted to fill her lungs with fresh air, but all she could smell right now was a mixture of freshly oiled teak wood, fish and human sweat.

She was aware that some members of the crew, who should be busily engaged in hauling aboard the remaining cargo, occasionally glanced in her direction and muttered under their breath to each other. She was used to men gazing at her, but she never ceased to be repulsed by such sordid scrutiny. Her skin was still pale and flawless, there was no trace of grey in her long, black hair. She was as slim as ever, and the blue and gold tunic she wore over a matching ankle-length skirt simply enhanced her attractiveness. Nevertheless, she had lost confidence of late and the way they looked at her made her feel like a piece of meat in the market. She moved away to seek a different view and searched the skyline for anything she could recognise.

'Are you looking for anything in particular?' a familiar male voice asked in Cantonese. Wing Yee turned to see Captain Lim looking at her quizzically.

'I'm not sure what to look for,' she replied. 'I've lived in Guangzhou for the last fourteen years but have very rarely stepped outside the confines of Madam Ong's establishment. I'm unacquainted with most of the city.'

The captain, who had always viewed her as a sophisticated woman, was taken aback, but didn't let his surprise show. He pointed out the Plain Minaret of the Huaisheng Mosque, which could just be seen in the distance. 'It's a shame you can't see the roof from here,' he said. 'That's what makes it unusual. And sadly, the Temple of Six Banyan Trees is also hidden, but look, there's the Zhenhai pagoda, you must recognise that surely? It's so tall, it can be seen from all over the city.' He turned to smile at her and waited for a response, but she remained silent. 'You're not regretting your decision to leave, are you?'

'What is there to regret?' she replied. 'I've been wanting to get away from Madam Ong from the very first moment my mother left me on her doorstep. You have simply provided me with an opportunity to fulfil my dreams.'

'I hate to disappoint you,' the captain replied, 'but life with Boon Peng may not be that good, he's old, over-weight, and not very handsome.'

'But I will be looked after,' Wing Yee said. 'That's why I agreed to be part of this scheme. As his concubine, I will have somewhere of my own to live and he will provide for me, even when he tires of me. I've worked for Madam Ong long enough to know how quickly men tire of women. In another year, I will reach my thirtieth summer, what will happen to me then? If Madam Ong decides I am no longer useful to her, I will be thrown out onto the street; I will have no home, no means of support. No, I need to leave Guangzhou before that happens.'

'But what will I do when you are no longer here?' the captain protested. 'You know how much I look forward to our times together. Whenever the *Golden Phoenix* returns to Guangzhou, my first thought is of seeing you. I ask for no one else. When you belong to Boon Peng, I will never see you again.'

'Yes, but that is how it must be,' Wing Yee snapped. 'A man like you, a *daban*, has a life bound to his ship, that is your world. This is my chance to have a different - a better kind of life. I've waited a long time for this; I have to make my own destiny.'

'Maybe you will fail in your task. Remember, Boon Peng wanted to choose from three women, and we are taking only one for his English friend. You need to make sure there is no trace of opium on her by the time we reach Singapore. If that part of the bargain isn't fulfilled, then no money will be exchanged. The Englishman won't get his mistress and Boon Peng will not be taking a new concubine. You'll have to stay on board with me,' he said, 'and sail on the high seas for the rest of your life!'

Wing Yee didn't know if the captain was serious, or if he was merely joking. She was sure she could hear him chuckling to himself as he returned to his cabin. His attitude irritated her. He pretended that he would like to have her all to himself, but they both knew the idea was impossible. She needed to concentrate on her plan. She would not be distracted by his frivolity. As soon as they left Guangzhou behind, she would gradually reduce the amount of opium available to Shu Fang. She was deter-mined to achieve her goal.

Wing Yee had never visited the harbour area of the city before last night. Life had been hard, but she had never let herself be seduced by the temporary relief of opium and found it difficult to sympathise with others who lacked her strong will. Neither was she beguiled by any of the men who told her that she was lovely. Almost from her first day in Guangzhou, she'd shut off from all emotion in order to protect herself and keep sane. Even when her status had risen, and she was required to welcome only a small number of select clients, her defences remained resolute; she made sure that no one ever got really close to her, not even Captain Lim.

Now, as she looked down on the ordinariness of the buildings that surrounded the quay, she allowed herself - for a short time only - to wish that her life could have been different. The newer buildings held no interest, but the makeshift structures in the centre of the square commanded her attention. Captain Lim had told her that farmers used them when they brought their produce to market. As a child, she had been happy living in the village. If her life had been different, she would have been content to live in the countryside, and maybe even to marry a farmer. She sighed, knowing the idea was ridiculous.

Her gaze travelled to the older establishments that bordered the square. All of them, had at least one elaborately carved dragon keeping watch over the soft, ochre patterns created by their rounded roof tiles. She'd discovered that these well-worn buildings, tall and thin, provided a family home as well as an open-fronted warehouse. Vast numbers of people, who all made their living out of the activities connected with a busy port lodged there, just as they had done for generations. Would she ever see such sights again?

A clattering sound attracted her attention, as hawkers - even at this early hour - began to set up their stalls on the quay below. She was aware, of course, that much of the food delivered to Madam Ong's establishment came from the street vendors, but having been confined within the house, she had never seen anything like this before. Each stand had a frame which extended above and across the top of the cooking area. She could see that the heat came from a charcoal burner hidden within the box-like base, and hanging from the crossbar, she could see onions, herbs, and baskets of eggs.

Behind one stall, she could see an elderly woman clothed in a floral blouse and the ubiquitous black trousers favoured by coolies and ordinary folk alike. The woman wiped her hands down the front of her all-encompassing apron. In front of her, Wing Yee could see a vast array of ingredients - basins full of peppers, bean sprouts, mushrooms, and other vegetables. Some sort of netting protected the chicken wings, preserved pork and sliced fish and the woman kept steamed rice and noodles warm alongside the bowls and chopsticks that her customers would need.

There was nothing wrong with Wing Yee's eyesight or her sense of smell. Mouth-watering aromas began to reach her, and she longed to venture down the gangplank for a simple bowl of noodles.

As she turned, she just avoided bumping into a young boy carrying a blue metal tiffin carrier, held firmly together within a wooden frame. It was almost as big as the youth. 'Captain say, give you food.' He turned to point in the direction of the opposite deck, but there was no sign of Captain Lim. The youth placed the container beside Wing Yee's feet and scurried back towards the gangplank. She watched him for a while, ducking and diving between the coolies as they continued to heave the remaining cargo on board. The youth then completely disappeared amongst the multitude of people along the quay.

Wing Yee carried the food to the entrance of her cabin and opened the door. The stale odour of bodies in a confined space – laced with the sweet suggestion of opium – wafted out to greet her. She seized a jug from just inside the room and went in search of water. As well as persuading Shu Fang to eat a little, she knew that it was vital to keep her hydrated.

She returned to the main deck, where she'd seen the water barrels situated, and filled the jug almost to the brim. As she was replacing the lid of the barrel, making sure it fitted properly, she noticed there was a cupboard just behind it. The door was hanging at a peculiar angle and remained slightly ajar. Wing Yee glanced inside, but the space was empty. She wondered why no one had noticed it, and why it hadn't been repaired. She presumed everyone was too busy doing other things right now, and it was only a small cupboard, probably of no significance on such a large ship, so she picked up the jug and carefully conveyed it back to the cabin.

'Look what I've brought for you,' she announced. 'Captain Lim had this food delivered especially for us. It's probably the last decent meal we'll have for some time so why don't you sit up and we can enjoy it together.' Shu Fang raised her head, then flopped back down onto her bed. Wing Yee sighed heavily and spoke to her in a sharp tone, but there was no response. Shu Fang's taste buds had been anesthetised by smoking opium, and that was all she craved right now.

Wing Yee decided to satisfy her own hunger first, she needed to keep her energy levels up if she was going to succeed with this uncooperative young woman. She lifted the lid off each of the four compartments in turn and was intoxicated by what she discovered inside. She took some noodles first, then helped herself to slices of lemon chicken, a mixture of delicious vegetables, and some steamed fish that had only recently been hauled out of the Pearl River.

Once Wing Yee had finished her own meal, she selected a small piece of chicken with her chopsticks and lifted it towards Shu Fang's mouth. This time, the girl parted her lips automatically, like the open beak of a young bird. Painstakingly, Wing Yee continued to feed her in this way, finally giving her a cup of cold water to drink. It was only then that she began to realise that the task she had set herself was going to be a bigger challenge than she had appreciated. She retreated to her own bed. The journey lying ahead was going to be hard work.

Wing Yee surveyed Shu Fang, who had now fallen into a deep sleep on her bed. She was only a few years older than Wing Yee had been when her own mother abandoned her. All she knew about this young woman was that she had been destined to marry out of her own community. From a very young age, her mother and various aunts would have been schooling her in all the requirements needed to make a good marriage. She would have been subjected to having her feet bound when she was only five or six years old. She had then spent much of her life embroidering slippers for the matriarch who would become her mother-in-law.

Wing Yee had no idea what had gone wrong, but there had been no marriage. Rumours circulated around Madam Ong's establishment, of course: she'd heard that Shu Fang had been jilted by a young man who had defied his family and run away with his childhood sweetheart. Another tale supposed she'd been rejected because her dowry wasn't large enough. Wing Yee doubted that anyone had ever asked Shu Fang what she felt about the proposed arrangements or consoled her when they failed to materialise. She had been brought to the brothel by her mother, like so many before her, under a cloud of shame.

Wing Yee had seen her tottering around on her *lily feet* and was glad her own father had insisted that his children should not be forced to follow this painful tradition. But in the end, what good had it done?

She too had arrived at Madam Ong's door without any explanation from her mother. She was shocked when she realised the establishment was no ordinary house. The role she would have there was not that of a governess or even a servant, as she'd supposed. All the freedom of her early life was gone forever. Other girls arrived on the same day. Some showed signs of terror, some remained unmoved by what was happening to them; most had already accepted the inevitability of their lot.

Initially, she had merely been required to wait on the older women who'd been there for years. They made it clear that they didn't like the newcomers, and it hadn't taken her long to work out why this was so. They had youthful good looks and agile bodies; this posed a threat to the older women, and so the bullying began. One girl was so unhappy, she'd hanged herself. This was something Wing Yee hadn't thought of for a long time. Hardly anyone smoked opium back then, it hadn't been an option. You either put up with your lot or you found some means of distraction. For her, it had been the invaluable knowledge she had about herbal medicine and the help it provided to Madam Ong in times of trouble.

All that learning had come from the long hours she had spent with her father and it made her aware how different her life would have been, had he lived. After his death, her younger sister, had been taken off to an arranged marriage. The money her mother had been given by Madam Ong for delivering the sixteen-year-old Wing Yee into her custody had provided the necessary dowry. She hoped her sister was happy, her own hardships and the life she'd endured would then have been worthwhile.

Wing Yee's musings ended abruptly. All around her, she could hear the sounds of creaking timber, doors being slammed, crates being dropped and moved into place, voices of the crew as they carried on with their tasks, and the lapping of water against the sides of the ship. Then, a noise that she didn't recognise - possibly something heavy banging against some-thing else? She opened the door of the cabin, casting her eye along the length of the deck. Nothing was immediately obvious, then she heard it again. She looked up, and there it was, a heavy rope banging against the mast as the breeze caught the sail and the boat moved up and down. She realised the ship was moving away from the quay. At last, she was on her way to Singapore.

CHAPTER 3
Guangzhou and the South China Sea

Following her conversation with Father John, Chin Ming's mind was in a complete turmoil. Would her plan work? Would she fall asleep and miss her opportunity to leave? She dozed fitfully; questions danced around inside her head, tormenting her all over again. There was no satisfactory conclusion. Eventually, she decided she would just leave a note for Father John.

Soon after dawn, she gathered together her small bundle and tiptoed down the stairs of the Mission house. She remembered, too late, that one of the steps squeaked. She froze, unable to move any further. The house remained quiet, and no one stirred. She forced herself to continue. Part of her was sad to leave, but she hoped her letter might help Father John to understand why she needed to go and that, one day, he would forgive her.

She moved without a sound from the bottom stair along the corridor to the kitchen. She could hear the gentle breathing of cook, and knew she must hurry, he would be rising soon to prepare breakfast. She placed the note on the table.

She was thankful that cook kept the hinges of the door kept well-oiled, it opened easily, and she slipped out into the cool, early-morning air. There was just enough light to see around the compound. Luckily, there was an exit into a small side street.

Her heart was thumping as she reached the gate that opened into Pwanting Street and quietly let herself out. She kept in the shadows as she walked along the lane until she reached the junction with the main road. Only then did she begin to breathe easily again. Even at this early hour, the neighbourhood was busy with the invisible people who emptied the night soil, swept the streets, and cleared away the dross of yesterday. As she neared the harbour, she saw market traders already busy setting up their stalls for the new day, and hawkers preparing breakfast for early risers.

Heady aromas circled around, tempting her taste buds. She was hungry but had only a few coins collected from errands run for Father John, she hoped they would be enough.

Her hair was tied up out of sight, but she still pulled her coolie hat as far down over her face as possible, tying it firmly under her chin. Her slight figure, clad in the unremarkable garments she'd chosen to wear, gave nothing away about her gender. She threaded her way between large wicker baskets full of fat cabbages. Then, she spotted a food stall near to the ship. She walked towards the hawker, hoping not to draw attention to herself.

Chin Ming chose four items. The steaming noodles slithered into the bowl like a snake hurrying to safety. Deep-fried aubergine, fried wontons, and green beans completed the meal. She carried it carefully to a low-slung wall, where she sat quietly, out of everyone's way.

She could see the *Golden Phoenix* clearly from here. No sails had yet been hoisted, but it still looked very grand. She watched as pairs of coolies - joined together with bamboo poles across their shoulders from which swung sacks of rice or flour and the occasional pig - scurried backwards and forwards like bees around a hive. Big, strong stevedores heaved large crates onto gangplanks, passing them to a chain of coolies who bent double under their weight, before dragging them up onto the deck for loading.

The whole quayside heaved with frenzied activity, people shouting in many different dialects, crates being dropped with their contents smashed, chains clanging, sails flapping, hawkers vying for attention - she was completely mesmerised. Then, she saw her chance. Everyone was busy, preoccupied with their own tasks. She hoped they might not notice her.

Her heart began to race. The muscles in her stomach tightened. She gathered up her small bundle and crept forward. The men loading the cargo looked enormous. There was no way she could blend in with them. Even the exhausted coolies looked much bigger now than when she'd watched them from a distance.

She began to panic. She thought her plan was flawed, that she would never be able to sneak on board without being seen. What if she was caught, what might happen? Even if she found a way onto the ship, where was she going to hide? How would she be punished if discovered? She hadn't thought this through properly, but neither could she bring herself to return to the Mission. There must be some means of getting onto that ship, of creeping past all this activity. She had to calm down and think it through carefully.

Chin Ming clutched her meagre little bundle, all the things she's dared to bring with her, and glanced longingly towards the rear of the ship. She was about to give up when she noticed a second gangplank. It was the one used by members of the crew not engaged in loading cargo. She watched and waited.

Only a few people used this approach, they ambled aboard casually, in no particular hurry. Dare she attempt it? What other option was there? She hesitated for a moment only, if she thought about it for too long her courage would fail.

Inwardly shaking, she fixed her gaze on the top of the gangplank and walked towards it. A middle-aged man arrived from nowhere. He looked at her briefly but said nothing. He turned towards the ship and climbed aboard. Then, she simply followed in his footsteps, just a little way behind as if she was his shadow. Only when she reached the deck did she become aware of the cold sweat that enveloped her whole body. The man disappeared through one of the many doors, leaving her shaking from top to toe.

Her first instinct was to creep under a nearby pile of rags and sacking for immediate cover, but she had no idea of their purpose or when they might be needed. She tried not to panic. Her legs began to feel weak, and she wanted to run back down the gangplank. She must find somewhere to hide before anyone spotted her. She turned, slowly and carefully, and as she did so, noticed a small open door quite close by.

She tiptoed towards it. Behind the door, she discovered a small cupboard that was completely empty. It smelt damp and musty as if it hadn't been used for some time, but as far as she could see, it was clean enough. As she crawled inside, she realised that the door was damaged. Maybe this was why the space had been left empty, it wasn't secure enough to protect any of the precious cargo.

The ship suddenly lurched. It rocked up and down for several minutes and then she realised the ship was moving. She sat on the floor; every sinew of her body tensed, every fibre of her being listening out for indications of danger. Was it going to be like this for the whole voyage, or just until someone found her?

A blast of air rushed through the gap where the door was loose. She lunged towards it, fearing it would be flung wide open and expose her to the crew. Her heart pounded against the wall of her chest and the thumping in her ears drowned all sense of reason. She settled down only when she realised the draught was probably caused by the ship changing direction.

Sometime later, she tentatively eased her cupboard door open a fraction. The air that rushed in was intoxicating. In the murky gloom, she could just make out the shape of one of the ship's crew, and she closed the door quietly, hoping that he hadn't noticed any movement. She curled up into a tight ball, first hugging herself and then rocking backwards and forwards.

She squeezed her eyes tight shut and covered her face with her hands to stop herself making any sound. She held her breath and prayed to the God the missionaries had so much faith in.

*****

Chin Ming remained cautious for the next two days. At night, she crept out from her hiding place to take in the fresh air. She moved to the edge of the boat to relieve herself, but only when the patrol was well out of sight, then hurried back to safety. She soon realised there was a regular pattern to the route taken by the guard and the time he took to complete a circuit. She watched carefully, silently counting between his arrival and his return.

On the third evening, she eased the door open as usual, when the sun had finally set. Her small supply of water was almost gone, and she was thirsty. She cast her eyes around the deck, searching for any signs of activity. She felt like one of the cats back at the Mission, who sat quietly in the shadows for hours, watching and waiting for an unsuspecting mouse.

As soon as tonight's watchman walked by, she began to count. She'd tested her theory several times to check its accuracy. Only then could she afford to take a risk.

'One, two, three.' She stared into the darkness as he disappeared into the shadows. 'Eight, nine, ten.' She could just make out his outline further along the deck. She fixed her eyes on him whilst still counting. When she reached one hundred, she eased herself into the open. The day had been particularly hot and the stuffiness within her confined space, making her feel drowsy. Now, the temperature had fallen sharply, her lungs drank in the cold, salty night air, and she thought they would explode. There was no moon and very few stars, but one or two oil lamps had been lit along the edges of the deck.

She kept her body low and searched the velvety darkness for anything useful. Still continuing to count, she felt around cautiously with her hands. A sharp stab of pain shot through her right thumb as she bumped into something large and bulky. She bit her lip as tears welled up in her eyes, but stopped herself from crying out.

As she rubbed the injured thumb, she felt the warm stickiness of blood trickle across her palm. Instinctively, she put her lips over the wound only to find a thin slither of something sharp protruding from the injury. It must be a splinter. Carefully, she removed it with her teeth.

The offending object had curved sides. She felt the coldness of what she assumed was a metal band holding the wooden sides together. It must be a barrel, but what did it contain? She walked her hands up its sides, noticing the slight concave effect as she reached the rim, then she felt around the edge for a cover.

It was heavier than she'd imagined and her hands shook as she eased it to one side. She held onto it firmly with her left hand. There was no smell, other than the dampness of the wood. She lowered her right hand cautiously and was relieved when she encountered the smooth iciness of a liquid. As far as she could tell, there was nothing else in the barrel. She withdrew her hand, brought it towards her nose and sniffed. There was no discernible odour. She licked her dampened hand and only then realised just how thirsty she was.

She'd stopped counting when the splinter had punctured her hand. How long had she been standing here? How much time remained before the watchman returned? Unconsciously, she cupped her hands together and scooped the cold liquid into her mouth. She would like to have washed, but that was too risky. Then, she remembered her flask. Why hadn't she brought it with her so that she could fill it with fresh water? She couldn't risk staying here, she must return to her hiding place. She'd stumbled against the barrel after only a few paces, so it couldn't be far away. Her eyes, accustomed to the darkness now, focused on the shadowy hollow that was her cupboard. Carefully, she felt her way back towards its safety. The door was shut, but she opened it without making a sound and squeezed back into her solitary cell. Shortly afterwards, she heard the heavy footfall of the night patrol. He walked straight past, returning after only a few minutes.

Chin Ming began to count again, but she hadn't even reached twenty before she fell into a deep, exhausted sleep.

*****

She awoke with a start. It was already light and the business of sweeping the decks and checking that everything was in order had begun. She could hear a cacophony of voices close by, people shouting in dialects that she found indecipherable. She froze. She could feel the hair at the nape of her neck lifting and her hands became clammy. Despite the stuffiness of her hiding place, she felt cold and beads of sweat lined up along her top lip. What was happening? What had they seen? A million questions swam around inside her head.

'See marks,' a deckhand said. 'What make happen?'

The bosun strode towards him to examine the small, dark spots the sailor pointed to. The lid of the water barrel was slightly askew. He barked orders, and demanded to know who had been on watch during the night. Others appeared on deck. After a while, the sleepy night-watchman who'd been dragged out of his hammock, joined them. A tirade of questions and opinions offered by others, turned the whole deck into a state of pandemonium. Captain Lim appeared, demanding to know what was going on.

Chin Ming heard the footsteps. Something heavy hit the meagre door and it was flung open. She desperately hoped that no one would see her in the gloom.

'Search that cupboard,' someone in authority demanded in Cantonese.

It began with a gentle prodding. She backed into the

corner as far as it was possible to go. A large baton of some sort - she couldn't see it clearly - was sweeping backward and forwards across the small confirmed space. She wanted to scream, but when she opened her mouth, her terror choked even the smallest sound. The pole came back again, this time with more force and caught her foot as it did so. She pulled her knees as close to her body as she could and held her breath.

'There's something in there,' someone yelled, 'I heard it move.'

'Well find it man,' came the reply, 'get in there, let's see what we're dealing with!'

Everything went dark in front of Chin Ming. Even the smallest chink of light was blocked by someone crouching down in front of the cupboard door. Then, she was being dragged; someone had reached inside, grabbed her foot and was pulling her out onto the deck. She went rigid, and as she was pulled across the hard surface of the floor, something rough cut though her blouse and into her shoulder. All her pent-up fear, supressed for so long, exploded into a high-pitched scream.

The bright light dazzled her. She automatically shielded her eyes with one hand, whilst tugging at her torn blouse with the other, trying to cover her bleeding shoulder. More voices shouted and argued above her head. The strength of the sun, even at this early hour made her blink. She began to tremble again just as a large man, with a red face, grabbed her injured shoulder and dragged her onto her feet. A sharp pain shot down her arm, nearly causing her to fall, but the man now grabbed her other arm, holding her so tightly that she thought she might faint. He yelled something in a dialect she couldn't understand and the more she failed to respond to his tirade of questions, the louder he shouted.

Another man stepped forward, pushing the others side. She recognised his voice as the one who'd given the order. He spoke firstly in Cantonese, then in Mandarin. She was too terrified to respond. 'How did you get onto my ship? Who are you? Speak, or I will have you flogged.'

'Honourable sir,' she began, 'my ... my name is Chin Ming.'

'Well, Chin Ming, how did you get on board? What are you doing here?'

She didn't know how to respond. If she told the truth, would he believe her? Would he throw her overboard? Something she daren't even think about.

'I'm waiting,' he barked at her in Cantonese.

'Sir, I am sorry to hide away on your magnificent ship ... I need to get to Singapore ... to find my father ...'

'So, can you pay me - that's if I allow you to stay, maybe I'll just feed you to the fishes?'

Members of the crew began to smirk. They could think of a few ways a pretty girl like this could pay her way. The captain turned to face the murmurings and glared at them.

'Stop that,' he ordered. He looked at her closely and he began to calculate what the cunning old towkay in Singapore might pay for her.

The crew began to return to their work; there was no point in hanging around.

'Honourable sir,' Chin Ming began, 'I have no money, but I'm willing to work. My father is a *Shenshi*; he taught me to read and write - and to speak English. I can show you,' she offered. 'If there is paperwork needing attention, I could do that for you.'

Captain Lim paced around for a while, then he stood in front of her, looking hard into her eyes. She held her breath and waited. She could see that he was thinking about the hindrance she had caused and what course of action to take. 'We reach Cho Lon in two days to take on fresh water. That's when I'll decide what to do with you. In the meantime, you must stay with the other women.' He gestured to the bosun. 'Take her away!'

Chin Ming tried to protest, but he was already halfway along the deck. The bosun, a tall and muscular man, grabbed her arm again. Her wounded shoulder was throbbing painfully, she had no strength to resist. She yelped as he pulled her along the deck and pushed her into a small, stuffy cabin.

A sweet sickly smell coupled with the stale odour of unwashed bodies pervaded the atmosphere. After the bright sunlight on deck, this space was dark and airless. Chin Ming felt nauseous. She squinted into the gloom and shuffled her feet forward just an inch or two. When she adjusted her gaze to the dimness, she was aware of two sets of eyes staring back at her. No one uttered a sound, then one of them stepped forward. She was an elegant woman, dressed almost entirely in red. Her eyes blazed, and she looked angry.

When she reached Chin Ming, she gulped. 'What? Who?' she shouted in Cantonese. 'Who are you? What are you doing here?'

Chin Ming remained rooted to the spot. She was far too terrified to speak.

CHAPTER 4
South China Sea

The woman stepped closer. She continued to look angry. Her cold eyes stared at Chin Ming; she held her chin high.

'Who are you, what is your name?' she repeated, still speaking in Cantonese.

The girl swallowed hard. 'My name is Chin Ming,' she said.

The woman hurled question after question at the girl but made no attempt to introduce herself. 'There is no space for another body,' she snapped. 'It's already too crowded in here.'

Wing Yee then swept passed Chin Ming and marched out onto the deck. She failed to acknowledge the man who had been left to guard the cabin and gave a withering look to any members of the crew who looked up in astonishment as a flash of red tore along the deck.

'Take me to Captain Lim,' she demanded when she caught sight of the bosun. He put out his hand to restrain her, but she would not be deterred. As he tried to block her path, they both saw the captain looking down at them from an upper deck. Before anyone could stop her, Wing Yee had climbed the steps to confront him.

'What do you mean by forcing that girl onto me? That wasn't part of our bargain. Who is she anyway?'

Captain Lim stood perfectly still. Wing Yee knew that he would be shocked by her behaviour. She was aware that some of the crew stared in their direction, curious to know what would happen next. Lim took Wing Yee by the arm and led her into a small cabin.

'We found her hidden in a cupboard,' he said. 'I've no idea who she is or what she is doing on my ship. I'll make it worth your while if you can find out anything about her. It will help me to decide what to do.'

'What do you mean?' Wing Yee said.

'Well, it would be easy to get rid of her when we reach Cho Lon, but better still, I might let her stay - I'm sure I can get a better price for her in Singapore.'

Wing Yee glared at him. She thought she knew this man well, but he was just like everyone else. Women are a mere commodity and of no consequence other than the price some- one was willing to pay for them.

She had been put off-balance when Chin Ming was shoved into the tiny cabin. Her first thought was of her younger sister, Yan Yee; the girl looked just like her. When she realised her mistake, anger had come bubbling to the surface. Shu Fang was already draining her energy and she had no real privacy. Her gut reaction was to be annoyed with Captain Lim for imposing yet another body into her care, but her disgust at his attitude towards the stowaway now replaced her anger. For the moment, she decided not to reveal her feelings, instead, she began to consider how she might benefit from befriending the fugitive.

'I'll see what I can find out,' she said, 'but I will expect a suitable reward.'

When she returned to the cabin, Chin Ming was standing in exactly the same spot, just inside the door of the cabin.

'Well, it seems I am stuck with you,' she said, 'you'd better tell me something about yourself. Did one of the crew smuggle you on board, or perhaps someone promised to pay for your passage in return for special favours, is that it? Don't look so shocked, men do that all the time, it's the way of the world. What you have to do, is learn to play them at their own game!'

'No. No, it's not like that at all. I came onto the ship in secret ... I've been hiding in a cupboard ... but this morning, they found me, and now they're very angry.'

'That's because you made them lose face. It was quite a clever trick though.' Wing Yee said. She realised the cupboard might well be the one she had noticed an hour or so before they sailed. 'How on earth did you manage to get on board without anyone seeing you?'

Chin Ming recounted the story of how she'd spotted the second gangplank.

Wing Yee thought the girl had guts but was still annoyed that the meagre rations allotted to them would now have to be divided between three instead of just two. She wondered if the girl had managed to smuggle anything on board that might be useful to them.

'And how have you been living for the past three days?'

'I brought a few things with me ... some bits of food ... some fruit ... a spare set of clothes ... but I didn't have much water left.' She then went on to tell the woman how she'd watched the night patrol and crept out to find water the previous evening.

'I stumbled against a large object ... I caught my hand against the rough wood and got a splinter in my thumb...it started to bleed ... I thought I'd been careful, but I couldn't see properly in the dark,' Chin Ming said.

Wing Yee was now convinced that it was the same cupboard that she'd seen that first morning.

'So, that's how they discovered your hiding place?'

'There was a lot of shouting. They broke down the door and pulled me out - I hurt my shoulder when someone dragged me along the floor.'

Wing Yee examined the broken flesh, it was starting to weep and needed to be cleaned.

'We'll need to get that seen to,' she said. 'Wounds like that can go bad in these sorts of conditions.'

'I don't want to get you into any trouble,' said Chin Ming.

As she carefully wiped clean the graze on the girl's

shoulder and dressed it with a salve laced with yarrow and juniper leaves which she kept for occasions such as this, Wing Yee realised that it might not be as bad having her around, as she'd first thought. The way Chin Ming spoke, the way she'd planned this trip and her obvious determination meant that she wasn't stupid. Besides, there was something in the girl's spirit that reminded her of her younger self. If she could convince Lim that the girl could be useful to both of them, he might let her stay.

'Don't worry about me,' Wing Yee replied. 'I have an arrangement with Captain Lim. He needs me to get this one clean before we reach Singapore.'

'I don't even know your name,' Chin Ming replied. 'Could you get me clean too? I haven't been able to wash properly since we left Guangzhou.'

'I am called Wing Yee. And I don't mean clean in the same way that you do - take a closer look at her.'

Wing Yee watched as Chin Ming stepped further into the room so that she could see the prostrate figure. The woman hadn't uttered a single word since her arrival. She was sitting against the wall, covered by a grubby sheet, and staring into space. When Chin Ming looked closely, she could see that the woman was holding onto a long, black pipe that rested against her lips.

'What's her name?'

'She's called Shu Fang - she's actually quite pretty when she's more alert.'

'Why does she look so sleepy?' asked Chin Ming, 'it's not yet midday.'

'She's developed a liking for opium. Quite a few young women think it helps them to forget the shame they believe they've brought on their families.' She could tell that the girl didn't really understand what she was talking about; by the look of her she'd had an easy-enough life. Why then, had she smuggled herself aboard this ship - and why was she so determined to get to Singapore?

'But I thought the sale of opium was illegal?' Chin Ming said.

'Since when has making anything illegal stopped greedy men from making money? Instead of selling the stuff openly, it just gets smuggled into China from Bengal. The situation is getting worse, but it's a good source of revenue for the traders, especially the British.'

Chin Ming looked curiously at Shu Fang and the strange-looking pipe she was holding.

'You've never seen it before, have you? You must have led a very sheltered life. Take a closer look - there's an oil lamp next to her, can you see it? The heat from that turns the opium in her pipe to vapour, and that's what she inhales.'

'Is that what I could smell when they pushed me into this room?'

'That and the rankness of people who have been in a confined space for too long. We, like you, have not had the privilege of decent washing facilities since we came on board,' Wing Yee replied. 'You'd better get used to it. It's a long journey to Singapore.'

'The captain may not let me stay,' Chin Ming confessed. 'He said he'd think it over and make up his mind before we reach Cho Lon.'

'Well, if you're willing to help me, maybe I can persuade him to change his mind,' Wing Yee replied.

'What do you mean, what do you want me to do?' Chin Ming said.

'You'd like to stay on board, is that right?' Wing Yee asked. Chin Ming nodded quickly. 'Well then, you can begin by telling me why it's so important for you to get to Singapore. Come over here, you can share this mat with me for the time being.'

Wing Yee admitted that she'd hoped to have made more headway in reducing the amount of opium Shu Fang was using by now, but it had been more difficult than she envisaged. The first time she'd tried to feed her had just been slow and laborious, but since then it had become more of a challenge. Most of the food ended up slithering down Shu Fang's tunic as she often refused to co-operate. Wing Yee told Chin Ming, she had been on the point of losing her temper on more than one occasion, but she knew that would achieve nothing so she'd gritted her teeth, tried the best she could and then found a damp rag to wash down the soiled garments. She went on to admit that having someone else to keep an eye on Shu Fang, to try to make her eat something and just keep her distracted would help a great deal.

Chin Ming was aware that Wing Yee had felt antagonistic towards her when they first met, but she as beginning to feel more relaxed now that a way of helping had been identified.

'Do you think I'd be able to help the captain with his paperwork,' Chin Ming asked, 'as a way of paying for my passage? Papa always said that most of the ship's captains he'd ever met loved travelling from country to country but hated writing reports and dealing with inventories.'

Wing Yee realised that it might not be so bad having Chin Ming around, as she'd first thought. The way Chin Ming spoke, the way she'd planned this trip and her obvious determination meant that she wasn't stupid.

*****

Chin Ming began to tell Wing Yee all about her life up to the point when she left the Mission a few days ago. The older woman listened carefully; she was particularly interested in hearing about Chin Ming's education and the languages she had learned to speak.

Wing Yee smiled to herself. What she had learned about this girl in the last hour indicated that she would indeed be useful to both the captain and herself. The new life she'd been promised as the concubine of a prominent towkay would come with certain benefits, but now she began to think it could be even better. She spoke Cantonese and she understood a little Mandarin, but hardly any English. She could only write words associated with traditional medicine. Maybe this girl could teach her to write her name and much more besides? She would make sure that Captain Lim kept Chin Ming on board.

Wing Yee realised that, whilst the young girl's good fortune appeared to have run out, it looked as if, at last, luck might be about to turn in her own favour. She almost felt sorry for Chin Ming. No one would say the girl was beautiful, she thought, but there was something about her that compelled you to look again. She had an oval face with a small, upturned nose and flawless skin. Her large, vivacious eyes burst with life when she talked about her father. She certainly had determination. Wing Yee knew that her motives might not be entirely altruistic but nevertheless, she decided to make sure that no one bullied the girl or took advantage of her vulnerability.

*****

The *Golden Phoenix* reached Cho Lon three days later; it was early October. Captain Lim went ashore at first light and spent the whole day exchanging news with officers from the other ships, anchored offshore. It had been almost twelve months since he'd last visited Singapore and he was anxious to learn whether the fledgling settlement had continued to prosper. The majority of the reports he heard pleased him greatly, but there was one story circulating that gave him cause for concern. It was rumoured that Stamford Raffles would be returning to the town any day now. Some thought he may have already arrived.

Raffles' reputation went before him amongst the merchants who regularly criss-crossed the trading routes of the South China Sea. He was said to be a person with high ideals, an honourable man who was kind and considerate, but they also knew that he detested slavery in all its forms. Captain Lim recognised that he would need to be cautious when he handed over the women to the towkay, especially if he was to persuade him to take Chin Ming as well.

He'd already let himself be persuaded, by Wing Yee, that it would be advantageous to let the runaway remain on board. When he returned to the *Golden Phoenix* later in the day, he handed over a bundle of papers and told her to deal with them. Most of the material was routine administration, but she was to tell him immediately if any of the documents mentioned the name Stamford Raffles.

*****

Chin Ming stiffened when she heard the name spoken out loud; every muscle felt rigid but she tried to make sure no one noticed her interest. This must be the same man that Papa had told her about - why was Captain Lim so interested in him? Each day, she methodically scrutinised all the documents that he handed to her. She examined each piece of paper carefully but found nothing to report. She would like to ask Wing Yee why the captain was so anxious to find any reference to Raffles, but she didn't yet know her well enough to risk such a question. Some days, she caught a wistful expression on Wing Yee's face and began to think that she really enjoyed her company. At other times, she believed her presence was resented. During those moments, she tried to keep herself to herself and not upset anyone. The best time, however, was when they worked together to wash and feed Shu Fang. That's when she felt she was being treated as an adult and not some spoilt brat who knew nothing about life.

*****

41

Wing Yee made it her business to accompany Chin Ming whenever she was required to undertake any work for the captain. She insisted that as Chin Ming was so young, she should act as her chaperone. The work that Chin Ming was required to do took very little time, but they both enjoyed the opportunity to temporarily escape the confines of the stuffy cabin. As they began to know each other better, they looked for other reasons to linger on deck.

'I know only a few English words,' Wing Yee said one day. 'Could you teach me some more? I think it might be very useful, when we reach Singapore.'

A smile gradually spread across Chin Ming's face, showing her delight in being asked to share some of her own learning with this woman whose company she was beginning to enjoy. Each morning was spent in Captain Lim's cabin, where the girl copied out lists, read documents, and wrote letters for him. In the afternoon, she began to teach Wing Yee some basic English and to write a few simple sentences. On each occasion, Chin Ming chose five objects around which she could weave a story.

Today, she'd asked Captain Lim if she could borrow a birdcage that lay empty under a cupboard. She used it to tell Wing Yee the story of the *Emperor and the Nightingale.*

At first, Wing Yee protested. 'I am never likely to need either of those words,' she said.

'Maybe not,' Chin Ming said, 'but listen carefully and then tell me how many new words you recognise that will be useful.'

Wing Yee was an able pupil; by the end of the story, she had added - garden, trees, flowers, sunrise, sunset, and several more words to her vocabulary. She learned to memorise each new story she was told, and Chin Ming asked her questions in English. The more time they spent together in this way, the more Wing Yee's confidence grew and the closer the two of them became.

Back in the cabin, Wing Yee reverted to her detached self.

She was aware that the girl craved affection, but she had spent too long hiding her emotions to begin displaying any warmth towards another human being, just yet anyway. What she was able to provide was a certain schooling in the ways of the world. She knew some of this information came as a shock to Chin Ming; she could see the girl struggling to conceal her astonishment, not wanting Wing Yee to laugh at her ignorance. She would never do that, of course, it was good to realise that there was some innocence left in the world. When she looked back, however, she realised that it was during these long, shared conversations that Chin Ming moved to adulthood very rapidly.

When they began to approach the coast of the Malay Archipelago, the wind got up and the sea became very rough. The pile of rags that Chin Ming had thought of hiding beneath was brought into service as additional sail. Both women watched the crew as they busily engaged in this activity and the *Golden Phoenix* changed direction. Anything that was likely to move was tied down as sheets of water lashed the sides of the ship and torrential rain beat down upon them.

For the next few days, all the women were totally ignored. On the third evening there was a flash of lightning that tore across the sky towards them like a great silver arrow. It was followed by an enormous bang and then the wind sighed and thrashed around the tops of the masts. Another curtain of rain beat down upon them throughout the night, but as the light crept over the horizon the following morning everything became calm.

The captain told them that the storm had pushed them off course towards the islands of the Philippines. There was much clearing up to be done and food would now be rationed as the journey would take much longer than originally planned. Both Wing Yee and Chin Ming had turned out to be good sailors, but Shu Fang had suffered badly. She had spent much of the last few days wallowing in her own misery and the stench was overpowering.

Wing Yee sent Chin Ming to beg for some rags from the captain so that they could begin the process of cleaning. On the older woman's instructions, they each tied one of the pieces of cloth over their mouth and nose before beginning to wash out the cabin, but still the stale, sour remains of vomit and excrement made them heave so much that their chest hurt. Shu Fang was feeling too ill to care about what was happening around her.

'We need to strip her and wash away all this filth, 'said Wing Yee.

'I heard the bosun say that some of the water barrels had been swept overboard,' Chin Ming replied. 'We'll have to use sea water.'

'I don't care what we use, we need to get her cleaned up. We still have to share the cabin with her for the rest of the voyage and I can't bear this awful stench. Besides, she needs to arrive in Singapore looking reasonable, otherwise the man who is expecting her will be upset. And if he's upset, Captain Lim won't be paid. He is already worried because he was asked to bring three women for the Englishman to choose from - and we only have one left.'

'But you only had Shu Fang when I met you,' Chin Ming said.

'True,' Wing Yee replied, 'but I had managed to find two others - about the same age as Shu Fang and only recently arrived at Madam Ong's. They mysteriously disappeared about an hour before we came onboard the ship - probably scared off by Madam Ong herself. Hence, the one we do have really needs to please the Englishman!'

Chin Ming kept her thoughts to herself and went to find water. Meanwhile, Wing Yee set about removing the stained and stinking garments from Shu Fang.

When she returned to the cabin, Chin Ming caught her breath and looked quickly away from the naked body lying limply on the floor. Wing Yee heard her gasp and turned around.

'This is not the time to be shy, Chin Ming. I need you to help me. You can begin by getting rid of all this mess.'

Briefly, the girl remained frozen to the spot, then she pulled herself together and moved towards the garments that had been cast aside. She wrinkled her nose and tried not to breath too deeply. The dress that had once been the pride and joy of its owner was now contaminated with her own filth. Chin Ming picked the dress up gingerly and held it at arm's length before taking it and several other discarded garments out onto the deck. As soon as the bosun saw her, he grabbed the offending clothes and threw them overboard. Chin Ming hurried back to the cabin to tell her friend what had happened.

'I thought we would need to wash everything,' she said, 'what will she wear now?'

'Even the best laundry would have found it difficult to get that bundle of rags clean,' said Wing Yee, as she finished drying the hair of the limp body in front of her. 'If you look in that cupboard - no, the one to your right - you will find some clean tunics. I was planning to save them until we reached Singapore, but she'll have to wear one of them now, we have no other choice.'

Together, they lifted Shu Fang's uncooperative limbs and helped her to dress. Chin Ming would remember that pale and scrawny frame for a long time afterwards, no longer embarrassed by what she saw. The storm had inadvertently helped with the cleansing process and all the poison had been expelled from Shu Fang's body. Whilst she was vomiting up the last remnants of opium, Wing Yee had collected a few hidden pouches of the drug that had survived the storm. She made sure that every last grain of it, together with all the paraphernalia needed for its indulgence disappeared forever.

CHAPTER 5
October 1822, Singapore

Dick had only been asleep a short while when he was woken by the sound of raised voices; his arms and leg muscles tensed, and he began to shake. At eighteen, there were times when he still lacked confidence - usually when there was cause for alarm and the shadows from his unhappy childhood came flooding back. Shortly after the death of his mother, he'd been snatched from his village on a remote Pacific island and taken to Bali by a foul-mouthed Dutch trader. The man had a quick temper and delighted in brandishing an ironwood stick to torment the six-year-old. The bullying escalated during the next six years when the man tired of 'his pet monkey' and grew more and more irascible as the petrified child evolved into a tall, silent slave.

He was twelve when Raffles had rescued him from that tyranny and only a few months later they had travelled to England together. During the long voyage, Raffles had taught him to speak English. Soon after their arrival in that cold, damp autumn, formal adoption papers had been completed; the young man, who until that point had always been called *Boy*, then chose for himself the name Dick and asked to call the man who signed the adoption papers, Uncle.

Now, another six years had now passed. A week ago, they had arrived in Singapore; Raffles had been away in Bencoolen for three years, but for his wife Sophia and Dick it was their first visit.

For the time being, they had accepted an invitation to

move in with Raffles' sister Mary Anne and her husband Captain Flint. Their home was the harbour-masters' house and not large enough to sleep so many extra guests. Having been used to a large and airy room of his own, Dick had chosen to sleep in the shadow of the main dwelling rather than on its crowded veranda. He found the smell of rice and dried vegetables comforting and the storehouse offered him privacy with sufficient space to curl up on his mat each evening.

But now, even that space was being invaded by the sound of raised voices and the thud of boots pacing up and down on the floor above; he sat up with a jolt. He strained to hear what was being said. One of the voices was Uncle's, the other one he didn't recognise; both were high pitched and vehement. Dick covered his ears, but it didn't block out the noise of the commotion above him.

'God knows, I only ever had one simple objective,' Uncle's voice then became indistinct as he moved away from the edge of the veranda.

'... lack of Company support ... it's a tradition ... visiting ships ... presents ... Temenggong ...' Dick could distinguish odd snippets and even then, he had to strain to hear the other person.

Then Uncle's voice became more discernible again and he continued, 'But you have gone against my specific instructions - you've allowed a few favoured individuals to build their houses and warehouses wherever they want!'

The pacing continued, someone thumped their fist on the table and the whole house shook in response. Dick was immediately reminded of his slave-master, who used to shriek his displeasure whenever things had not gone to plan. His hands automatically flew to caress the scar on his back that would forever be a reminder of those childhood days. He shivered.

The visitor moved to the edge of the veranda; the unfamiliar voice became even more agitated.

'Och, you're a dreamer, Raffles, you've been back here no time at all and you're already criticising me. How else was I supposed to raise enough revenue to run the place, answer me that? You have no idea about how much things cost.'

'Maybe, if you'd kept to the plan we agreed when I left ...'

'Aye, a plan that was flawed from the start, you have no idea about ...' the visitor's voice became inaudible again as he moved further away.

Dick couldn't imagine what the argument was about, or why it was happening. Who would be visiting Uncle at this time of night, and what had caused them both to be so upset? They spoke in English so it wasn't any of the Chinese merchants, nor the Temenggong - the visitor must be from the European community. He thought he detected a slight accent, the lilt he'd come to recognise as Scottish, but most of the Europeans he'd met here came of Scottish descent, so he was none the wiser.

The footsteps continued to pace about on the floor above. The noise persisted for several more minutes. The two men continued to yell at each other, each believing his opinion was the right one; both having gone beyond accepting any alternative viewpoint.

'... the merchants who came here didn't want to build on the west bank, I tell you, it was far too swampy. I'm afraid I agree wi'em,' the visitor insisted

'Surely the land could have been drained?' Raffles responded. 'You're an engineer, and you know, full well, the land on this side of the river was reserved for government buildings.'

'I had enough to do dealing with the rats and the mosquitos after you left. I didn't have the cash for people to haul mud out of the mangrove swamps. Besides, word had spread; people had heard about the opportunities here and flooded in from all over - there was too much to do to worry about trivialities!'

'I don't call the allocation of land a triviality,' Raffles said. 'And anyway, it's not just about the land. You brought in chests of opium from Calcutta, and allowed them to be sold here, knowing full well how people become addicted to the filthy stuff. You condoned bringing slaves here too and allowed them to be sold like bags of rice. You must be aware that the slave business is illegal in any British settlement, even if you didn't know just how much I loathe it.

'I've had enough of this, I'm going,' the unknown voice spat into the shadows and heavy boots could be heard striding across the veranda towards the staircase. 'Damn you Raffles - you and your idealism. Your ideas are unrealistic and impossible to achieve. You demand too much!'

Dick looked up from his sleeping mat to see the long legs he now recognised as belonging to the Resident, Colonel Farquhar, thumping their way downwards. The older man pulled his bright red coat tight across his chest, then strode out across the compound, muttering to himself as he disappeared into the darkness.

When he could no longer see the retreating figure, his instinct was to draw his knees up close to his body and clutch his arms tightly around them. He hated arguments; they always made him feel uneasy.

He waited. Eventually, his breathing calmed down. The only noise now was the comforting hum of the cicadas. He wondered what was happening above him on the veranda. Was Uncle still there - had Colonel Farquhar lashed out at him? Might he be lying motionless on the floor; might he be hurt? He needed to find out. He raised himself to an upright position and strained his ears. No, nothing apart from the chorus of insects. It was very dark, with only the sliver of a moon and very few stars. The glow at the top of the steps indicated that the oil lamps were still lit. Slowly, he walked towards the staircase and one step at a time, made his way upwards.

On the veranda, he found Raffles slumped at a table with his head in his hands. Dick looked across to see the man he idolised weary with disappointment and his face consumed with anguish. An empty wine glass sat amongst a pile of papers. He tiptoed over to where Raffles sat and put a comforting hand on his shoulder.

'Oh Dick, you made me jump. I was miles away ... I'm sorry if the shouting woke you, I'm afraid Colonel Farquhar and I had a bit of a disagreement.'

'What about?'

'Oh, nothing for you to worry about. Some of the things I wanted him to do, he hasn't done, and some of the things I didn't want done, he has done, that's all.'

Dick sat quietly, waiting for Raffles to say more.

Instead, he got to his feet, took a deep breath, and sighed loudly. 'Let's talk about it tomorrow,' he said. 'You should have been asleep hours ago. I've got a shocking headache, and right now, all I want to do is put my head on my pillow and go to sleep.'

Raffles placed his arm tenderly around Dick's shoulders and walked with him back to the comfort of his sleeping quarters. 'I'll tell you all about it in the morning, I promise.'

*****

Raffles slept only fitfully. His mind was in torment, and his head was throbbing. As soon as it was light, he rose from the bed, leaving Sophia to continue with her dreams. He dressed quickly in his usual black breeches and light cotton shirt, made his way along the veranda, and then crept down the outer wooden staircase. He didn't want to disturb anyone, most of all Dick.

Right now, he decided he needed to clear his head, but later on he must try to find something to occupy Dick's time - to make him feel useful and involved in everything that is going on.

Before the heat of the day became too intense, he hurried

away from the house. He was exhausted and needed the peace and quiet that he knew he would find at the top of Bukit Larangan. It was where he'd decided to build his own house and the fresh air at the top of the hill would blow away all the cobwebs.

He reached the beginning of the pathway quickly. It curled around the hillside, between ancient trees that disappeared into the dazzling morning light and dense foliage that was content to huddle in their shade. Every so often, where the bushes had become thick and overgrown, he needed to push his way through the lush vegetation, before continuing upwards. Occasionally, he snagged the ample sleeves of his shirt on vicious barbs but managed to avoid ripping his flesh. He could already feel the warmth of the day on his face, but it hadn't yet reached the intense heat and humidity that many of the European residents complained about. The path occasionally fragmented into a rough track, suddenly vanishing beneath fallen and rotting branches. He looked up to search for the sky, but all he could see was a vast green canopy of foliage interspersed with shafts of golden light. The roots of some of the larger trees curled and twisted towards him, as if mocking his slow progress.

Eventually, he began to see daylight again and when he reached the clearing at the top, a chorus of unseen birds made him welcome. He slumped onto the ground, under the shade of a banyan tree and began to go over the events of the previous evening in his mind.

After a while, he rose to his feet. Farquhar's right, he thought, I am an idealist, but what's wrong with that? All I want is to establish a great commercial emporium here - to restore Singapore to the successful settlement it was in the fourteenth century. My dreams have only ever been about trade, about establishing a free port. The Company, on the other hand, have always been scared that the Dutch would want to add this place to their other possessions. They've given us very little support and I suppose that's why Farquhar let himself be bribed. Maybe I've been unfair to him.

'I'll try talking to him again - we need to be able to work together,' he said out loud to an audience of inquisitive mynah birds that had gathered around his feet. But with no sign of food on offer and a sudden noise coming from the path below, they took off in a flurry of feathers to a place of safety.

*****

It began with the snapping of twigs and the rustle of leaves. There was no wind and no obvious sign of animals moving around. That didn't mean, of course there wasn't a rat or a snake snuffling around in the undergrowth or one of the tigers who occasionally swam over from Johor in search of food. Up here, all alone he would be fair game. He kept still and listened.

The noise was too regular to be an animal stalking its prey, which meant the slow, steady steps must belong to another human being, but who might that be? He was beginning to feel a little uneasy when the foliage parted and, to his immense relief, it revealed a head of short, tightly curled black hair that identified the visitor as Dick.

'What brings you up here, young man?' he asked.

'I overslept, Uncle. I went to the Company office, but no one had seen you. Then, I went to the quay, but everyone just shook their head when I asked about you. I was about to return to the house, when one of the fishermen called me. He said he'd seen you early this morning, walking towards the path that leads to the top of the hill. I decided to see if there was any sign of you - and then I just kept going.'

'It was quite a risky thing to attempt on your own. The jungle can be quite treacherous until you get used to it. Remember you've only been here just over a week. It would have been easy to get lost.'

'You're not angry, are you?'

'No, not angry, just concerned about you losing your way. Until we get this track made into a proper road promise me you will always tell someone if you come up here again.'

'I promise, but you shouldn't worry. Finding my way along some of the rural tracks in Sumatra taught me to be wary. I am always careful. I only came because I was worried about your quarrel with Colonel Farquhar. Last night, you looked so miserable.'

'Yes, you're right, I was distressed - I still am, but I need to talk to Farquhar again. I think I was a bit too harsh on him.

'What do you think made Colonel Farquhar go against your wishes?'

'It could be any number of things. You see, he didn't choose to come here. He was due to return to Scotland, but three years ago Lord Hastings persuaded him to help me find a new base for a trading post south of the Melaka Strait. Farquhar thought the Carimon Islands would be a good spot, but the anchorage there was totally unsuitable.'

'Are you saying, he ignored your wishes because he didn't agree with your choice of Singapore?'

'The idea has crossed my mind, but no, I think he had a hard time here early on and he was simply too worn down by the pressure to make a stand.'

'I don't understand,' Dick said.

'There was nothing much here, apart from the fishing village and the Temenggong's kampong, when we first arrived. Farquhar was left with a few sepoys and not much in the way of funds when I had to return to Sumatra. I truly believed that the Company would be pleased with this choice of location and would send all the help we needed. Instead, they believed the Dutch would stake a claim to the island; they are still reluctant to invest in the place.'

'Colonel Farquhar must have come to like it here, don't you think?' Dick said, 'otherwise he wouldn't have stayed.'

'That's right - and maybe his Malay wife had some influence on the situation. I doubt whether he would have taken her back to Scotland. We exchanged letters throughout the whole time I've been away; I wrote to him in January, when I suspected he was turning a blind eye to certain things, but he offered no explanation to the questions I asked. Maybe it's my fault - maybe I should not have stayed away so long.'

'But the people in Bencoolen needed you. You appointed Colonel Farquhar as the Resident because you trusted him, and it sounds as if he's let you down.'

'Don't get me wrong, Dick, Farquhar has achieved a great deal - come let me show you.'

Raffles strode over towards the very edge of the hillside and chose a comfortable spot amongst the fallen tree trunks. Dick followed and sat next to him. From this vantage point they could observe the whole panorama of the developing town below, and beyond it to the ocean.

'You see what I mean,' Raffles said. 'Look at all those ships out there - all wanting to take advantage of our free port facilities. The popularity of the place is a lot to do with Farquhar's hard work at the beginning.'

'It looks like a forest, made up of sails,' said Dick. 'It could even be a second town sitting on the water down there.'

Raffles smiled, amused that Dick had caught his own enthusiasm. He pointed out the European ships with their square rigging, the Chinese junks with their characteristic horseshoe-shaped sterns and the outlines of other vessels from all around the region.

'I know you hate slavery, Uncle. I'm glad of it, otherwise I might still be trapped in Bali, but what else has Colonel Farquhar tolerated that upsets you so much?'

'I loathe slavery and everything that goes with it,' Raffles said. 'The men who come here from China to work in the *gambier* plantation often arrive owing the cost of their passage to someone or another. They send money back to their families and gamble away what is left in an effort to pay off their debts; when that doesn't work and their debts increase, they seek solace in opium. It helps them to forget, but it's a vicious cycle.'

'And does that apply to the prostitutes too?' Dick asked.

Raffles looked startled.

'Don't look so shocked, Uncle, Captain Flint told me all about Madam Ho - and her ladies. And don't worry, I have no desire to visit the place!'

'In my opinion, women who are forced into prostitution are just as much oppressed as anyone else forced to into a life of servitude. All these things mount up together and the trouble is, once you've allowed bad things to happen, it difficult to get rid of them.'

Dick didn't know what to say. He wished he could do something to help, but had no idea where to start, there was no easy solution. He decided to change the subject.

'Why don't you show me the spot where our new house will be built?' he said.

They walked towards a place where the jungle had recently been cleared. The building work was due to start any time soon and with luck, they would be able to move in before the end of the year.

'I think it's wonderful, Uncle, there's so much space and it has a good feel about it, but why has no one else thought of building here? Is it because of all the superstitions about the hill?'

'What have you heard? Raffles said.

'All I know is that Bukit Larangan means forbidden hill and the locals are afraid to come here' Dick replied.

'Hundreds of years ago, the kings of Singapore built their palace here. I daresay none of the ordinary people were allowed to come anywhere near the place then and that's why all the superstitions have developed.'

'But there are graves here too, aren't there? Won't some

people be upset if we build so close to a burial ground?'

'Don't worry, the burial site is a long way from this spot, and I certainly have no intention of disturbing such an important part of local history,' Raffles said.

'What about the other Europeans, they've all built their houses down on the Plain or near to the river, don't you want to be near to them?'

'No Dick, I prefer to be somewhere cooler. Have you not noticed the way they are always complaining either about the heat or the humidity? We'll be much better off up here, on top of the hill. There's a lot more breeze for a start, the air will be able to flow through the house freely. It will be cool and the trees will provide plenty of shade. Not only that, but we'll also have fine views of the river and the sea.'

They returned to the edge of the hill, choosing a spot that provided a view of the quay. Raffles focused his gaze on the area just beyond the river; the portion of land that he'd intended to form the hub of the port. True, it was covered in low-lying mangrove swamps, but Farquhar hadn't attempted to drain even a small part of it. Surely, once people saw its potential, it would be easy enough to persuade the merchants to build their warehouses on that side. He needed to make it more attractive, then they would be happy settle there.

Just beyond the quagmire, the land rose again in a series of significant peaks. He hadn't paid them much attention, but he began to envisage what might be possible if some of the soil and gravel from these hills could be moved. The germ of an idea was beginning to form in his head when Dick interrupted.

'Is something wrong?' he asked.

Raffles turned towards Dick with a smile that lit up his whole face and made him look much younger than his forty-one years. 'I think I may have a come up with a solution to one of my problems. It will cost a good deal of money, so I'll need to convince the people in Calcutta - and others in London - that the investment is worth their while.'

Dick looked at him thoughtfully.

'Remember Uncle, in Sumatra, I sketched nearly all of the animals and plants in your collection before you sent them back to England?'

'Yes, you've always had a talent for drawing.'

'I could sketch the Settlement; to illustrate how it looks at present,' Dick said. 'I can show the far bank of the river covered in mangroves, the warehouses that have been built on this side of the water, the haphazard nature of the bazaar, and the complete jumble of hawker stalls.'

'That's not a bad idea,' Raffles said. 'I'm thinking of moving the soil from those hills over there, then using it to fill in the swamp. Your drawings could help to convince people the scheme is worthwhile.'.

Dick's face was alight with enthusiasm. 'I could include the Malay kampong - and best of all, views from this hill to complete the whole panorama.'

'I could send your drawings, together with the new town plan that Lieutenant Jackson has made, to Calcutta. It will show them where changes need to be made - and how these ideas will transform the whole Settlement. That way, everyone will benefit,' Raffles said.

'So, you'd like me to do it?'

He nodded, and Dick's expression showed how pleased he was. But, having given his approval, Raffles now had to fend off a myriad of questions from Dick about paper and ink and when he should start. However, he was glad to have discovered something that obviously interested him so much.

'Slow down,' he said. 'You can begin tomorrow if you like - and you can get all the materials you need from the Company office. But first, I think we should go and talk to Lieutenant Jackson. You need to look at the plan he's drawn and then we can decide the best place to start. Let's walk back into town together and see if we can have a word with him.'

*****

Dick felt as if he was on a magic carpet as they made their way back down the hillside. All the roots, fallen tree trunks and other hazards he'd encountered on his way up the slope had apparently disappeared from view, together with all the haunting spirits from his past. They had somehow waltzed away into the shadows and, for the moment, no longer troubled him. He had his own dance now and that was all that mattered.

CHAPTER 6
Singapore

After their conversation at the top of the hill, Raffles took Dick to the Company office. There, Dick was introduced to Lieutenant Philip Jackson. Large charts, showing the new proposals covered three trestle tables and Dick moved from one to another amazed at the level of detail shown. He recognised the place where the newly-constructed bridge crossed the river but was fascinated to see new sites: one marked for a church, another showing an open square, and another for a court house.

'It's very different to the way things look at present,' he said. 'It's all so neat and tidy.'

'It's your Uncle's plan really,' Jackson replied. 'What I've drawn here is all based on his vision for the Settlement.' He moved nearer to Dick so that he could explain the details 'That area between the river and the stream is reserved for government use. The European town will be next to it and beyond that, the Bugis and the Arab communities - right beside the Sultan's kampong.'

At this point, Raffles joined them. 'I'm not sure everyone is going to like these ideas, Uncle,' Dick said.

'I've set up a Town Committee to examine the proposals,' Raffles said, 'and they will consult representatives from the Malay, Chinese, and other communities. I'm not expecting everyone to approve at first, but I hope to convince them that they will be better off in the long run. Once the Town Committee have given their approval, we'll start to clear the swamps. After that, we can begin to build.'

For the next few days, Dick went to the Company office each morning and then proceeded up the hill. On his first trip, Raffles went along too, it was more to convince himself rather than Dick that the route was clear. When they reached a place where the path divided, he told Dick to avoid the buttress roots of a kapok tree, and pointed to its seed pods surrounded by fluffy, yellowish fibre. The next time the path split, Raffles pointed out a cluster of torch ginger lilies, with their large, deep pink petals fading to a lighter shade at the margins. Finally, there was a tembusu tree, whose large lower branches spread all around at ground level. Its bark, a distinctive dark brown shade had deep fissures that made it resemble a bitter gourd. Dick had to admit that looking out for these markers would make the route easier than it had been on the day he'd struggled up the hillside in search of Raffles. Then, he'd fallen into thickets, taken several wrong turns, and had almost given up - not that he would admit this to anyone. These landmarks would help to speed up his journey, and he knew the route would soon become so familiar that he'd wouldn't need any help at all.

Raffles, meanwhile, was busy conducting meetings. Alexander Johnston, George Bonham, and Captain Charles Edward Davis of the Bengal Native Infantry - who made up the newly-formed Town Committee - needed little convincing, but Colonel Farquhar still presented a problem. He was intent only in justifying the reasons for his actions during the last three years and it felt as if he was not at all interested in seeking any common ground.

*****

It took several visits for Dick to capture the different views from the top of the hill. Towards the end of the third afternoon, he gathered together his collection of sketches and took one final look out towards the harbour. The sky was beginning to darken, and he decided to hurry back before it started to rain. Just as he reached the lower slopes, he heard the first low rumble of thunder in the distance and saw the storm clouds gathering. He decided to head for the Company office in order to avoid the deluge.

Almost immediately, he bumped into Abdullah, Uncle's secretary. Even though Abdullah was seven years older than Dick and their family circumstances were so very different, the two had become good friends.

Abdullah had been born in Malacca of Arabic descent and was the only surviving child of five sons. His mother had tried to spoil him, but his father had been a strict disciplinarian and had made him learn to read and write in Arabic at an early age. He'd shown an aptitude for languages and now he loved to teach others.

He always dressed in the usual style of Malacca Tamils: baggy trousers, a long-sleeved shirt with a stiff upright collar, a check sarong tied around his waist, a square skull cap placed firmly on his head, and sandals on his ample feet. Dick, whose own attire tended to be more European than Malay, envied Abdullah his loose-fitting garments that looked both cool and comfortable.

Dick glanced around the office. He soon realised there was something different about it today. Everyone was smiling, shaking each other by the hand, and generally looking pleased with themselves. He turned towards Abdullah, looking for an explanation.

'The Land Allotment Committee have just announced their approval for the relocation plan. I am to draft the notices that will be sent out tomorrow. They'll be posted all around the town in both English and in Malay. Everything seems to be going well,' he said.

*****

Dick tucked his shirt into his breeches. Everywhere he went, these days, he heard people talking about the dinner party Uncle had decided to host. Fortunately, his sister Mary Anne was happy to accommodate such an occasion. Abdullah had been asked to send out the invitations, and Dick had helped him to deliver them. He sometimes caught sight of people looking at him as he walked along beside the quay with his sketchpad under his arm; he wouldn't give them an opportunity to criticise him by looking dishevelled.

*****

Dick arrived early. Raffles had suggested that they sat together, but Dick had asked to be excused. His English was as good as his Malay, but with the guests being so much older than him, he felt nervous about engaging such important people in conversation. Instead, he'd managed to persuade Uncle that it was a good opportunity for him to capture the great occasion by making some sketches of the people attending. To do that he would need to be able to move around freely.

Earlier in the day, some additional tables and seating, borrowed from other European houses had been delivered. Now, during the space of a few hours, the whole place had been transformed. The rattan chairs and every-day clutter had disappeared. In their place, a long banqueting table had been created on the veranda. It was covered in crisp white linen and set out with both knives, forks, spoons, and chopsticks to accommodate the different needs of all the guests. The jugs of freshly squeezed fruit juices made him feel thirsty and he wondered if anyone would notice if he helped himself. He noticed carafes of wine, but as he'd never tried the deep red liquor, he decided now might not be the time to experiment. He looked up to see huge swathes of coloured fabric elegantly draped from the rafters. It all looked so pretty - quite unlike anything he'd ever seen before.

Dick finished his drink and settled himself at the side of the veranda with his sketchpad. He looked up to see the glasses sparkling in the candlelight. He took a deep breath and was immediately intoxicated by the aroma from the frangipani blossom, silhouetted against an indigo sky packed with stars. He thought, surely, no one could fail to be captivated by this magical atmosphere.

He saw Uncle emerge from his quarters and walk to the head of the stairs, ready to welcome each of the guests in turn. When he saw Dick, he said, 'I expect most of the people coming tonight will be here out of sheer curiosity. However, it's my intention to fire their imaginations. The plans we have in mind will benefit everyone and I truly believe that it can all be achieved.'

Dick smiled at Raffles in the most encouraging way he could manage. He too hoped that the people attending the feast would, by the end of the evening, feel suitably optimistic. Maybe once the new development started, Uncle would get fewer headaches. Dick knew he still had a lot to learn, but he was no longer a child and longed to be of help - if only Uncle would ask him. Nowadays, they seldom got to spend any length of time together when such things could be explored. For the time being, all he could do was make sure every one of his drawings were good enough.

Dick watched closely as, one-by-one, the guests began to arrive. He couldn't help being impressed by the splendour of their beautiful clothes and sparkling jewels. No matter what anyone said to the contrary he thought this banquet was just as magnificent as any of the grand occasions he had attended in London with Uncle, a few years ago.

With the exception of Colonel Farquhar, all the European gentlemen dressed in formal evening attire. The Chinese tailors had profited greatly from events such as this evening, by supplying dinner jackets, breeches, and shirts in silk or other materials much lighter than those brought out from England. Baba Tan, the most influential of the Peranakan merchants was wearing western clothes, which he preferred to do when he was with Europeans.

Dick began to sketch Sophia. She had come to stand beside Uncle now and it was easy to quickly capture her outline. He then began to fill in the detail, showing her distinctive curls just below her ornate turban-like headdress. It was decorated with tiny pearls and he thought she looked very elegant. He drew long lines to represent the way the folds of her yellow and blue silk dress fell from the nipped-in waistband. She wore her favourite necklace, which sparkled in the soft light of the oil lamps. Tonight, it was displayed to perfection above her fashionably low-cut neckline.

Only a handful of Europeans wives had joined their husbands in Singapore, but two of them had seized the opportunity to buy new gowns and show them off. One appeared to drift along the veranda in a froth of sprigged muslin, whilst the other walked more purposefully in her pale blue lace creation. Both had intricately embroidered silk slippers and a pretty arrangement of flowers in their hair.

Dick had just finished sketching the outlines of both ladies when he noticed the arrival of the Temenggong and the Sultan. Neither man had brought an escort. He knew, from something Uncle had said, that the Temenggong's wife was long dead, and the Sultan would not dream of bringing his women amongst European men. He also knew that it was the Malay custom for men and women to sit separately when dining formally. He was not surprised, therefore, to see both men seated at the far end of the table, well away from the few women present.

Dick was amused to see several of the European men glancing in the direction of these latest arrivals. He heard some people talking about the magnificence of their attire, but one voice was more strident than the others. He couldn't quite make out who was speaking, but he knew not everything he heard was entirely complimentary. The man was making pointed remarks about the colours worn by the two gentlemen, and their similarity to those chosen by Sophia.

When everyone was seated, Dick put down his sketch pad for a moment and watched Uncle rise to his feet, offering an official welcome. He invited everyone to enjoy the good food and liquid refreshments.

Mary-Anne's usual helpers had, this evening, been supplemented by servants from other households and now they appeared, resplendent in their best apparel, to offer the celebratory feast to all the guests. The different aromas that floated towards Dick made him feel hungry as one by one the different platters passed in front of him. There was Bengal mutton with Java potatoes; traditional Chinese rice and noodles, dishes with chicken or fish and bird's nest soup; Peranakan dishes flavoured with coconut milk, green chillies and lemongrass; various curries and bread. Then came his Malay favourites, beef rendang, nasi goreng and nasi padang.

He decided to slip out for a while and help himself to some of the food set aside for the helpers. When he reached the kitchen, he saw one or two of the servants squatting down on their haunches, tucking into their favourite dishes. Someone indicated to help himself and he quickly filled his bowl.

When he returned to the banquet, this time at the opposite end of the veranda, he noticed even those with the heartiest appetites could eat no more. A few moments later, Uncle rose to his feet again.

'We're here tonight, ladies and gentlemen,' Raffles said, 'to celebrate the approval of the Town Plan by the Land Allotment Committee and to look to the future of this amazing settlement. Please join me in raising your glasses to - our on-going success.'

All the guests shuffled their chairs out of the way and rose to their feet. Most - but not all - joined with Raffles in repeating, 'Our on-going success.'

'I know some of you are reluctant to move from the east bank of the river,' Raffles said once they had returned to their seats. He paused for a while, then continued, 'A short while ago, I found myself looking at the town from the top of the hill, and I marvelled at the way it has grown on this side of the river ...,' he turned to smile at Dick, as he remembered the day the two of them had stood there together looking at the whole settlement.

'It seems to me that the only sensible way to develop the west bank is to use the earth from the hill at South Point and fill in the swamp. I discussed the idea with Lieutenant Jackson over there and he agreed that it could be done. Now, I'm glad to say, the Land Allotment Committee have given their approval too.'

Smiles of appreciation spread around the room and everyone began to relax. Then, somewhere out of Dick's line of vision, he heard some low muttering. He glanced across at Raffles who was looking uneasy, but there was no way of telling if the commotion came from some guests continuing their own conversation or whether it signified genuine disquiet.

'But what about those of us who have already invested in building our houses and godowns on this side?' one of the merchants asked. His speech was already slurred from a surfeit of alcohol. He tried to struggle to his feet, but the man sitting next to him put a restraining hand on his arm and whispered something inaudible in his ear. Raffles knew that the man who had spoken was called Sidney Percy; he had been warned that Percy was a potential trouble-maker but had hoped that he would not cause any trouble this evening.

He'd learned from Colonel Farquhar that Percy had arrived in Singapore from Malacca just over three years ago, but no one knew much about him.

'As you know full well, Mr. Percy,' Raffles emphasised the name, 'Colonel Farquhar granted only temporary leases on that land to you all.'

Several pairs of eyes turned to look at Farquhar, but his head was cast down and he refused to comment.

Dick noticed Sidney Percy glaring at the other European merchants, but they all remained silent.

'And where is the money for all this activity coming from?' Percy continued.

'I will have to draw on some money from Calcutta, but I'm sure I can convince them that their investment will bear fruit,' Raffles responded. 'Each of you will be assessed on your current property, but don't worry gentlemen, you will be properly compensated for any losses according to the current value of your businesses. The new land leases will be put up for auction in the New Year. We will then require half of the money in advance, and the other half when you have moved to your new locations. The port is free, gentlemen, but that does not mean everything else is free too,' he added, looking directly at Sidney Percy.

During the remainder of the evening, many more questions continued to be asked. Dick tried to make a rough sketch of each of the men as they rose to their feet, some to pose a challenge and others to offer words of encouragement. The majority of the guests supported Raffles in his enthusiasm for the new venture, but a few members of the gathering remained sceptical.

A low rumble similar to the grumbling noises heard earlier in the evening became more audible. Most of the whispers came from the merchants who had foolishly assumed that the land leased to them by Colonel Farquhar was a permanent arrangement. Dick distinctly heard the arrogant voice of Sidney Percy saying that the East India Company had no intention of sending funds to make Singapore a permanent settlement.

He looked anxiously at Uncle, but whether the comment had travelled to the far end of the table or not, Raffles chose not to be drawn into an argument. Instead, Dick watched him walk towards the Temenggong and the Sultan. Dick knew that Uncle trusted neither of them particularly and wondered what he might be about to say in order to gain their loyalty.

'Gentlemen,' Raffles said as he looked them both in the eye and continued to address them in Malay, 'with your help, I believe that this place can be even more successful than it is at present. In the last three years, we have already established a great location for free trade, but to develop even further, I need your support.'

The red-toothy grin of the Sultan beamed back at Raffles and the eyes of the Temenggong continued to sparkle. Someone at the other end of the table shuffled their chair and sighed loudly. Dick worried that Sidney Percy might be about to make more fuss, but Raffles ignored the interruption and continued with his speech.

'Gentlemen, the plan that has been agreed by the Land Allotment Committee will require the co-operation of everyone. The European town needs to be located east of the Bras Basah stream; it will extend out towards your Istana at Kampong Glam, Sultan Husain and it will stretch inland as far as the foothills of the Rochor River. There will be land reserved for the Arab community in the vicinity of the Istana, and the Bugis community will be moved further east, to the mouth of the Rochor River. This means that your current village, Temenggong, will need to move to a much larger plot of land at Telok Blangah, about a quarter of a mile west of the Chinese township.'

'The land at Telok Blangah is good, I think,' the Temenggong replied. 'But how are we supposed to move a whole village?'

'I will arrange for some sepoys to help with both the dismantling and the rebuilding of your houses, but you will supervise which buildings are the first to go and how the layout of the new kampong will be arranged.'

'And what will we receive in return for our co-operation?' the Sultan interrupted.

'You will both receive a regular payment, a large sum of money, from the East India Company in return for the right to further develop the British settlement.' Both men grinned back at Raffles and quietly nodded their assent.

Dick finished his drawing just as Uncle took a deep breath and turned back to address the entire assembly. Raffles was anxious not to give Sidney Percy, or any of his cronies, the opportunity to upset anyone else this evening. He continued, 'Ladies and gentlemen, this is just the beginning - and not just of a new design for the town. We will also establish a system of justice and we will create an educational institution of higher learning so the noble civilisation that formerly existed here will be great again. May I ask you once more to raise your glasses and join me in a toast ... to the future success of Singapore!'

CHAPTER 7
Singapore, Early November 1822

Chin Ming and Wing Yee awoke one morning to hear the slow, grinding sound of chains as the anchor was being released. It was exactly one week after they had been thrown together during the storm, and October had turned into November. The junk shuddered when it was finally secured to the seabed. Soon after, the sound of footsteps - running, sliding, stamping - above and around their small abode began to form a regular pattern, indicating the intense activity of off-loading cargo had begun. Chin Ming looked at Wing Yee. The bond that had begun to develop between them meant that no words were needed. They both knew they had, at last, arrived in Singapore. It was the destination they had both dreamt about, but what did it really hold in store?

Chin Ming felt just as she did when she'd first boarded the ship. The muscles in her stomach had tied themselves into a knot, her legs began to shake, and her body felt tense; she was listening for the moment when they would be summoned. The waiting was endless.

The warmth of the afternoon sun seeped through the door of their cabin and Shu Fang was becoming drowsy in the corner. A few moments later, the door was flung open, and the unaccustomed brightness blinded them all. The bosun appeared and beckoned them forward.

It needed both Wing Yee and Chin Ming to help Shu Fang to her feet and encourage her to move any distance. During the voyage, she had only been out of the cabin for short periods to relieve herself and hastily toss a modicum of water over her body from a communal bowl. The opium had gone from her body, but she had eaten very little since the storm and was now quite weak. She tottered around in great discomfort, having not walked any distance for so long. She had not been privileged with the long periods of fresh air that Wing Yee and Chin Ming had enjoyed whenever they visited the captain. The older woman had continued to accompany the younger one whilst she worked on the documents Captain Lim handed to her each day. Wing Yee sometimes made other solitary visits, those that took place late at night, when Shu Fang and Chin Ming slept.

Chin Ming looked around as Wing Yee helped Shu Fang to the side of the junk. She could see the last of the bumboats, heavily laden, making its way from the junk towards the shore. Below the ship, bobbing around in the water was another craft with only an oarsman and one member of the crew on board. They beckoned to the women. On the deck of the junk, the bosun pointed to the rope ladder and instructed them to make a move.

Wing Yee looked around for any sign of Captain Lim, but he had chosen to absent himself from any formal parting. She shrugged her shoulders and began the descent. The ladder swayed slightly as she put first one foot, then the other, onto the rickety supports.

'Keep looking at me, don't look down,' Chin Ming shouted.

Once Wing Yee was in the bumboat, she encouraged the others to follow, but Shu Fang was too terrified to begin the descent. The bosun eventually hoisted her over the side of the ship and lowered her, unceremoniously, into the waiting lighter. She lost her balance and fell directly on top of Wing Yee; the small craft rocked precariously from side to side until they had scrambled to their feet and crawled towards the stern. They sat across from each other, each clinging on to the side of the boat. Chin Ming stepped forward. She took one last look at her surroundings; the scrubbed decks with their coiled ropes, the water barrels now empty and the oil lamps extinguished after their night-time vigil. The flapping noise of the sails attracted her attention. They had already been lowered after their weeks of hard labour; only the long red flags on the central mast now remained. She smiled and was glad that they had arrived safely, whether or not it had anything to do with these so-called lucky charms.

'Hurry,' shouted Wing Yee. 'Why are you dawdling? I thought you'd be first in line to get off that hulk and see what Singapore has in store for you!'

Chin Ming was conscious that the bosun was staring at her. Fearful that he might grab hold of her, or even worse, push her overboard, she swung her light frame over the side of the junk and found her footing on the ladder. The few possessions that she'd managed to retain - a few rags of clothing and her father's precious scroll - were already tied in a piece of cloth around her waist.

She settled herself onto a seat alongside Wing Yee, with her back towards the *Golden Phoenix*. She was thankful that she'd survived the journey, but the junk now represented the past; her future is what lay ahead.

One of the men lifted the oars and the boat began to pull away. Chin Ming filled her lungs with the refreshing sea air and gazed across to the golden sands that bordered the island. What she saw was a blur of small hills covered in green vegetation and a small collection of buildings that might be the town. Her father had told her many stories involving princes from Java and Sumatra hundreds of years ago that romanticised the origins of Singapore. He'd also told her about the island being recently settled by the British. Even so, she hadn't expected it to be so small, with no obvious signs of its glorious past.

*****

Raffles never thought of his secretary as anything but an equal. He'd been surprised, therefore, when Abdullah had preferred not to attend the dinner party. Instead, he'd continued to work in the Company office until the light became too poor to see properly. News had been received in the afternoon that a large junk from Guangzhou was due to anchor the following morning. He'd promised to accompany Dick to the beach, so that they could watch the bumboats going to offload the cargo and bring it back to the godowns along the river. He wanted to make sure that all his work was up to date.

They met, as agreed, just before noon in the Company office. Dick was still sleepy, having not got to his sleeping mat until late. He yawned as he greeted Abdullah.

They talked about the previous evening for a while, with Dick enthusiastically describing the beautiful clothes, the sparkling jewels, and the magnificent feast. He omitted to say anything about the disruption caused by Sidney Percy, choosing instead to focus on the splendid speech that Raffles had made at the end of the evening. Abdullah smiled at Dick's excitement as they began to stroll towards the mouth of the Singapore River. They arrived just in time to see the beginning of a flurry of activity.

'Look, over there, all those lighters heading out to sea in such a hurry. The new arrival from Guangzhou must be ready to off-load. If we walk along the beach a little way, we'll get a better view,' Abdullah said.

Several of the fishermen from the kampong had already gathered. They greeted Abdullah and pointed in the direction of the junk, anchored some way off. The outline of the ship was still magnificent, even with its sails taken in. Their sandaled feet sank into the soft, hot sand as they made their way towards the edge of the water. They could see several ships anchored in the bay, but the Chinese junk was the one that commanded most attention.

'Why do they fly those long red flags?' Dick asked.

'The sailors believe they protect the ship and themselves from danger,' Abdullah replied, 'some sort of good luck charm I suppose.'

'Look, some of the lighters are beginning to come back,' said Dick. 'Do you think they've loaded up already, or could they be coming back empty?'

'Junks have lots of different compartments. The cargo is placed in specific parts of the ship, and that makes it easy to offload as quickly as possible,' Abdullah said. 'The sooner they get the cargo to the warehouses, the quicker the captain will be paid.'

A group of men, whom neither of them had noticed before, began to move towards them to observe the growing activity more closely. They said that the ship belonged to Lim Tse Poh, a merchant from the south of China. He always came around this time of year, just before the monsoon set in. He usually brought silks and ceramics, sometimes other things. When Dick asked "what other things" the men looked shifty, shrugged their shoulders and moved away.

Over the course of the next two hours Dick counted nearly twenty fully laden bumboats return to the go-downs along the east side of the river. Some went back and forth to the junk two or three times before all the activity eventually went quiet. They began to turn away, ready to make their way towards the town when Dick noticed something strange.

'Something else is happening,' he said. 'Look, there's another boat out there - it's not a bumboat, it's much smaller. There are people getting into it.'

'I expect that's some of the crew who are due for some shore leave,' Abdullah said.

'No,' said Dick, 'they're not men, they're too small. Well, there are two men - one's doing the rowing, the other one is just sitting in the bow, but the others look like young boys ... they might even be women? They don't look very happy, whoever they are. Let's wait here a bit longer and see what happens.'

They had to wait quite a long time before this last boat was close enough for them to be sure about its passengers. Sitting slightly apart from the rest, an arrogant-looking Chinese man kept his gaze firmly on his precious cargo. Dick counted three women. Two of them sat close together; they appeared to be inspecting the shoreline, but he couldn't decide whether they looked anxious or excited. The other woman was slumped against the side of the boat; maybe she was weary after the long journey. Dick hadn't told Raffles any of the details Captain Flint had divulged about the *Ah-Ku* women who came here from China to provide entertainment in the town's brothels. But when he took a second look at the three women in the boat, he wondered whether they could be the 'other things' the fishermen had referred to earlier on.

He stared at the boat as it changed course and headed into the mouth of the river. Now, closer to the shore, he could see the women more clearly. One of them in particular seemed to be gazing in his direction; she was much younger than the others, perhaps about his own age. He instinctively waved, and he thought she noticed him. He was sure she had smiled, but then she looked quickly away, as if embarrassed.

As the boat slowed and turned into the entrance to the river, it became steadier and ceased to rock from side to side. Dick waited to see if the girl would glance in his direction again, but she was now engaged in conversation with the woman sitting next to her. He wondered what they felt as they approached their new home. Maybe excitement, maybe a little sadness? They might be glad to leave their past life behind them, but perhaps they remembered happier times?

Abdullah had drifted over towards a couple of fishermen who had remained behind. This gave Dick an opportunity to gaze at the solitary boat without any comment from his friend. He had never seen anyone quite like her, the young girl who had shyly returned his greeting. Her long, black hair turned the darkest shade of blue as the sun's rays put her in their spotlight. Instead of the pockmarked skin he'd seen amongst the coolies, hers looked fresh and unblemished. She had dark, almond-shaped eyes, but she was oblivious to everyone around her as she searched the faces of the many by-standers along the length of the quay. Dick glanced at the woman sitting next to her; she was, he imagined, older than her companion. Something about her reminded Dick of someone he once knew. A faint image of another beautiful woman crept into his consciousness. The figure was emerging from the muted shadows of his past, his mother maybe, but the recollection remained intangible and shallow.

The boat was now very close to the quay. He saw the girl look around as she stepped ashore, but was reprimanded immediately by one of the men accompanying them; maybe he was the person in charge of them? She was then pushed towards the other two women and propelled along the walkway, disappearing into the anonymity of the crowd. The whole scene made Dick feel uneasy. There was something about this girl that made him think she couldn't possibly be an *Ah-Ku*, not yet at least. If that was the case, maybe she could be rescued. He knew Uncle was trying to stamp out prostitution - after all, that was part of the disagreement with Colonel Farquhar. He instinctively wanted to hurry to her side and protect her from whatever fate lay in store. He turned to Abdullah.

'What's going on?' Dick asked. 'What are they doing to those poor women? What's going to happen to them?"

'I think they want to get them out of sight quickly, before anyone in authority notices. It's likely that they've been brought here illegally. If there's any chance of finding out what's going on, we'd better hurry,' Abdullah said. 'We need to get to the quay before they are taken away.' They both quickened their pace, heading back towards the godowns.

Dick needed no encouragement. The image of the young

girl being pushed and prodded as she'd emerged from the bumboat was distressing enough, but he could tell from the forlorn expressions on the faces of the other two women that none of them was particularly happy. The one who had been sitting a little way apart from the other two walked in a strange way, as if she was finding it hard to keep her balance. She took tiny steps, tottering from side to side as she tried to keep pace with the others. In contrast, the younger one walked with grace and poise. He wondered whether this was just her youth, a naturally defiant spirit or whether there was something he had yet to learn about Chinese women.

Then, he noticed the man thrusting his stick into the young girl's back again, but he didn't see her wince with the pain. Neither did he see her force back the tears that welled up in her eyes, but he could tell, even at this distance that something was wrong. He and Abdullah continued to fight their way through the crowd, but they had no more sighting of the three women. They simply disappeared amongst the throng of coolies busily engaged in moving the last remnants of cargo from the many other bumboats on that part of the river.

Dick kept bumping into Abdullah as they made haste towards the quay. They tried to speed up, but the busy hawker stalls in the bazaar had already started to prepare their specialties for the evening. They had to tread carefully, avoiding bowls of shrimp, baskets of vegetables and the occasional live chicken. It took some time to reach the new Monkey Bridge, which Lieutenant Jackson had just finished building, linking one side of the river with the other. They crossed the road and hurried along the quay on the Chinese side, but being unfamiliar with these warehouses, they had no idea where to start looking. Their disappointment rose when they discovered that most of the bumboats bobbing about on the water had now been unloaded, and their cargoes already stored safely in the godowns.

There was no sign of anyone who might be able to tell them about the dubious human cargo they sought. All that remained of the intense activity from a short time ago, were some labourers unloading bags filled with pepper and gambier, everyone else had disappeared. It was no use asking these coolies for any information, they would only be able to converse in their native tongue - Hokkien, Cantonese, or another dialect from their home in China. Neither Dick nor Abdullah could hold a meaningful conversation with them.

They looked at each other in despair. 'I'm afraid we're too late,' Abdullah sighed. 'We may never know what happened to those women - I've heard that such people just disappear, never to be heard of again.'

'But we can't simply give up!' Dick said. 'Besides, Uncle will be very angry when he finds out what's been going on.'

'Yes, my friend, I'm sure the Tuan will be very unhappy indeed, but I'm not certain what difference that will make,' Abdullah replied. 'The people who organise these sorts of transactions are very cunning; they cover their tracks and leave little evidence behind. It will be too difficult to prove that what we saw -or thought we saw - today was anything underhand.'

Dick refused to believe there was nothing Uncle could do, after all, he'd said only last night at the dinner, that he was going to put everything right. Surely, he wasn't just talking about the layout of the town, it must include all the other things that hadn't gone according to the original plan. Dick needed to find him quickly. He was sure that Uncle would be able to get to the bottom of it all. He said a hasty goodbye to Abdullah and began to make his way towards the Company office.

The light had started to fade and very soon it would be completely dark. One or two oil lamps had already been lit. Dick began to run. He wanted to catch Uncle before they returned home for the evening. He burst in through the door and startled Lieutenant Jackson, who was carefully rolling up some papers with his most recent designs and proposals for the new roads.

'Whatever is the matter?' the Chief Engineer enquired. 'What's happened to cause you to run in this humidity, are you alright Dick?'

'I ... I was looking ... I was looking for Uncle,' Dick gasped.

'I'm afraid you've missed him. He left about an hour ago. He's been feeling unwell all day. This morning, he woke up with one of his bad headaches and it's been getting worse all through the day. I tried to persuade him to leave earlier, but he insisted on drafting a letter to Calcutta and finalising the paperwork for the Town Committee.'

Dick flopped onto the floor. If Uncle was in that much pain, he knew from previous occasions that he wouldn't be able to speak to him this evening. As soon as he got his breath back, he thanked Lieutenant Jackson for the information, pulled himself to his feet and said he must be getting home.

As expected, when he reached the house, he found that Uncle had already retired into a darkened room. Everyone was going about their business quietly so that he wouldn't be disturbed. Dick couldn't quite believe that only twenty-four hours ago the place had been bedecked for the evening celebration, with guests beginning to arrive and everyone in such a jolly mood. Then, he remembered the anxious look on Uncle's face just after the man called Sidney Percy had muttered his final grievance. At the time, Dick thought Raffles had ignored the disturbance, but now he thought it might well have been the cause of today's headache, the first Uncle had suffered for some time.

Dick too went to bed early, but his thoughts muddled around and about his head; he couldn't sleep. He tossed and turned, going over the scene he had witnessed over and over again. He was convinced that something dishonest was going on and he was determined to get to the bottom of it.

Maybe Uncle would feel better in the morning, then he could tell him about everything that had happened today. If there was no improvement, then maybe he'd just have to look for some clues to the mystery all by himself. Eventually he drifted into a fitful and restless sleep, interspersed with dreams of female figures being dragged out to sea, ships being smashed on treacherous rocks, doors being closed and the haunting image of a young girl holding out her arms.

CHAPTER 8
Singapore

On their arrival, the towkay's men hauled the three women from the bumboat and hurried them away from the quay. Chin Ming dawdled behind the other two, trying to examine her surroundings but whenever she slowed down a sharp pain shot along the length of her spine. The man who brought up the rear of the procession prodded her with a long metal rod as if she was an animal about to stray from the rest of the herd. Finally, all three found themselves being herded towards the door of an unsavoury-looking dwelling that overhung the water. Once inside, one of the men showed them to a room at the back of the house, completely bare apart from some rattan sleeping mats and some folded sarongs.

'I come back in morning - take you to towkay,' he said in Cantonese and then withdrew. Before anyone had time to comment, the door opened again, and a Malay woman appeared with their supper. Having been at sea for so long, Chin Ming longed for some meat or perhaps some fruit, but bowls of rice with a few meagre vegetables was all that was offered. When the women appeared to collect their bowls, she pointed to the pile of sarongs.

'Put these on,' she said in Malay, but none of them understood her and they remained seated. Then, she picked up one of the sarongs and wrapped it around herself; when it was firmly tied, she put her head against her folded hands and pointed to the mats.

'She wants us to change into them, I think,' Wing Yee said

and picked up a garment for herself. The Malay woman nodded and left them alone.

The room had obviously been closed for some time. It was hot and stuffy, but Chin Ming felt cold and frightened. Why did I ever embark on such a hopeless task, she thought. I have no idea how to go about finding Papa and it looks as if I won't even be given the opportunity anyway. The whole idea is impossible. I wish I'd stayed with the missionaries in Guangzhou. Papa would want me to be brave, of course, but right now everything seems so hopeless.

She slid down onto her haunches against the wall, into which she wished she could just disappear. She drew her knees up in front of her, pulled her sarong tight and put her head into her hands so that no one could see the tears.

Wing Yee turned down the lamp.

'Ch ... Mi ... Chi ... Min ...,' these whispered sounds began to penetrate the girl's consciousness, eventually forming into what she now recognised as Wing Yee calling her name. 'Chin Ming, come ...'

She looked up at the woman who, although so much older, she was beginning to think of as a friend, or the elder sister she had never known. Wing Yee beckoned and held out her hand; Chin Ming crept over to the corner that the older woman had claimed for herself. Wing Yee patted the space next to her on the mat and invited Chin Ming to sit down beside her. The warmth of Wing Yee's arm, as it was wrapped her shoulders, was reassuring. When was the last time she'd felt the affection of another human being? Wistfully, she remembered the touch of her mother when she was a child. Each night, Mama would lovingly brush her hair, before tucking her into bed and telling her a story. Perhaps the last time she had enjoyed such comfort had been over eight years ago, a few days before a snake had bitten her mother, causing her early demise.

'What will happen to me?' she asked, speaking in Cantonese. Wing Yee's English wasn't yet up to a lengthy conversation.

'Remember,' Wing Yee cautioned, 'no one here in Singapore was expecting you, so they won't have decided what to do with you yet, but they will see you as a problem. When I see Towkay Boon Peng in the morning, I'll see what I can do. Once I've handed over Shu Fang, I will talk to him.'

'Not ... not working in the brothel. Please,' pleaded Chin Ming.

'I can't make any promises, because I don't know the man, but I will try to convince him that you could be useful in other ways. Remember how I persuaded Captain Lim to let you help with his papers?'

They continued to talk in hushed tones until Chin Ming's eyelids began to flutter. It took only a few more moments before she fell into a deep sleep and Wing Yee sighed, stroking the young girl's lustrous, dark hair. She searched her mind for ideas that might work. First of all, she needed to make contact with the towkay, to find out what he was like and then decide whether or not she would be able to ask him for favours. Nothing could be done until the morning, but before she too drifted into unconsciousness, some plans that might benefit both of them had started to form.

*****

The following day, just after dawn, Wing Yee woke. The sunlight gradually pushed its tendrils through the cracks in the walls of the flimsy abode and soon the floor was decorated in silver stripes. A key turned in a lock somewhere beyond the room, a door opened, footsteps, muffled voices and then, the man who had escorted them from the quay opened the inner door.

'My name Lu Tong,' he said in Cantonese. 'I work for Towkay Boon Peng; he send for you now.'

Wing Yee turned to rouse Chin Ming from her slumber, but Lu Tong strode over to her mat before she was able to do anything. 'Not that one,' he said. 'Master say you bring woman for Englishman, not stowaway. She, maybe come later.'

How did she know this man was speaking the truth? What would happen if she left Chin Ming now? How could the girl set about finding her father if she had nowhere to live?

'Get your things - quick, quick! Get other girl and follow me,' Lu Tong said, already turning in the doorway.

Wing Yee took what little opportunity she had. She knelt beside Chin Ming and whispered in her ear. 'The servant-man has come to collect me and Shu Fang. I am to escort her to the towkay but he says you are not to come yet. I will come back for you when Shu Fang has left with her Englishman. Don't worry, I won't abandon you.'

Lu Tong came back into the room. 'Hurry, hurry,' he said. 'Englishman very impatient. You bring that girl quick, quick.'

Wing Yee had no idea whether Chin Ming had understood what she had quickly whispered; there was no hint of recognition other than a slight whimper - and now she had to leave, her chance to say anything further had gone.

A cart was waiting in the empty street. Lu Tong bundled Shu Fang in first and then pushed Wing Yee and her belongings in behind. He climbed up in front and urged the reluctant pony to move forward. There had been no time to change out of their sarongs and the morning air was still cool. Wing Yee reached into her bundle for a shawl to protect her shoulders; she held it close as the cart rumbled over the uneven surface and nearly dropped it when they came to a sudden stop. She looked up to see gaudy red and yellow lanterns hanging over the entrance to a building that could only be the local brothel.

Lu Tong jumped down and was greeted by a woman dressed entirely in black. 'Girl get out here,' he said. Wing Yee looked at him in astonishment.

'You said you would take us to the towkay,' she said. 'This cannot be where he lives.'

'I deliver girl here. Englishman will come for her later.'

Wing Yee had a sinking feeling in her stomach. She did not like the idea of leaving Shu Fang here, not knowing where she was going and with whom. Thank goodness Chin Ming had been left behind; she wouldn't want this wizened looking woman to get her hands on the young girl. Lu Tong helped Shu Fang walk the short distance to the large red door and all Wing Yee could do was to watch.

Lu Tong returned, climbed onto the cart and they clip-clopped on their way. They doubled-back and then turned down a side street, ending up at the far end of the quay. She couldn't see the rickety house from here, but she knew it couldn't be that far away. Then, Lu Tong beckoned, she climbed down from the cart and followed him towards a large teak door. He pulled out a set of keys from his robe and released the lock. They crossed a pleasant courtyard and entered the rear of the building. From the outside, it had looked like a warehouse, very similar to all the rest in this part of the town, but as she walked into the shadows at the far end, she realised it had been cleverly adapted into something entirely different.

The towkay was obviously a wealthy man. He folded his hands within the long sleeves of his black silk gown. His *queue*, tied at the end with bright red ribbons, hung down behind his shoulders. On his feet he wore slippers decorated with gold braid and seed pearls. He leant against the back of his black wooden chair, inlaid with the most beautiful patterns in mother-of-pearl. As he rubbed his hands together, Wing Yee saw his long, curving fingernails; on his each of his fingers the large, vulgar rings confirmed his opulence.

'You bring woman for English?' he asked. Immediately, Wing Yee realised that this man might be wealthy, but his dialect betrayed his humble beginnings and lack of education.

His command of Cantonese was poor and he often relapsed back into his native dialect.

She stepped forward and bowed towards him. He grinned, obviously liking this acknowledgment of his power, but it also showed that he was pleased with the look of this woman.

'And she is clean, as promised?' he continued.

'She is. There was a storm at sea, and she was very sick. She was not a good sailor and was very ill for several days. During that time, all the poison left her body, and every trace of opium was removed.'

The towkay looked puzzled. 'You say she is sick?'

'Not anymore,' she replied quickly. 'The rough sea made her vomit, but now she is well; she will please your friend.'

'Good,' said Boon Peng, 'you do well. I give you this house for when I come visit.'

She wanted to ask what would happen to Shu Fang, but now was perhaps not the moment. Instead, she said 'I was lucky to have some help - without that it would not have been so easy.'

'What help? Maybe Captain Lim? You will be my woman now. No like if other men have you.'

Wing Yee chose to ignore the barbed remark. 'No, the captain was too busy keeping the ship afloat. It was a very bad storm,' she said. It was, she thought, an honest reply to the question being asked, and she was desperately searching for some reason to introduce the subject of Chin Ming. 'There was another young woman on board, she helped me.'

'Lu Tong tell me about girl. She some run-away child who hid on ship and no one see her?'

'They found her just three days out from the port,' Wing Yee said. 'Captain Lim said he might leave her behind when we reached Cho Lon, but by the time we reached that port he realised how useful she could be.'

'How useful? You tell me more,' said Towkay Boon Peng.

Wing Yee saw the greed in this man's eyes and thought

this might be her opportunity to sow the germ of an idea. If she could show the old man how valuable Chin Ming had been to the captain, then maybe she could also persuade him to consider having the girl do similar tasks for him. After all, a powerful man with little or no education could surely find it beneficial to employ someone with Chin Ming's talents.

She knew she needed to be careful; after all, she didn't yet know Boon Peng or anything about his business dealings. Maybe she should wait a while and get to know him better, before putting forward the plan that had begun to form in her mind. He was probably more likely to support her suggestion if he believed it was his idea in the first place. As anxious as she was about leaving Chin Ming behind, she thought it would be worth it in the long run. Boon Peng had readily accepted her as his new concubine; the house had been promised to her and he would only visit her occasionally. This gave her confidence, but she would bide her time.

*****

Chin Ming took a long time to escape the arms of slumber that morning. At first, the sound of waves lapping against the wooden stilts upon which the house was built, and the sound of its creaking timber led her to believe she was still on board the ship. She vaguely remembered afterwards a noise that could have been a latch dropping or a key turning. She remembered thinking it was a strange sound for the ship to make. Slowly, she stretched her arms above her head and rubbed her eyes. There was a warm patch beside her that, until relatively recently, Wing Yee had occupied. She remembered thinking it was curious and became confused. Normally, they slept on opposite sides of the cabin. Then, she realised there was no movement, no sound either. She sat bolt upright and looked around the unfamiliar room - then she remembered their unceremonious arrival at the quay and the urgency with which they had been brought to this house.

Where was Wing Yee? Where was Shu Fang? Had they abandoned her? Thoughts continued to race around in her head, struggling to understand what was happening. She remembered Wing Yee saying that she would have to take Shu Fang to meet the towkay, but she hadn't realised that meant leaving her behind. She tried hard to recall the last thing they had said to each other the previous evening, but the only thing she could remember was an impression of Wing Yee kneeling beside her side, whispering.

'Why was she kneeling?' Chin Ming said out loud. Wing Yee had called her over to share her sleeping mat, she remembered that quite clearly. They had sat together and talked for a long time and then she supposed she must have fallen asleep. So, when was it that Wing Yee was kneeling by her side? Did it really happen, or was it a dream?

She scrambled to her feet, listening for any signs of life in the rest of the house but heard nothing. The shirt and trousers she wore yesterday had disappeared, but the small bag containing her other possessions was still hidden away out of sight. Her sarong had become loose during her disturbed dreams. She pulled it up to her armpits, wrapped it tightly around her body and knotted it firmly into place. Then, she crept across the floor as stealthily as an animal tracking its next victim and peered around the screen that revealed an open door leading into the next room.

'Ah so, you wake up?' A woman, clad entirely in black silk, swung round to greet Chin Ming in a mixture of Cantonese and stilted English. 'Welcome, my dear,' she purred.

The woman beckoned Chin Ming to come forward by simply flicking the index finger of her upheld right hand. She had dark, lifeless eyes that stared at the girl, her skin was sallow and the teeth - visible only when she opened her mouth to issue a command - blackened and broken. Over her plain trousers, she wore a tightly fitting tunic, that had a tiny motif embroidered onto each sleeve. The yellow threads that once formed a pair of intertwining snakes, had become frayed and shabby. Her face was plastered with white make-up. Two other women joined her and peered at Chin Ming. None of the women said another word, but all three moved steadily towards the terrified girl. The old crow pinned her against the wall. The trio formed an oppressive semi-circle and examined her for a long time.

'Eyes clear. No addict,' the woman in black declared. It was obvious that she was the person in charge and the other two, in attendance to do as she directed. Eventually the woman stepped away and indicated to the others to do the same.

'Yes, Madam Ho,' they chorused in Cantonese.

Chin Ming didn't know where to look and started to fidget. Then, the woman moved forward again and extended her arms towards her. Chin Ming took a small intake of breath, before becoming completely rigid; Madam Ho placed her arms on Chin Ming's shoulders.

'You keep still,' she snapped, looking hard into the girl's startled face. The alien arms moved like the tongue of a lizard exploring its prey, as they travelled over Chin Ming's body.

'Good bones, soft flesh,' she announced as she stood back to inspect the girl again.

'Pretty hair. This good also,' she added. The other two women, standing in the corner of the room giggled. Madam Ho then turned towards them, clicking her fingers as she did so. The giggling stopped immediately, and the women stepped forward to take hold of Chin Ming's arms. She wriggled to escape their grasp, but they held on tightly as Madam Ho's hand slapped her across her face. She screamed.

'Keep still and be quiet!' Madam Ho screeched back at her.

Chin Ming opened her mouth in an effort to protest, but as she did so, Madam Ho thrust a grubby lump of rag between her teeth. She gagged and tried to expel the offending item, but it was too firmly wedged. She slid to the floor, but the women managed to keep a tight grip. The trembling that had begun earlier now returned and her whole body started to shake violently. She had no idea why these women had come here, nor why they held her down. Where was Wing Yee? What had happened to Shu Fang?

She felt light-headed and thought she might pass out, but just then, Madam Ho nodded to her accomplices. Each one held one of in Chin Ming's arms with one hand, whilst grabbing her legs with the other. They lifted her off the floor and laid her flat on a table in the middle of the room. She tried her best to wriggle free but both women simply tightened their grip and made it impossible for her to move. Madam Ho grabbed her squirming ankles so tightly that the combination of pain and shock forced her to keep still.

The women then transferred their grip. One held both of her arms firmly together whilst the other one moved towards Madam Ho. She pulled at the hem of Chin Ming's sarong and tried to make the girl bend her knees.

'Bend knees up,' Madam Ho demanded. When she didn't move, the woman who had snatched at her sarong now took charge of Chin Ming's ankles in turn, gripping them tightly and pushing hard. Chin Ming tried kicking, but it was no use. The woman was ready for her and grasped each of her flailing limbs, before forcing her legs to bend. She then applied her weight to Chin Ming's knees and pushed her legs into the required position. The examination was crude, but quick.

'She intact,' Madam Ho announced.

They dragged her off the table, leaving the sarong behind. Chin Ming curled into a foetal position to hide her embarrassment. She was still shaking as one of the women held out a shirt and what looked like the trousers worn by a coolie. She felt dirty and longed to be able to wash away the sense of shame. Still terrified, she grabbed the garments and scrabbled into them as fast as she could manage, wanting to cover her misery as well as her humiliation. She hardly noticed when they tied a rope around her ankles and then fixed it to a chain that was attached to a metal spike. One of the women pulled the rag out of her mouth and tossed it into the corner of the room. She coughed and spluttered for a while, but there was no fight left in her and she curled into a ball against the wall. Madam Ho snapped her fingers when she was satisfied that Chin Ming had been firmly restrained and the two women scurried to her side. Without another word, all three turned and left the room.

Chin Ming remained transfixed. She daren't move, she daren't speak. Without realising what she was doing, she pulled her hair over her face and dropped her chin to her chest. Behind her hair, her face burned, and she was oblivious to the tears that ran down her hot cheeks. Even when she squeezed her eyes tight shut, the memory of her encounter with the women would not go away and she let out a low moan.

CHAPTER 9

Dick woke with a start. His body was hot and clammy, and his skin began to tingle all over. It was already light, but he hadn't lived in this house long enough to be familiar with the shapes and shadows that pranced all around him. He didn't even know where he was at first. He was like an animal looking around warily, in case anything was about to pounce. Then, the memory of his dreams came flooding back. The events of yesterday drifted through his consciousness like the shadow puppets he'd seen so often when he lived in Bencoolen. He rubbed his eyes and stared into the room. He listened, but he could hear nothing and there was no movement from the family in the house above. Maybe everyone was still asleep. He relaxed a little, stretched, and yawned ... threads of sunlight began to form a pale golden mantle above his head. Normally, Uncle would be getting up around this time, but on mornings following one of his really severe headaches, he was often slow to rise.

Dick decided to remain on his mat for a little longer, wondering how long it would be before he heard some movement. Only then would he be able to find out whether or not Uncle's malady had diminished overnight. A few minutes passed and then he saw the shadow of one of the servants moving across the veranda - the house was beginning to stir.

Dick dressed quickly, anxious to find out whether Uncle was feeling any better. He leapt to his feet and hurried to splash water over his face before bounding up the stairs to the veranda. Initially, he thought he was alone.

Then he turned around and bumped straight into Sophia. She was coming from the direction of the kitchen, carrying a bowl of water. When she saw Dick, she put it down on a table and placed the index finger of her right hand across her nose and mouth, indicating that he should not make any undue sound.

'Is Uncle no better?' he whispered.

'I'm afraid not, Dick,' she said in the softest voice possible, 'he seems to be in a great deal of pain. I have sent for the doctor, though I fear there is little he will be able to do other than give my husband the usual potion of opium mixed with a little brandy.'

She disappeared in the direction of their bedroom and Dick was left on his own. Sophia was always kind, but he often wondered what she really thought of him. After all, Uncle had arranged to adopt him before they married, and she'd had no choice in the matter. He walked the length of the veranda, wondering what he could do next. The smell of freshly baked bread and a pot of coffee lured him into the kitchen. Cook, as usual, was glad to see him and invited him to help himself to some food.

Normally, Dick would be ravenous at this time of day, but this morning he could work up no enthusiasm to eat. After a couple of bites, he thanked cook and wandered back onto the veranda. He looked across aimlessly towards the river. His focus alighted upon the fishermen who had already embarked upon their daily tasks. Beyond them, lay the warehouses - the European ones sitting firmly on this side of the river and a few, less substantial Chinese emporiums, on the opposite bank. It was this area which was about to undergo the greatest amount of change. Dick hoped that his drawings would be as useful when Uncle tried to convince the authorities in Calcutta to finance the new developments. He wanted Raffles to be proud of him - to give him other things to do, to help relieve some of the stress. A great deal of the tension would be eased, of course, if the Company was more enthusiastic about the Settlement, and men like Sidney Percy ceased complaining. If Mr Percy stopped complaining, it would be so much easier to pacify any other merchants, ready to copy his constant criticism.

Since Raffles had first suggested the drawing project, Dick had completed a range of views from the top of the hill. He knew that it was now time to move on to the area around the quay. Everywhere he went, people knew that Raffles had asked him to make the drawings; wherever he went with his sketchpad under his arm, no one ever questioned his presence. Positioning himself along the quay would offer several new vistas to record and also give him the perfect excuse to observe the activities around the warehouses; no one would think anything of it.

By mid-morning, the beginnings of a plan started to develop. He decided to begin with the European warehouses on the eastern side of the river. From there, he would be able to glance across to the other side and keep a lookout for anything that appeared suspicious. Later on, he would examine some of the Chinese warehouses soon to be relocated around Telok Ayer. He needed to get on with the task quickly if he was going to complete it before the sepoys started moving the soil from South Point and filling-in the swamp. He felt better already; his idea enabled him to complete an important part of his drawing schedule whilst providing the perfect opportunity to observe all the activities along the river—the place from which the women disappeared - last night.

His heart was now beating fast. He couldn't wait to get started, hoping that he would find something incriminating to present to Uncle as soon as he was well again. Uncle was bound to be proud of him if he could solve this mystery all by himself. He bounded down the stairs, gathered his charcoal, his pencils and his sketchbook and made his way along the side of the river towards High Street.

He began by making a rough sketch of the merchant godowns, the bazaar and the residency compound. These buildings occupied most of the east bank between Bukit Larangan and Ferry Point. Then, he made more detailed drawings, starting with the huge dwelling, which had its own warehouse, at the eastern entrance to the harbour. When he was satisfied with his effort, he moved on to another one, built on a plot of land between High Street and the river. When he'd finished, his curiosity to explore the Chinese godowns got the better of him and he decided to ignore the other European buildings for the time being. As he headed back towards Monkey Bridge, he met Alexander Johnston, the man who had established the first European company in the Settlement. Dick held a secret admiration for this man. Uncle had told him that, shortly after arriving in Singapore a couple of years ago, one of the first things Johnston did was to purchase a European girl from a Bugis trader, in order to free her from slavery.

'Good morning, young man,' said the merchant as he greeted Dick with a broad smile. 'I see you've been busy already today.'

'It's my first attempt here at the quay, Mr. Johnston. Most of my other drawings have been done from Bukit Larangan, but I thought it was about time I began on the fine detail - before the building works starts across the river.'

'That's probably very wise,' Johnston said. 'They're already making good progress draining the mangrove swamp. Mind you, if we get any of the downpours that are usual at this time of year, they might have to start all over again. Where are you heading now?'

'I thought I'd just wander amongst the Chinese godowns while everyone is still busy. I want to find a place from which I can show the whole panorama - what it looks like right now - unless there is anywhere you would recommend?'

'Well, I'm on my way to visit Baba Tan. You may

remember him from your Uncle's dinner party. He looks Chinese, but he always wears western clothes when he is with Europeans.'

'Yes, I do remember. The man with the roundish face who wore small, wire-rimmed spectacles? He looked very kind. I don't think he joined in the conversation very much. Does he not speak English?'

'Far from it. He learned to speak English when he grew up in Malacca and because of his mixed-race background, he also speaks Malay, Hokkien and a little Cantonese. All that is invaluable in dealing with some of the Chinese junk captains.'

'Has Baba Tan been in Singapore very long?'

'He came here shortly after the Settlement was first established.'

'Isn't that when the man called Sidney Percy arrived?' Dick said.

'I suppose that's right, but they couldn't be more different. Baba Tan began quite modestly. He bought live chickens, fresh fruit, and vegetables from farmers in the outlying areas. Then, he transported them to sell to the people living in the town, as it grew bigger and bigger. He's now accumulated enough money to invest in other enterprises and has started talking to some of us European merchants about joint ventures. Such an enterprise could be very interesting, I for one am keen to talk it through with him,' Johnston said.

'But why does Baba Tan want to work with the British if his own business is so successful, what's in it for him?' asked Dick.

'A very good question, young man,' Johnston replied. 'Baba Tan is Peranakan - his ancestors are Chinese men who came to this part of the world and married non-Muslim women - most of them Hokkiens from ports such as Amoy. Over the years, they've developed a culture all of their own, incorporating some ideas from China and others from Malaya. Quite a few Peranakans adopted English ways of working and their businesses have expanded as a result. Being able to speak English gives Baba Tan an advantage over the Chinese merchants who can usually only speak their own native dialect. Why don't you come with me? I'll introduce you.'

When they reached the entrance to Baba Tan's warehouse, Dick was immediately enthralled by the rows and rows of multi-coloured textiles that had recently arrived from China. His eyes widened and his lips parted; he took a deep breath. This is what he imagined Ali Baba's cave to look like. The kaleidoscope of coloured silks almost made him feel giddy. He had never seen such a rich array of tints before, and it momentarily made him forget his reason for coming to this part of the town.

He sat, mesmerised as Johnston and Baba Tan began to talk. The Peranakan was wearing European clothes, just as Johnston had described. His long, flowing Chinese gown, fixed together at the shoulder with tiny bow-like buttons made from woven thread was worn only when he was relaxing in the privacy of his own home.

Tea was served in minute porcelain cups, but even its refreshing taste failed to bring Dick back down to earth. Johnston was amused to see him completely captivated by his new surroundings and supposed it had something to do with encountering such riches for the first time. When their business discussions began, Johnston suggested Dick might find it more interesting to look at some of the other warehouses further along the quay; he could then decide which ones he might like to draw. Dick jumped up from his seat, realising that the two merchants probably needed some privacy. He was pleased that he was actually being given permission to explore; what better reason could he have to look for some clue or other about yesterday's mystery cargo.

He took his sketch pad with him and began to search for a good place to sit; he wanted to capture the activities of as many people as possible going about their daily business. He strolled away from Baba Tan's premises, to a place that he had never visited before today. Some of the towkays looked at him quizzically at first, but most took little notice. Beyond the first cluster of buildings there was a solitary warehouse, slightly set back from the rest. Strange sounds of men engaged in heated discussion emerged from inside; one voice, speaking English, was high-pitched and angry. The other person spoke in a mixture of Cantonese and broken English. Dick's curiosity got the better of him. He moved forward very quietly. He could just see two men in the shadows, towards the back of the warehouse, one was Chinese and the other appeared to be European. Along the side of the warehouse, he could see a door which was slightly ajar. He edged his way along and crouched down to listen more intently.

'... he now bring two women only - one for me, one for you,' said the Chinaman.

'That was not the arrangement we made. You guaranteed you would provide find me with three women so that I could choose the best one for myself. Why have you not managed to do that?'

'Captain say two run away. This one very good, very young, very pretty; I keep older one, she my concubine.'

'You lying cheat! Why should I trust you? How do I know this girl is everything that you say she is?' the other voice yelled.

'There is one more girl,' the Chinaman replied. 'She stowaway. You can have for special price. You pay now?'

'You can have your money when I see the goods, but I will only take one woman. The other one is your problem. How did a stowaway get on board? I certainly don't want to risk having her,' the agitated English voice continued.

'They say she hide on ship, have no money. I send Madam Ho looksee.'

'You'll have to be careful,' the European continued. 'It's been bad enough since Tuan Raffles arrived with all his high-minded ideas, you know that. Farquhar was always willing to turn a blind eye to our little projects; he was content to condone more or less anything that brought in revenue. Lord High-and-Mighty is a different matter, however. He thinks he knows better than the rest of us and is hell-bent on getting rid of the brothels and anything else that he disagrees with for that matter. The man is quite mad - these are all the things that generate money to run this place! And, have you heard his latest crazy idea? He's going to drain the swamp and move all the warehouses. You, my friend, will be just as affected by all his madcap schemes as are we Europeans!'

Dick couldn't believe his ears.

The European; he sounded very much like the one who had been so disgruntled all through the dinner party. It was the same man, he believed, who had brought on Uncle's latest headache. Could it really be Sidney Percy inside this warehouse with the unknown Chinaman? Dick hadn't liked his behaviour a couple of evenings ago, but he'd tried to dismiss his conduct on that occasion as merely rude. Now, here he was talking to the person who was obviously responsible for bringing young women to Singapore, probably to work in the brothels. He knew that Uncle would be angry when he found out, but how long would it be before he could tell him what he'd overheard? He pressed his ear against the wall of the warehouse, eager to pick up any additional information, but now there was only silence.

Dick remained crouched beside the wall for a while, but all the signs and sounds of activity within the building had ceased. His felt his legs shaking as he slowly raised himself into an upright position. His mouth was dry, and he kept swallowing hard to overcome the terrific thirst he'd developed. He was terrified that the men would suddenly emerge from the warehouse; it was the time of day when they might go to the hawker stalls in search of lunch. They would then discover his whereabouts and realise their discussion had been overheard. He knew he should be getting back, but the effort of moving from this spot took every bit of his willpower.

Making sure no one was watching, he retraced his steps to the corner of the building where the clandestine meeting had taken place. He checked in both directions. Then, when he was confident that the coast was clear, he hurried back along the quay to the magical world of Baba Tan's emporium. Mr. Johnston was just emerging onto the quay, rubbing his eyes as he adjusted to the bright sunlight. Baba Tan followed, with a broad grin on his face. The two men turned to each other and bowed, then they shook hands, covering all cultural niceties. Dick too bowed to their host before turning on his heel and joining Johnston.

'You're very quiet,' Johnston said. 'What have you been up to?'

'Oh, I just wandered along beside the river, looking at the other warehouses,' said Dick.

'And did you decide what you might want to draw?' Johnston enquired.

Dick hesitated before he replied. Although he liked the Scotsman, he didn't know him very well. He didn't feel confident enough to share any of his concerns.

'I saw lots of produce being unloaded - baskets piled high with nutmegs, others overflowing with gambier, as well as the usual array of vegetables and live chickens spilling out all over the quayside. But none of the other warehouses look as colourful and exciting as Baba Tan's godown. I think I might go back and start sketching from there,' he told Johnston. 'Thank you for introducing me to such an interesting man.'

Towards the end of the afternoon, Baba Tan walked across to the place where Dick had been sitting for the last few hours. He moved carefully so as not to interrupt the young man, though he was curious to see what he had been drawing all afternoon.

'Your uncle told me that you had talent,' he said, 'but I had no idea that you are so skilled. You make our humble building look quite respectable.'

Dick smiled. 'I'm glad you like it sir,' he responded. 'Would you, perhaps, let me draw you, standing outside your warehouse tomorrow?'

'My Chinese side would not allow that,' said Baba Tan. 'You might be taking away my spirit.'

Dick looked alarmed. 'I apologise if I have caused any offence,' he said. 'I was ...'

'You have not upset me,' the merchant replied. 'When I am working, I wear European clothes. My European side would be most honoured to stand beside my humble business. Tuan Raffles can show all the important people in Calcutta that the warehouses in Singapore are doing well. Now, come inside young man, I have made some jasmine tea. You must rest for a while, out of the sun.'

The older man and the young boy spent the next couple of hours talking and sharing their memories. Baba Tan told Dick about his life in Malacca and why he'd decided to come to Singapore. Dick was eager to know all about the early settlement and the adventures that had taken place whilst Uncle had been busy in Sumatra. He listened attentively to stories of rats and centipedes, of rogue tigers and leeches. Finally, Baba Tan described how they had survived the floods when the river overflowed its banks during a really bad monsoon season.

Dick felt completely at ease in the older man's company. He soon found himself telling the merchant a little of what he could remember of his own early life and the last eight years spent in the company of Raffles. Talking to Baba Tan was effortless and undemanding. Maybe, if Uncle's health didn't improve in the next day or two, he would tell Baba Tan about the things he'd seen yesterday. He already believed he was a man who could be trusted.

The following morning, he went back to the warehouse, as

promised. The sketch didn't actually take that long, but Dick wanted to test out his instincts regarding the merchant. His mind had been drifting back to two men whose conversation he'd overheard the previous day. No matter what he did to obliterate it, their words kept going around and around in his head. Was Sidney Percy really involved in smuggling women and girls into Singapore? And what of the girl he had seen? Was it possible that she was the stowaway they talked about? Dick wished he had some way of finding out what was really going on before he talked to anyone else. He needed to find out where the women were being held, but he had no idea where to start looking. Should he, perhaps, ask Baba Tan to help him?

'Is the drawing not good? Baba Tan asked as he appeared at Dick's side. 'Have I been moving about too much? You look distressed.'

CHAPTER 10

During her first couple of days with Boon Peng, Wing Yee made sure she did everything she could to please him. Captain Lim's description of the man had been correct, yet he wasn't repulsive, just the product of over-indulgence and laziness. She needed him to like her well enough, so that he would be anxious to please her. Only then could she start to ask for favours.

On the second evening, she introduced Chin Ming's name into the conversation again, but said nothing further. When he visited on the third afternoon, she used all of the charm and trickery from her former way of life to beguile him. When she felt that he was safely in the net, she began to sow the seeds that might convince him that Chin Ming's knowledge of languages and her ability to read and write might be useful to him.

'The young girl who travelled with us,' she said, 'have you thought what to do with her yet?'

'I pay good price for her. Madam Ho say sailors pay more for young body,' Boon Peng said, looking as if he was already calculating the dollars he might collect.

Wing Yee looked away so that he would not notice her anger. When she had regained her composure she said, 'I can think of a way that she could make you even richer.'

'How so?'

'During the voyage here, she helped Captain Lim with all his paperwork.' She spoke to him in Cantonese, hoping that he could follow what she was saying. 'You've already told me that you find it difficult to understand all the official documents that are issued by the British. She understands English. If she read all your paperwork, you would be able to send an immediate response. She could write back in English on your behalf. You would stand a better chance of getting government contracts as well as knowing what everyone else is doing.'

'This good,' Boon Peng said, 'she read notices from Tuan Raffles and send reply. It necessary for Englishman to know wishes of important Chinaman.'

He looked very self-satisfied, and Wing Yee was pleased that he obviously believed he'd thought of the idea all by himself. Wing Yee could see that he was entirely convinced, and she knew he might, at any moment, simply commit Chin Ming to a life of servitude in the town brothel. Even worse, he might send her out to placate the poor souls working in the gambier plantations. Just as she was beginning to think that she'd won him over, he added, 'Men who come here like pretty young women.'

When Wing Yee had first encountered Chin Ming, she could think only of the benefits the young girl might bring to herself. Chin Ming, after all, didn't even realise that the learning she had acquired was anything unusual. In offering to chaperone the girl, she'd been able to spend time away from the claustrophobic atmosphere of their cabin. Then, she'd realised it also provided an opportunity for her to learn to speak English. It was all meant to be a means to an end, but unfortunately, she let herself grow fond of the girl. The more she got to know her, the fonder she became.

Boon Peng was still muttering about the additional money he'd had to pay for Chin Ming and what she might now be worth. Wing Yee was determined to do everything she could to prevent the girl getting ensnared by Madam Ho and being forced to entertain strangers in the way that she herself had been compelled to do so at a similar age.

Her brain was working fast as she began to rub a mixture

of soothing oils into the towkay's broad shoulders. She'd discovered, soon after her first encounter with him, that he particularly enjoyed this slow, tactile form of contact before they embarked upon anything more demanding.

'She is very young and completely inexperienced, you know,' she purred into Boon Peng's right ear. 'Maybe you could use her in other ways.'

'How so?' Boon Peng replied, turning over to look at her and showing from the expression on his face that he was obviously interested.

Wing Yee adjusted her position, with her legs astride his broad frame and her hands gently stroking his shoulders. She smiled at him innocently, as an idea began to develop.

'The men in the lighters that you send out to greet the newly arrived ships are told to tell the crew about the delights awaiting them in the port, is that not so?'

Boon Peng nodded in agreement.

'Well,' she said as she poured a little of the oil onto his chest and smoothed her hands over his torso, 'if you let them have sight of what might be on offer, so to speak, they are more likely to hurry into town quickly looking for Madam Ho and her young ladies.'

His face revealed that she had caught his attention now, but he said nothing, waiting for her to go on.

'Maybe Chin Ming could be dressed in a way that would interest men. She will need some new clothes made for her; in the best silk you can get hold of in Singapore. I could style her hair in a way that would make her look older - more appealing to men - you could then send her out in one of the lighters whenever a new ship arrives in the harbour. All the men onboard will see her. They will like what they see. She could entice special customers, who would be willing to pay above the normal fee. You would soon get your money back.'

'What she say to sailor?'

Wing Yee realised that she would need to explain her plan

in more detail if she was going to make him understand and go along with her suggestions. 'She wouldn't say anything. She would just look across to their ship.'

'What then?' Boon Peng asked, still not entirely understanding what she had in mind.

'The lighter would circle around the ship a few times, just long enough for her to be noticed. I could go with her to make sure they understand she is special. If you think it necessary, I could speak to the crew - make sure they know special means expensive and perhaps, maybe only on offer to the officers.' Her thoughts raced and the more she let her imagination fly, the more ambitious the idea became.

'We could give her a new name, one that was particularly seductive ...,' her voice drifted into silence to allow him time to take in what she was saying and to appreciate this opportunity to make more money. It also gave her more time to think. When she began this conversation, all she had in mind was some way of saving Chin Ming from a future in the brothel. The more she'd talked, however, the bigger and bolder her ideas became. If she could convince him that her idea would make him wealthier, then both she and Chin Ming would benefit.

'Maybe the officers on the larger ships, men who have been at sea for some time, might like her,' she continued. They might say it's only the common sailors who crave sex when they come into port, but the captains and the bosuns are just as hungry themselves.'

'How you know?' he demanded, getting agitated.

This was the second time that he had shown her that he could be a jealous man. She realised that she needed to be careful what she said next.

'The women that I knew in Guangzhou, they told me such things happen,' she said as innocently as she could manage.

'But this girl virgin, what can do?'

'That doesn't matter. She will never actually meet the men

from the ships.'

'Why not? Men want special girl they see on ship. I not understand.'

'And what they'll expect is someone who is very experienced and able to please them. Chin Ming has no experience, she will not please them. I presume the rooms in the brothel are not well-lit, no one will know that the woman who gives much pleasure is not the beautiful creature they saw from the deck of their ship.'

Boon Peng rolled on his side and grinned at Wing Yee. 'You clever woman.'

Wing Yee allowed herself to smile, thinking that she had won him over.

'What if find out?' Boon Peng asked, still not entirely convinced by the idea.

'If you are careful - and not too greedy,' Wing Yee waved her finger at him, pretending to scold him, 'that will not happen. We must choose one of the younger women, maybe more than one, who are about the same size as Chin Ming. As long as they are experienced -and paid a little extra perhaps - so that the officers have a good time, then no one will care about anything else.'

'Maybe, come back for more.'

'Maybe, maybe not. We want them to believe the time they spend with the young woman is exceptional, not something that's available every day.' Her mind raced as she continued to think how she could prevent Chin Ming getting involved in any of this other than to act as a magnet. 'You could make a rule that only one visit is allowed,' she said. 'The officer concerned could spend the whole evening with the woman we choose - she can be available to him for the that one evening, but no more.'

'You think this work?' he asked.

'It will add to the mystery, word will spread about the delights of this very special *Ah-Ku* - there will be no shortage of customers,' Wing Yee reassured him. 'How long do the ships stay in the harbour?'

'Few days only,' he replied. 'Only longer when weather bad.'

'Good, then most of the customers will move on quickly. By the time they return to Singapore they will not remember what Chin Ming looked like, all they will remember is that they had a good time.'

Boon Peng sat up, rubbing his hands together and imagining the silver dollars he might be about to accumulate. 'Also write letter,' he said, just to make sure Wing Yee understood he expected to get full value for his money.

Wing Yee nodded, cautiously hoping that she had, at last, managed to convince Boon Peng to do as she suggested.

'I think about all you say,' he continued, as he roughly pulled Wing Yee towards him. She knew then, that for the time being, the conversation was at an end.

*****

During the time Wing Yee was working to persuade Boon Peng that her idea was feasible, Chin Ming was left in total isolation. The first few hours, after the women departed, left her feeling numb and dazed. She became conscious of her surroundings only slowly and tried hard to block out every single memory of what had really happened. There was no sign now of either the woman in black or her two companions, and she even began to think that it had all been a terrible nightmare. However, she could not ignore the fact that beneath the garments she'd been given, her arms showed signs of being badly bruised, a rope had been knotted around her wrists and another one tied her legs tightly together. The binding around her ankles was fixed to a length of chain, which was padlocked to a rough stake on the opposite wall. Finally, she focused on the sarong, which lay twisted and dishevelled in the corner of the room and she knew the that the whole, disgusting experience had indeed been real. The memory of the woman's creeping hands, accompanied by the giggling chorus made her head spin, she felt dirty and ashamed.

Had it not been for the ropes and chain that held her fast, she might well have thrown herself into the river. She knew now that Father John had been right all along - she might never know what had happened to her father. Still, she wasn't ready to believe that he was dead, but neither could she believe that he would have come to this terrible place. Coming here herself had all been a terrible mistake.

Later in the day, she heard the door unlock and she froze, thinking that the horrible woman in black had returned. She backed herself against the wall, as far as the tightly stretched chain would allow, petrified of what might happen next. The door opened slowly, and quietly. It revealed an elderly Malay woman. She was accompanied by a young boy, who offered Chin Ming a bowl of soup with pieces of fish and a few vegetables. Slowly, the woman untied the ropes that bound her arms.

Ching Ming hadn't eaten all day, but she remained cautious, wondering what sort of trap this might be. The boy gave her a spoon and mimicked the action of eating. She tentatively took some of the liquid from the bowl and sipped it slowly. Two pairs of eyes watched her. The fish was very tasty and made her realise how hungry she was; she ate the remainder of the meal quickly.

The woman had dark skin and was dressed in a long blouse over a loosely pleated sarong. The blouse was pale yellow, and the sarong was made from a length of batik fabric. A shawl was draped loosely over her head and neck. When the meal was over, the woman loosened the ropes around Chin Ming's ankles. Nothing was said, but she indicated that Chin Ming should stand.

Her limbs had stiffened during the time she had been

curled up against the wall and when she tried to get to her feet, she felt unsteady; she held onto the wall until she regained her balance. The woman guided her towards the balcony, which was balanced precariously over the river. The woman then squatted on her haunches to indicate that this was the time and place for Chin Ming to relieve herself. When she was finished, the boy appeared with a bucket of water. She was encouraged to wash her hands and face and was then led back to the sleeping room. Beside the mat, she found some fresh clothes, the type of shirt and trousers worn by peasants in the rice padi.

'My clothes,' she said as she turned to the woman. 'Please, can I have my own garments to wear?' The woman spoke only Malay and simply pointed to the garments left beside the sleeping mat. Once Chin Ming had finished dressing, the woman re-tied the ropes around her arms and ankles, then replaced the chain and fixed it back into position. She closed the padlock and made sure that it was secure before picking up her lamp and leaving the girl alone in the darkness.

Each morning the boy appeared again with some rice or some noodles, which he helped her to eat, and in the evening, he was accompanied by the elderly woman. She went through the routine of loosening the ropes and leading Chin Ming to the place where she could relieve herself. After the ropes and chain had been replaced, she was left alone again, with the sound of water plopping against the wooden stilts of the house and frogs croaking away in the distance.

She spent the majority of each day, curled up into a ball, trying to obliterate the memory of the woman in black. The visits from the boy and the woman continued in a regular pattern, but despite this her muscles tightened every time she heard the slightest sound, never knowing what to expect next. Often, she was drenched in sweat and became light-headed. She wished she could just see something other than the ancient cobwebs in the rafters of this brown house on stilts, with its tiny gaps between the shrunken strips of attap. The space, that would afford a window in a more substantial house, had a shutter that was pushed open and held in place by a wooden pole, but she could see nothing more than a vast expanse of sky, vivid blue during the day and deep indigo at night.

Sometimes she summoned up enough energy to be angry. She was furious with herself for getting into this situation, but mostly she felt hurt and disappointed with Wing Yee for abandoning her. Each evening, when the level of her distress had burned itself out, she found herself imagining countless different voices, some from her past and some much more recent. The voice of her father was the one she heard most often and whenever this occurred, she began to fret about the disappearance of the garments she'd been wearing when she first arrived. It was not that there was anything special about them, of course. After all, they had been taken from the collection of clothing acquired by the Mission. It was the fact that the scroll, given to her by her father, was sewn into the hem of the shirt. She'd managed to keep it safe throughout the whole of her journey here, not even sharing that secret with Wing Yee.

Sometimes, she imagined she could hear Wing Yee whispering into her ear, telling her that she would come back. She still couldn't decide whether this was an actual memory or just wishful thinking. Other older memories crept across her mind too - a vague impression of her mother painting yellow chrysanthemums, the look her father always gave when he was teaching her something new. When she calmed down, the recollection of these jumbled images strengthened her resolve; it was her duty to both her parents to somehow stay alive, she must not let them down. Each night, these thoughts clung to her and tormented her before she eventually drifted into intermittent sleep.

The dark-skinned boy who brought her food spoke neither

Chinese nor English and she spoke no Malay. On the second day, she thought he gave her a lop-sided smile and was reminded of the boy she'd seen on the beach when the bumboat that brought her here was approaching the mouth of the river. The colour of their skin was similar, but the one on the beach was taller - definitely much older - and it was only their smile that they actually had in common. She remembered how she'd blushed when the other boy had waved to her. She wished he was here now. Perhaps he could speak in a language she could understand, perhaps she would be able to tell him her story, perhaps ... but in her more lucid moments, she knew this was a ridiculous idea. There was absolutely no reason why the boy on the beach would be able to help, just as Wing Yee had been unable to do.

She found it hard to believe that the woman she'd come to think of as a friend had abandoned her altogether. Of course, she may not have had any choice in the matter, Chin Ming thought. The fact that she'd disappeared without a word might indicate that she had been forced to leave in a hurry. However, the vague memory of Wing Yee's whispered message continued to haunt her. Was it real, or was it merely imagined?

During the length of their voyage to Singapore, Wing Yee had told her a little about her arrangement with Captain Lim, but she had never really understood the nature of the contract her friend had entered into, only that Wing Yee believed her life in Singapore would be better than how she'd been forced to live in Guangzhou. If Wing Yee had been taken away, how much longer would she be left alone in this house? Would she be sent back to China, or would the awful woman in black come back to collect her?

On the third morning, Chin Ming sat in the far corner of the room, staring at the ropes around her feet; her dull and lifeless eyes encircled by the shadows of sleepless nights. The house was very quiet, and she suspected that she was still all alone, but there was no way of telling. Occasionally, she could hear sounds in the street and on the river. There was a mixture of voices, most likely those of the merchants, the hawkers, and the fishermen, but even if she'd plucked up enough courage to shout out, would anyone hear her above all that noise? She still had ropes firmly tied around her wrists and ankles. The short chain to which the rope was attached jangled if she tried to move too far and pulled against the metal stake that was fixed firmly to the wall. There was no possibility of escape, even if she had the energy. All the courage she'd had back in Guangzhou, and during the voyage, had melted away in the hot Singapore sun.

CHAPTER 11

Chin Ming was beginning to doze as the stuffy, hot morning air dulled her senses. She thought the house was empty, but there was no way of telling. Then, she heard a new noise. It was coming from just outside in the corridor and it caused her to sit as upright as her bonds would allow. She heard two distinct voices; it sounded like a man and a woman, but she could not make out what was being said. It was some time since the boy had delivered her morning bowl of noodles and although there had been no sign of the woman in black since that first day, Chin Ming still dreaded her return.

Her whole body began to tremble. The knuckles in her clenched fists went white. She listened hard but everything had gone quiet. All she could hear was the sound of her own heart pounding like the drums used to herald the lion at Lunar New Year. She could feel the panic rising within her as the image of her father disappearing into the crowd swam before her. She closed her eyes tight and held her breathe. But no matter how hard she tried, she could neither relax nor let go of her terror. After what seemed like an eternity, she heard a door quietly closing. Whoever had been in the house had now left. Her breathing began to ease. Later on, a key clicked in the lock. She tensed as footsteps advanced in her direction. The door opened slowly; its unoiled hinges complained. She forced herself to look, hoping it was the boy who brought her food. Then, the man who had collected them from the quay burst into the room.

'You stand,' the man, whose name she later discovered

was Lu Tong, yelled at her. He spoke in a mixture of Cantonese and some other dialect that she didn't understand. After a while, she worked out that he had been sent to collect her.

'You stand,' he shouted again.

She tried to roll onto her knees, but the ropes made it impossible to do so without assistance. After several failed efforts, Lu Tong came over and grabbed her arm. He dragged her onto her feet and thrust her against the wall. She caught her elbow against something sharp.

'You big nuisance,' he continued to shout as he began to untie the ropes. 'Should throw you in sea to feed fish, you worthless girl.'

Chin Ming cast her eyes down and let him rant at her for as long as was necessary. There was no point in arguing or trying to speak to someone who had no interest in hearing anything she had to say.

'Master say you read and write,' Lu Tong looked at her accusingly. 'He say, this good. I get you clean up; you write many letters for Master. If good, he take you for boat ride,' he added.

Chin Ming was relieved that the man's anger had calmed down a little and she would, indeed, be glad of a good wash. She thought about writing letters for the man he called master, just as she had done for the ship's captain. Such an occupation wouldn't be too bad. It would give her time to think about finding of her father. She had no idea what he meant by, boat ride, but maybe his master lived on one of the smaller islands? She just hoped it didn't mean she would be thrown into the sea if she displeased them. If only Wing Yee was here to ask.

She raised her head and looked Lu Tong straight in the eye, waiting for him to issue further instructions. 'How does your master know I can read and write?' she ventured.

'Master's new woman, she speak for you. You lucky.'

'What is the name of this woman?'

'She called Wing Yee,' Lu Tong replied. 'Master like her.'

After all this time, the mention of Wing Yee's name took her by surprise. If her friend had been able to speak to this man's master, it meant that she hadn't abandoned her after all.

'Oh,' she gasped. 'Where have Wing Yee and the others gone? When will they be back?'

'Not your business. You wash now, then you have rice. After that, I take you to Master.' He continued to untie the ropes and threw them, along with the chain and the stake, into the corner, then he pointed to the door.

Down the corridor from the room which had been her prison for the past few days, she now discovered there was a rough space that served as a washroom. In the corner, there was a vat containing rainwater and beside it a small bowl.

'Take off clothes. Use bowl, scoop out water, make clean,' said Lu Tong. He continued to stand and stare at Chin Ming, smiling in a way that made her feel very uncomfortable.

'I will wash as you say,' she said, 'but you must wait along the corridor. My father would not like to think that a man who is not my husband has looked at me.'

'Your father not here,' yelled Lu Tong. 'I stay. You wash NOW! You lucky get this chance. You refuse, then fishes have good feast tonight.'

She turned slowly away from him. Her face had turned ashen, and she began to shake, but she knew there was nothing she could do. If there was any possibility of finding her father, of seeing Wing Yee again, she needed to obey this man. Keeping her back towards him, she slowly untied the fastenings on her blouse and lifted it over her head. Next, she loosened the cord around her waist that held her trousers in place and let them fall to the ground.

Still shaking, she snatched at the metal bowl, scooped it through the water and through it over her hair and the rest of her body. She repeated this movement three or four times until every inch of her was drenched. There was nothing visible with which she could dry herself, but she refused to turn around in front of this man to ask for a cloth. Instead, she reached for her blouse, then rubbed it over her shoulders and legs.

She struggled to drag her trousers over her still damp skin. Then, she screwed her sodden blouse into a rope-like mass, squeezing it as tight as she could manage to wring out as much water as possible. Then, she gave it a final shake before tugging it over her head and with great difficulty, pulling it down over her torso. She twisted her long, dark hair into a coil to rid it of excess moisture, then twisted it again - this time into a knot - but she had nothing to fix it in place on top of her head. All she could do was let it slip down her back, where it clung to her, like a shiny black snake.

She took a deep breath and turned around. Lu Tong was sitting in the corner of the wash house with a smirk on his face. She felt angry and wanted to lash out. Even the small amount of water she'd been able to wash with had given her renewed energy, but she knew it would be foolish to upset this man, who might still refuse to take her to his master.

She was given the bowl of rice she'd been promised as the sun reached its zenith, but still nothing else happened. She was beginning to feel drowsy in the late afternoon heat when she heard the gently snoring of Lu Tong, as he sat with his back set firmly against the door. The sound blended in with usual creaking of the rickety house. When, she wondered, would he be taking her to see his master? Still nothing happened. The usual voices that drifted across from the busy harbour began to fade along with the light. A few moments later, Lu Tong was awake.

'It dark, we go now,' he announced. 'Come, we go quick. Come, come!.'

Chin Ming grabbed her bundle and walked towards him. He held her firmly by the wrist and pulled her across the fragile plank that led from the ramshackle house onto the wharf. It swayed as they crossed from one side to the other and she was glad when her feet felt solid ground again. The darkness made it difficult to see any detail amongst the shadows that danced around her, but as her eyes got accustomed to the light, she could just make out a row of more permanent structures across the street. She was led to the one at the end of the row. It appeared to be on at least two levels, but even that was difficult to establish in the gloom. A cart, piled high with sacks of rice, had been left at an angle directly in front of the entrance to the building. This made a convenient screen and would have prevented anyone who happened to be standing on the wharf from seeing inside. The front of the building turned out to be a warehouse and Chin Ming needed to tread carefully as Lu Tong propelled her between the crates and other packages. Towards the back of the building, there was a green wooden door that was firmly shut. Lu Tong knocked three times, then he waited and knocked again. He repeated the action once more before they heard a strong male voice uttering the word, 'Enter,' in Hokkien.

Lu Tong pushed the door wide open to reveal a man who commanded authority. He reminded Chin Ming of similar-looking figures that she'd seen in Guangzhou. Papa had told her that such men met together to decide the fate of the law breakers and the destitute. He sat, very upright, on a carved wooden chair that was decorated with dragons. He beckoned her to come forward. She took one or two tentative steps, then flinched as she heard the door behind her being firmly closed.

'Come, let me look,' the man said, now managing to speak in Cantonese.

She edged towards him trying not to stare, whilst struggling to discover what sort of man he might be. He was dressed from top to toe in black silk and when she caught sight of his long fingernails, she realised that he was a person of some importance. She kowtowed before him.

'Good, you taught to respect elders,' the man said. 'Stand up, come, come here so I see you, light here not good.'

She raised her head, saying nothing, but looked straight into his eyes. He told her that his name was Towkay Boon Peng, and he was one of the most eminent merchants in Singapore. He smiled an odd sort of smile, then told her that he had been surprised to learn she had arrived here on the *Golden Phoenix*; that she was not expected. Chin Ming remained quiet.

'I'm told you read and write - you useful to captain on ship - is correct?'

'My father taught me,' she whispered.

'Cannot hear what you say,' he replied. 'You read to me notices from Tuan Raffles. He use English or Malay. You tell me what he say, then write answer. Can do?'

'I can read and write in English sir, but I do not yet know Malay - but I can learn,' she continued in a quiet, unsteady voice. The mention of the name Raffles made her feel light-headed. This was the name written on Papa's scroll, this was the man to whom the letter should be delivered.

'Speak up child!' Boon Peng barked back at her.

Chin Ming nodded eagerly. 'I would like to help you, sir,' she said.

'I get you new clothes - very pretty. You ride in boat - see ship in harbour,' he grinned as he spoke, thinking again of all the money that Wing Yee's scheme could bring to him.

At the mention of the word boat, she remembered Lu Tong's threat. It no longer sounded like a punishment, but she had no idea why she would be given nice clothes and taken out to see the ships in the harbour. Chin Ming frowned and pursed her lips, waiting for an explanation. Boon Peng repeated something about looking pretty and riding in a boat, but her fear of something terrible being about to happen prevented her from making any sense of what it all meant. She was on the verge of asking a question when Boon Peng strode to the side of the room. He drew back a long gold-coloured curtain that concealed a stairway and shouted something which Chin Ming couldn't understand.

There must be someone else in the house. A few minutes later, a woman wearing an elegant yellow tunic appeared. She didn't recognise the woman at first because she had changed the way she wore her hair. When she looked again, there was something familiar about the way she held her head. For a fleeting moment only, Chin Ming could have sworn the woman standing before her was Wing Yee. She was puzzled, as the woman walked towards Boon Peng and stood beside him. There was no hint of recognition, not the slightest hint of a smile. The two of them spoke in a dialect that Chin Ming didn't recognise. Finally, she heard the woman say in Cantonese, 'Let me talk to her on my own, I think you've frightened her.'

He shrugged, as only men with no real interest in putting people at ease can, and walked across the room. When he reached the door, he turned and said, 'Tomorrow. Make right by tomorrow.' With that, he opened another door and disappeared into the back lane.

Wing Yee put her index finger to her lips, indicating she should remain quiet for a little longer. She waited a few moments and then walked to where Chin Ming stood trembling and held her in a long embrace.

'It's alright, Chin Ming, I'm here. It's best Boon Peng doesn't know we are already friends. He will listen to me if he thinks I have no interest in you.' She spoke in Cantonese as the English she was beginning to learn was not yet extensive enough to express what she wanted to say.

Chin Ming drew back, looking alarmed. 'I can assure you; everything is going to be alright,' Wing Yee continued, replacing her arms around Chin Ming's shoulders

Chin Ming began to weep. All the pent-up fear of the last

few days was released and try as she might, the tears wouldn't stop. She felt light-headed as she was enveloped by her friend's embrace and wondered if this was yet another dream. Wing Yee took Chin Ming by the hand and led her towards the staircase, then guided her carefully up the steps to the room above. She sat her down on some cushions and helped her to dry her eyes.

'Your elbow is bleeding. Come, I will bathe it for you,' Wing Yee said quietly.

She smiled as she fetched a small bowl of water to wash the offending wound, adding 'it seems there is always some part of you that needs mending.' After carefully drying the flesh, she produced a salve containing herbs which she gently rubbed it into the wound.

'I seem to be always bathing your wounds,' she said, trying to lighten the mood, but Chin Ming didn't return her smile. 'I'm sorry that I had to leave you alone for so long,' Wing Yee said, seeing the haunted, far-away look in Chin Ming's eyes. She sat beside the girl and stroked her hand until she was sure she had calmed down a little. 'I had to find out what sort of man the towkay is and then think of something that would capture his attention.' She spoke slowly, trying to make sure that Chin Ming understood. 'He is a greedy man - in more ways than you could imagine - so I had to think of something that he believed would make him either wealthier, or more powerful. I'm sure he thinks the proposal I've suggested will satisfy both of these desires, at least for a little while.'

'But I don't understand,' Chin Ming replied, looking anxiously at her friend. 'What is it you want me to do - and why did that awful woman come to see me?'

'What woman?' Wing Yee said, much alarmed by Chin Ming's question.

'She was dressed entirely in black - a bit like the towkay, but not as smart. She had two other women with her, I can't remember much about them, but they giggled a lot. It was horrible, Wing Yee, she kept touching me, stroking my arms, then my legs and then ...'

'What did she do Chin Ming? Tell me, what did she do to you?'

Little by little, Chin Ming described the bare bones of her ordeal, but the memory was still raw and she hung her head, feeling ashamed all over again.

'I can't believe it, I told him there was no need. I thought he'd agreed not to send that old crow to check I was telling the truth.'

'But who is she?'

'Her name is Madam Ho; she runs the brothel here in Singapore. The other women are probably two of her *Ah-Kus*.'

Chin Ming shrank back and looked alarmed.

Wing Yee took the girl's hands between her own and gently kissed them. Then, she slowly stroked her back until she relaxed. 'Look at me,' she said. 'Come on, look at me. It's' going to be alright. I will take care of you; I'll make sure that it will not happen again, you will not be made to work in the brothel.'

'How can you be so certain?' Chin Ming asked. 'Especially if you have to pretend not to be my friend.'

'I've persuaded Boon Peng that it would be a waste of your talents and he can make more money in other ways.'

'But who is he?' she continued to ask, 'and what is it that he wants me to do?'

'He is a man of influence. He has business arrangements with the British and with a number of the Chinese merchants who come here from Guangzhou.'

'But how do YOU know him - and why did you leave me in that awful house?'

'I'm afraid I had no choice. The man who came for us would only take the people he said his master was expecting. I did try to tell you, as I was leaving, that I would speak up for you and that I would come back for you. But I couldn't wake you and I had no idea whether you'd heard me whispering to you or not.'

'I thought it was a dream ...'

'So, you did hear, I am glad of that at least.'

'But you didn't come back. What happened to you?'

Chin Ming, do you remember - during our journey her - I told you that I had agreed to bring several women here? In the end, there was only Shu Fang'

She nodded, still not seeing what that had to do with her and why she had been held in the house by the water.

'Well,' Wing Yee continued, 'that first day, we went to the women's house, only a few streets away. That's when I met Madam Ho. She asked a lot of questions and I took an instant dislike to her. We had to leave Shu Fang with her. First, she and Lu Tong said the Englishman was waiting for her inside, then they said he would collect her later. I wasn't sure of the truth. I was worried that Shu Fang might be expected to join the other Ah-Ku ladies.

After I arrived here, I talked to Boon Peng and he assured me that the money had been handed over, as arranged and Shu Fang had been taken to the house of a European gentleman, Unfortunately, Lu Tong had told Madam Ho about you—she wanted to get her hands on you straightaway. I pleaded with Boon Peng; I told him that you are an innocent young girl who had come here to find her father, that you would never be any good as an Ah-Ku. I asked him to bring you here so that that Madam Ho couldn't touch you.'

'I don't understand,' said Chin Ming.

'There is probably a lot you don't understand Chin Ming. I will try to explain, but not tonight. You look exhausted and it's time for us both to sleep.'

CHAPTER 12

It had been light for nearly two hours, but Wing Yee continued to wait patiently. She realised, as she looked at the sleeping figure before her, that Chin Ming reminded her of her former self - the young woman she might have been. She had tried to bury the growing fondness she had for the girl and so, the concern she had experienced during the time they had been apart had taken her by surprise. She now recognised that she was beginning to think of Chin Ming as the younger sister she had lost. She had given up all her own hopes and plans so that Yan Yee's future would be secure; now she would do everything she could to protect Chin Ming.

The events of the previous day and all the emotion it stirred up had caused Chin Ming, eventually, to collapse into a world of swirling seas, crowded streets and endless flights of stairs that twisted and turned, before disappearing into an abyss. Now, she struggled to climb out of this deep slumber, her eyes would not cooperate, everything was out of focus and her mind was in a total muddle.

Gradually, she became aware of another person sitting beside her. Her first reaction was to recoil and retreat into the corner of the room., thinking the awful woman in black had returned.

'It's only me, Chin Ming - no need to worry,' whispered Wing Yee trying to sound as calm as possible.

The girl looked startled. She sat up and looked around, and then she remembered the previous evening; the shock of finding Wing Yee again and being told things she didn't entirely understand.

'We will spend today quietly,' Wing Yee continued, 'and I'll tell you more about what life here has to offer us. Listen to me carefully. Do as I say and the bad dreams will eventually go away.'

She spent the morning coaxing Chin Ming to eat and drink. She showed her where to wash and made sure that the girl had some privacy whilst doing so. She brought salves to heal her physical wounds and wished that it could be as easy to mend the girl's emotional scars. She sent a note to Boon Peng, telling him that she needed more time to prepare Chin Ming for the role she was to play in his business affairs. She was much relieved, therefore, to receive a message from him in return, telling her that he would be occupied with one of the European merchants for most of the day.

By late afternoon, Chin Ming had listened to her friend describe all that would be expected of her. Wing Yee told her about the towkay and the influence he had amongst the Chinese merchants. She welcomed the idea of writing letters and translating documents for him, but she remained puzzled about the trips out to sea. Why was it necessary to do this? Nevertheless, the thought of getting out into the fresh air would be very pleasant. She decided she would just have to trust Wing Yee for the time being.

*****

The next morning, Chin Ming was rested and more at ease. Wing Yee told her she needed to leave her alone for a short while but assured her that she would return as soon as she possibly could.

'Where are you going?' Chin Ming asked, with a hint of panic in her voice.

'I've persuaded Boon Peng that if we are to look attractive when we visit the ships in the harbour then we should be wearing a *pien fu*, not an ordinary-looking *qipao*. He reluctantly agreed and now wants me to accompany him to a warehouse where I can choose some suitable fabrics.

Together, they worked out that they would need three *bu* of silk for each of Chin Ming's outfits. Being that much taller, her own garments would require four and a half *bu*. Wing Yee wondered how many dollars Boon Peng was prepared to invest in this enterprise and how persuasive she was going to have to be.

Chin Ming dozed a good deal whilst Wing Yee was away, but as soon as her friend returned, she was anxious to hear all about the visit, everything she'd seen along the quay and all that had happened.

'We visited a godown, not that far from here, belonging to a very polite gentleman. He is one of the Peranakan merchants, but I wasn't introduced to him, so I don't know his name,' she told Chin Ming. 'I've never seen so many bales of silk in my life - such lovely fabrics, so many different colours.' Chin Ming asked her to describe every single detail of the visit, envying Wing Yee her freedom to leave this house, even if it was under the escort of the towkay.

'So, what did you choose in the end?' she asked.

'There are six lengths of material altogether, three for you and three for me. I've chosen light green for the *pien fu* you'll wear when we go out in the bumboat. It's really pretty with tiny gold flowers woven into the design and it will be trimmed in a way that I hope you'll find pleasing.'

'What fabric have you chosen for your own *pien fu*?'

'Dark blue silk, with chrysanthemums embroidered throughout the fabric in silver.'

'But you said there was more material. Will we be getting more new clothes?' Chin Ming asked excitedly.

'That's what I'm really pleased about. I managed to persuade Boon Peng that we would need new dresses to wear every day. The others will be simpler, of course, but good quality all the same; one in light blue, one in pale lilac, one in red and the other is an extremely pretty shade of dark peach.'

I can't remember which I intended for you and which for me, but it doesn't really matter, we're both going to have a complete set of new garments to wear.'

*****

In the evening, when they began to prepare some food together, they heard the first crash of thunder. The noise made Chin Ming jump and she grabbed her friend's arm. Seconds later, the whole room was flooded with a brilliant shaft of silver light; Chin Ming's grasp became tighter, and her eyes widened into an incredulous stare.

'It's just a thunderstorm, nothing to be scared of,' said Wing Yee. 'Come over here, we can watch through this window.' She moved to the far side of the room and threw open the shutters to reveal the havoc being caused by the wind and the rain. Another clap of thunder, and Chin Ming rushed to her side.

'Aren't you frightened?' Chin Ming asked.

'Not at all, and neither should you be. It will clean the air and make everything fresh again. I love it; it makes me feel alive, excited and full of energy.'

Together they peered outside, but it was raining so hard by now that nothing could be seen clearly, and the thunder was so loud that they couldn't hear each other speak for a long time. Chin Ming had never seen Wing Yee look so elated.

'I've never met anyone who enjoys storms as much as you do,' Chin Ming shouted over the noise.

'During that storm at sea, on the way here, there was so much to do for Shu Fang,' Wing Yee said. 'Do you remember how sick she was and how we had to clean her up all the time? But it was the strength of the storm that gave me the energy to deal with the mess. I had no idea that thunder and lightning upset you so much.'

Chin Ming smiled, remembering that night and the following days at sea. She recalled Wing Yee issuing orders and telling her not to be so shy. She had liked being treated as an adult and had been determined not to seem weak by showing her fear of the tempest. It was in the days after the storm that Wing Yee had begun to take a real interest in her.

'My enjoyment probably has something to do with when I was born,' Wing Yee laughed, as the noise of the storm began to abate. 'A Chinese dragon is said to be extraordinarily powerful and when it flies it is usually accompanied by lightning and thunder. You've heard about the dragon and the turtle who helped the ruler, Yu the Great, I take it?'

'I don't think so,' Chin Ming replied.

'The story goes that the great leader was at his wits end because the flood water was devastating his kingdom. A dragon, with the help of his friend the turtle, managed to control the water and turn it into a better irrigation system. A dragon always overcomes obstacles, you see!'

Chin Ming didn't believe a word of it, but it made her smile. The noise made by thunder had always filled her with alarm, but recently it had become more terrifying. It sounded like the pounding drums she remembered from the spring festival and the unhappy months that followed. She didn't know which was more disturbing, being reminded of those events or fear of the wind and the rain outside. However, she'd always loved to hear the old stories from China's distant past, so now she tried hard to concentrate on Wing Yee's fantastical tale and eventually she forgot to be afraid of the storm as it continued to strut all around them. When the world became settled again and they had finished their meal, she asked, 'How do you know about the story of the dragon?'

'Like I told you, it's my birth sign,' Wing Yee replied, 'I was born in the Year of the Dragon.'

Chin Ming looked quizzical. Her father had told her all

about the twelve animals that made up the zodiac, but she had never paid much attention, and had no idea which animal was associated with the year in which she had been born.

'The year of my birth and the hour I entered this world make me who I am,' Wing Yee continued.

'And who is that? You know, you've never told me much about yourself - I don't even know where you were born.'

'I'll tell you one day, I promise, but the storm has given me an idea and I want to see what you think.'

'What sort of idea?'

'It's to do with the boat trips we'll take out into the harbour. I told Boon Peng that you should have a new name and ...'

'But why?' Chin Ming interrupted 'If Papa is here ... if he tries to find me, he won't be able to if I have a different identity.'

Wing Yee explained that the crews of the ships arriving in Singapore would most probably have been at sea for several weeks, if not months. 'Most of the men will have been looking forward to their time in port for the last few days of the voyage. One or two may want to visit the opium dens, others may want to gamble away their meagre earnings, but quite a few of them will be eager to spend their leisure time with a beautiful woman.'

Chin Ming gasped.

'Hear me out,' Wing Yee said. 'Our job will be to entice the officers to come into town and spend their money with Madam Ho.'

'But you promised,' Chin Ming began.

'That is all we have to do; make it know that such facilities exist and that they would be welcome. When they see how lovely you look, some may ask your name and we don't want them asking for you at Madam Ho's do we? It will be like playing one of the characters in *Xiqu*, but you won't have to sing,' Wing Yee said with a broad smile, trying to get the girl to relax a little.

'It won't really be changing your name, just something for men on the ships to know you by.'

Chin Ming remained puzzled. She still wasn't sure why Boon Peng wanted her to do this, but if it enabled her to continue to live with Wing Yee, she was happy to go along with it and the fact that she would be given some new clothes to wear was certainly a bonus.

'So, what is this new name that you've thought of?' she asked.

Wing Yee laughed. 'I think it would be amusing if we call you Te Shui. It means *something special coming from the water*,' Wing Yee announced, feeling quite proud of her inventiveness.

It was Chin Ming's turn to join in the mirth now. It was the first time she had laughed in a very long time.

*****

Chin Ming now wanted to know more about the agreement Wing Yee had entered into with the towkay. He certainly wanted value for money as far as she was concerned, but what other promises had her friend made to this man in order to stay alive?

'You promised that you'd tell me all about yourself some time. I don't understand why you left China, why you had to accompany the other three women, or how you know this Boon Peng man, for that matter?'

Wing Yee looked across at Chin Ming for a long time before answering. When the girl had first arrived in her already cramped quarters on board the junk, she had been extremely irritated. When she started to find out something about her background, she quickly realised that the girl might prove to be useful. Her ideas certainly hadn't been entirely altruistic when she started to take her under her wing. She realised once again, how much everything had changed. The more she got to know Chin Ming, the more she realised the protective shell she'd built around herself over the last few years was slowly beginning to soften.

She would do anything she could to prevent Chin Ming having to lead the lifestyle she'd been forced to adopt when not much older than the girl was now. She wouldn't wish that on anyone. Her knowledge of herbs had been useful in helping her to prevent becoming pregnant, but she would always regret not having a child of her own, not having a daughter.

'I will give you just one answer as it deals with all of the questions you have asked,' she said thoughtfully. 'It is to do with the fact that I am now approaching my thirtieth summer. So, let me tell you a story. Back in Guangzhou, I'd been living and working in the ... the women's house ... for over twelve years. I was aware that soon, men would tire of me; they will want young girls who are more attractive, more agile than me ...,' her voice trailed off as she hesitated to explain in any detail the exact nature of her lifestyle.

'I've been there since I was two years younger than you are now. I've known nothing else since I was sixteen. I knew it couldn't go on for much longer and I was worried about being on my own, about being poor and having nowhere to live.'

Chin Ming moved closer to Wing Yee, anxious to know more.

'I was one of three daughters, 'she began. 'My father was the herbalist in a small town near Guangzhou. I was his favourite, always fascinated by the plants he grew and the potions he made and the fact that he could make people well. He taught me to read by having me help with his remedies. I always wanted to help him; I wasn't interested in the marriage my mother was trying to arrange for me. My elder sister was already married, and she kept saying it was my turn next.'

'So, what happened?'

'Just after my sixteenth birthday, my father was accused of poisoning someone. The man was very important in our small town and his family was very influential. It wasn't true, of course, my father would never have made such a mistake, he was far too conscientious. However, rumours spread and the family of the young man I was due to marry asked to be excused from the arrangement. My father couldn't prove his innocence; he had lost face and was so ashamed. He took his own life.'

Chin Ming gasped. She didn't know what to say, or what to do.

'I had a younger sister,' Wing Yee continued. 'She was only ten and very pretty. The marriage broker told my mother that a good marriage could be arranged for younger sister, but they would have to move away, and she would need to raise money for the dowry. It was the marriage broker who suggested selling me to the brothel.'

Chin Ming was horrified. 'But how could your mother go along with that?'

'She was desperate, I realise that now. The marriage broker made all the arrangements, and I eventually became a high-class courtesan. At first, I was very miserable. I hated every minute of it. I missed my father and my easy-going life, but there was nothing I could do to change what had happened. I worked my way from being an everyday girl to the one who was reserved only for the wealthier gentlemen.'

Chin Ming remained silent.

'For the last four years, I became the favourite with a certain sea captain. When he came to Guangzhou last year, he told me he'd been approached by one of Singapore's more influential towkays - a man he dealt with regularly. The towkay himself was acting on behalf of an Englishman who wanted three young women, from whom he would choose just one to live with him in Singapore. It was all very mysterious. He told me the women must be Chinese, must be young and most importantly, they must not be opium addicts. But that was the problem, Lim couldn't find anyone who met these criteria.'

'When he returned to Guangzhou in August this year, I discovered that he still hadn't found anyone suitable. I'd reached my twenty-ninth summer and was beginning to wonder how long men like Lim would continue to find me attractive. I came up with a proposition and he was so desperate to deliver the goods that he eventually agreed. I was to select three women from the brothel and accompany them to Singapore, but as I told you, only Shu Fang came with me in the end. It was essential to make sure she was free of the opium habit by the time we arrived here.'

'But wasn't that an enormous gamble - and what was in it for you? I still don't really understand that part of the arrangement.' Chin Ming said as she began to find her voice again.

'When Captain Lim first told me about the scheme, he also said that the towkay involved in the deal was looking for a new concubine. That's what settled it for me; I saw it as an opportunity for something better. Even if the old man tires of me, and he will, I know I will be looked after - just as the wife he's left in Malacca is looked after. In exchange for making sure Shu Fang arrived here drug-free, I would become the concubine of one of the most prominent towkays in Singapore. I was prepared to take the risk. I thought it would give me a certain status. I knew I would have nice clothes to wear, enough food to eat and somewhere of my own to live. The temptation was too great. All that was, of course, was long before I met you.'

CHAPTER 13

The demons inside Raffles' head continued to beat their drums for over three days. In the worst of his fevers, he told Sophia that - should he not survive this attack - he would like to be buried alongside the ancient kings of Singapore on Bukit Larangan.

Dick, meanwhile, continued with his drawings. Each morning, he woke wondering if Uncle would be feeling any better and, in the evening, he returned to the house with the same wish. To cope with his daily disappointment he worked industriously, so that he would have a whole range of scenes to show to Uncle once the headaches had abated. He worked his way all along the river, capturing the various activities of the merchants, the fishermen and the hawkers in the bazaar, but all the while he sketched, he searched for any clues that might tell him what had happened to the girl he'd seen disappear into the crowd.

At the end of each day, Dick found himself wandering in the direction of Baba Tan's warehouse. Their conversation was easy as the Peranakan merchant had a good command of both English and Malay. He couldn't fail to notice that something was troubling the youth but waited until their second evening together before he asked any questions. By then, he had gleaned enough information to build the bare bones of a story, and Dick felt comfortable enough to share some of his worries.

He began by telling Baba Tan about the junk being off-loaded, and what he had seen at the quay. The merchant listened carefully and noticed the anguish on the boy's face. He put his hands together, interlacing his fingers as he folded them over each other and stared at them for what felt like an eternity. Eventually, he looked up and swallowed hard.

'I know bad things go on. You understand what I mean when I talk about a place called a brothel?'

Dick nodded.

'I'm told another one has opened in town. If true, it won't be hard to find new customers. You've seen how hard the coolies work. The majority arrive here owing money for their passage and they are required to repay their debts from the pittance they earn. Once that is done, they're expected to send money back to China. No one earns enough to support what is demanded of them, and so they turn to gambling believing it will solve all their problems. When that doesn't work, they seek solace in opium, or they visit Madam Ho's young ladies. I'm afraid it's a vicious circle and there are always unscrupulous people ready to exploit anyone who is vulnerable. What you saw - a few women being offloaded and pushed around by a bully - isn't so unusual when a new ship arrives here. Maybe you don't know about these things, maybe this why you are so upset.

'It's not just the slavery thing,' said Dick, 'though Uncle will be very angry about that, when he finds out. He's already had words with Major Farquhar about such matters.'

'So, what is it about this particular group of women that concerns you?'

Dick began cautiously, but quickly became engrossed in his tale. He talked about how the girl reacted when he waved to her; said he thought a regular *Ah-Ku* would not be shy in the way that she had been. Then he told Baba Tan about how she had hung back, when they reached the quay, before being pushed towards the other women. He spoke faster and faster, and he knew he was making no sense.

Baba Tan wondered why Dick had decided to divulge this

information to him rather than to his guardian. He realised the Tuan's adopted son had been in Singapore only a short while. He may not yet have had the opportunity to make new friends and Sir Stamford was, of course, a very busy man. The fact that the young man had developed a personal crusade to solve this mystery he found rather endearing; he was flattered that Dick had chosen to confide in him but wasn't sure how he could help.

Finally, Dick's fury came to a head. 'The day I met you, I heard two people arguing in a warehouse further along the quay. Only odd phrases, of course, but they definitely said something about women - and a boat. I'm sure they meant those I'd seen in the bumboat.'

'Slow down, slow down,' said Baba Tan. 'Now, you say the girl was taken away with the other women, is that correct?'

'Yes, the last I saw of her was when she disappeared into the crowd. By the time Abdullah and I crossed the bridge there was no one to be seen - just a few coolies unloading some sacks of pepper. All three women had simply vanished.'

Baba Tan asked more questions. Dick went over it all again, including what he could remember about the conversation he'd overheard.

'There's something else that's been worrying me,' Dick added. 'One of those voices, it was vaguely familiar. I'm sure I'd heard it before.'

It took Baba Tan a little while to get him to say whose voice it was, but when the name was revealed, the merchant shook his head sadly from side to side and told Dick that he wasn't exactly surprised.

'We must tell the Tuan all about this as soon as he is well enough, of course. In the meantime, I will talk to some of my friends. Someone is bound to have noticed something unusual. There must be a clue somewhere that will help us to discover what happened,' he said.

Slowly, Dick began to smile. He suddenly felt terribly tired, but it was such a relief to be listened to and to be taken seriously.

'Leave it with me, young man,' Baba Tan said. 'I will come and find you the moment I have some news. Now, why don't you go home to see if the Tuan is feeling any better.'

*****

During the next two days, whilst Raffles remained out of action and Baba Tan consulted his contacts, Dick decided to visit the Malay kampong. He had seen the Temenggong only once and that was from a distance. Raffles' plans for the town involved relocating the village to Telok Blangah, so the sooner he could make some sketches of the existing site, the better.

By the time he arrived, the track winding through the kampong was drenched in full sunlight and he could feel the tingling heat of the sand through his thin soles. It went unnoticed by the group of bare-footed children who, as soon as they noticed Dick, abandoned their games with shells, a rattan ball, and stones. He greeted them in Malay, but only one or two responded; the others offered shy smiles and padded softly in his wake.

Dick, followed by the children whose curiosity he had aroused, made his way towards a line of coconut palms surrounding a house much grander than the rest. It was easy to recognise as the one belonging to the Temenggong and he wanted to ask permission from the headman before he began his drawings. Now, engulfed by the shade from the trees, his feet felt more comfortable again. At the top of the steps that led to a long veranda, he saw a proud figure whom he recognised as the Malay Chief.

The Temenggong was no longer wearing the impressive robes he'd flaunted at the dinner party a few days ago, but Dick recognised him immediately. He was about the same height as Dick, with similar wiry black hair, but it was his eyes that made him so distinctive. Each one, a deep-set black sapphire that took on a golden lustre when he smiled. Today, he was dressed in a plain white *baju* over a simple blue and yellow sarong, with a matching piece of cloth tied round his head. One of the children took hold of Dick's hand and pulled him up the steps, where he was instantly greeted by a broad grin and large, smiling eyes that made him feel welcome.

'I see you have met my grandson,' the Chief said in Malay. 'He obviously likes you, so will you please join me for some refreshment?'

Within seconds, a young girl appeared carrying a pitcher of coconut water, which she poured into earthenware drinking vessels.

'May I see your drawings?' the old man asked.

Dick handed over his sketchbook and gulped down his drink. He heard noises of appreciation as, one by one, each of his drawings was carefully scrutinised.

'You have a gift,' the Temenggong said in Malay. He coughed, then paused for a few seconds before continuing. 'I hear you made a special drawing of the Peranakan merchant beside his godown.'

Dick nodded, wondering what would be said next.

'I would like you to make a drawing of me, sitting on my veranda. We will move from this place in a few months' time, I want to remember this house, where I have lived for most of my life.' he said.

'I would be honoured, sir,' Dick responded. 'Perhaps I could come back tomorrow morning, if that would be convenient?'

The Temenggong nodded his assent.

'My grandson will escort you back to the river when you have finished drawing the village,' he said, indicating that their meeting was now at an end.

Dick spent most of the following day making several sketches of the Malay chief, dressed once more in his blue and silver regalia. The jewels in his elaborate headdress twinkled in the bright sunshine and Dick was pleased with his efforts to capture their splendour. When the Temenggong inspected the finished work, he was obviously delighted with all of the sketches, but Dick invited him to choose the drawing he like best. He then promised he would arrange for it to be framed so that it could hang in the Chief's new home.

*****

On the fourth morning after Raffles took to his bed, his eyelids fluttered open. Instead of the blurred vision, interspersed with flashing lights he'd experienced during the height of the migraine, he was pleased to be able to focus and even more delighted when he realised the figure sitting beside the bed was his wife. 'Sophia,' he whispered.

She looked up from the book she was reading and smiled.

'You look tired, my dear,' he said, 'how long have you been sitting there?' He had no recollection of the hours she had spent bathing his forehead, administering the laudanum and trying to make him comfortable.

'It's nothing,' she replied. 'More importantly, how are you feeling today?'

'I feel hungry,' Raffles said, pulling himself into a sitting position. 'How long have I been lying here?'

'It was Friday evening when you took to your bed. Since then, you've passed in and out of consciousness. It is now Tuesday.'

'That long? None of the other attacks have lasted more than two days. I must get up immediately. I need to find out what's been going on in my absence.'

'Do you not think it would be wise to take it quietly, at least for a day or two? I worry that you push yourself too hard.'

'But there is so much to accomplish.'

'Dearest husband, you know how much I admire

139

everything you do, but what is it that drives you? This compulsion to put everything right is taking its toll on your health; it was the same in Bencoolen. I had so hoped life in Singapore would be different.'

Raffles knew that she was right. His doctor had warned him that the only way to rid himself of these days of agony was to return to England and its cooler climate. In some of the letters he'd written to close friends in England he'd admitted his physical frailty and he knew he'd not last more than another year or two in the Indies, but would that be long enough? In establishing this settlement, he had achieved a long-held ambition and he was determined to see it through. He was happy here; he was on good terms with the Temenggong and most of the merchants. The climate was healthier here than in Sumatra and when they moved to their own house, up on the hill, it would be better still.

Sophia interrupted his musing, trying her best to understand. 'My dear, I know from Mary Anne your early life wasn't easy,' Sophia said, 'did something happen then that led to the values you hold so dear? I once asked her about your childhood, but all she could remember was your fondness for animals and plants. She said you had a small garden of your own and loved to visit local nurseries. And when you were older you would spend a whole shilling, at a menagerie just off the Strand, just to see wild animals from faraway countries.'

Raffles smiled, remembering the pleasure those excursions had given him.

'I assume that's when you became fascinated with natural history,' she continued, 'but it doesn't explain your other passions. You've worked hard for everything you've achieved, but maybe it's time to put your personal life - our marriage - first.'

A silence fell between them. She wondered if she had said too much. What did other women, married to idealists, say to their husbands? How did they balance their desire to support all the efforts being made for the benefit of others with their own feelings of neglect and isolation?

Raffles considered her words for a while before attempting to reply. Sophia had been so strong during the time they'd spent in Sumatra, but it had affected her health too. Perhaps he'd taken her too much for granted of late, but what she was asking him to tell her, he'd never spoken about before. He pulled the sheet towards him and began to twist it around in his hands. 'My childhood was cut short,' he said. 'At fourteen, family circumstances forced me to leave school; I had to support my mother and four sisters. An uncle found me a position at East India House, but I was determined to continue my learning in the evenings.'

'You have more in common with Dick than I realised,' Sophia said.

'I never suffered the humiliation of slavery as he did; my family wasn't wiped out!'

She nodded, aware that she had hit a sensitive nerve, but hoping he would feel able to continue.

'I worked hard, but still it took almost ten years before my first chance of advancement came; I was lucky enough to be chosen as assistant to the Chief Secretary when the Company decided to expand its base in Penang.'

She remembered him telling her about his life in Georgetown when they first met. Perhaps she should have asked more questions then, but she knew only eighteen months has passed since the death of his first wife and it hadn't seemed appropriate to probe too deeply. Then, when they met again, he was already talking about returning to the East. Theirs was such a whirlwind romance, there was no time to ask many questions and she was already caught up in his own enthusiasm.'

'I learned to speak Malay on that first voyage,' Raffles said. 'It was useful in Penang as few other Europeans spoke anything other than English. It's always been useful of course, but I suppose it's where my interest in the literature and history of this part of the world began.'

'And you've been conducting a love affair with the Orient ever since,' Sophia said, pleased that his usual fervour was beginning to return. 'But none of that explains why you are so fanatical about injustice.'

Raffles rubbed the back of his neck and underneath the sheets his toes curled up. He took a deep breath. 'Until I was born, my father spent many years trading in the Caribbean; rum, sugar - and I'm ashamed to say, slaves. I didn't realise what that meant until I went to work in Java; I met so many local people there who had been exploited by the greed and self-interest of others. Some had family who had been sold as slaves and taken to the Dutch colony in South Africa.'

'And it's become a personal crusade,' she said, feeling a mixture of pride in her husband and guilt for wanting him all to herself occasionally.

'It's important to get the fundamentals correct,' he said. 'We must make sure that the foundations are strong enough for future generations to build upon. If we get that right, others can complete the task and make this place so much more than a midway port, a convenient stopping place between India and China.'

Sophia sat quite still, waiting for him to carry on. His impassioned words might sound like rhetoric to anyone else, but she was all too aware of the arguments he'd had with the Company about the future of Singapore and how much he wanted to restore its to its former glory.

'For that to happen,' Raffles continued, 'I just need to sort out the land reclamation, the distribution of plots, the problems created by the inappropriate licenses Farquhar has handed out - and yes, I would really like to establish a school here before I leave. Am I being unreasonable?'

Sophia picked up his hands and squeezed them between her own. It was his energy, his enthusiasm and his vision that had captured her heart when they first met; nothing had changed.

'I will have cook prepare some breakfast for you,' she said. 'Then, maybe we could walk down to the Company Office together.'

*****

Towards the end of the day, as the light started to fade, Dick gathered up all his belongings and began to make his way back towards the town. He was just approaching the river when he saw Baba Tan hurrying towards him.

'Someone told me they had seen you heading off towards the kampong, but I wasn't sure which way you would return. I wanted to see you before you returned home, so I waited here, at the crossroads, just in case.'

'Have you got some news?' said Dick. 'Has one of your friends been able to tell you something useful?'

'Better than that, I think,' Baba Tan replied. 'Have you got time for a cup of tea?'

'Of course, I have,' said Dick, 'I'm not expected home for a little while yet,' and he hurried along the quay beside the Peranakan merchant, full of hopeful anticipation. As soon as they reached the warehouse, Baba Tan busied himself making tea and Dick paced about, anxious to hear his news. The scent of jasmine and bergamot drifted on the air and filled their lungs with its distinctive fragrance. The tea was sipped slowly, Baba Tan regained his composure and Dick waited patiently.

'Earlier today, I had a visit from Towkay Boon Peng.'

'Who is he?' Dick asked. 'Is he one of your friends, does he know anything?'

'I'm sure he knows a great deal,' replied Baba Tan, 'but he will not confide in me. He knows I am friendly with the British. He may even know that I'm about to go into partnership with Mr Johnston.'

'I don't understand,' said Dick, taking another sip of his tea.

'Towkay Boon Peng is a very wealthy and powerful man. He owns the licences for most of the gambling dens and at least one of the brothels. He came here from Malacca about three years ago. He has contacts with the Chinese captains, with the Bugis traders, the Sultan and with Colonel Farquhar. More importantly, it is believed that he has also formed an alliance with a European called Sidney Percy. They seem to be spending a great deal of time together and it is rumoured that they have some sort of business arrangement, but no one knows any of the details.'

Dick moved to the edge of his chair, anxious to know more. 'Why did the towkay come to visit you?'

'The towkay was not alone. He was accompanied by an attractive Chinese woman - no, it couldn't have been the girl you saw, this one was a good deal older.'

'What did they want? And what has this to do with the women on the boat?' Dick said.

'They wanted to purchase some of my best fabrics. Boon Peng had me bring down several bolts of silk from my store for him to look at. The woman took them into the sunlight to see their true colour and check their quality. Eventually, they chose six lengths of material - two very ornate and the others much simpler, but in pretty colours.

'Baba Tan, why are you telling me this,' Dick asked, completely at a loss as to where this conversation was going.

'Two reasons,' he replied. 'I asked them about making the material up into garments and whether they knew a tailor who was used to working with such fine fabric. The towkay's response was very guarded, but something the woman said made me feel that not all of the material was for her alone. She muttered something, then she turned and asked me if there was a particular tailor who I could recommend.'

'So, what did you say?'

'I thought about all my contacts and considered who would be the best at making the garments - and keeping secrets, should it be necessary.'

'You really think the towkay and his wife might know something?'

'First of all, she is not his wife. His wife stayed in Malacca and, like many of the men living here, he gets lonely, bored, or possibly both. I've heard that there was a concubine a couple of years ago, but she died in childbirth. Maybe this lady is his new companion.'

'But what's all that got to do with the girl I saw?'

'I'm not sure, Dick. It's only a hunch. I would be surprised to learn that Boon Peng is so generous that he would spend all that money on clothes for just one woman. I gave them the name of only one tailor - my friend, Lim Chow - and I've already been to see him. He will let me know if either the towkay or the woman pay him a visit.'

'Do you think Lim Chow might be asked to make garments for all of the women I saw on the boat?'

'It's possible. And if that happens, they will have to go along to the workshop for a fitting. Even the best tailor in the world would need to make some adjustments if he was going to create quality garments out of all that expensive material,' Baba Tan added.

'And you've asked Lim Chow to tell you when he makes arrangements for the outfits to be tried on?' Dick said, checking that he had understood properly.

'Correct,' said Baba Tan. 'All we have to do now, is wait for word to be sent to me from my friend - and then we will see what happens.

'You said earlier you had two reasons for concern, what is the second?'

'At your uncle's dinner party - it was Towkay Boon Peng along with Sidney Percy who caused all that trouble. Their business interests are known to be dubious. It could be that the heated conversation you overheard was conducted by these same two men.

*****

Dick walked along the quay, feeling as if an enormous weight had been lifted from him. He spoke to one or two of the merchants he'd got to know in the last few days and lingered for a while on Monkey Bridge, looking across to the east bank. It was the end of the afternoon. He tried to imagine what the town would be like once Uncle's plans had all been put in place. It was difficult to think of some of these more permanent buildings being taken down and rebuilt on the opposite bank, but already the swamp was being filled in and if the rain held off the new building would start very soon. Even the more temporary godowns, built by the Chinese merchants on this side would be moved, of course. He felt sorry for those who had already established a thriving business for themselves.

The less substantial ones, however, like the ramshackle building he couldn't fail to notice, hovering over the edge of the water, were a different matter. Such eyesores ought to be got rid of as soon as possible, he thought. But still, he would ask Uncle to make sure that Baba Tan would be able to secure a good site for himself, once the land auctions began in January.

Small pieces of debris began to skip around his feet when he reached the far side of the bridge, lifted by a playful wind. By the time he reached High Street, its good-humoured game had turned into something more menacing. It had already gathered momentum and every cloud looked as if it was spoiling for a fight, gradually changing from a brilliant white to a dull grey. In the distance, Dick could hear a low rumbling sound and he knew, at once, a thunderstorm was imminent and he'd better hurry back home.

The faint rumblings soon became more distinct. Just as he reached the house at the end of the harbour, the noise grew louder, and the eastern sky had turned an inky black. Within a few minutes, he felt a cool wind blowing from the sea, while the whole of the darkened sky was swirling about in a frenzy. It reminded Dick of the pictures of Hades he'd seen in the books used by the missionaries to persuade wayward coolies they could be forgiven their many sins, by converting to Christianity. Looking back to the end of the road, he could see the recently planted Angsana trees bending precariously to one side and thought they might, at any moment, either snap in half or be uprooted and blown away like feathers on the wind.

As he began to climb the stairs to the veranda, he was much relieved to see Uncle standing there. No mention was made of the headaches, nor the days they had occupied.

'I'm glad you made it back here before the rain started,' Raffles said to him. 'You look as if you have quite a collection of drawings there, it would be such a pity to ruin them.'

Dick grinned. It was so good to see Uncle up and about again. They heard a very loud roar above the rumbling of the thunder and Mary Anne's baby began to howl, along with the wind. The roar intensified as it reached a crescendo and even Uncle, who had lived in the tropics for nearly twenty years, looked alarmed. Moments later, the house was engulfed in a curtain of water as the rain beat down on the attap roof and shook it around relentlessly. The storm was now in full swing. Lightning lit up the darkened sky and cracks of thunder echoed an immediate, deafening reply. Mary Anne and Sophia tried to comfort the baby, Dick covered his ears with his hands - and Raffles prayed a silent prayer. When he dared, Dick tried to look out to sea, but the white blur of the rain had cut visibility to no more than a few feet outside the window. Just beyond the veranda, the rain was being driven at an acute angle, followed in hot pursuit by the wind. No one spoke, which was just as well, because they wouldn't have heard each other above the pounding and relentless noises on the roof. All they could do was wait for the storm to blow over - and hope.

Raffles feared that all the hard work done clearing the swamp would now be wasted. The coolies had only just begun to fill the quagmire with soil and stones from the adjacent hills and it was likely that they had now been washed away. Dick worried about Baba Tan and all the lovely fabrics stored in his warehouse. He thought about the girl too. He hoped that, wherever she was, she felt safe and not too frightened by the violence of the storm,

It raged for about an hour. Then, as suddenly as it had started, it rained itself out, the wind gradually dropped, and the evening sky softened to a pale indigo. When it was over, Raffles and Dick stepped out onto the veranda to breathe in the cool air and gaze at the stars as they began to appear, one by one. The aftermath of the storm filled them both with a feeling of exhilaration. Everything was now washed clean; the air was fresh, but they wondered what damage had been wrought by the deluge and if the swamp had regained control of the east bank. Whatever the answer, nothing could be done now; better wait until the morning.

CHAPTER 14

The following morning, everyone woke to pale sunshine. Dick's thoughts turned once again to the possible havoc created by last night's storm. He decided he might climb to the top of Bukit Larangan after breakfast to see the extent of the devastation for himself. Just then, Raffles appeared.

'I'd like you to accompany me to the south side of the river today,' he said. 'I've arranged to meet Lieutenant Jackson and Colonel Farquhar at the quay so that we can examine the devastation caused by the downpour.'

Dick was pleased to be included in the expedition and when they had both finished eating, he followed Uncle onto the veranda. 'Don't forget your sketchpad,' Raffles said, 'I'm afraid many of those improvised buildings along the riverbank might be damaged, making them unsafe. If that's the case, I'd like you to capture the scene before we start pulling them down, and before anyone gets hurt.'

Dick followed Raffles down the steps to the small garden below. Immediately, he felt his feet sinking into the path, made slippery by the rain. The road remained extremely wet, and he had to pick his way carefully between huge pools that filled the many potholes which had appeared as a result of the storm. By the time they reached High Street, Dick's feet squelched musically in his sandals and the rain-soaked branches he'd brushed against along the way made his shoulders feel damp. Raffles, however, strode ahead intent on reaching the south bank quickly and Dick doubted that he'd even noticed the mud that had covered his shoes and spattered onto his coat.

As soon as they reached the far side of the river, one of the sepoys, who had been supervising the coolies stepped forward to give a brief report. Raffles was in the process of thanking him when Lieutenant Jackson and Colonel Farquhar arrived. All three men wanted to see the extent of the damage for themselves and moved closer to the area which had suffered most.

Raffles walked away from the others when he saw the muddy water swirling around in the recently excavated ditches. He thought he'd mentally prepared himself for a setback, but what he witnessed was overwhelming. It would take many days to drain away the surplus water and even longer to collect enough soil from the surrounding hills to make the ground firm enough to commence the building programme. His brow was deeply furrowed when he returned to the others; he expected them to be equally distraught. Jackson and Farquhar's annoyance about the wasted effort was obvious, but as the settlement's engineers they had already dealt with many a disappointment over the last three years.

The three men had just begun to plan a way forward when Sidney Percy arrived.

'Your hairbrained schemes are looking pretty silly now, hey Raffles?' he taunted.

'I fail to see what you are talking about, sir,' Raffles replied, refusing to be harassed. He recognised this man; he was the same obnoxious individual who had caused the disturbance at the dinner party. Best not to rise to the bait or show his annoyance by the disturbance.

'I'm referring to your ridiculous idea to fill in the swamp and move all the merchants over to the south bank, of course.' His words ran together, but this did not prevent his continued harangue. 'That, and your fancy plans for the different communities living here. You have no right, sir, to impose your ludicrous, liberal ideas on this settlement.'

Raffles wrinkled his nose and took a step away. Fumes of alcohol pervaded the air; the man's breath was unsavoury, and his speech slurred, even at this early hour. His appearance was dishevelled, and a dark stubble covered his jaw. He'd probably spent the previous night at the brothel and was now trying to find his way home. Deep down, Raffles knew he should have ignored him, but instead he felt it necessary to uphold the things he held dear – the values he believed to be fair and reasonable.

'As Governor of the settlement, I have every right,' he said, 'though I would prefer it if you, and all your friends could find it in your hearts to support me. Your desire to cause dissent amongst the Chinese and Malays has been noticed. It is not only unwelcome; it is very short-sighted.'

'I have no idea what you mean,' Sidney Percy said in a disparaging tone, before turning on his heel and striding off in the direction of Hill Street.

Colonel Farquhar, acutely embarrassed by the whole conversation, was trying to disassociate himself from the criticism.

'Ignore him, he's an arrogant pig,' Lieutenant Jackson said. 'Whenever he comes into town, it's always to make trouble.'

Raffles looked across at Dick. He'd expected to find him busily engaged in his drawing - something he often did when he was feeling embarrassed - -and was surprised to see him rooted to the spot. With an incredulous expression on his face, he was staring at the place that Percy had just vacated.

Dick thought he'd heard that voice before; he certainly recognised the face. It was one of the people he'd sketched at the dinner party; the same person who kept trying to argue with Raffles. And here he was, being rude yet again. What concerned him now was the thought that his voice sounded very similar to the European he'd overheard quarrelling with the Chinese merchant - but he couldn't be certain.

Before Raffles had chance to ask Dick what the matter was,

one of the sepoys who had been directing the reclamation work came running up. He was agitated and kept pointing to the ramshackle building Dick had seen from the bridge on the evening of the storm. One of the rattan walls was now hanging from a wooden pole that was about to give way.

'Get back!' Raffles shouted at the small crowd who had gathered to witness the drama.

Their attention was rewarded a few minutes later when the side of the building broke away from the rest and plunged into the river. Until then, there had been hardly any movement and no discernible odour, but not anymore. As the syrupy, black water swirled around, the rankness of decay filled the air. Only those with a strong constitution resisted the urge to gag when the suffocating stench filled their nostrils. The displaced water swept silently over the muddy bank, washing the feet of those standing close to the edge of the path. The remaining onlookers listened - for any indication of the water rising, for cries from anyone trapped in the mud, for further movement of any kind - but there was nothing, apart from the uncanny stillness.

'We'll have to pull the rest of it down before it does any damage,' Jackson said, moving towards what remained of the house to get a better look. He was joined by Raffles and Dick, but Colonel Farquhar remained a discreet distance away.

'What's that, hanging over the edge?' Dick asked.

'It looks like a metal chain, with something attached to it, I think it might be a piece of rope,' Jackson replied. 'Goodness knows what that was being used for - who does this house belong to?'

No one knew the answer. Raffles looked around for Colonel Farquhar who should have a record of all the property leases, but he'd now disappeared. Raffles sighed. He'd hoped the Resident's engineering experience might be put to good use here and that it might help to overcome some of their differences, but obviously, it wasn't to be.

'Get a gang of men to help you take it down,' Raffles said, 'and the sooner the better. Dick, I'd like you to sketch the monstrosity-then the people in Calcutta will see why we need to get on with the new building programme.'

Dick pulled open his sketchbook again.

'Make sure you stay at a safe distance,' Raffles said. 'I don't want to hear that you've been hurt by flying debris, or anything else, for that matter.'

It wasn't long before a gang of coolies arrived, and the dismantling work began. They started with the roof, then the remaining outer walls. Shortly afterwards, they began to hurl various pots and a few odd plates onto the bank of the river. Then, some cushions and three sleeping mats followed. What an odd assortment it was, thought Dick.

He was hastily scribbling, adding the last detail to the corner of his drawing when something landed at his feet. It looked like a collection of rags. He continued working for a while and then curiosity got the better of him. He poked at the small bundle with his toe, but it remained intact. No one noticed when he scooped up the package and started to unfold the wrapping; he lifted out the items it contained, one by one. Just a water flask and some items of clothing. From its shape and design, the water flask was clearly Chinese and he supposed the owner got it from a mariner on one of the junks. Next, came a small pair of peasant's trousers and a plain grey shift. Something about the shift troubled him. It triggered a blurred memory, but he couldn't hold on to it long enough to bring it into focus.

He began to put the garments away, when he realised the hem of the shift felt odd; it was much thicker at the front than at the back. He looked around to see if anyone was watching before he turned the shirt inside-out and began to examine it in more detail. Something was hidden inside the hem. The stitching all along the front of the garment was different - the thread that had been used was lighter in colour and the stitches themselves, much closer together than the rest. He checked once more to make sure no one was watching then carefully returned each of the items to the piece of rag in which he'd found them. He placed the bundle out of sight, under his sketchpad. The idea that someone had hidden an object - maybe a treasured keepsake - in their clothing made him feel curious, but instinct told him to keep the discovery to himself. He needed to take the items away from the frenzy of the quay and find a place where he could examine them in private.

Raffles had already returned to the office, leaving Jackson in charge of the dismantling operation. It was not yet noon and Dick knew the Company office would be busy. His feet automatically turned in the direction of Baba Tan's godown.

'No news yet, I'm afraid,' said the merchant as soon as he saw Dick. 'It's three days already since the towkay and his friend came to buy the material. If they decide to take up my recommendation, I think they will visit the tailor very soon.'

'That wasn't the reason I came to visit you,' Dick said.

'Well, it is good to see you any time Master Dick.'

'I've been down at the wharf with Uncle and Lieutenant Jackson. The storm damage, where the swamp has been filled in, needed to be checked It's very muddy and quite smelly, but it's not as bad as they expected.'

'I see you've got your sketchbook with you. I would imagine the storm-damaged buildings look quite dramatic - all that the mud and the debris?'

Dick nodded, but held the sketchpad close to his chest, keeping the small package out of sight for the time being.

'Would you like some tea?' Baba Tan asked.

This was the invitation that Dick had been hoping for. He wanted to share the news of his discovery straight away, but he'd learned this was not the Chinese manner and in these matters Baba Tan liked to practise the usual traditions. They sipped their tea slowly, taking time to appreciate the delicate flavour and Dick waited patiently.

'What is it you're hiding under those drawings?' the merchant eventually asked.

Dick grinned. 'I thought you'd never ask!' he replied. 'You know that dilapidated house that hangs out over the river - the one right at the end of the quay?'

Baba Tan nodded. 'I walked past it only yesterday and noticed that it was in a very bad state of repair - and I suppose it's even worse following the thunderstorm.'

'Part of it plunged into the river not long after we arrived there this morning. Uncle gave the order for it to be taken down, so that it wouldn't cause any harm. He wanted me to make a sketch of it - something that would be good for the collection.'

'And ...,' said Baba Tan, waiting for Dick to reveal what he was obviously hiding.

'When the coolies began to take the house apart, they flung stuff all over the place - and THIS landed at my feet. I'm not sure what it means.' He took the package and placed it in front of Baba Tan. 'I've had a quick look and I think there is something interesting about it.'

'What sort of thing? It just looks like some old clothes and a flask to me.'

'It's the shirt,' Dick said. 'Something's hidden in the hem - look, it's much thicker here and the stitching is different.'

'We had better take a look then,' Baba Tan said, handing Dick a pair of very small, very sharp scissors.

'I don't want to damage anything that might be inside, it might be valuable,' Dick responded. 'You're used to cutting expensive fabrics and fine pieces of lace, could you open it, please?'

The merchant felt along the hem of the shift, picked up his scissors and used a single blade to loosen the first stitch. After that, it was easy to pull through the remaining cotton thread and fold back the edge of the material.

'I think it's a piece of parchment.' Baba Tan removed the tiny scroll and untied a fine golden thread that held it together very carefully.

'What does it say?' Dick asked.

'As you can see, it is written using Chinese characters, and I suspect it has been written by a scholar.'

'What makes you say that?'

'The brush strokes are very fine, there are no blotches, no mistakes made. It is beautifully decorated around the edges. I suspect that it contains some very special sentiments and means a lot to its owner. I think it has been written with a great deal of care.'

'Can you understand it Baba Tan?' Dick asked as he moved closer to examine the writing himself.

'The dialect I spoke when I was growing up was Hokkien. I also speak Cantonese and even some Mandarin, but as I said this is the hand of a scholar. Some of the characters I can pick out - all Chinese languages are written in the same way, you see. The problem is, because this is so sophisticated, many of the characters mean nothing to me. It would be foolish of me to attempt an interpretation; it needs someone who can understand it as a whole.' He pointed to particularly ornate parts of the text. 'See what I mean?' he added.

Dick moved even closer to scrutinise the document. Its calligraphy was exquisite and the drawings that decorated its borders, quite beautiful. He was just about to express his admiration, when he noticed something incongruous. Right at the bottom on the scroll, there was one word that leapt out at him. The word was in English—and the word was RAFFLES.

'That's Uncle's name. Why would his name be on such a document? What does it mean?'

'It is indeed very strange,' Baba Tan said. 'In China, the calligraphy is written from the top to the bottom of the page like English, but the difference is that it is done from right to left, not left to right. The fact that your uncle's name is written at the bottom of the page, using English, leads me to believe that this document is actually addressed to him.'

Baba Tan stood up, leaving the scroll on the small table in front of him. 'Did anyone see you take these things?'

'I made sure no one was watching when I first looked at the package. When I packed up my things to leave, everyone was too busy making sure the remainder of the rickety old house didn't collapse. I don't suppose you know who owns it, do you—that might give us a clue about the origin of the scroll?'

'Yes, I do know Dick, but I didn't like to say. Now, I feel concerned, and it makes me think we should find someone who is able to translate this whole document for us as quickly as possible.'

'You think it's important then?' Dick asked.

'Perhaps. I think there may be a link between the scroll and the girl you are wanting to find. I know that particular house has a bad reputation - and not just because of its state of repair. In the past, it was the place where they took the women being brought into Singapore from China, but I didn't know it was still being used that way.'

At that moment, someone knocked very quietly at the door of the warehouse. The sound made both of them jump.

'Hide the scroll - and the rest of the things - under those bales of fabrics,' Baba Tan whispered.

Dick hurriedly bundled everything together, covered it with the original piece of rag and carefully placed the package between two bales of yellow silk. Baba Tan went to the door and was relieved to discover his friend Lim Chow waiting outside. He ushered in his visitor, but as soon as the tailor saw Dick, he hesitated.

'This is the young man I told you about,' Baba Tan said in Hokkien, 'you can speak freely in front of him.'

Dick had no idea who the visitor was, neither could he understand anything that was being said. The conversation continued in hushed tones, with both men getting very animated. When it was over, they bowed to each other and the visitor left.

Baba Tan went to the door of the warehouse and locked it. More tea was made, and Dick was invited to sit. The tea was tasted and savoured. Dick knew better than to ask any questions until Baba Tan was ready to talk.

'That was my friend, Lim Chow,' he said quite calmly. 'He is the tailor I told you about, and there has been a visit - this morning.'

'Who?'

'It seems that Towkay Boon Peng and his lady-friend called on Lim Chow today. The woman told him about the garments he was to make and asked him lots of questions. When she was satisfied with the answers, she gave Lim Chow a list of measurements and Boon Peng informed him that the lengths of silk would be delivered by a messenger, early tomorrow morning.'

'So, the material was for Boon Peng's woman, after all?' Dick said. 'We are no further forward.'

'That is where you are wrong,' Baba Tan said, with a smile gradually spreading across his face. 'Lim Chow described the woman; I am sure it is the same person who came here with the towkay to purchase the silk. She handed over two lots of measurements and instructed my friend to make six sets of garments; she said three would be for her own use and the other three are for a young friend who is unable to visit the tailor herself.'

Dick's lips fell apart and his hand flew to cover his open mouth. This was replaced, moments later, with a tentative smile that gradually developed into the broadest of grins.

'So, we might be able to find out where they live?'

'We can certainly discover who the other garments are intended for,' Baba Tan replied. 'There is no guarantee, of course, that it is the girl you are hoping to find.'

'But it's good news, is it not? Dick stood up, all at once full of energy. 'Tell me what else Lim Chow had to say. What will he do once the material has been delivered?'

'He will begin to cut the material according to the measurements given to him and then he will piece them together. He says he always suggests there should be at least one fitting session for his customers.'

Dick put his head on one side and held a slightly curved index finger to his lips.

'It's a good idea, but what if the towkay or the woman says the other person is still unable attend?'

Baba Tan muttered to himself as he considered one or two possibilities, and after a little while he said, 'We will have to think of some other way of finding out where the women are staying. The one with Boon Peng, who I'm assuming is his new concubine, must be fairly strong-minded. I'm sure she'd want to try on her own garments, to check that they fit well—so maybe I could follow her if she turns up alone. I'd have to be very careful and keep out of sight, but it's highly likely that she will go straight back to her home. I assume both of the women are living together somewhere.'

'And you think it's possible the other one could be the girl I saw on the boat' Dick said.

'If I'm wrong, and she's living somewhere else, the woman in yellow might still deliver the other garments to your young lady.'

'She's not my young lady!'

'She is your young lady in the sense that you spotted her and thought she looked distressed.'

Dick let that statement stand, although his cheeks still felt hot. He tried to change the subject. 'Just before the tailor arrived you said you thought the girl might have been held in the rickety house and that it had a bad reputation. Is that why you think she has something to do with the package - because she may have been staying there?'

'If I'm right, she is likely to have brought the package with her from Guangzhou.'

'But the building was empty this morning. If the scroll is as important as you think, why would she leave it behind?'

'Maybe she was moved in a hurry, possibly because of the storm...I'm not sure. The only thing I am certain of is the connection between the man who owned that building and the woman in the yellow dress,' Baba Tan said. 'And the point is,' he said, looking directly into Dick's eyes, 'that house is just one of the properties owned by Towkay Boon Peng.'

CHAPTER 15

Following the selection of material for their new garments, Wing Yee had hoped both she and Chin Ming would be allowed to visit the tailor themselves once he'd worked his magic with the lovely silk and produced their new wardrobe. She regretted the fact that Boon Peng had allowed only her to accompany him on that first visit, but she'd relished the opportunity to get out into the fresh air. Hopefully, another such occasion would arise when the garments could be fitted; if not, she knew the towkay would permit no more outings until a ship, suitable for their money-making scheme, arrived in the harbour.

Now, the days had fallen into a regular pattern, which was beginning to shape their lives. Each morning, she and Chin Ming spent at leisure, telling each other stories. The more they talked, the more they shared some of their secrets and the greater the trust between them grew.

In the seven years since her mother's death, Chin Ming had built a protective wall around herself, blocking out any feelings of sadness, nostalgia, or sorrow. Instead, she had concentrated on being a good daughter, accompanying her father wherever he went, listening to his words and learning from his wisdom. The trauma of his disappearance had opened a small fissure in her defences, but with the hope of finding him decreasing with every passing day, the crack was turning into a chasm. She longed for the warmth and understanding of another human being and increasingly, she dared hope she had found it in her relationship with Wing Yee.

She continued with Wing Yee's English lessons, but at other times they spoke Cantonese. Eventually, she told her friend about the missing scroll.

'Just before I left the Mission,' she said. 'I hid it in the hem of my tunic, I kept it safe throughout the whole of the voyage, and I know it was still sewn into my shift when we reached Singapore.'

'You wore a grey cotton shift, along with your coolie trousers on the day Lu Tong brought you here.'

'Neither of them belonged to me. It's what the Malay woman brought for me after Madam Ho's visit. That first morning I was wearing the sarong I'd slept in. After Madam Ho and the other two women left, I managed to pull it around me again, but when the Malay woman arrived with some food, she let me wash and gave me clean clothes. I kept asking her for my own things, but she didn't understand. I never saw my clothes or any of the things I brought from the Mission again.'

'What is so important about the scroll?'

'Papa gave it to me to take care of, on the morning we went to the docks. I hadn't looked at again until the evening before I left the Mission. I can't remember the details but do know there was something about a man who had to leave China in a hurry. I think Papa was sending some sort of warning. The last thing he told me was to come to Singapore and deliver the letter to the man called Raffles. He's someone Papa trusted. If I could only meet him, I would ask him to help me find out what happened to Papa, but without the letter what chance do I have?

Wing Yee was about to reply when they heard the distinctive click of a key turning in the door. Chin Ming still hadn't got used to the sound; it was a vivid reminder of her days in the rickety house over the water. She instinctively tensed and held her breath until it was clear that the visitor was, as usual, Boon Peng.

'Time stop talking, time for work,' Boon Peng announced

as he stepped through the door.

'We talk later,' Wing Yee whispered softly, practising her increasing use of English.

Chin Ming went to sit at the table, wondering what paperwork he had brought for her to work on today. She considered all the things that he'd delivered over the last week. Initially, she'd felt overwhelmed by the bulk of the correspondence, but as she read through them, it was obvious that they had been issued over several weeks and Boon Peng had not replied simply because he didn't understand what they contained. He came now, each afternoon, with something new for her to work upon. She was grateful to be kept busy during the hours he spent in Wing Yee's company, it helped her to forget bumps and murmurings that floated down from the room above her head.

She was expected to have his papers ready to collect by the time he reappeared downstairs. The nearest he'd come to telling her that he was pleased with her work was the previous evening. He'd asked her to write a letter, in reply to a note he'd received from *Munshi* Abdullah about the development of the south bank of the river. He'd given her only a few words as the basis for the response, but she had conjured his sentiments into something more comprehensive and articulate.

'This good,' he'd said, when she explained in Cantonese what she had written in English. 'This Governor, he now listen to Boon Peng. He think Boon Peng important man.'

Wing Yee smiled at him before saying, 'The Europeans will also recognise your status when they see your new concubine and her beautiful companion in their new clothes. How soon before they are ready?'

'I go see tailor now,' he said. Her question had obviously triggered his greed again. The sooner the garments are ready, the sooner the two women would be able to lure the mariners towards the pleasures of the port.

*****

Early the following morning, Lu Tong arrived with their new clothes. He dumped them, unceremoniously, in front of Wing Yee. 'From Master,' he said, in Cantonese. 'You lucky women.' Then, he hurried to the door, stepped out into the warehouse, and turned the key in the lock. They remained trapped and alone, once again.

Wing Yee was disappointed that there had been no opportunity to try the dresses on and have any adjustments made, but it was now obvious that Boon Pang didn't believe in such refinements. During the hours she and Chin Ming had to themselves, they enjoyed playing card games, sewing and practising any newly acquired English words. However, they both longed to get out of the house into the fresh air, especially Chin Ming, who had not been allowed outside since the evening she'd been brought here.

Despite that particular regret, Chin Ming couldn't hide her eagerness to examine the garments. She picked up first one, then another. Wing Yee quickly joined her, anxious to see how the instructions she'd given to the tailor had turned out.

'This is the *pien fu* that you will wear when we go out to greet the ships.' She carefully lifted the skirt first, handing it to Chin Ming who in turn held it against her waist. Next, she picked up the matching tunic and rested it close to Chin Ming's shoulders.

'Why not try it on? We need to know that it fits properly and if the length is right.'

Chin Ming stepped out of her drab coolie pants and into the soft green skirt. As soon as she fastened it around her waist, the luxurious fabric made her feel very grown up and a shy smile spread slowly across her face. By the time Wing Yee had helped her pull the tunic over her head, and smooth down the fabric, she felt radiant. The *pien fu* was made of the finest quality silk and shimmered, like the peridot gemstones her mother used to wear, as she walked around.

'It's the colour of fresh leaves,' Wing Yee said. 'It suits your complexion perfectly.'

'I love it all,' Chin Ming said, ''but especially the decoration on the sleeves?'

Wing told her that she'd chosen this fabric because of the way it was trimmed as much as for the colour.

Chin Ming examined the cuffs and borders of the tunic more closely. It was festooned with white peonies encircled with tiny, pink plum blossom.

'It's really beautiful,' she said. 'I hope the water will be smooth when we go out in the lighter. I couldn't bear the sea-spray to spoil it.'

Wing Yee laughed. 'I'm glad you like it,' she said. 'The men on the ships won't appreciate its symbolism, but it amused me to choose that particular design.'

'What do you mean?'

She reminded Chin Ming that both the lotus and the plum blossom represent purity.

'The peony represents, amongst other things, wealth - and we both know that's all Boon Peng is interested in. Just as we chose your new name for a particular reason, I selected the fabric because the symbolism of the design amused me.'

Chin Ming laughed. 'So, what sort of material did you choose for yourself?'

Wing Yee's *pien fu* was the colour of the night sky. As she held it against her body, the light fell upon the silver thread of the chrysanthemums, embroidered all over the tunic.

'And did you choose this design because of the way it's decorated too?' Chin Ming asked, looking closely at the collar and the edging of the garment. 'You have peach blossom and bamboo on the border of the neck and cuffs. What does that signify?'

'Each part of the peach tree is important. Bamboo represents strength and resilience because it can survive in the hardest of conditions. Both symbolise longevity - and I do intend to live for a very long time,' she smiled as she looked at Chin Ming.

'Can we look at the other garments now?'

'There should be two *qipaos* for each of us, to wear as everyday garments. I thought the lilac and the pale blue would be good for you; the red one and the dark peach colour are for me. Why don't we choose one to wear straight away?'

Chin Ming looked at both garments and marvelled at their detail. Finally, she opted for the lilac *qipao*. It was embroidered with sprays of cherry blossom in a dark shade of violet; around the neck and cuffs she noticed the fine detail of sun symbols in gold. Wing Yee helped her into it and fastened the frogging at the neck. It hung loosely to Chin Ming's ankles and the wide sleeves allowed easy movement. She danced around the room, twirling around so that Wing Yee could admire her.

'It is so beautiful,' she said. 'I feel like the Empress of China herself.'

'Maybe this new life of ours won't be so bad, after all,' Wing Yee said.

*****

When Boon Peng arrived at his usual time later in the day, he was obviously pleased to see Wing Yee in her red *qipao*. He glanced at both of them in their new attire but was more anxious to inspect the *pien fu* garments.

'You show me,' he said. 'Make sure tailor do good job. You wear now,' he insisted.

Both women withdrew to the bedroom and slipped into their *pien fus*. When they reappeared at the bottom of the stairs, a satisfied smile stretched from one ear to the other.

'You, clever woman,' he said to Wing Yee. 'I make many dollar when sailor see you.'

He told them to walk around the room several times, so

that he could view the from all angles. Finally, content with his investment, he handed Chin Ming the usual pile of paperwork and moved towards the staircase. Wing Yee knew that the time for frivolity was over and now she must accompany him to the bedroom.

Chin Ming wished she could change back into her *qipao* as it was much more comfortable than the more formal *pien fu*. She knew, however, that she would now have to wait until Boon Peng left, later in the afternoon. All she could do was lift the tunic over her knees, enabling her to sit down more easily. She stared at the pile of letters he had left with her and sighed deeply. Now she was used to the routine, she found the work fairly monotonous, but was relieved that she didn't have to do the things that Wing Yee had to put up with. She picked up the first document and tried to block out the strange noises coming from the bedroom. She needed to concentrate.

When he departed later that afternoon, Boon Peng made an announcement. 'Ship from Calcutta come soon. It arrive next few days. Lu Tong arrange you visit.'

*****

As promised, Lu Tong arrived to collect the women and guided them to the quay. Chin Ming felt very self-conscious as she walked the short distance to the bumboat, but there was a frenzy of activity in front of all the go-downs and no one paid them any attention. Lu Tong insisted that Chin Ming boarded first as he'd been instructed to make sure she could be easily seen. She felt nervous as she stepped into the bow of the boat and looked back anxiously at Wing Yee, now seated at the stern.

The oarsman pulled away from the quay immediately and manoeuvred the small craft from the mouth of the river into the harbour. Chin Ming was glad that the sea was calm. She looked back at the warehouses and remembered the day they had arrived here; their first sight of the settlement. I was so full of hope then, she thought. I was convinced if I could find the man called Raffles, then he might be able to help me to find Papa. So much has happened since then; those terrible days when I was left tied up in that old house over the water, but I have to admit it's been better since they let me live with Wing Yee. Whatever happens now, I'm absolutely determined to survive. I want Papa to be proud of me.

They approached the Indiaman whilst she was still engrossed in her reverie.

'Look across at the ship and smile,' Wing Yee instructed. 'That's all you have to do. We'll circle the boat once, then when we come around again you should wave to anyone on board who notices us.'

She did as she'd been told. When she smiled at the men leering down at them from the deck, she thought again about the day they arrived in Singapore and the young man who'd waved to her from the beach. She'd smiled at him too; he'd looked so friendly - but then she'd felt embarrassed and looked away. Now, she had a role to play, no time to feel modest. She waved and smiled, trying not to show how she felt inside. As predicted, one of the men staring down at her asked her name.

'She called Te Shui,' Wing Yee shouted back in English. 'You ask for Te Shui at Women's House, you not disappointed.'

With that, Wing Yee nodded to the oarsman. Slowly, he turned the boat around and headed back towards the quay. Chin Ming began to shiver and feel slightly nauseous.

Lu Tong was waiting for them on the quay. 'Be quick,' he said as soon as they reached the top step. 'Master say, hurry back house now,'

Once inside the door, Chin Ming couldn't wait to change back into the comfort of her lilac *qipao,* glad that the ordeal was over. Her only regret was the relatively short time she'd been able to be outside in the fresh air.

When Boon Peng visited that afternoon, Wing Yee

reported the details of their trip which pleased him no end. She wasn't required to amuse him that day and he left almost immediately. He was eager to tell Madam Ho to expect at least one man from the Indiaman, who might come asking for Te Shui that evening. If the visit went well, he knew that others would follow every evening the vessel was in port. Satisfaction covered his entire face as he walked back along the quay.

Subsequent visits over the next few weeks, also involving large ocean-going ships, followed the same pattern as first excursion. Boon Peng told Wing Yee that their scheme was working well. Each occasion resulted in several of the officers from the visiting vessel coming ashore looking for a girl called Te Shui.

At the beginning of December, yet another East Indiaman arrived from Calcutta. Amongst its passengers was a missionary on his way to China, but he had gone ashore by the time the Chin Ming and Wing Yee arrived. Following the usual pattern, someone would ask to know the name of the young girl who smiled so enticingly; the moment after Wing Yee provided an answer, the lighter turned back towards the shore.

'You look upset,' Wing Yee said, as soon as they moved away from the ship.

'I keep thinking about the women who work for that horrid woman, Madam Ho,' Chin Ming said. 'When these men ask for Te Shui the women who work for her don't have any choice; I don't like the idea that I'm responsible for wat happens to them - especially if any of the men hurt them.'

'It will be one of her regular girls and it won't be the same girl every single time. There are several that are around your age.'

'It seems so unfair,' Chin Ming said. 'Some poor soul is being forced to spend time with these men just so the towkay can make even more money.'

'We are in no position to argue,' Wing Yee replied. 'We are

merely chattels as far as these men are concerned. Boon Peng is greedy, you know that. No matter how good you are at writing his letters and translating his documents, he will never think that alone is enough. Besides, he's paid for our new clothes; he wants to get his money back. You need to understand that men like him always want more; you must learn to be patient. We just need to bide our time.'

'But ...,'

'Some of these girls may not be as unhappy as you think. The life they led previously was likely to have been far more precarious than what they have now.'

'But what about their future?'

'Some may hope that one of the sailors might want to marry them, I suppose. There are very few women in Singapore, remember, so it's not impossible. Their best prospect is probably to hope that someone will want them as their concubine - it's not so different to the choices I have had to make.'

CHAPTER 16

Dick now visited Baba Tan each day to see if there was any further news. Both he and the kindly Peranakan merchant suspected the towkay might be involved in something underhand, but nothing could be proved. Towards the end of the following week, just as Dick arrived, he saw a man who was vaguely familiar, scurrying away from Baba Tan's warehouse.

'Was that Lim Chow I saw leaving,' he said. 'Did he have any news?

'Indeed, it was - and yes, he did come to tell me something, but I'm afraid it isn't good news.'

The air was filled with foreboding and Baba Tan looked completely downcast. He proceeded to tell Dick about Boon Peng arriving at the tailor's workroom the previous evening and leaving Lu Tong to oversee the completion of the garments. 'Lim Chow worked all night and Lu Tong took them away this morning,' he said. 'Unless they need to be altered, the women won't be coming to Lim Chow for a fitting - and maybe not even then. I'm afraid we have no way of finding out where they are living.'

Dick collapsed down onto his haunches; it was just as if he had been punched in the chest. It felt as if all his efforts to find the girl had come to an end. Baba Tan could see how devastated his young friend was, but he too felt at a loss.

'Master Dick, I understand how upsetting this must be. I know the Tuan has brought you up to hate injustice, but I have to ask you again, what is it about this particular girl? Why does she mean so much to you?'

Dick furrowed his brow and shrugged his shoulders. He didn't know how to answer Baba Tan's question; he'd never really thought about what impelled him to keep on searching for her.

'Did you think she had been brought here against her will? Perhaps seeing her in the boat bring back memories of the man who snatched you from your village and forced you onto his ship?'

'I was only a child, and it was a long time ago,' Dick said.

'I think I understand now why you are worried about the girl,' Baba Tan said. 'Something is obviously not right. Maybe it's time to tell Tuan Raffles what you saw at the harbour that day and why you feel anxious about the fate of those women.'

'Yes ... you're probably right,' Dick said. 'I know he would be upset and I'm sure he will want to help, but perhaps we're already too late? Perhaps, like Abdullah said, there is nothing that anyone can do.'

He waved goodbye to Baba Tan and wandered along the entire length of the quay. His eyes continued to search, but his determination was gone. He watched the coolies unloading cargo from the bumboats and thought they looked like clockwork toys. The noise of their high-pitched boasting floated over his head; the smell of sweat from their half-naked bodies caused his nostrils to twitch, but he remained in a daze. The tantalising smells of chicken, pork, and fish, drifting across from the hawker stalls would, on previous days, have claimed his attention, but today there was nothing that could penetrate his anguish.

He walked slowly back to the harbour-master's house, only to find that Uncle was not yet home. When Raffles did arrive, he brought with him Lieutenant Jackson and Mr Johnston. Talk over dinner was of the imminent arrival of an East Indiaman from Calcutta. Raffles had renewed energy and was full of enthusiasm because he expected to receive extra supplies that would keep both the merchants and the sepoys happy. When the ship made the return journey, it would take with it a detailed report on the proposed new developments and a complete portfolio of Dick's drawings.

Dick felt his last ounce of energy drain away when he realised there would be no opportunity to talk to Uncle tonight. He went to his sleeping mat early and curled up into a ball whilst Raffles and his visitors talked enthusiastically about the imminent arrival of the ship from Calcutta. Dick couldn't hear any of the details, neither could he summon up enough enthusiasm to be interested; eventually he drifted off into a fitful sleep.

*****

Throughout December, Raffles was busy supervising land reclamation and compiling reports for the Company; visitors continued to appear each evening and Dick began to think an opportunity to speak to him alone would never arise.

On Christmas Day, the small European community gathered at the quay. They stood next to each other with the tropical heat beating down upon them, whilst the austere-looking preacher tried to impress the crowd with his fire and brimstone sermon. The faces of those nearest the front of the gathering turned from pink to crimson. Some used their handkerchiefs to swat away the flies and mosquitos whilst others used them to mop away the continual dampness from their brows.

Dick began to fidget as the temperature increased and the sweat trickled down the back of his neck. He didn't want to upset Uncle, but his concentration strayed, first to the well-established godowns on this side of the river and then towards the less permanent Chinese warehouses on the other side of the river. He wondered what Baba Tan was doing today. His gaze eventually wandered out over the sea, attracted by all the colourful craft in the harbour. He remained in this stance for nearly an hour, with his back set firmly against the odd collection of godowns that fringed the edge of the river. The minutes passed slowly, and he remained oblivious to the fact that he, and the crowd he was standing amongst, was being observed by two Chinese women locked in a house not far away.

Raffles frequently glanced in Dick's direction whilst the sermon was droning on, but Dick was unaware of that too. The young man's faraway look made Raffles feel uneasy and he wondered what was demanding so much of his attention.

Afterwards, everyone was anxious to speak to one another, to shake Raffles' hand and offer him their Christmas greetings.

'Let's hope that the rain holds off and we can get on with clearing more land in the New Year,' Lieutenant Jackson added to the season's pleasantries. Raffles smiled and nodded his agreement, glad to hear such positive enthusiasm and eagerness to get on with the work.

Some of the merchants who had overheard this comment nudged themselves forward to reiterate Jackson's sentiments. However, Raffles knew many offered their support only to curry favours, hoping to obtain a preferential site once the land was up for auction.

Eventually, the hand-shaking ceased and everyone began to drift away to their homes, to celebrate Christmas in their own way.

Raffles put his hand on Dick's shoulder. 'Is something troubling you?' he asked. 'I've been watching you and I know it's not easy to stand for so long in the mid-day heat, but I there's more to it than that; you look as if you have the worries of the world on your shoulders. What's upsetting you, Dick, you haven't been your usual cheery self for some time - what can I do to help?'

Dick pursed his lips and his head hung down. Now the

opportunity to unburden himself had presented itself, he was unsure how to begin.

'There is something. It's something I've been wanting to tell you for a while, but first of all your headaches made you unwell and then other things kept getting in the way ...'

'Are you not happy here?' Raffles looked closely into his eyes. Just occasionally, during the seven years Dick had lived with him, Raffles wondered whether, one day, Dick would want to return to the island where he'd been born.

Dick looked alarmed. 'I'm very happy to be here with you and I'm looking forward to the new house, but ...'

He so much wanted to find the right words to tell Raffles about the arrival of the junk all those weeks ago and what he'd witnessed. But, he hesitated, was this really the right time? He knew how everyone had been looking forward to Christmas. It was a day when Uncle should be able to relax and not be burdened with the challenges of the Settlement yet, here he was, about to do just that.

'It can wait until tomorrow,' he said, 'I don't want to spoil the celebration and the meal Mary Anne and Sophia are preparing.'

Raffles took Dick by the arm and guided him to the shade of a banyan tree. 'Take your time,' he said. 'We are not needed back at the house for quite some time yet. We won't be eating until this evening when it is cooler. I daresay they're all caught up in telling each other stories of Christmas's they've shared with other people, in other places, in other circumstances. They won't miss us for some time.'

There was a long silence and then Dick took a deep breath. 'You remember the day after the dinner party? You developed a really bad headache and retired to your bed for several days?'

Raffles nodded. The memory of the pain was all too clear. It had started with needles jabbing into his temples; he'd tried to ignore the discomfort and concentrate on the letters that needed to be written, following the events of the previous evening. As the day progressed, so did the pain; creeping around to the nape of his neck and progressing slowly upwards to encompass all of his skull before weaving its way to pound his temples. By the time he reached the house, it felt as if a metal band had been fixed around his head and was getting tighter and tighter. During the hours of darkness, the stabbing turned into throbbing and in his more lucid moments he began to realise that it might be time to take his doctor's advice and return to England.

'I didn't know you felt unwell,' said Dick. A particularly magnificent junk arrived that morning; Abdullah and I went down to the beach to watch the bumboats plying backwards and forwards; I took most of the day to bring the cargo ashore.'

Raffles could understand Dick's enthusiasm, such spectacles always aroused interest when you witnessed them for the first time, but he was beginning to wonder where this was all leading. I'll need to be patient, he thought, if Dick is going to tell me what is really on his mind.

He hadn't long to wait. Dick recounted seeing the women come ashore in the last boat and the expressions on their faces. He described every single detail of what he'd observed, how he and Abdullah had made haste to the quay only to find it deserted apart from a few coolies.

'Abdullah told me things like that happen all the time, but I couldn't get their expressions out of my head; they looked tired, sad and sort of shocked all at the same time. I couldn't accept his answer and I knew you wouldn't either,'

'So why has it taken you so long to tell me?'

Dick reminded him, once again, that he been around to tell. 'I talked to Baba Tan,' he said. 'He agreed to help me and then I suppose I wanted to solve the mystery myself so that I'd have something good to tell you so that you would feel proud of me.'

He then went on to tell Raffles as much as he knew about the towkay's involvement, about the bundle of clothing he'd found and the mysterious scroll discovered inside one of the garments.

'Dick, the first thing I want you to know is that I am proud of you. You spotted something was wrong, you persisted when others would have given up and you tried your very best to put it right.' Raffles put his arm around the youth in an effort to comfort him. Deep down, he was furious, but it would do nothing to help Dick if he revealed his true feelings right now. If only Farquhar hadn't made it so easy for brothels to be established here, then it would be more difficult for the people who profit from trafficking young women to operate.

'There's something else,' Dick said. 'There was one word which Baba Tan and I could both read, it was your name - written near the bottom of the page.'

'My name, are you sure?'

'Absolutely, it was the only word in English - and written in capital letters.'

Raffles knew immediately this was an indication that the scroll was addressed to him, but he had no idea what that meant. Tomorrow, he would ask Dick to show him the scroll, and then he would begin to make some enquiries about the comings and goings in the harbour. 'I daresay Colonel Farquhar might know more than he's prepared to tell me,' he said almost in a whisper, then he turned back to Dick and said, 'I'll need to tread carefully, if I'm going to get to the bottom of it. But get to the bottom of it, I will. This has to stop!'

*****

Heavy downpours throughout the following week prevented Raffles starting his investigation. Each morning began with a watery-looking sun doing its best to push through the sombre clouds, but by early afternoon it had failed to make any headway and accepted defeat. Some days the rain continued well into the evening, dampening everyone's spirits and soaking their attire. Raffles had planned to move to the new house on Bukit Larangan, but the paths leading up to hill had turned into squelching mudslides. His frustration was increased by the fact that most of the people he most wanted to talk to, following his discourse with Dick, were fully occupied drying out their premises.

The weather, during the days that led up to the end of one year and merged with the beginning of the next was mixed, but the heat of the sun lasted a little longer each morning; muddy paths solidified, shutters on houses opened and musty odours died away. One Thursday evening in early January, a final thunderstorm cleared the air and washed away all the loose stones and fallen twigs lying in its way. The ground was swept clean. Friday was overcast, but no more rain fell. Saturday morning dawned to pale sunshine determinedly pushing its way through any lingering grey clouds. Everyone woke in an optimistic mood and Raffles decided to go ahead with moving their belongings from the crowded conditions in Mary Anne's house at the harbour, to their new vantage point at the summit of the hill. He left most of the ordering of the house to Sophia, Dick and some Malay helpers, so that he could get on with investigating any illegal conduct in the town and discover who was most likely to benefit from such undertakings.

*****

Dick stopped what he was doing to glance at Sophia opening the boxes; the sheer delight on her face as she rediscovered the possessions they'd brought with them from Sumatra was a joy to observe. It had never felt right to call her Aunt, in the same intimate way that he referred to Raffles as Uncle, but he found her company pleasant and comforting. Instead of helping with the unpacking, he very much wanted to pick up his sketch pad and capture her distinctive charm.

The four years they had spent together in Bencoolen, before coming to Singapore, had been challenging for all of them and Dick often wondered how Sophia had endured. Perhaps it was the example set by her husband that enabled her to discover her own inner strength. Shortly after their arrival in the failing and forgotten colony, Raffles discovered the Company owned three hundred slaves; he was appalled. He called a public meeting, gave the slaves their freedom, and set up a school for their children. Public cockfighting and gambling had been stopped too, all to the annoyance of the complacent and arrogant European community. Now, he was having to deal with very similar problems here. Deep down, Dick's worried that the information about the Chinese women would only add to all the other troubles and might even cause Uncle's debilitating headaches to return.

He completed the outline sketch, looking across at Sophia again before filling in any of the detail. He found her gazing at a small, lace shawl; her moist eyes betrayed the thoughts of babies she had lost, and his heart missed a beat. A pleasant breeze, enriched with the scent of frangipani, played with a loose strand of her hair; she put the shawl to one side. Dick hoped that this time the climate might be kinder to them both and now they had begun to settle, she would conceive again, and Uncle's headaches would cease.

Sophia looked across at him and smiled. 'Come along, young man,' she said, 'we can't spend any more time day-dreaming, we have work to do.'

*****

Raffles first of all sought out Baba Tan. After the usual pleasantries had been exchanged, they sat down to share what each of them knew about the business activities of Boon Peng and consider whether any of it might be connected to slavery and prostitution. The conversation that Dick had overheard added weight to their suspicions, but they had no tangible evidence. Baba Tan promised to enquire discreetly, once again, amongst his regular customers about any dealings they'd had, or heard about, involving the towkay. He would report back as soon as he had any significant news.

None of the Europeans merchants who Raffles trusted could throw any light on the matter of Towkay Boon Peng. They had all heard colourful tales, but actual facts remained in short supply. Finally, Raffles decided that he would need to meet with Colonel Farquhar again. After all the antagonism that had arisen between them, he knew the Resident would be on his guard, and any questions asked would need to be delicately phrased. An opportunity arose towards the middle of the month when Farquhar arrived early for a meeting to plan the auctioning of new plots of land.

'I anticipate a great deal of interest in the sale,' Raffles said. 'It might be useful to know something about the types of business some of the merchants want to establish.'

'I'd ha' thought ye' knew all that by now,' Farquhar replied.

'The European merchants, yes,' Raffles said. 'You've been very meticulous in recording such information, but the details on some of the Chinese merchants is a bit sketchy, perhaps you can fill me in.'

Farquhar looked uneasy, and Raffles knew he needed to tread carefully. 'We know about the Peranakan merchants, of course, but not much about - these for instance. He handed Farquhar a list of Chinese names, with Boon Peng's appearing about half-way down the page. I believe that most of them came here from Malacca early on, so I'm presuming you got to know them during your time as Resident there.'

Farquhar studied the list thoroughly. 'The first three all have similar interests,' he said. 'They import cheap cotton goods from India and sell them to the Malays. The next man,

Chong Chin Lo, imports herbs from China and spices from the Moluccas. Those at the bottom of the list are mainly interested in tea, spices and porcelain, as far as I know.'

'What about this one?' Raffles said, noticing that Farquhar had avoided saying anything specific about Boon Peng.

'Don't know a great deal,' he replied. 'He deals in a number of things as far as I can make out - fingers in many pies, so to speak. He's definitely from Malacca though - left his wife there - quite a matriarch, I believe. He owns several houses along the waterfront and the gambier plantation, of course.'

'Ah!' Raffles said, 'the waterfront and the gambier plantation. Am I right in thinking there are brothels in both locations? Does Boon Peng own both establishments?'

Farquhar's face reddened. 'I suppose you're going to have another go at me for selling licenses for these places. I told you before, with lack of support from the Calcutta, we needed the revenue!'

Before Raffles could reply, three other members of the Town Committee joined them, their conversation was over, and Raffles was no further forward.

CHAPTER 17

The seasonal monsoon winds prevented both the larger Company vessels from Bengal and the Chinese junks from Guangzhou or Amoy from reaching Singapore at the turn of the year. Boon Peng's frustration grew as each day passed and the lack of income made him more and more irritable. None of his enterprises was bringing in revenue, least of all the venture Wing Yee had talked him into. His characteristic greed prohibited his ability to think straight.

Today, he had surprised both Wing Yee and Chin Ming by arriving in the middle of the morning, instead of his usual afternoon visit. He hurled a pile of documents at Chin Ming without giving any hint of what she was to do with them. She sat, watching him pace about in front of Wing Yee, muttering to himself.

'Why you say this girl good thing?' he demanded, pointing at Chin Ming. 'New clothes cost me many dollar. Not many sailor come. Not get money back. You say I make more money - not true.' Boon Peng usually spoke Hokkien, but it was a dialect with which Wing Yee was unfamiliar and despite the time he had spent in Malacca and Singapore, his Cantonese remained awkward.

Wing Yee tried to placate him. 'But next month, things will change, 'she said. 'When the winds move round to the south, there will be lots of junks coming from China. The captains of all those ships won't be able to resist the temptation, trust me. Chin Ming's new name, Te Shui, will already be well known to them. The Indiamen will already have spread the word.'

'Maybe you right,' Boon Peng said, 'but need money now. Lunar New Year next month, cost lot of dollar.'

'But that's weeks away, there's bound to be a vessel arriving before then. Once the junks start to arrive, I'm sure there will be plenty of opportunity for you to make a lot of money. By the time you see the moon herald in the new year, you will have forgotten all this vexation; you will be a very rich man.'

Boon Peng rubbed his chin thoughtfully. Maybe she spoke the truth. This new concubine was different to the others he had known. Unlike most women, she had a good understanding of business.

'Why don't you let me help you to relax a little,' Wing Yee said in the softest tones she could manage. She was keen to take his mind off this obsession for increasing his wealth; she needed to steer him away from any negative thoughts he might be having about Chin Ming and the money he'd invested in her. 'You always feel better after a relaxing massage,' she said. 'You say how much calmer it makes you feel, when I rub my special oils into your body.'

He shrugged his shoulders and followed her out of the room. He had no desire to return to his warehouse, where he knew he was likely to be confronted by Sidney Percy. He'd received a note from him only yesterday, stating that the woman he'd paid good money for was unsatisfactory. It was only a matter of time, before the man turned up on his doorstep, demanding his money back.

As far as the harbour trade was concerned, Wing Yee was correct; nothing could be done right now, so why not benefit from what had turned out to be the very best part of his latest investment.

*****

Chin Ming remained at the table and set about translating the papers the towkay had left with her. Most of the work was all too easy and she often found her thoughts drifting to the life she had left behind in Guangzhou. Today, she was wearing her pale blue *qipao*. Of the three dresses the towkay had provided, it was her favourite. The material, decorated all around the hem with tiny butterflies, reminded her of a silk skirt, favoured by her mother. She rose and moved away from the table, walked up and down the room, then twirled round and round at the point where the sunlight was at its strongest. The minute gold and green wings of the creatures shimmered with her every move Her store of childhood memories had faded rapidly as the years since her mother's death multiplied; any recollection that floated into her mind nowadays, no matter how intangible, was comforting. It conjured. up an image of happier times, when her life had been uncomplicated, and anxiety unknown.

Boon Peng had made it clear that he was reconsidering his decision to allow her to live in his house alongside Wing Yee. His early arrival today had in itself been alarming, but she was much more troubled by his fit of temper. On previous visits, she had never witnessed such an outburst and it had unnerved her. Wing Yee had been able to pacify him on this occasion, but how long would it be before it happened again? She must work even harder - maybe she could make some suggestions about the replies he sent to his letters. He was apt to avoid making decisions, tending rather to invent excuses for his actions. She needed him to see that his investment in her was worthwhile, even without the harbour visits.

She returned to the table and the document in front of her. It was obviously a contract of some kind and she couldn't afford to make a mistake. Occasionally, she found an English term difficult to translate and the usual murmurings coming from the room upstairs made it difficult to concentrate. She heard a bump directly above her head, much louder than normal. She shivered at the thought of what might be happening. She would never understand how Wing Yee could bear to let this elderly, overweight man come anywhere near her, but she knew it was pointless to question the motives of her friend.

She covered her ears in an effort to concentrate; and as she tried to distract herself by remembering one of the poems her father had taught her; one particular verse kept repeating itself in her head:

Colours blind their eyes, sounds deafen their ears,
flavours spoil their palates, the chase and the hunt craze their
minds,
and greed makes their actions harmful.
And so the sage will avoid extremes.

She wished that, like the sage, she could be wise, but even wisdom would not help to overcome Boon Peng's greediness. Everything now depended on the arrival of a large enough trading vessel before the spring festival. If, for some reason a ship was delayed, due perhaps to bad weather, what would be the consequence? Would Wing Yee be able to distract him yet again?

'Chin Ming! Chin Ming!' It was Wing Yee calling her name. The tone of her friend's voice was unusually high, and her words came in sporadic bursts. Chin Ming caught her breath and a chill surged through her veins. She ran towards the curtain that covered the staircase and pulled it back. She looked up to see Wing Yee clinging to the banister and looking very pale.

'He started to get angry again,' she said haltingly, barely able to get her words out. Chin Ming rushed up the stairs as fast as she could. She took hold of Wing Yee's hands and persuaded her to sit down.

'He kept ranting about money, about the cost of our dresses, and so few ships in the harbour,' Wing Yee said.

'Then ...' she paused to take a ragged breath.

Chin Ming stroked her friend's hand and waited.

'... he was half-way through a sentence, when his words started to sound strange, like men who've had too much alcohol. He kept swallowing and his face looked very odd - as if someone had pulled his mouth to one side. I tried to get him to sit down, but it was as if he hadn't heard me. Then, he collapsed onto the floor. I've been trying to get him to tell me what's wrong, but there's no response. I think he's dead!'

Both women remained in the same position, staring at each other - unable to speak or move. Chin Ming couldn't believe her ears. Wing Yee's face had turned ashen, and she was shaking from head to foot. Chin Ming edged closer and put her arm around Wing Yee's shoulders. They sat close together, like the statues in the temple, oblivious of time,

'Do you think I should take a look?' Chin Ming eventually whispered. 'Maybe he isn't dead after all, maybe he just passed out.'

The sound of Chin Ming's voice jolted Wing Yee back into consciousness.

'We'll both go. I don't want you to be alarmed by what you see.' She stood up. 'But you're right, we do need to check to see whether he is breathing or not.'

The room was stuffy. It was dimly lit - only the more persistent shafts of sunlight penetrated gaps in the shutters, illuminating the centre of the room. Dust particles danced in the spotlight that hovered above the prostrate figure beside the bed. Maybe the bump I heard was Boon Peng falling onto the floor, Chin Ming thought as she hurried towards him and knelt beside his body. His mouth was twisted, and his eyes stared straight ahead. It did indeed look as if all the life had drained out of him. She began to straighten his clothing, in preparation for the ritual washing that a dead body must receive, when she noticed a small movement in his chest. She placed her hand below his nostrils, the way she'd seen Father

John check the abandoned children so often dumped outside the Mission. She smiled, as she felt a feather of Boon Peng's breath flutter across her fingers. 'He's alive,' she said to Wing Yee. 'It's only very slight, but he's still breathing - we need to get some help!'

'But we're locked in. Does anyone apart from Lu Tong know the towkay comes here every day?'

'There must be a key, hidden somewhere on his body,' Chin Ming said, suddenly becoming the one to take charge of the situation. 'Help me to search his clothing.'

Wing Yee hesitated, unable to move.

'Quickly,' Chin Ming shouted. 'If we can find the key, we can get out of here - and we can find someone who might help.'

These words made Wing Yee spring into action. They delved into the many pockets - some obvious and some hidden - in Boon Peng's various garments. Chin Ming's hands moved like lightening; occasionally bumping into Wing Yee as she did so.

Despite all their efforts, no key was found. Together, they struggled to turn the body, so that they could explore underneath his heavy frame. They repeated their search but found nothing; Boon Peng's breathing remained shallow.

'Where's the robe he was wearing when he arrived?' Chin Ming said.

Wing Yee lifted the reddish-brown robes from the stool where it had been carelessly flung. Chin Ming was at her elbow now, looking anxious. The coat had two deep pockets; it was the second one in which they found not one key, but a whole bunch of them.

'Should one of us stay here with Boon Peng?' Chin Ming asked.

'I think we should both go to find help,' Wing Yee said. 'My English is not good enough to explain to anyone in authority what has happened - and I don't want you to be out on the street alone. It will be safer if we go together.' She eased a cushion under Boon Peng's head; his breath was still shallow, but he was alive. Wing Yee covered his body with a sheet, taking one last look at him before she followed Chin Ming down the narrow staircase to the room below.

Chin Ming reached the door first. She took the keys from Wing Yee and tried the one that looked mostly likely to fit. It slipped into the lock easily enough, but it wouldn't turn in either direction. She tried each of the keys in turn, but they all failed to engage with the stubborn lock.

'Let me try,' Wing Yee said.

Without taking the care that Chin Ming had demonstrated, she hastily tried each key in turn. She was beginning to feel jaded when, on her sixth attempt, there was some movement. She continued turning, then she heard a loud click. The lock was set free, and the door swung open.

Both women stepped over the threshold into an area piled high with sacks of pepper, gambier and rice. 'I'd forgotten there was a warehouse out here,' Wing Yee said.

When they reached the far end of the go-down, a pair of large wooden gates mocked them, barring their way.

'What now?' Wing Yee said.

'Quick, try all the other keys until we find one that fits,' Chin Ming said. 'You see there, on the left-hand side, there is a small door cut into the larger one.

Chin Ming took the keys from her friend and once again systematically went about finding the one to match the lock. She tried to hurry, but her fingers felt clammy and the more she hurried, the more difficult it became.

A loud knock, and the door shuddered. Both women jumped back. There it was again, louder still this time. Chin Ming looked questioningly at Wing Yee, but she didn't utter a word.

The noise on the outer door changed from what had initially sounded like an anxious knock to more agitated hammering. Chin Ming's skin began to tingle, her heart started to race. The banging continued. Wing Yee was frozen to the spot.

Who was out there? The voice was that of a man, but what did he want and why was he so insistent?

'Who can it be?' Wing Yee whispered. 'No one ever comes here. Boon Peng meets the other merchants and his business partners in his office. No one visits us apart from Boon Peng - and occasionally Lu Tong.'

'It can't be Lu Tong,' Chin Ming said. 'He has his own key to the outer door. He used it when he brought me here.'

'Boon Peng, I know you're in there,' an angry European voice yelled. 'Lu Tong told me.'

There was silence and then the haranguing started all over again. 'He says you come here to see your woman. Lucky you, that's all I can say! She must be better than the one you sold to me. You cheated me, you old crook - you tricked me out of fifty dollars and I want my money back!'

'We should hide,' Wing Yee said.

'Whoever it is, he's angry. If we don't let him in, he'll either get Lu Tong to open up or ...'

'Or he'll break the door down himself,' Wing Yee added.

The knocking started all over again. 'I'm not going away, so you might as well let me in, you old fool!' the unknown voice shouted, even louder than before.

'Wait,' Chin Ming shouted back. 'We need to find the key.'

'Who's that? Let me in.' The visitor continued to thump on the door as Chin Ming tried to find the right one and fit it into the shuddering door.

When she felt a slight movement, she gave Wing Yee one last look. This would not end well, and Wing Yee's expression confirmed her own fear. Wing Yee gave her a small nod.

She turned the key. A loud click, and she almost lost her balance as the door was thrown open from the other side. A tall, swarthy *Ang Moh* burst in.

CHAPTER 18

Neither woman had ever seen Sidney Percy before, nor did he introduce himself on this occasion. To them, he looked much like any other *Ang Moh*; dressed flamboyantly in dark European clothes,

'So, where is he - and what are you doing out here with a bunch of keys?' the man yelled.

Wing Yee and Chin Ming remained motionless; they both stood, rooted to the spot, unable to utter any form of response. Wing Yee's skin tingled all over and her heart raced. Chin Ming stared at her, looking alarmed. Who is this man, she thought? What does he want, and why is he so belligerent?

'I suppose he's drunk,' the man said. 'And you thought you'd take the opportunity to run away, is that it? Well, you wouldn't get very far, even if I hadn't come calling - you'd stick out like a sore thumb out there on your own.

Wing Yee winced. 'Boon Peng,' she began, but he interrupted before she could continue.

'Yes, that's who I'm after, the good-for-nothing-towkay; show me where I can find him.'

Wing Yee's fleeting courage failed her, and she remained still.

'Where is he?' the *Ang Moh* yelled.

Wing Yee pointed to the green door that opened into the house. She hurried after the man, as fast as her long skirt would allow; Chin Ming followed in their shadow. Once inside, she said, 'He not well - something happen,' she said in her limited English. 'He fall on floor; we look for help.'

The *Ang Moh* stared at Chin Ming. 'Is this true?'

She nodded, then she pointed to the staircase.

'Stay there!' he insisted, as he strode across the room; he pulled back the curtain and ran up the stairs.

Wing Yee wanted to follow him, to tell him about Boon Peng's shallow breath and ask him to get some medical help, but instinct told her to be wary. She dreaded what might happen next; she felt cold and miserable as she waited for the man to reappear.

They could hear the sound of heavy footsteps above them, then everything went silent. Wing Yee started to move towards the stairs, but Chin Ming restrained her. 'I think we should wait,' she said. When the *Ang Moh* reappeared, his anger was cloaked in a mood even darker than before.

'You,' he pointed directly at Wing Yee. 'I assume you are the concubine he told me about. Tell me what happened.'

Wing Yee hesitated. In broken English, she told him that Boon Peng was upset when he visited them that morning. She made no mention of the cause of Boon Peng's anger. 'I help him relax,' she said. 'He like me to massage - after little while, he more happy, he enjoy rubbing with oils. He grow calm.'

As she was talking, Sidney Percy studied her carefully. He'd heard that Boon Peng's latest concubine was good-looking, but he hadn't expected to see anyone quite so striking. She was taller than most Chinese women he'd encountered and above the fine cheek bones, her dark, defiant eyes shone like black sapphires. Her hair hung down her back in a thick cascade, and he knew instinctively what pleasure he would derive in breaking her spirit. No wonder the old man had kept this one for himself. His mind came racing back to the words she was uttering, words that might easily be twisted, if it suited him.

'And ...?' Sidney Percy looked at her reproachfully. He wasn't interested in the towkay's preferences or what amusements he indulged in with this woman.

'At first, he pleased ...but he get upset again.'

'What happened?' her interrogator persisted.

'His face look strange, twisted, then he fall on floor. Cannot make him hear me. Not know what to do, but he still breathing. We find keys, go look for help.'

'What makes you say he was breathing?'

Chin Ming stepped forward, but he didn't notice. 'His chest was moving up and down slowly,' she said. 'I could feel his breath on my hand.'

'Well, he's not breathing now,' the man said, looking accusingly at Wing Yee. 'He's dead!'

Both women gasped. They looked at each other in horror, and all the blood drained from their faces. Sidney Percy stared at Wing Yee. Her face was pale and he knew she was scared. A woman like her had no status and with no witnesses, she might easily be accused of killing the old man. Now was his chance to take her and he wouldn't even have to hand over any money. He believed it to be a reasonable recompense; after all, he'd paid over the odds for one woman, and she had proved to be totally useless. That's why he'd come looking for Boon Peng - to confront him about being cheated.

The towkay had insisted that Shu Fang was all he could wish for. She was pretty enough, and she was obviously used to pleasing men - but no one had mentioned the noise she would make as she clattered around on the tiny apologies she had for feet. He had already arranged for her to be taken to the gambier plantation.

He put his hand on Wing Yee's shoulder. 'Stupid old man. Old and overweight, no wonder he suffered a seizure,' he said. 'But don't worry, I'll get Lu Tong to deal with all the fuss and while he makes arrangements for the burial, I will take you away from here. I will protect you.'

Wing Yee turned towards Chin Ming and for the first time, Sidney Percy appeared to become aware of the younger girl. He looked her up and down. He couldn't believe his luck. Not only was the concubine his for the taking, there also was an even prettier young thing that he could have as well. It would be easy enough to persuade them that he had only their best interests at heart. There was no need to tell them that he lived on the outskirts of the town, and the house he'd built there was so remote that none of the other Europeans knew where it was located. No one would know where the women had gone, and he doubted that anyone would even care.

Everything was happening so quickly, neither Wing Yee nor Chin Ming knew what to say. Wing Yee worried that people might accuse her of killing the towkay; Chin Ming worried about her friend. What could either of them do, other than accept the offer that was being made? They knew no one in this town. If only she'd been able to find the man Papa had told her about - the man called Raffles.

'It will be best if you stay here while I go to find Lu Tong,' the *Ang Moh* said. 'I will tell him what's happened and make sure he starts to make the arrangements as quickly as possible. While I'm away, I want you to pack up your things. It's important that I get you away from here quickly before the body begins to stink. We will go tonight.'

Wing Yee tried to protest, but he ignored her. He picked up the bunch of keys that Chin Ming had left on the table. 'Hurry,' he said, 'I need you to be ready to leave when I return.'

They watched as he walked away from them and let himself out. The next thing they heard was the familiar click of the key turning in the lock.

'I shouldn't have opened the door to him,' Chin Ming eventually said.

'It would have made no difference,' Wing Yee replied, reverting back to Cantonese. 'He would have broken the door down. We had no chance of getting help for Boon Peng - and now he's dead. It's all my fault.'

'It's nobody's fault,' Chin Ming said. 'What else could we have done in the circumstances. We had no choice!'

'Just as we have no choice now, apparently,' Wing Yee added. 'But I don't trust that man. I don't trust anyone who can't even be bothered to tell us his name. I think we should get our things together and be ready to leave here as he says, but we should look for a chance to get away from him as soon as possible.'

Both women needed all their courage to return to the room where Boon Peng's body lay, but finally they ventured up the stairs together. They each had only a few possessions to take with them - the garments Boon Peng had paid for and some remaining scraps that had come with them from Guang-zhou.

Chin Ming tried not to look at Boon Peng's body, but the *Ang Moh* had removed the sheet they had draped over him. The towkay's forehead, nose and ears were dark pink and his cheeks had taken on a purplish hue. It felt as if he was staring at them both from enormous pupils, made even larger by the yellowing whites of his eyes. There was a small trickle of blood staining his mouth. Chin Ming had never seen a dead body before and she stood, as if struck by lightning, in front of him.

Wing Yee bundled all the *pien fus* and *qipaos* together, grabbed a few odds and ends and then noticed Chin Ming's immobile state. She took her hand in her own, and gently steered her out of the room and down the stairs.

They sat quietly together, waiting for the *Ang Moh* to return. 'I don't trust him,' Wing Yee whispered. 'When he takes us away from here, try to remember the route. Listen out for any sounds, memorise any smells ... anything that might help us to recognise our whereabouts.'

'What are you saying?' Chin Ming said.

'Be careful, that's all I mean. Why should he take any interest in us? We are just two of Boon Peng's women who are in the way ... why should he want to protect us unless ...'

The click of the door being unlocked made them jump.

'The wagon is just outside,' the *Ang Moh* - who still hadn't told them his name - announced. 'Get into it quickly and lie down flat. We don't want anyone to see you leaving the house of a dead man.'

'But ...' Wing Yee started to protest.

'But nothing,' he said. 'Believe me, I'm doing this for your own good.'

She took Chin Ming by the hand and led her to what turned out to be only a small cart. Almost as soon as they had settled themselves on its floor, Sidney Percy threw a piece of sacking over them. He had chosen a time of day when not many people frequented this part of the town, but he still took the precaution of making them invisible to anyone who should pass by.

Wing Yee squeezed Chin Ming's hand. She was convinced that the *Ang Moh* was untrustworthy, but what option did they have, other than to go along with his plan? If I try to escape, she thought, people might think I was instrumental in Boon Peng's death. And what would Chin Ming do? If she comes with me, then she might also be accused of foul play; if she is left alone with the Ang Moh then she is surely damned. No, we'll have to go along with him for the time being. Maybe he'll tire of us; maybe we won't suit him? Her thoughts continued to ramble but led to no satisfactory conclusion.

Sidney Percy drove the cart away from the house for a short distance only. It stopped abruptly and everything went quiet. They lay perfectly still under the stale odour of the hessian; there was no way of knowing how long they waited.

'Listen,' Wing Yee continued to whisper in Cantonese. 'I think I can hear the movement of oars. There's a particular squeaky noise they make. I remember it from our visits to the ships in the harbour.'

Both women strained their ears to listen for any further clues, but as they did so, Sidney Percy flung back the cover and told them to get out. The light was already fading, and one or two oil lamps had been lit. As they quickly gathered their belongings together, he pushed them in the direction of a waiting sampan. He indicated that they should get in. When he followed, his weight caused the small craft to rock from side to side. Chin Ming looked alarmed, but once he was seated everything settled down again. He remained, firmly installed on a plank towards the prow of the vessel, looking them up and down. He crossed his arms, thrust out his chest and tilted his head backwards. Wing Yee noticed a faint smirk cross his lips before he gave an order to the boatman to depart. The small craft slid silently along the river towards its mouth, bobbed up and down at the point where the current changed and then turned, to make its way eastwards parallel with the beach.

Wing Yee and Chin Ming looked at each other as the glow from the lamps along the shoreline faded from view. They had now gone beyond the boundary of the town. No one said a word, but Wing Yee squeezed Chin Ming's hand again and was glad when she received a comforting response. As the journey continued, she found it more and more difficult to keep still, she was uncomfortable and extremely thirsty. Where was the *Ang Moh* taking them? Why so far away from the town? Perhaps he intended to throw them overboard? She couldn't swim and neither could Chin Ming. The water would be cold, and it was already dark. Maybe she should have given more serious thought to escaping; there might have been a possibility when they stood on the quay, waiting for the sampan to pull alongside? Now, it was too late, and if what she suspected was correct, they had little chance of survival.

The oarsman continued to row, until they reached the mouth of another river. He looked round at this point and the *Ang Moh* nodded. The vegetation on both sides of this new waterway was thick and the boat needed to be guided carefully. Eventually, they turned and pulled into the margin; they had reached a solitary house, built in the Malay style. The oarsman jumped out into the water and pulled the small craft alongside the riverbank. Sidney Percy stood up. The boat rocked once more, as he too jumped into the shallows. When Wing Yee and Chin Ming hung back, he simply came back to the sampan and lifted each of them unceremoniously onto dry land.

'Follow me,' he ordered.

They looked at each other and tried to examine their new surroundings. There was a rough path along one side of the river, but it was too dark to see where it might lead. Beyond the house itself, all they could see was the dense blackness of the jungle.

The lamps had been lit inside the house and it almost looked welcoming after everything that had happened to them in the last twenty-four hours. It's remoteness, however, coupled with the attitude of the *Ang Moh*, did nothing to alleviate Wing Yee's fears. She had been thinking about Boon Peng's involvement with this mysterious European, and wondering what type of business arrangements they shared. His complaints and obscure references to the woman he had recently purchased led her to believe that he might be the man to whom Shu Fang had been delivered.

'Hurry!' shouted Sidney Percy.

They scurried up the steps to the veranda, and a Malay servant beckoned them to follow her. They both looked from right to left as they walked from a spacious living area, following the woman along a wide corridor to a room at the back of the house. There was no sign of Shu Fang. After a while, the same servant brought them a bowl of chicken rice and some soup. Neither Chin Ming nor Wing Yee had eaten anything since the previous morning; suddenly, hunger clawed at their insides.

The servant returned to collect their bowls sometime later. 'Master say you sleep now,' she said. 'I go back my village.' Surprised that the woman spoke even a little English, they did as they had been instructed. They lay together, with the lights dimmed, on one of the low wooden beds. They held each other tight; neither having any idea what might happen to them in this place so far away from the nearest habitation. They listened hard, wary of any sudden movement, but there was none. Their only distraction was the lapping noise of the river and occasional entertainment provided by a loud chorus of chirping crickets. They saw nothing further of the *Ang Moh* that evening.

CHAPTER 19

It was already light. The intensity of the heat in the room already indicated that it was well past the middle of the morning. Wing Yee and Chin Ming had seen very little of the house when they arrived yesterday evening, but the impression left in Chin Ming's mind, as they'd been bundled through to this room, was of something more impressive than the living quarters they'd inhabited in Boon Peng's abode. She thought Wing Yee might have been wrong in her superstitions about this strange European. The house was unlike either of the other places they'd been held. She touched Wing Yee gently on the shoulder, but her friend was already awake. There was no sound, other than something rustling in the rafters above their heads, accompanied by exuberant birdsong.

'Why don't you wear your coolie trousers and save your *qipao* until we get out of here?' Wing Yee suggested. She had spent most of the night thinking of ways they might be able to escape. Eventually, she decided that if her unease about the *Ang Moh* was correct, it was unlikely that they would both be able to get away and Chin Ming would have a better chance on her own. Her simple peasant garments would make running easier and hopefully, the *Ang Moh* would be less likely to pay much attention to her.

'But what will you wear?' Chin Ming replied.

'Never mind that, I'll find something later,' she said. She knew instinctively that the girl would refuse to leave without her, but somehow, she would have to make her understand. She picked up the grey shift and helped Chin Ming to slip it over her head and pull it down over the trousers before she raised any more objections. Wing Yee chose the yellow dress with white cherry blossom that she had worn the day Chin Ming had been brought to Boon Peng's house. It was a slender cotton garment that showed off the shape of her body, but it also had frog-buttons with tight loops at the neck and all down the side. Each one was beautiful to look at, but difficult and time-consuming to unfasten. If her distrust of the *Ang Moh* was correct, she hoped that such intricacies would provide a necessary delaying tactic.

As soon as they had finished dressing, they opened the door of their room and checked that there was no one about, before tiptoeing towards the main room of the house. They looked around, but there was no obvious sign of either the man who had brought them here or his Malay servant.

'The *Ang Moh* who brought us here,' Chin Ming whispered, 'have you any idea who he is? And why have we been moved so far away from the town?' she continued. 'Do you think that he's he gone away and left us here all alone?'

'I very much doubt that,' Wing Yee replied. 'I'm sure he has his reasons for bringing us here and I still don't trust him. Why has he never told us his name? I can only assume - from the way he behaves and from some of the things he was shouting about yesterday - that he is one of Boon Peng's business partners. I believe he may even be the person who paid for Shu Fang to be brought here from China,' Wing Yee replied.

'So, where is she?'

Before Wing Yee had a chance to say anything further, the *Ang Moh* strode into the room. 'The woman you speak of has gone, she did not satisfy me,' the loud, booming voice of Sidney Percy made them jump. 'Not that it is any of your business.'

Their faces turned pale, and their hands became clammy as they wondered how long he'd been listening to their hushed conversation. He was wearing only a sarong and his skin was still damp from washing in the river. He towered over both women, scrutinising every inch of their bodies. They shrank back against the wall, holding each other's hands tightly, but neither of them could stop shaking. Sidney Percy focused his gaze on Chin Ming. He looked her up and down as if examining an animal brought to market, then he abruptly announced, 'No, she did not satisfy me at all, but I think you, little girl - when I get you out of those appalling clothes - I think you might satisfy me a great deal.'

'No!' Wing Yee shouted back to him in English. She moved rapidly to stand between the man and Chin Ming. Her ruse to divert his attention away from her friend had not worked. Her suspicions had been correct; his intentions now obvious. She'd seen people like him in Guangzhou - totally selfish, intent only on their own pleasure and she was determined to protect Chin Ming from such brutality.

'Get out of my way, you trollop,' Sidney Percy yelled back, pushing Wing Yee aside. She stood her ground and refused to let him anywhere near Chin Ming.

'No,' she insisted, pulling Chin Ming behind her. 'You cannot have her; we had an agreement with Boon Peng. She came here as my companion. He agreed that she could stay in return for translating documents and writing letters for him - sometimes we both went out to welcome the new ships in the harbour. It was all agreed. He promised,' she added hastily.

'Boon Peng took on a woman called Wing Yee as his concubine - I presume that is you, madam. Any arrangement he came to later is no longer valid.' He looked Chin Ming up and down. once again. 'Tell me your name, young woman,' he said.

She remained stubbornly silent. How dare he demand to know her name, when he hadn't even told them his own.

'I said, tell me your name,' he yelled, 'NOW!'

She took a deep breath and looked him straight in the eye.

'My name is Chin Ming,' she said, 'I am the daughter of Li Soong Heng ...'

'What did you say? What is your father's name?'

'Li Soong Heng,' She repeated defiantly. 'He ...'

'I know who your father was!' He kept his eyes fixed on her for a long time; neither she nor Wing Yee dared to speak. The silence felt endless. Finally, he stepped away from Chin Ming and turned towards Wing Yee. 'Boon Peng is dead; he owed me the money I paid for that worthless woman. He was supposed bring three women, so that I could choose the one I wanted, but no, he tells me there is only the one and she is very special. What he failed to tell me was that special meant she had such an ugly excuse for feet!'

'In China, small feet believed beautiful,' Wing Yee replied. Call them *lily feet* and have much value .'

'We are not in China! The sight of them made me feel ill and the noise they made as they clattered over the floorboards drove me insane. No, Boon Peng owes me; the two of you will compensate for the other women I was originally promised - I think I'm entitled to take what was his.'

'Then take me,' Wing Yee continued in English. 'You correct; I am concubine. I not unattractive,' she said as she moved towards him. 'And my father, he think no need to bind my feet.' She edged closer to him and pulled the hem of her dress over her ankles, to reveal a pair of small, perfectly healthy feet. Despite the shaking inside, she looked up at his face and smiled. 'Men say I give much pleasure,' she said in the softest, most seductive voice she could manage.

'I am not Boon Peng,' he scoffed. 'I am considerably younger and have a ferocious appetite.'

'And I make men happy - from China, from Europe - for long time,' she continued, hoping against hope that she could distract him and that he would take the bait.

*****

Chin Ming was shocked. Why was Wing Yee behaving like this? She said she didn't like this man, that she didn't trust him - and yet here she was behaving like a common prostitute. Why was she flaunting herself in front of this man? She looked at her friend in disbelief, and it was only when she heard the next part of the proposition that she realised why her friend was behaving in this strange way. Wing Yee was trying to protect her.

*****

'This girl has just eighteen summers; no experience with men. I will please you, not her.'

Sidney Percy considered his options. He could, of course, have both women - and he fully intended to, especially now he'd discovered that one of them was the daughter of the man who had betrayed him to the authorities in Guangzhou. If it hadn't been for Soong Heng and his precious principles, there would have been no need for him to leave China in such a hurry. The past few months had been particularly boring; his lust grew as each day passed and the recently arrived young woman had been sadly disappointing. 'Maybe I will take you up on your offer,' he said.

'Wing Yee, you can't ...' Chin Ming reverted to Cantonese and moved quickly to her friend's side.

The older woman turned towards her. Knowing that the Englishman would not understand, she replied, also in Cantonese, 'I have come to think of you as my sister; I will do anything to protect you. It will be alright. I know what I'm doing. I can smell alcohol on his breath, even at this early hour, so he will probably tire quite quickly. Once he is asleep, we must begin to prepare our escape, but for the time being, I need you to act normally. Do not try to intervene or to stop him. Remember,' she concluded, 'I am a Dragon, I am strong, and I can survive this.'

A feeble smile crossed her lips. She was determined not to show Chin Ming that she too was scared. They held each other whilst Sidney Percy stepped across the room to secure the shutters; then, he fixed a padlock on the door. He reached out and grabbed Wing Yee by her hair, pulling her towards him. She made herself smile, hoping that the skills she'd learned from Madam Ong would enable her to divert his attention away from Chin Ming. He stared at her with unfeeling eyes, but his appetite for her grew as he began to drag her towards his bedroom

'You stay there,' he yelled at Chin Ming. 'And speak in English, or not at all. I'll come back for dessert later.'

Chin Ming remained rooted to the floor. She was unfamiliar with the word *dessert*. What did he mean? She slumped onto the floor, feeling helpless and frustrated. What had seemed not such a bad existence a few days ago had now turned into a nightmare. She couldn't even begin to imagine what it was like to be with a man, let alone someone like this monster. Who was he? What hold did he have over Wing Yee? Surely no one would really believe she had deliberately killed Boon Peng?

Her frustration turned into anger as she became aware of the low, grunting sounds that came from the bedroom. It reminded her of the pigs in a farmyard. She listened for Wing Yee's voice, but heard nothing other than the loud, demanding and, at times, vicious tones coming from the bully in the bedroom.

Once again, she began to ask herself questions. Why had this man come to Boon Peng's house yesterday morning? What was the connection between them - and why had he reacted so angrily when she mentioned her father's name? Surely, there must be something in this room that would provide an answer to some of the questions buzzing around in her head.

She looked up, suddenly conscious of the diminished light.

The closed shutters obscured the outside glare, and it took her a while to become accustomed to the gloom. Then, as odd shafts of sunlight found their way into the gaps between the wooden panels, she identified a circle of rattan chairs, covered in cushions, and draped in hand-woven brocade. She scrambled to her feet, intent now on finding out the name of their captor. She made her way across the room, being careful to keep to the rich and colourful rugs, scattered all over the dark, polished wooden floor. She made hardly a sound.

When she reached the ornate wooden sideboard on the far wall, she was shocked to see her own reflection in its mirror. Whatever would Papa think if he saw her now? He might not even recognise her; she had changed so much over the past few months. She began her search by running her fingers over the surface of the dresser and then she opened first one drawer and then another. The smaller, outer drawers contained a collection of chopsticks, pieces of string, some European cutlery, and an odd collection of items - most of which she didn't recognise.

The middle drawer was heavy and more difficult to open, but eventually she managed to pull it out. The first thing she saw was two large ledgers jammed on top, making the drawer harder to release. Once that was achieved, Chin Ming lifted each of them out and placed them on top of the dresser. She turned the pages carefully, looking for anything that might reveal the name of the *Ang Moh*, but all she found was merely a record of business dealings. She glanced briefly at the entries, but there was nothing there of interest. Underneath the ledgers, she found several bundles of papers, each of which was tied together with string.

She lifted out the first bundle, untied the knot and examined the contents. Most of them turned out to be copies of notes to Boon Peng, but one described the dealings between the towkay, Captain Lim, and a man called Sidney Percy. The last name meant nothing to her, but she thought it might well be the *Ang Moh* - and when she inspected them further, it was clearly evidence concerning the arrangements to bring Shu Fang from China. She tried to release the string on a second bundle, but the knot was tight and even her slender fingers felt awkward and clumsy. She was still struggling with it when the bedroom door opened and the *Ang Moh* shouted something incomprehensible. She remained rooted to the spot, unable to move.

*****

'Bring me water, girl,' he shouted. 'And some more wine, you'll find them in the kitchen, behind the blue curtain.

Chin Ming felt herself tense and her heart pounded against the wall of her chest. For a brief moment, she wondered if the servant had returned and maybe the man was directing his demand to her, but then she heard him shout again, this time more aggressively.

'Girl! Did you not hear me?' he yelled at the top of his voice. 'I want something to drink - and I want it NOW. Hurry!'

She feared he might come looking for her at any moment; there was no time to return the papers back to the drawer so she moved quickly, hoping that the water and wine would pacify him. It didn't take long for her to locate what he wanted. A jug of water and a flagon of wine had already been laid out on a tray. She picked it up and hurried along the corridor. The bedroom door was closed again. 'I have your drinks,' she said, 'I'll leave them outside your door.'

She stood, looking at the bedroom door from the safe distance of the living area. Minutes passed before the *Ang Moh* appeared; his sarong was loosely knotted around his waist, his hair dishevelled, and his torso drenched in sweat. He picked up the tray without a glance towards Chin Ming and withdrew back into the room. She heaved a sigh of relief.

CHAPTER 20

When she thought it was safe to do so, Chin Ming tiptoed back to the bureau and picked up the second bundle, then she put down again. If I was trying to hide something significant, she thought to herself, I would make it more difficult to find. If he has engaged in anything else underhand, as Wing Yee seems to suspect, then any evidence will be well hidden. What else can I discover about him? Is his name really Sidney Percy? And how does he know Papa?

She removed each of the bundles in turn, being very careful to keep them in order, but they all looked similar and of no particular interest. Right at the back of the drawer, she found another book, this one was much smaller than the ledgers and when she examined it, she found the pages completely blank. She felt frustrated; maybe there was nothing else to find, after all, and yet, she couldn't stop exploring - just a little while longer. Every so often, she stopped her search; the low rumble of the man's voice coming from the bedroom made her wonder how much time she had left. She looked up and listened again. The bedroom noises continued.

As she slid the book back into place, she realised there was what looked like a small package hidden behind everything else. It turned out to be a bundle of letters, written to the man called Sidney Percy from someone in Guangzhou. Each one of them was written in English and her interest was immediately aroused. Mostly, they contained general comments about politics and investments, then there was something that made the hairs on the back of her neck stand on end. The writer said: *'Always remember that I have your best interest at heart and have arranged for the man responsible for chasing you out of Guangzhou to be dealt with.'* The next letter she pulled out was dated February 1822 and there she found another phrase that leapt out at her: '*... the matter is now over.'* It went on to describe riots at the harbour during Lunar New Year: *'Another triumph by ...'*

Then, towards the bottom of the first sheet of paper, a single name leaped off the page; it was that of her father Li Soong Heng. The rest of the letter described how someone had led Papa to believe a passage could be arranged on a ship. This same man had been instrumental in inciting the riot and when trouble broke out, the narrative went on to describe how he'd pushed through the crowd, knocking Soong Heng's daughter out of the way and seizing Soong Heng himself. *'Before he knew what was happening,'* the letter read, *'we had him bound and gagged and on the way to Amoy, where he was locked up in the hold of the Tek Sing. It sailed earlier this month but was grounded on a reef between Belitung and the Bangka Islands. It sank almost immediately. You can rest assured, my friend, Soong Heng will not be coming to Singapore or going anywhere else from now on. The matter is over and done with.'*

*****

Chin Ming began to tremble. It was all too obvious what this letter meant. She felt numb; how likely was it that Papa could have survived a shipwreck? Instinctively, she knew that she must hide this letter; it was the only information she had about her father's disappearance. Still with her hands shaking, she carefully folded it as small as she could manage and slipped it into the pocket of her trousers.

She hurriedly tried to tidy the drawer and put everything back as she had found it. She had almost pushed it back into place when she realised that all the noise had stopped. The house was entirely silent and all she could hear was the song of a bird from somewhere out beyond this prison, a song of freedom from the unknown.

It reminded her of an old Chinese proverb - and it gave her the courage to creep along the corridor towards the *Ang Moh's* bedroom. There was still no sound at all coming from the room. She pushed the door open very slowly. She could see the man, collapsed onto the bed; he was snoring loudly. At first, she failed to detect Wing Yee, but as her eyes adjusted to the shadows, she saw her curled up on the floor at the side of the bed. She rushed forwards to discover that she was badly bruised and had a deep cut over her left eye.

'Shhh,' Wing Yee whispered, 'don't wake him. Can you... can you help me stand? Can you find some water so that I can wash?'

Chin Ming held onto her friend and supported her weight as she got to her feet. The *Ang Moh* turned onto his side and grunted loudly. They froze, thinking that he would wake up any second and try to grab one of them. It was only when she was satisfied that he'd sunk back into oblivion, that Chin Ming carefully guided her friend to the main part of the house.

The young girl did everything that Wing Yee requested. She asked no questions and made no comment. Wing Yee removed her torn dress, cleansed her cuts, and pulled a fresh *qipao* over her head. 'That man is evil, she said, 'somehow, we have to get away from him or he will kill both of us!'

'You must be exhausted,' Chin Ming said. 'We can't leave until you feel stronger. Let me try to find some food while the man is sleeping.'

'Every moment we stay here increases the danger,' Wing Yee said. 'We can't break that padlock on the door, but it might be possible to force the shutters open. He was already inebriated when he closed them, and they might not be fastened properly.'

Wing Yee winced as Chin Ming helped to her feet again; she supported her weight, helped her to cross the room to the nearest set of shutters and lowered her onto some cushions. Then, she turned her attention to the slatted screens. She pushed them gently at first and then put more force into the effort, but the first two sets of shutters would not yield. Neither would the next pair budge at first, but when she looked more closely, each was held in place with only a simple wooden pin. It was quite easy to prise it out of position. Very slowly, she eased the shutters open fearing they might make a noise that would alert the *Ang Moh* to their task. Fortunately, the hinges were well-oiled, and the room was immediately flooded with the cool, evening air. She stood, for a second only, enjoying its freshness.

When Chin Ming turned around, Wing Yee had managed to smile. She knew there was no way she would be able to squeeze through that small space. If there was any chance of survival, she must persuade Chin Ming to leave without her.

'Help me up,' she said. Just as she'd managed to stand, they heard a loud snort, followed by heavy breathing from the room along the corridor. They stood, frozen to the spot until the snoring stopped and a regular breathing pattern could be heard; only then could they be sure it was safe to move again. 'You go first,' Wing Yee whispered.

Chin Ming's slight frame had no trouble at all squeezing through the narrow space that served as a window. She lowered herself down onto the ground below and prepared to help Wing Yee.

Her friend looked down at her through the shutters. 'I'm not going to be able to squeeze through that small space,' she said. 'It's fortunate that you are wearing those peasant clothes, my tunic and skirt are too cumbersome and I'm so much taller than you, I'm sure to get stuck. Chin Ming, I must ask you to go by yourself—go and get help!'

'I am not leaving without you,' the girl replied. 'I'll climb back in to help you.'

'No, you must go - go now. If the *Ang Moh* wakes, I no longer have the strength to keep him away from you.' She gritted her teeth and fought back the tears that began to surface. The *Ang Moh* had been violent; she was cut and bruised, but the shame she felt was weighing more heavily than anything else. All her energy had oozed away, and she didn't much care if she lived or died - but Chin Ming still had a chance. She had to persuade Chin Ming to leave.

'But what about you? I can't leave you with him. You have done so much to help me since we met, and you took an enormous risk persuading the towkay to let me stay with you. It would have been so much easier to let me go to a brothel and forget about me. It's my turn now, to look after you.'

'Then go and get some help - that's the only way - please,' she said, 'I will try to distract him for a short while, but you must hurry. Every moment you stay here increases the danger. Say no more, in case he hears us. You must go now.'

With that, Wing Yee used all her remaining strength to reach for the shutter and pull it towards her. Now, it was firmly closed, and there was no way that Chin Ming could re-enter the house.

Chin Ming was shocked. 'What are you doing?' she said.

She swallowed hard, not quite believing what Wing Yee had done. At first, no words would come and then she began to feel giddy, but she knew she had no choice other than to do what her friend had asked. Finally, she whispered, 'I promise, I'll find someone who can help. I promise I'll try.' Then, to reassure herself as much as her friend, she added, 'Remember what you said - you are a Dragon, you must be strong. I've lost too many people I care about. I cannot lose you too.'

With that, she stumbled down the steps and looked out into the darkness. They had arrived here by boat, but she could see no sign of any craft of the river now. The clouds parted just long enough for her see the moonlight on the water and the direction in which the water was flowing. Common sense told her that if she followed the river, she would eventually come to the shoreline. She looked back to see if she was being followed, but already the house had disappeared from sight. Her legs felt weak, and her heart was racing; she wasn't even sure this was a proper path, but she continued to push her way through knee-high vegetation.

Earlier in the day, she was convinced she could hear drums in the distance and imagined that there might be a village nearby. If she could find such a place now, then she could ask for their help - but even if she could find its whereabouts, would the people who lived there be able to understand her?

As she continued to stumble along, she remembered her first sighting of the settlement all those months ago. As they'd travelled from the junk in the bumboat, she remembered seeing the young man who had waved to her from the beach. If only she could find that golden stretch of sand, then she could follow it; and if she followed it, she would ultimately reach the edge of the town. If she could get herself there, then there would definitely be people who spoke English, or Cantonese. Maybe someone would know how to find the man called Raffles?

The moon teased her, playing hide and seek between the clouds. Once, in a patch of total darkness, she nearly fell into the water. Later, she felt a slimy slithering creature glide across her foot; she remained rooted to the spot, her body became totally rigid, and for a while, she was too scared to move an inch. It was only the greater worry that the *Ang Moh* might be following, that eventually caused her to go on.

During the remaining hours of darkness, she moved as fast as she could manage along the uneven ground. She stumbled when sharp stones cut into her bare feet and winced whenever the *lalang* grass sliced against her legs. Once, when a leaf fell from overhead and a cobweb ensnared her face, she wished that she'd heeded Father John's advice and had never left China. She wiped the strands of spider's web away with her sleeve and told herself not to be so silly. But she continued to turn around constantly, still terrified that the *Ang Moh* might be in pursuit. Her determination to find help for Wing Yee, however, gave her the resolve to keep going- -and to find it as quickly as possible.

Eventually, the false dawn arrived, and she thought she saw the outline of a village in the distance. She had no idea how far she had come, nor how far she still had to go. Then she realised, that instead of the rough grass and the mud she'd been walking on beside of the river, her feet now dug into soft, golden sand. Fatigue overcame her, but she still tried to walk. Her stubborn streak forced her to continue for as long as possible, but just as the sun appeared over the horizon, she sank to her knees in a state of utter exhaustion; she could go no further.

CHAPTER 21

Wing Yee listened hard for any indication that the *Ang Moh* had emerged from his drunken stupor, but the only sound was the regular clicking of the cicadas and an occasional whooping noise from what she imagined was a bird. She heaved a sigh of relief. Chin Ming had a better chance of survival out in the jungle, than in this vile house.

A sharp pain brought her back to the present moment. It ripped through her whole body - from the sore throbbing sensation between her legs, right to the top of her head. She swallowed hard and tried to control her self-loathing. 'I brought all this upon myself,' she thought. 'I couldn't see what was right in front of me, what was obvious. If I hadn't offered myself so freely to him, maybe ...'

'I must get myself back to the bedroom,' she said to herself, when she was able to think more clearly, 'or he will notice straightway that Chin Ming is missing, and he will know I helped her to escape.' She closed her eyes and took a deep breath before extending her left hand out onto the floor. Slowly, she turned, bringing her right hand across to join it. Then, she pushed with all her remaining strength to raise herself onto her knees. A wave of nausea swept through her and she began to feel faint. She bit down on her bottom lip and clutched her stomach.

She listened carefully and was relieved when all she could hear inside the house, was the regular breathing and occasional snort of the *Ang Moh*. Her resolve strengthened. She took a deep breath before placing one hand at a time in front of her and then forcing her knees to follow in a straight line. Her progress across the room was slow, as each movement she made caused great pain and she was still petrified that the *Ang Moh* would suddenly appear in front of her.

When she reached the passageway, she looked up and listened again. Another sharp, stabbing pain seared through her body and with it, the nausea returned. The door of the man's room was slightly ajar, and she could just make out the shape of his body, slumped across the bed, in much the same position as he'd been in when Chin Ming found her there. Her pulse began to race, and she felt clammy all over.

Wing Yee took a deep breath once more and gritted her teeth. No matter how much she loathed the idea of him touching her, she must think of some way to distract him again, so that Chin Ming had the best possible chance to get away.

Slowly and steadily, she pulled herself along the last few yards to the room they had briefly shared. Her ears continued to strain all the time, listening for any give-away signs of movement. Finally, she reached her mattress and with one last effort pulled herself onto it. Now, while she waited for her tormentor to appear, she must try to think about delaying tactics.

Wing Yee passed in and out of consciousness several times as images of the *Ang Moh*, forcing himself upon her over and over again, continued to torment her. In her more lucid moments, she remembered thinking that she had never experienced anyone so callous, so cruel, so animal-like as this monster. She dreaded the moment when he would wake up; she knew once he failed to find Chin Ming, that he would take out his anger on her. She wished she could have found some weapon that she could use either to defend herself or to attack him, but with all her physical strength now gone she knew that it was impossible.

*****

Now, she was wide-awake; it was already light. Somewhere beyond where she lay, she could hear the distinctive sound of squeaking floorboards. It could only mean one thing, the *Ang Moh* was conscious and moving around. Was he still in his bedroom or had he gone to the front of the house expecting to find Chin Ming? How long would it take for him to discover that she was missing? Every sinew of her body tensed, and her heart raced. A solitary ant, taking a short-cut home tickled her left hand; she instinctively flicked it away. She strained to listen, but there was nothing other than the subdued sound of someone walking up and down; she was now certain the *Ang Moh* was no longer just along the corridor. It was likely that he had donned fresh clothes and returned to the communal living area. This thought was verified when she heard a distant shout, 'Damn them!' She flinched. She wanted to run, but she had neither the strength nor a means of escape. Besides, she needed to stall him for as long as possible.

He was still moving around - pacing backwards and forwards, it seemed. Then, she heard a different sound, a rattling noise; maybe he was checking the shutters. Thankfully she had replaced the wooden pin, closing those through which Chin Ming had escaped, once she was sure her friend was on her way to get help. The subsequent sounds were harder to decipher. Intermittently, she could recognise the *Ang Moh's* voice, but it was impossible to decipher the words. All she could hear was a confused murmuring, interspersed with the occasional loud expletive.

Wing Yee craned her neck sideways, straining harder to understand what was happening - what the man was doing and when he was likely to appear in front of her. She thought her eardrums might burst very soon with the effort of trying to work out what was taking place. There was a period of silence, then a scraping sound, as if he was moving furniture about. Surely, he didn't believe that he would find Chin Ming and herself cowering behind that heavy and ornate-looking bureau she'd seen in the corner of the room.

For a while, she could make-out nothing at all. Had he stopped looking for them? Had he left the house? All she could hear now was the pitter-pat of mice in the rafters and birdsong somewhere far away; she was almost starting to relax. Then the silence was shattered.

'That damned girl must have taken it!'

It was the unmistakable voice of the *Ang Moh*. Had a visitor arrived or was he talking to himself? The volume was lower now and she could only hear the occasional word or two, but it was sufficient for her to know from the tone that he was extremely angry and, very soon, his wrath would be propelled in her direction.

'... just coincidence ... hidden at the back ... her father ...'

It made no sense, and she could catch nothing more. There was another long silence, then she heard his heavy boots moving in her direction; he would arrive at any moment. Her throat was dry, her hands shook, and her body was rigid. She knew he would demand answers. She lay perfectly still, clenching her fists and screwing her eyelids firmly shut whilst she waited.

It was not long before the noise of his boots on bare floorboards stopped; he was right beside her; his shadow fell across her bed; she lay absolutely still.

'Where have you hidden the girl?' he bellowed at the figure below him. Wing Yee opened her eyes slowly and stared at him. All the colour had drained from her face, her throat felt parched and no matter how hard she tried, no words would come.

'The girl, where have you hidden her, you worthless woman?' he shouted even louder than before, using only English and expecting her to fully understand him.

He paced around the room. He snatched at the shutters,

prodded the bundles of clothing they had brought with them and pulled the bed apart, tossing Wing Yee onto the floor. 'I'm waiting,' he said, towering over her. His arrogance reminded her of members of the Imperial Guard in Guangzhou, when she'd seen them searching for an escaped prisoner.

Wing Yee waited in silence. She hoped all his strutting and probing would dissipate his rage, or at least take the heat out of his fury. Meanwhile, she struggled to her feet and backed herself against the wall. It was obvious that he was now intent on taking Chin Ming, raping her for the sheer satisfaction of destroying her virginity. She hated this man. This pale, pathetic creature who cared about nothing and no one, but himself. She had no idea about how far away Chin Ming might be by now, or the route she would have taken, but the longer she could distract this bully, the better. She refused to respond to any of his questions, but raised her head to look him straight in the eye.

He glowered back at her. Then he lifted one of his vulture-like hands and brought it down with force across her face. 'How dare you,' he yelled. 'You think because you come from a high-class courtesan house, because Boon Peng was foolish enough to take you as his concubine, that you have anything to interest to me – other than to tell me where you've hidden the girl.'

Wing Yee forced herself to stare straight at him, but still said nothing. He began to move towards her. All his life he'd had his own way and he would not have these ignorant women make a fool of him.

He took a step closer. 'She's stolen something, she's been through my papers!' he said, 'or perhaps it was both of you, madam. Have you been looking at my private correspondence?

'Not know what you mean,' Wing Yee retorted, in genuine indignation.

'Then it was the girl - did you plan this together? What did Boon Peng tell you about me, what have you heard?

'I not know you until two day ago,' she said, 'still not know your name.'

'Well, your evil little friend knows. She has stolen something - a very important letter. You're nothing but scheming, ignorant women and you will regret trying to make a fool of me! I'm not going to ask again, tell me now, where is she hiding?'

'But you search house already? I hear you. If you not find, then maybe she use magic powers!'

He stared at Wing Yee. She remained impassive to those dark eyes boring into her face. No doubt, he was thinking how insolent she was, but she was determined to be strong; to hold out for as long as possible. She knew he had no idea how many hours it had been since Chin Ming escaped, but he would be aware of the amount of time he'd spent sleeping. Rather than attributing his exhaustion to pure greed and selfishness, he would no doubt get round to blaming her for his drowsiness

'The two of you had had long enough together to search through my belongings and try to escape. But why has your friend left you behind, maybe she is still hiding?'

He didn't wait for a response. He hurried back to the living room and began to pace around again, this time rattling each of the shutters, but none of them appeared to be loose - Wing Yee forced herself to follow him and wondered what he would do next. She stood perfectly still and waited.

She watched him check the lock on the door, it too was still firmly fastened. She saw him touch the key, held in place by a piece of string around his neck. She'd seen it earlier, of course, but hadn't realised then that it might have provided a route to freedom.

'Which means,' he said, glaring in Wing Yee's direction, 'that somehow, your cunning little friend must have managed to get out through one of the windows and you shut it again once she was outside.'

He examined each one in turn. Finally, he came across the

one which had a faulty pin. He swung round towards Wing Yee with a face as black as thunder. As he approached her, he raised his hand again with the obvious intention of hitting her, but before the full force of his anger and frustration landed, she tossed her head back and spat straight at him.

He gasped and his fingers went straight to the spittle running down his cheek. He swore at her. 'Damn you, bitch,' he yelled, 'you will be sorry you did that.' His vanity and arrogance couldn't bear being humiliated, especially by a woman, and a Chinese woman, at that. 'You will regret defying me, madam,' he continued, 'just as you will regret your part in helping the girl get away. She is a common thief, and you are nothing but a whore! She may have managed to get out of my house, but I assure you she won't have gone very far, we are completely surrounded by the river and the jungle. When I bring her back, I will make both of you pay for trying to make a fool out of me!'

He grabbed Wing Yee by her shoulder and forced her onto a chair. She had no strength left to resist any of his actions, but mentally she was pleased that she had been able to stall him, even for a short while. She remained determined not to give in to this brute of a man. As he took her arms and twisted them behind her body, she couldn't help wondering what it was that Chin Ming had taken. The girl must have been searching through his papers while she and the *Ang Moh* had been occupied in the bedroom, while he was raping her. Chin Ming had said nothing in the brief time they'd had before she'd been persuaded to leave, but she wondered why. Then, she remembered that she'd led Chin Ming to believe that they would both be leaving. Probably, she'd intended to tell her about whatever it was that she'd found, once they were on their way.

Wing Yee winced as he tightened the ropes around her wrists; she pressed her lips together and ground her teeth, determined not give him any hint of her pain. He tightened the rope again and lashed it to the back of the chair. He looked around for some more rope to tie her feet in the same way, but there was nothing to hand, and in the end, he realised she was too weak to get very far. He needed to leave, to follow the track through the jungle in order to find the girl, and his missing letter.

'It won't take me long to find her,' he announced as he turned the key to open the padlock. 'I know these paths and tracks like the back of my hand.' He glared at Wing Yee, adding, 'Then we'll see what you have to say for yourself, madam. Maybe you would like to watch?' A shaft of yellow light filled the room, revealing his steel-grey eyes and menacing grin. 'Yes, you can watch as I slowly undress her ...' He laughed, as he slammed the door behind him and fixed the padlock to the outside.

Moments later, she heard a horse whinnying, followed by the sound of hooves gathering speed; then the noise gradually dissolved into nothingness. Chin Ming had several hours start on him, but would it be enough? Specks of dust danced about in the sunshine; she hoped it was a good sign.

CHAPTER 22

Following the discussion with Farquhar early in January, Raffles made it his business to talk to as many of the merchants as possible. Ostensibly, he asked them questions about the Town Plan and their preferred locations across the river, but then he slipped in another question, relating either to prostitution or to gambling. He made sure that he was never seen to criticise, hoping that he would learn more about the people who frequented these establishments. He knew there was no point in questioning Farquhar any further. The Resident always became defensive and there had already been too many arguments. The way he always averted his eyes, shifted his weight from one foot to the other, and his short temper was indication enough for Raffles to think that he'd been correct to suspect Farquhar of taking bribes.

One or two of the Chinese merchants told Baba Tan they'd heard rumours of a boat that went out to greet any ship that new into harbour. Others talked about two beautiful women, occasionally seen on a bumboat in the harbour, but no one had any details and it all sounded like a game of smoke and mirrors.

Raffles arranged for some sepoys to search the town's brothels and, when nothing unusual was found there, they went out to the gambier plantation. The trek there was long and arduous, but the report Raffles received after the expedition lacked any substance.

Reluctantly, towards the end of the month, he decided to interrogate Farquhar again. The Resident was very sheepish about people who flaunted the law, but he continued to remain loyal to his own circle of friends.

'I've told you before,' he told Raffles, 'I had no choice. During those first couple of years, there was no substantial funding available from Calcutta. It was you who insisted on establishing a free port, but then you went back to Bencoolen and left me to get on wi'it - where was I supposed to get the money to run the settlement, eh? The Company was too worried about upsetting the Dutch; they refuse to acknowledge our success, even now. The only option I had was to sell licenses for the activities that would keep everyone happy.'

'In Bencoolen, the public expenses accrued in one month are less than you spend here in twelve,' Raffles said. 'Your excuses merely demonstrate your inability to stand firm against corruption and your readiness to turn a blind eye to the establishment of brothels, gambling dens and the use of slaves,' he continued.

'But ...'

'But nothing. The first thing I did in Bencoolen was to get rid of these evils. I intend to do the same here, but I need your co-operation. Tell me everything you know about the towkay called Boon Peng.'

The blood drained from Farquhar's face; he felt like an animal that had been stalked for days and was now finally trapped. He was searching for small pieces of information that would satisfy Raffles without giving away too much information away about the people from whom he'd accepted bribes.

'He's the Chinaman I told you about when we'd been here merely twelve months. He's the one who said, even then, that he'd be happy to give five hundred thousand dollars in exchange for the revenue of Singapore five years hence. To me, that shows he saw a future in the place, so when he wanted to invest in property, I saw no reason not to agree.'

'So, which establishments does he own - and who are his business partners?'

'He has a few properties along the quay, some investments

in the gambier plantation and, I believe, he still has property in Malacca. He left his wife there when he moved to Singapore.'

'Is that where he has gone to now?' Raffles asked.

Farquhar was puzzled. How did Raffles know that Boon Peng hadn't been seen for a while - and what did he want with him anyway?

'I haven't seen him for a day or two, but I've had no reason to. I wouldn't think he would visit Malacca until the spring festival and that's still a few weeks away. Why do you ask?'

'I have some questions to put to him. I want to ask him about the business arrangement he has with the man called Sidney Percy.'

'Oh,' Farquhar laughed, 'young Percy is a bit of a hothead. I know you and he got off to a bad start, but he's harmless enough.'

'What makes you say that; how much do you know about him?'

'He knew Boon Peng in Malacca,' Farquhar said, ' - they came here at roughly the same time. Before that Percy was in China I believe. The man can speak Dutch, I thought he would be useful to have around, if ever the Hollanders did try to invade Singapore.'

'I suppose it was men like Boon Peng and Percy who convinced you not to drain the land on the west side of the river?' Raffles said, looking Farquhar straight in the eye. 'You complain about the shortage of funds, but if that land had been drained and made available from the start, when the population was small, it would have saved both time and money. During the last few weeks, labour costs have been increasing every day. You've visited the site yourself each morning, and sometimes I've been you there as many as three times in a day to supervise the work. Every single evening, I've had to send money in sacks to pay the men. All this could have been avoided if only you hadn't listened to people like Boon Peng and Percy.'

Similar conversations prevailed each time Raffles and Farquhar met, and their relationship continued to deteriorate. Farquhar dug his heels in and refused to give Raffles any information that was remotely useful, and Raffles found it impossible to confide his real concerns about the missing women to the Resident.

During all this time, Dick tried to keep himself occupied. He helped Sophia unpack more boxes and listened to her whenever she mourned the death of three of her four children. He tried to cheer her up by talking about Ella, the little girl who had been sent back to England in the charge of her nanny. Dick had loved playing with all of the children, and he was glad that the youngest was still very much alive, safe from the ravages of tropical disease.

Some days, he took his sketch pad and wandered amongst the merchants, the hawkers and the coolies, always busy along the quay. When the sale of the new plots of land began, he was there too, ready to record the frenzied scene. He still hoped that he might see something or hear some gossip that would be useful. Whenever he asked Uncle for news, he was reassured that an extensive search was being made.

*****

Towards the end of month, Dick suffered one of his really bad nightmares. It was some time since he'd undergone such an ordeal and he'd even begun to believe that his memories of childhood horrors had finally been driven away, but on this particular night all that changed. During his brief periods of slumber, he'd been tormented with images of floggings, beatings, and other forms of cruelty. He had no idea what had provoked this anguish or caused this restlessness, but he knew it was pointless to linger in bed any longer. He pulled on his clothes and stepped out onto the veranda. Each morning, since moving to this new house, he'd enjoyed walking around in the clear, fresh air that enveloped the hill at this time of day. The distinctive screech of the cicadas was no longer to be heard, but the birds that frequented the trees around the house had already begun their daily chorus.

Now, he wandered out of the house and down the track that led to the harbour. The path had been made much firmer now and it was easier to negotiate than it had been a month or two ago. He drifted along Hill Street with no particular purpose and as he rounded the corner, almost bumped straight into Raffles leaving the Company offices.

'If you've come to ask if I have any more news, I'm afraid I've nothing to tell,' Raffles said, 'but I'm continuing to work on it. I'm asking questions all the time, and I have been able to find out one or two things that may be helpful.'

Dick looked hopeful. 'I was taking a walk - just to clear my head,' he said. 'I didn't sleep very well last night ...'

Raffles looked quizzical. Dick had, of late, become quite a sound sleeper. He wondered if the nightmares had returned, and if so, what was the cause.

'Your sleeplessness and your bad dreams - have they anything to do with that girl you're still worrying about?' Raffles said. 'Does her disappearance remind you of your own abduction? I'm sorry I hadn't made the connection before now.'

Dick reassured him that there was nothing beyond his concern for the girl and her companions troubling him.

'I haven't got to the bottom of the mystery, but you know I will keep trying to find her. In fact, I'm determined to know what happened to all of the women you saw that day. Colonel Farquhar maintains that because I gave no specific instructions regarding slavery, it was reasonable for him to turn a blind eye. He insists that it was a legitimate way to raise money for the colony. All this bluster is to cover his own back, but he still won't give his cronies away. So, I have to tread carefully around some of the people who are most likely to know something - those who have money invested in the brothels and gambling dens.'

Raffles put his arm around Dick's shoulders in order to reassure him. 'How about we take a walk along the beach together? I could benefit from some exercise and there ought to be a cooling breeze coming off the sea at this time in the morning. It will blow away the cobwebs in both our heads.'

Dick smiled, glad to have Uncle to himself, if only for a short while.

The two of them walked in silence at first. They left behind the busy sampans and tongkangs that conveyed the noisy local crews about the harbour and glanced, for a moment only, at the ships anchored offshore. The sandy beach that stretched before them was already beginning to sparkle with hints of gold, as their feet sank into its softness.

'That day, when you saw the women arriving in the bumboat,' Raffles began, 'did you see anyone else around?'

'We met some fishermen on the beach, but they'd gone by the time we saw the women. When Abdullah and I reached the quay, only a few coolies unloading cargo further along the wharf remained, no one else.'

Together, Dick and Raffles went over every piece of information they'd been able to gather, including the conversation Dick had overheard when he'd wandered off from Baba Tan's godown.

'It's a pity you didn't hear all of that conversation,' Raffles said, 'Baba Tan is convinced that one of the voices you heard that day was a Chinese towkay called Boon Peng. It seems very likely, and it fits in with everything else Baba Tan has told me about the man's business dealings. I'm still not absolutely sure about the other man's identity - but I have I have a very good idea. I just need some actual evidence before I can make a move,' he continued.

'Can't you find some reason to question the towkay?' Dick

asked. 'He might give you the name of the European is if he thinks it will help to get him out of trouble.'

'That, I'm very keen to do,' said Raffles, 'and I've been trying to track him down for the last two weeks. The day before yesterday, Baba Tan's tailor recognised the towkay's servant - you know, the man you told me about, who came to collect the garments. The tailor followed the servant to a house near the river. It turned out to be quite close to the site of that house we demolished. As soon as Baba Tan came to tell me the news, we went to visit the house together.'

'But you didn't find anyone?'

'It was completely empty and when I asked about the towkay, no one had the slightest idea where he might be. I spoke to several of the merchants in the vicinity, but none of them had seen him for a while. The man seems to have disappeared and no one has any idea where he's gone.'

The more they went over the small snippets of information they had at their disposal, the more hopeless it seemed. Dick felt completely drained. After he'd first shared his concerns with Uncle on Christmas day, he'd begun to feel a little easier in his mind. Initially, he'd been sure that Uncle would be able to sort it all out, but it was obviously now proving to be a major problem, even for him. Maybe Abdullah had been right, after all - such goings-on happen here all the time; he was beginning to believe that he would never get to know what had become of the girl and her companions.

By the time Dick and Raffles had finished their conversation, they had gone beyond the place reserved for the building of the European town, past the Sultan's palace, past Kampong Glam and had almost reached the entrance to the Rochor river.

'I think we should sit down for a while, before we begin the journey back. We've come quite a distance,' Raffles said. 'I'm sorry we haven't yet solved the puzzle, Dick, but believe me, I haven't given up hope. I'm not willing to go along with the notion that such things are peculiar to Singapore, people don't just disappear. I intend to find out who is at the bottom of all of this - and hopefully, we can put a stop to it.'

It was so good to hear Uncle speaking like this, so full of enthusiasm, so reassuring in his attitude. His smile was infectious too and Dick, although weary, felt better already. He should never have doubted him.

'I think your sleepless night is beginning to take its toll,' Raffles said, 'you look exhausted. Let's see if we can find some shade to rest in for a while.'

They made their way to the top of the beach, where a line of coconuts fringed the sand. What looked at first like a dark shadow was, as they got nearer, more like something that had drifted in on the tide. Something that had been thrown overboard from a passing ship, perhaps.

They approached the pile of rags cautiously. As they got close, they could see a leg protruding from the clothing. It was caked in mud and covered in scratches, which had been bleeding. Mosquitos had already begun to enjoy a feast.

Raffles bent down beside the body. He could see a gentle rising and falling movement, indicating that the body inside the dishevelled clothing was still alive. He didn't want to frighten the youth but thought it unsafe to leave whoever was lying there alone; he could already feel the increasing warmth of the sun on his own back. Very, very gently he began to turn the body over.

Chin Ming remained semi-conscious, but, as Raffles turned her onto her back, her hair fell out of the knot she'd tied it into. They both drew a deep breath as they realised the solitary body was that of a young woman.

Dick couldn't believe his eyes. His hands flew to cover his mouth before he whispered, 'That's her ... that's the girl I saw on the bumboat.'

Raffles raised his head and scrutinised Dick's face. 'Are you sure?'

'I'm absolutely sure,' Dick replied.

'Then we'd better get her away from here as quickly as possible,' Raffles said. 'I've no idea how she got here, but from the state she's in, it looks as if she was running away. Someone is bound to come looking for her and this spot is far too isolated to start an argument.' With that, he gently scooped her up and hoisted her over his shoulder. 'Quickly,' he said to Dick, 'we must move as fast as we can. Keep within the cover of these trees; their shade will protect us from the sun - and we won't be so easily seen.

CHAPTER 23

They had gone hardly any distance at all before Raffles began to struggle. Despite the fact that Chin Ming was very light, he had to put her down and rest for a short while before continuing. The uneven terrain and the increasing heat put additional pressure on him. Occasionally, she made a muffled noise, and he was worried that, if she regained full consciousness before he could get her to safety, she might struggle to get away. He stopped, just for a moment to catch his breath. 'Dick - I want you - can you run ahead?'

Dick nodded. 'What do you want me to do, Uncle? Where do you want me to go?

Raffles struggled for breath, but just managed to say, 'See, where those nets are drying - on the sand? That's, that's the Temenggong's kampong. Find him, ask him to send someone to help ...'

Dick needed no further instruction. He sped off along the shoreline, his bare feet kicking up a cloud of sparkling golden dust in his wake. He raced down to the water's edge, where the sand had been dampened by the tide; it was much firmer than the softer substance at the top of the beach. He ran as fast as he could towards the fishing nets. Sweat gathered on his forehead and cascaded down his face as he gathered speed and he gasped at the salty air as it rushed past him. At one point, he nearly stumbled, having failed to see an old tree trunk that was almost buried into the sand. He leapt over it at the last minute, feeling as if he was beginning to fly. He ran, as if he was being pursued by a great tsunami.

A small group of fishermen, who had come to check that their nets, stood warily to face whoever was approaching them in such a hurry. As he got closer, they recognised Dick as the adopted son of the Tuan and waited to see why he was so agitated.

'The Tuan,' Dick puffed, 'we found a young woman, further along the beach. She's injured, can you help?'

The fishermen looked at each other, not sure how to react. Dick's Malay was perfect, but in case they hadn't understood, he repeated his plea, this time more slowly. 'The Tuan told me to find the Temenggong and ask for his help, but it would save a lot of time if you come back with me now.'

They whispered amongst themselves for a few minutes. Then, one of them took the lead and began to organise the others. He sent the youngest member of their party back to the village, to warn the Temenggong to expect visitors. Then, he pointed to the drying nets. 'We could use these to make a sort of *buaian*,' he said. The others looked perplexed at first. 'Like the swing-hammock the women put the babies in, but big enough to carry a woman,' the first speaker added. Together, they followed Dick to the place further along the beach, where Raffles was resting, cradling Chin Ming in his arms.

She moaned again as they lifted her onto the improvised hammock, but she was still too exhausted to be fully aware of what was happening. With two men at each end of the improvised bed, they made good progress. Raffles began to tell the other fisherman what had happened as they made their way towards the kampong. Dick followed in their wake.

When they reached the edge of the village, groups of children who had been playing in the shade between the houses accosted them. The youngsters delighted in the small cavalcade, beginning to dance all around and in front of the procession. They hurled questions at the fishermen as they did so. Dick recognised one of them as the Temenggong's grandson.

'How fast can you run?' he asked him.

'I am faster than any of the other children in the kampong,' he boasted.

'Then show me,' Dick said. 'Run as fast as you can, tell your grandfather, tell him we're here. Tell him we need help.'

Several other Malays began to appear, but the procession continued to make their way, through the gathering crowd, towards the Temenggong's house. The headman was already being pulled down the stairs, by his grandson when Raffles and the rescue party reached him.

'My apologies for disturbing you,' Raffles said in Malay, 'but I'm afraid this young lady badly needs our help.'

'You are very welcome Tuan,' the Temenggong said, 'but may I ask why you have chosen to help this person, I'm told she is a thief.'

'What makes you say that?'

'I've had another visitor; he was looking for a young Chinese woman. He said she was his slave and that she had stolen something belonging to him, then run away.'

'Who was this man?' Raffles asked.

'Another European. He did not introduce himself and was not very polite. I thought I recognised him though. If I'm not mistaken, he was the man who was very rude when we attended the dinner party you gave last November.

'I believe the man we are both talking about is called Sidney Percy. He is not to be trusted and may even be dangerous.'

'Aya! When he couldn't find what he was looking for here, he rode away in a great hurry. I think he went straight into town, he assumed that's where she had gone. What do you want us to do, Tuan?'

The makeshift hammock rocked slightly as Chin Ming began to stir. Raffles and the Temenggong continued to talk in subdued voices, discussing how to proceed. Only Dick noticed the movement. He knelt down beside her and took her hand.

She was muttering something, but he couldn't make out anything specific. He wasn't even sure what language she was speaking.

She slowly became aware of the sound of human voices that surrounded her. The first thing she saw when she opened her eyes was a dark-skinned boy; had he been holding her hand - or had she imagined that. He looked vaguely familiar, but she couldn't remember why. He spoke softly but his words floated away and everything around her felt as if it was slowing down. She became aware of a few other people; two men and a group of women, all of whom looked like the Malay woman who had brought her food when she was locked up in the rickety house.

Raffles and the Temenggong turned immediately once they realised that the girl was awake and Dick was trying to talk to her. It was then that she realised there was a European amongst the on-lookers. She tried to scramble to her feet, searching as she did so for a means of escape. She trusted no one; she needed to run as far away from these people as possible. A sharp pain shot up her leg from one of the cuts on her feet & she began to stumble. Raffles caught her just in time, but she tried to pull away from him. She lashed out with her legs, kicking up loose earth into Dick's face as she did so.

'Hush,' said Raffles,' you are safe, we will not harm you. We only want to help.' He spoke in English, hoping that she might understand.

She glanced towards the dark-skinned youth, he had a kind face, but she still couldn't think why she felt there was something familiar about him.

Continuing in English Dick said, 'We know you're frightened.' He took hold of her hands in his. 'Please try not to worry. This is my Uncle,' he pointed towards Raffles, 'we really do want to help you.'

'Help, I need help,' said Chin Ming, also using English.

'We found you on the beach,' Raffles said, bending down

onto one knee. 'You are injured and obviously exhausted. Can you tell me what - or who - you have run away from? Can you tell me what happened?'

'I need you to help me,' Chin Ming repeated.

'That's what we all want to do,' Raffles said. 'We'll take you somewhere that is safe.'

She wanted so much to believe that these people really meant what they said, but it might be a trick. They might be working for the *Ang Moh* and now simply waited for him to collect her.

Hoping to put her at ease, Dick said, 'When you arrived in Singapore, you sat in a boat with two other women. It was me who waved to you. The friend I was with told me many women are brought here from China, but you looked unhappy, and I thought maybe you hadn't chosen to come here. We came to the wharf, but by the time we arrived everyone had disappeared. I've been trying to find you ever since.'

'You ...'

'I was on the beach - with my friend Abdullah. We'd been watching all the cargo being unloaded and then we saw the last boat coming ashore. The women beside you stared ahead, as if in a daze, but you kept looking all along the shoreline; as if searching for something. That's when I waved.'

'Need help quickly,' Chin Ming said, yet again.

'Yes, we want to help you. We found you on the beach,' Raffles repeated, 'so we carried you here, with the help of some fishermen. I assumed you had escaped from something that had frightened you, or harmed you in some way. I thought I ought to get you away from danger you as quickly as possible.'

'No, need to get help,' she implored.

Dick and Raffles looked at each other, both still puzzled by what the girl kept repeating. They kept trying to reassure her, saying over and over again that they would help, but she didn't seem to understand. Raffles tried a few words of Malay, but she ignored him. Dick decided to try one or two of the limited Cantonese words he's picked up from some of the merchants he'd met along the quay. He wasn't sure that he had the intonation correct, but thought he'd try anyway.

'Help,' he said as clearly as he could manage. 'We ...' He moved his hand towards Raffles and then touched his own shoulder. 'We - help you,' he said, now pointing his hand towards her.

She still looked worried but nodded briefly before continuing in English. She had to take a risk now and believe that these men really did want to help. That they had nothing to do with the *Ang Moh* she had run away from. 'It's not me who needs help. My friend - she is in danger - locked in a house. The Englishman, he will hurt her.'

'Where is your friend?' Raffles asked. 'Where did you come from, can you give us directions so that we can find the house you speak of?'

Before Chin Ming could answer, Dick cut in with, 'Do you know the name of the Englishman?'

'He never told us his name, but I think I might have found it out, I'm not sure,' she sighed. 'He took us to his house by sampan two - maybe three - days ago, when it was dark. We started out from the harbour.'

'Where have you been living since you arrived in Singapore?' Raffles said. 'I know it was not in the - um - the house run by a woman called Madam Ho. I had that placed searched only two weeks ago.'

Chin Ming winced when she heard the name of the woman she dreaded - the woman who had treated her so badly. 'We have been in a house owned by Towkay Boon Peng,' she said, 'but, something happened; the towkay is dead. The Englishman came. He was angry because he said Boon Peng owed him money. Then, he said he would take us away - he said he would look after us, but he lied, he is a bad person.'

'Do you remember anything you saw, anything you

recollect about your boat ride?

'It was dark, but I saw lamps burning in a village on the outskirts of the town. We turned into the mouth of a river. I'm not sure how far it is from there to the house. When I got away, I was trying to follow the river. I thought if I could get back to the beach, I might be able to find the village. I tried to run along the riverbank, but it was overgrown. There was mud everywhere and I kept slipping. The house is locked. I got out through one of the shutters, it wasn't fastened properly. My friend couldn't leave, he has hurt her badly. I promised I'd find help.'

'Does the Englishman have a gun?' Raffles asked.

'I don't know, sir, do you think ...' her voice drifted into nothingness and she turned very pale.

The Temenggong, who had been standing quietly, listening to everything that had been said, stepped forward. 'Why don't you send the boy to get help Tuan?'

'An excellent idea,' Raffles said. 'Dick, I want to you run to the Company office as fast as you possibly can. Find Alexander Johnston - tell him that I need Lieutenant Jackson to come here with some sepoys straight away.'

'But can't I stay here Uncle? They might not take any notice of me.'

'Dick, I need you to do this. Tell them that I have sent you and they are to make haste. I need to stay here just in case the Englishman returns. He will not dare to take this young lady away if I am here to stop him.'

Dick knew Uncle was right. He listened carefully and memorised the messages he had been charged with. The girl looked imploringly at Dick. 'Please go quickly,' she said. 'My friend is in great danger; we will both be so thankful,, please run.'

'Tell Lieutenant Jackson that he should bring the sepoys here and then we will discuss how best to find the house. Mr. Johnston needs to come too; as magistrate, he will need to issue a formal arrest.'

Dick needed no more persuasion. He moved quickly away from the Temenggong's house and once he'd left the kampong behind, he gathered speed and headed back towards the town.

There was an awkward silence for the first moments after Dick's departure. The crowd had drifted away, but Raffles noticed the girl looking across at him. She was a little less wary now. One of the women brought her a bowl of soup and she took it gratefully. While she was eating, Raffles said, 'You must excuse me, young lady, we have not been properly introduced, my name is Stamford Raffles, I am the Governor of this small settlement.'

Chin Ming almost dropped her bowl. Some of the liquid spilled onto the floor, attracting a brigade of hungry ants within seconds. She looked up slowly and searched his face before speaking.

'Then you are the reason I came to Singapore, sir.' She looked him straight in the eye. 'My name is Chin Ming; I am the daughter of Li Soong Heng.'

'Forgive me, Chin Ming, but I do not recognise that name.'

'My father was a *Shenshi*. He was responsible for encouraging education and fostering Confucianism in our province. We moved from Shaoguan to Guangzhou six years ago, after my mother died. Papa and I went everywhere together. He was keen for me to learn too; it did not matter that I was not a son. I can speak several languages. Papa was also interested in your Christianity. He got to know the missionaries at the English factory very well.'

'This is all very interesting, but I still don't see what it has to do with Singapore,' Raffles said.

'Papa thought some of the other *Shenshi* in Guangzhou had become - what is the word - it means dishonest, I think. He had evidence that they had accepted bribes from foreigners. Papa discovered something about one particular *Ang Moh* which vexed him a great deal. The man was originally from

Java, but when he came to live in Guangzhou, he got involved in the opium trade. The emperor is trying to make the sale of opium illegal, and Papa reported what he found out to the authorities. The *Ang Moh* left China in a hurry and Papa discovered that he'd settled in Singapore. He wrote it all down in a letter that was addressed to you, Tuan. He gave it to me to take care of the day he disappeared.'

'And where is the letter now?' Raffles asked, his curiosity aroused.

'It was written on a scroll that I sewed into my shift, but I lost the few things I brought with me when I was moved to the towkay's house - the house I shared with Wing Yee. Wing Yee is the friend I need you to help.'

Raffles' mind was racing. He couldn't quite take in everything the girl was telling him, but as soon as she mentioned Towkay Boon Peng, he began to put two and two together. He wanted to know anything she could recall about either of the houses in which she and her friend Wing Yee had been held. So far, he'd had little to go on other than snippets of information gleaned from Farquhar and the rumours passed on to him by Baba Tan. Now he was convinced that the Englishman the girl referred to was indeed Sidney Percy. His behaviour at the dinner party had been appalling and everything he'd heard about him since that evening gave him reason to be suspicious. It seemed now that those suspicions might well be justified.

'And when the Englishman came to the towkays' house, you're sure he never told you his name?'

'No. When Boon Peng collapsed, Wing Yee and I searched his clothing and found some keys. We managed to get into the warehouse, but that too was locked. It was while I was searching for the right key that we heard someone banging on the outside, demanding to be let in. He did not tell us his name,' Chin Ming said. 'But I think he might be the man referred to in this letter.' She put her hand into the pocket of her shift and drew out the sheet of paper she'd taken from the bureau at Sidney Percy's house; she handed it to Raffles.

He took the letter from her and read it through. It was incredible, he couldn't believe his eyes. Two phrases stood out - *the matter has been dealt with* and *Soong Heng will not be coming to Singapore to expose you.'*

Raffles imagined Chin Ming most probably hadn't understood the full extent of the message and what it implied. He couldn't confront her with all that now, he needed to concentrate on finding Sidney Percy and arrange for both women to be taken to somewhere that was safe.

'I always thought the man was a scoundrel,' he said, 'but this is far worse than any of my suspicions. He is a very bad person and quite obviously no respecter of the law.'

'You will help Wing Yee, won't you,' Chin Ming implored. 'He has already hurt her and I'm sure she will be blamed for letting me escape. He will punish her even more. I only left her because she insisted; she wanted me to find someone to help us.'

'You can be sure we will do our very best,' Raffles said, 'Lieutenant Jackson will be here soon - then we'll head out towards the Rochor river to search for the house. I want to find your friend before this man - I think his name is Sidney Percy - returns. When he fails to find you in the town, he has two choices. He will either come back here to question the Temenggong, or he'll ride straight back to his house. My guess is that he will return to the house to demand that your friend tells him exactly how you got away. It is vital, therefore, that we reach the house before he does.' Raffles tried to smile, hoping that it would reassure her.

'In the meantime, I will ask the Temenggong to look after you. He speaks English - and I'll ask Dick to stay with you too, so you need not worry. I will come back to collect you as soon as Wing Yee is safe. I will then take you both to my house to meet my wife. She will be glad to have some female company.'

CHAPTER 24

After the *Ang Moh* had slammed the door shut, Wing Yee flinched. The slightest movement compounded the tension of the rope around her wrists. It rubbed against her bones and cut into her flesh. The hardness of the chair made sitting most uncomfortable, but the more severe pain was caused by her mental state. She believed there was now no chance of her being seen as anything but a common prostitute; there was no escape from her past and no hope for the future. She found herself praying again - the same prayer she had uttered earlier to the Lord Buddha - asking for the protection of Chin Ming and strength enough to hold on until help arrived.

Whether it was the realisation that she would be alone for several hours or the effect of sheer exhaustion she didn't know, but a strange feeling of light-headedness and numbness began to consume her whole being. She tried desperately hard to focus, to keep alert and to listen intently, but the stress of the last couple of days was overwhelming and she began to hallucinate.

*****

An image of Boon Peng stood in front of her. His head was larger than she remembered and he kept pointing his long, manicured fingers towards her face.

'Make more money,' he kept repeating. 'Many ship come from China. You and girl go visit ships. Sailor like pretty girls. Make more money, make more money!'

Then, a very clear image of Captain Lim appeared. It was

back in Guangzhou; it was the summer before last, long before she'd ever thought of coming here.

'You are as delightful as always, Wing Yee,' he said. 'I think you grow more beautiful every time I return here.'

'I'm glad I continue to please you. It is good that you do not tire of me,' a ghostly image of herself replied, 'even after five summers.'

A multitude of apparitions, from the life she had led in Guangzhou, swirled through her mind like the rapid movement of the multi-coloured ribbons used by the court dancers. Faces of men who had become her regular clients over the years - those who, on the whole, had treated her well - moved in and out of focus. Hot on their heels, faces of women loomed into her mind - those already well-established with their regular clients when she arrived.

'When you bring tea, you do not look at my gentlemen,' a woman from her nightmare shouted, taunting her. 'They choose me; want me, not you. Do not look.' The apparition, who wore shabby clothes and was rather overweight reared up in front of Wing Yee. It was just as she remembered them during her first months at the brothel, always bullying the younger ones.

*****

She was now totally enveloped in a kaleidoscope of faces and a multitude of memories, all dancing around inside her head. As one image from her past life faded, another came into focus. Total exhaustion finally took over and there was a brief period, when she actually slept, but this was brought to an abrupt halt when she became aware of a loud and constant commotion.

Her mind was spinning again, then the sensation changed. The noise in her head slowed down and transformed into an unidentifiable and continuous clamour. She had the notion that all the men and women she'd ever encountered now hammered on the walls of the house.

*****

Raffles, Lieutenant Jackson and the sepoys found the house quickly. Jackson knew that some of his men occasionally frequented the gambling dens and he'd managed to glean valuable information from one of them in return for a promise that the man would not be reprimanded. The sepoy in question had been present when Sidney Percy, having been lucky at cards and made careless by a surfeit of liquor, had boasted about his secret hide-away. The sepoy remembered the key elements of the story and had been able to lead the small group to their target easily enough.

They dismounted from their horses and led them into the shade at the back of the house, so that they would be hidden from sight and not troubled by the noonday sun. One of the sepoys was sent to survey the scene and ascertain whether or not the house was occupied. He reported that there was no indication of life; that the door and all the shutters were firmly closed and there was no sign of a horse tethered nearby.

'We know that he went into town on horseback,' Raffles said. 'If his horse is not here, then neither is Percy, but we need to act quickly.'

'I suggest we break down the shutters at the back of the house,' Lieutenant Jackson said. 'It will be less obvious when he does return; we don't want him to turn on his heel and get away.' Everyone agreed that this was a sensible plan.

They posted two sepoys at the front of the house, to keep watch. The others stayed with Raffles, Jackson and Alexander Johnston at the rear. They found another door, but it was obviously bolted from the inside. Jackson banged his fists on the door; he shouted out and beat loudly on the shutters with a wooden baton, but there was no reply.

'If she's still alive, she will be terrified,' Raffles said. 'Maybe she will respond if I call her by name?' The others nodded.

'Wing Yee - are you in there?' They all stood, listening carefully for some sort of response. 'Your friend, Chin Ming,' Raffles continued, 'she asked us to come and find you. Can you let us know if you are in there, Wing Yee?'

Again, there was silence. Chin Ming had told Raffles that her friend was able to understand English, so he repeated the question. After a while, a faint voice could be heard saying, 'I am here ... cannot move ... tied to chair. Chin Ming, is she safe?'

'Your friend is fine. Don't worry about her now. We need to get you out of there, quickly. We are going to break down the shutters. It will be noisy, but try not to worry.'

Raffles nodded to Jackson and together with the sepoys they began to prise apart the planks of wood that covered the rear windows. Once a gap was exposed, they lifted the bar that fixed the shutters from within easily enough. To make a larger opening, they prised out a few more planks and then, one of the smaller sepoys was pushed through the window, quickly followed by Raffles. He called out, to reassure Wing Yee that all was well. It took a few seconds for their eyes to adjust to the dim light, but by the time they reached her they had become accustomed to the gloom inside the house. Raffles tried not to show his shock when he saw the bruises that covered her face and arms. He began to untie the rope that bound her hands together. He moved swiftly whilst trying not to hurt her, but the rope was tight, and her hands had become numb.

Each circle of the cord left behind a deep welt in her wrists that looked, at first glance, like a series of bright red bracelets. She rubbed first one hand, then the other, but even that small movement was difficult after being forced to stay in one position for several hours. She hunched her tight and aching shoulders up to her ears, then tried to rotate them behind and down in order to ease the stiffness that consumed her.

'Can you stand?' Raffles asked. As she started to struggle to her feet, he noticed that her nose had been bleeding, her lower lip was torn, and another large bruise had painted itself all down the left-hand side of her face. 'Let me help you,' he said.

He scooped her up and moved quickly to the gash they had created in the rear wall.

'Johnston,' he called out, 'take this young lady. Make her comfortable while we decide how to get her away.' Wing Yee was gently handed from one man to the other, through the shattered wall of the house, out onto the open veranda.

'Surely, Percy will return the same way that he left,' Johnston said. 'How are we going to avoid him on the track that leads back to town? What we really need is a boat of some sort, then we could get away via the river.'

Wing Yee struggled to be put down. She coughed and spluttered at first, but then managed to say, 'He tell me he has small boat; he mock me, say not think of leaving - this just before he tie my hands.'

'Are you sure, where was it?' Raffles asked.

'He not say, but not see when arrive here; maybe on far side river.'

One of the sepoys was dispatched to search for the vessel. It was an age before he returned and in the meantime Jackson, Raffles and Johnston discussed whether to leave immediately or wait for Percy's return.

'We need to get her away now,' Raffles said. 'If there isn't a boat, then we should at least move her from the house and hide in the undergrowth. I will stay to confront Sidney Percy, but I don't want him to know, in advance, that we're here.'

'Tuan, I found the boat,' shouted the sepoy who'd been dispatched to scout the area. He ran up to the group, puffing a little. 'It's where the - er - lady said it was. There's a narrow path, it leads to a sort of jetty, very overgrown. The boat, it's small; but it looks waterproof; there's only room for three, maybe four, people at the most.'

'That's perfect,' said Raffles. 'Johnston, I want you to look after Wing Yee. Take the boat and get her back to the kampong. She can stay with Chin Ming and Dick until we've sorted everything out here. One of the sepoys is with them, so you should be safe enough and you can take another sepoy with you. The others will remain here whilst Jackson and I wait for Percy to return. Go now; take care but go swiftly.'

Raffles listened to the sound of the oars pulling the small craft away downriver. He prayed that they would be well away from here by the time Percy returned.

'Take up a position at the front of the house,' he said to the sepoy who had discovered the boat. 'You remain here, at the rear,' he said to the other. 'As soon as one of you hears the sound of a horse approaching you are to bang on the wall and then get yourself well out of sight.'

'Come, Jackson,' he said, 'we must be ready to confront this scoundrel. Position yourself just inside the main door, but don't do anything until I say so. Now we've got Wing Yee safely away, there's something I want to look for before Percy returns. Both men hurried back inside the house. Raffles quickly cast his eyes around the room that had formed Wing Yee's prison. He spotted what he was looking for almost immediately and strode over to the mahogany dresser. 'This must be where Chin Ming found the letter she gave to me,' he said. He looked across at Jackson, who was poised beside the door, and listened. The only noise that penetrated the thick silence was the occasional creak of the house stretching its timbers in the heat of the sun. 'There will be other documents hidden there, I'm sure of it 'he said.' I'll need everything I can find to convict him.' He took a step towards the bureau, but before he could open any of the drawers, he heard the hammering sound of wood on wood, indicating that the return of Sidney Percy was imminent.

Raffles nodded to Jackson, who remained beside the door. Then, he strode towards the chair vacated by Wing Yee. He lowered himself onto it, with his back to the door. He sat, with his arms lowered, his fingered entwined and waited.

*****

Almost immediately, Sidney Percy's horse was heard approaching the house. The pounding noise of hooves increased as it got closer, then ceased when it came to an abrupt halt. The animal had been galloped hard and his sleek, black body was drenched in sweat. Sidney Percy leapt from the horse, loosely tied the reigns around the balustrade and strode up the steps to the veranda. His arrogance was such that it didn't occur to him to check for anything amiss. When he reached the porch, he noticed patches of mud on the floor, but thought nothing of it. Boys from the nearby kampong frequently called by, trying to sell him some of their vegetables or fish.

He fumbled with the key, eventually managing to undo the padlock and flung the door wide open. A shaft of strong sunlight flooded the room, but then his body blocked it out again as he stood just inside the doorway. 'Where's the girl?'' he yelled into the gloom. 'I've been to the kampong, I've searched Boon Peng's house, I've even been to see Madam Ho - no one has seen her. Tell me now where she's gone, or you will surely wish you'd never been born!'

Raffles swung round on the chair 'And which girl might that be?' he said as calmly as he could muster.

It took Sidney Percy a few seconds to comprehend that the woman he'd left tied to the chair had transformed into the man he loathed more than anyone else in the settlement. He lurched forward. 'Damn it,' he yelled, 'what right have you to enter my home uninvited?'

Raffles stood up and faced Percy. 'As representative of British law and order in this settlement, I have every right,' he said.

'Oh yes, just like the rights you assumed when you landed in Java all those years ago,' Sidney Percy scoffed.

Raffles ignored this comment. 'You seem to take pleasure in flouting the law wherever you go,' he said. 'I'm informed that you escaped from China in a hurry, and I know you have held women in this house against their will. Slavery is no longer tolerated in Britain, thank God, and it will not be condoned in a British settlement.'

Sidney Percy's eyes had now adjusted to the low light within the house. He glanced around the room, searching for any signs of the Chinese woman he'd left tied to the chair. Then, he looked Raffles straight in the eye. 'And where are these women I'm supposed to have held captive?' he said.

'Don't be a fool,' Raffles replied. 'Both the women you brought here from Boon Peng's house are now safe and being cared for. When they are well enough, I'm sure they will gladly tell me exactly what you've been up to here. I know all about your gambling habits and liking for alcohol. I've suspected, for some time, that you are involved in illegal trade and very soon I will have sufficient evidence to have you evicted from the colony.'

At this point, Lieutenant Jackson moved sideways and quietly closed the door. The sepoys remained on guard outside. 'Sidney Percy,' Raffles began, 'I am taking you into custody for the crimes I believe you have committed. You will be interrogated, first by myself and then by the magistrates. Unless you can prove us wrong, you will be held here until the next East Indiaman arrives; the ship will take you back to Calcutta, where you will face a full trial.'

'You can't do that!' said Percy, glaring at Raffles defiantly.

'I assure you that I can, and indeed I have every intention of doing so,' said Raffles.

'You may be able to flaunt your authority over the British merchants - and even the local businessmen who are stupid enough to take any notice - but you have no authority over me. You see, SIR Stamford, I am not British!'

For a fleeting moment, Raffles was taken aback. He hadn't expected Percy to co-operate, but neither had he expected this blatant defiance.

'British or not - and you have certainly led people to believe so - you have behaved in a way that is totally unacceptable and you will be punished accordingly.'

Before Raffles had finished his sentence, Sidney Percy had begun to move back towards the door. He quickened his step, thinking that he could escape easily enough, but Lieutenant Jackson had anticipated this move and was already blocking his path. He grabbed Percy's wrists and forced them behind his back. Raffles picked up the rope that had been used to restrain Wing Yee. 'It's time to give you a taste of your own medicine,' he said.

It was agreed that Jackson and the two sepoys would accompany Sidney Percy to the barracks, where he would be locked up, ready for Raffles to interrogate later. One of the sepoys fetched the horses from their hiding place and led them to join the others at the front of the house. Sidney Percy was helped to mount his own steed and the long procession back into town began. Raffles rode at the head of the cavalcade and Jackson at the rear; a sepoy guarded Percy on each side. The party took the track that led them straight to the barracks, ignoring the path that went to the kampong. Sidney Percy was escorted to the rough wooden shack that was used for confining soldiers who misbehaved. Having remained quiet through the whole journey, he now began to shout and scream obscenities, but no one took any notice. He was told that he must stay here to await questioning. There was no other place in the settlement to imprison anyone.

'I need to return to the Temenggong,' Raffles whispered in Jackson's ear. Out loud, he said, 'I will return tomorrow morning, when Percy, or whatever he chooses to call himself, has had time to consider his actions.'

Jackson nodded. 'I will make sure that he is under constant guard. Rest assured, Sir Stamford, there is no way that he can get away from here,' he said.

*****

It took Johnston well over an hour to guide the small craft out along the Rochor river and through the surf towards the Temenggong's kampong. When he recognised the familiar sight of the coconut palms that fringed the village, he steered the boat towards the shore. Johnston leapt out, followed by the sepoy and together they dragged it up onto the sand. They looked around to make sure it was safe, then the soldier held the boat fast while Johnston lifted Wing Yee out. She tried to walk, but she faltered after only a couple of steps.

'We shouldn't waste any time,' he said. 'Let me help.'

With that, he lifted Wing Yee's fragile body and carried her as if she was a precious cargo of Ming porcelain. His long legs strode purposefully to edge of the village and the sepoy followed in his wake. The children, whom Dick had met earlier in the day, had gone for their afternoon rest, so the rescue party moved swiftly along the paths unhindered.

*****

The group was spotted first by the sepoy who had stayed to take care of Dick and Chin Ming. All three of them sat in the shade on the Temenggong's veranda; Dick and Chin Ming in deep conversation. The sepoy put his hand over his eyes to see more clearly. He was anxious to make sure that the people approaching the village did not include Sidney Percy. Dick noticed this movement and leapt to his feet.

'I think they've found your friend,' he said.

Chin Ming looked towards the group making its way in

their direction and clapped her hands in sheer delight. Before anyone could stop her, and forgetting her own injuries, she ran down the steps and straight across the compound. Dick was close on her heels.

'Thank you, thank you,' Chin Ming said. She was so overjoyed to see Wing Yee again that all she could do was keep repeating the same two words. She longed to throw her arms around her friend, but she looked so fragile - so tired and pale - that she felt unable to touch her. She was just grateful to be together again and to be alive, that was all that mattered now.

CHAPTER 25

The first thing that Raffles did when he reached the kampong was to check that everyone was safe. Chin Ming appeared remarkably cheerful and was busy chatting to Dick. Wing Yee, however, was not looking at all well. He sent a messenger to James Hagley, the doctor who had recently arrived in Singapore, to come and examine her. Then, he sent a note to Lieutenant Jackson reminding him to ensure that Sidney Percy was well-guarded throughout the night and not allowed any visitors. He hoped that by leaving the man alone for several hours, he might begin to reflect on his conduct and regret some of his actions. He would then be easier to deal with.

The doctor told Raffles that Wing Yee would need careful nursing but, in time, her physical wounds would heal, and she would survive. The medic also examined Chin Ming's cuts and bruises but was satisfied that the attention she'd received from the women in the kampong was perfectly acceptable. He did, however, suggest complete rest for both of them for the next day or two. Alexander Johnston offered to fetch his carriage, so that both women could complete their journey to Raffles' home in reasonable comfort. His suggestion was gratefully accepted and sometime later, Chin Ming helped Wing Yee transfer to the luxury of the landau. Johnston leapt up to take the reins. The party conveyed their thanks to the Temenggong and said their farewells.

Dick was charged, once again, with running ahead. By taking the path, rather than the newly constructed road that wound its way slowly up the hillside, he should arrive well ahead of the main party.

'Hurry,' Raffles told him. 'Make sure you reach Sophia before the carriage arrives. 'Tell my wife that I'm sending her two young ladies, who are greatly in need of her care. I will explain everything else that has happened later.'

It took Dick longer than normal to reach the bungalow. He had eaten very little since the previous evening. He'd walked the entire length of the beach and had raced most of the way back again, to the Temenggong's village. Then, he'd run to the Company office to find Lieutenant Jackson and Mr Johnston. His energy level was now low, but he forced himself to struggle up the track that led from Hill Street to the house. He knew how important it was that the house was ready to receive its visitors.

'Uncle sent me,' he puffed, as he flopped down in front of Sophia.

'Why, whatever is the matter?' she said in surprise. 'What's happened, Dick? You look exhausted. Has someone been hurt?'

'Well yes,' said Dick, 'but no one you know. There are two women - young Chinese women, they have both been badly treated. Uncle has rescued them.'

'And he's sending them here? Do you know why?'

Before he could answer, Dick thought he heard the carriage on the track below the house. 'Uncle said to tell you that he will explain everything when he gets here,' he said. He pointed in the direction of the procession, which was already in sight. It struggled up the final slope that led to the front of the house. Sophia just had time to compose herself and by the time the carriage arrived she was ready to welcome her new guests. She walked towards the landau as it drew to a halt.

'Welcome,' she began. Then, looking at her guests more closely, she understood immediately why her husband had directed them here. 'Oh, my goodness,' she said,' who did this to you?'

Dick helped Chin Ming out of the carriage and then Johnston carried Wing Yee the short distance to the veranda. Sophia fetched more cushions for the rattan chair she'd just vacated, positioning them to give maximum comfort. Johnston lowered Wing Yee very carefully onto the enveloping softness. There was no sign of Raffles.

*****

Having entrusted the care of Wing Yee and Chin Ming entirely to his friend Alexander Johnston, Raffles made haste to return straight back to Sidney Percy's house. He enlisted the help of one of the sepoys to systematically search the whole building. He made it his business to give particular attention to the bureau, but after a thorough examination it was clear that only one of the drawers contained any paperwork. He emptied its entire contents and packed it into a small crate.

Most of the material looked mundane; receipts and odd notes from people whom Percy might have known either here in Singapore, or in Malacca. Raffles was fairly sure anything that might further incriminate the man had been destroyed long ago and the chance of finding anything new, which might help convict him, was fairly slim. He started to push the empty drawer back into place, but he found it difficult to return it to its original position. Maybe the wood had warped over the course of time, causing it to swell slightly. He decided to remove it completely and start again. He was careful to hold the drawer so that it was completely straight, then he tried to insert it in the bureau once again. Despite his caution, however, the drawer could not be pushed in any further. Something must be preventing it from closing.

Raffles pulled the drawer out completely, all over again. Then, he knelt on the floor in front of the bureau and looked inside the cavity. There was nothing to be seen. He began to feel around the sides of the empty space; he ran his fingers along the smooth wooden runners at each side and then along the rougher wood at the back of the void. Something flitted across his fingers, tickling them as it did so. He removed his hand quickly, only to find a small spider, curled up in a state of shock between his thumb and index finger. He placed the creature on a nearby table and returned his hand to the cavity. This time, his hand brushed against something soft; it was well-lodged into a crevice right at the back. He tugged at it gently and released it from its place of refuge. What emerged was a small velvet pouch with several small sheets of paper inside. The writing was hard to decipher in the fading light. Raffles stuffed the pouch inside his ample coat pocket and then rose to his feet.

With the help of the sepoy, he made the house secure again, boarding up the damaged wall at the rear. Then, he fitted a new padlock to the door at the front. Only when Raffles was completely satisfied, did they make the return trip to town. The sepoy escorted him to the top of Bukit Larangan before returning to the barracks.

*****

Sophia gave instructions for a room to be made ready for Chin Ming and Wing Yee. In the meantime, cook brought them some tea and light refreshments, but the steaming liquid was too much for Wing Yee to manage, despite her thirst. Chin Ming poured hot tea from one cup to another until it was cool enough for her to offer to her friend. Even then, she had to hold the cup in a lopsided fashion in order avoid the swollen side of Wing Yee's mouth.

Raffles arrived to find them all in deep conversation. Dick was the first to notice his arrival and leapt up to greet him.

'I'm glad you are all getting along together so well,' Raffles said. 'I'll join you very shortly, but first I need to have a word with Dick.'

The youth excused himself, leaving the women to continue their conversation.

'That scroll you found near to the rickety house, the one you showed me, do you still have it or is it with Baba Tan?' Raffles asked.

'Yes, Uncle. It's hidden in my room. Baba Tan hasn't been able to find anyone to translate it for us.'

'Can you get it for me? We need to show it to Chin Ming. If, as you suspect, it does belong to her, then she may be able to tell us what it says.'

'I'll get it straight away.' Dick said.

Raffles re-joined the women, and they all spent the evening together. A light meal was served, but Wing Yee struggled to eat; the cut resulting from Sidney Percy's temper was still tender and she winced whenever anything touched her lips. Sophia suggested that she should rest, in the hope that she would feel better in the morning. She helped Wing Yee to her bed and Chin Ming made ready to follow along behind.

'Before you retire, Chin Ming' Raffles said, 'there's something that I'd like you to look at.' He gave her the scroll that Dick had handed to him only a short while beforehand.

As she took it from him, her hands began to tremble. She loosened the familiar gold thread and unrolled it slowly. 'Where did you find this?' she asked. 'I brought it with me from Guangzhou, but I lost it. I thought I'd never see it again.'

'Dick found the scroll amongst some clothing that had been tossed aside down beside the quay,' Raffles said, 'I don't mean to upset you.'

'It came from a place that was being demolished after a bad storm,' Dick added, 'but there was no one living there, and I had no way of finding out who owned it. I showed it to a friend of mine, to find out what it said, but we've not been able to find anyone who could translate it.'

'Dick showed it to me a few weeks ago,' Raffles continued,

'but we've not found anyone to tell us what it says. One of the reasons that I've been concerned is because it has my name written within the rest of the calligraphy. Do you mind telling me how you came by the document, and more importantly, can you decipher it for us?'

'It was written by my father,' Chin Ming replied. 'He handed it to me for safekeeping the last time I saw him - alive - on the morning we went to the docks - the day that we got separated.'

Raffles felt uncomfortable. The girl was obviously distressed, but he needed to know why the document contained his name, written in large capital letters.

'It was almost a year ago,' Chin Ming began, 'we went to the harbour - in Guangzhou - to see the parade; to see the Lion Dance. At least, that's what Papa told me.'

'What happened?'

'Papa said that he had arranged to meet someone, a man who was able to arrange a passage for us to travel to Singapore. The people who had gathered to see the Lion Dance suddenly became agitated; others arrived and began to push and shove. Papa looked worried; he reached into his pocket and gave the scroll to me. It all happened so quickly. The last thing I remember before I lost sight of him was his voice telling me to get the letter to a man in Singapore. The name of that man was Raffles - your name sir,' she said looking straight at him.

'When I lost sight of Papa, I stared into the crowd, searching for him, but he was nowhere to be seen. I lost my footing, got swept along in a sea of bodies and - I'm not sure what happened afterwards. The next thing I knew, I woke up in a bed at the Mission - Father John told me I'd been left on their doorstep.'

'Do you know why your Papa was planning to leave Guangzhou?'

'He told me he'd upset some of the other *Shenshi*; he'd

criticised their behaviour and ...'

Raffles nodded, allowing her to take time to explain.

Chin Ming began to examine the scroll. 'It's not really a letter,' she said, 'it's more like a report, but it's definitely addressed to you sir.' She glanced at it again. 'It's similar to what I said earlier, but Papa says the man who was helped to escape was a Dutchman. Papa says he heard good things about you and that's why he decided to come to Singapore. He wanted to warn you about the Dutchman.'

Raffles felt wretched for the girl, but he was confused. What had her father's interest in a Dutchman got to do with what she'd said earlier about the Englishman; was he also involved with the corrupt members of the *Shenshi?* Why did her father want to contact me, what did he want to warn me about, and what is the connection with Singapore?

Raffles mind raced. It was obvious that Chin Ming loved her missing father a great deal, but I can't help her with that right now, he thought. I'm intrigued by her reference to the Dutchman though; could there possibly be a link with the man I've had locked away? Was that the reason that he made such a fuss about not being British.

'Does your father say anything else Chin Ming?'

She studied the scroll. The simple act of handling something that Papa had touched, had written, had handed to her, made her heart miss a beat. She spent several minutes reading the words he had drafted, considering carefully how she would express his sentiments in English.

'There is something else about a Dutchman,' she said. 'His name is Pieter Steffens. He arrived in China from Java - after the British took over. Papa says the man visited Guangzhou frequently, but he thinks he lived elsewhere - maybe Whampoa, or even Macao. He came to Guangzhou several times each year and always brought great quantities of opium.'

She looked up to add a comment of her own, 'That is against the law, but there is a lot of smuggling.' She returned to the letter and some moments later added, 'Papa says he reported Mr Steffens to the authorities, but before anything could be done, he discovered that the Dutchman had already left China.'

'And does your papa say where this man called Pieter Steffens went to?' Raffles said.

Chin Ming looked at the document again. 'He says he heard many rumours - some said the Dutchman boarded a vessel bound for Malacca, others said that he went to South Africa. Papa says he found further evidence that confirmed some of the other *Shenshi* - those who had become involved with the opium trade - helped Mr Steffens get away in a hurry. He says these men became angry when they discovered what Papa had done and for the last three years have made life difficult for him.'

Her shoulders drooped and her voice changed to a monotone as she looked at Raffles and added, 'He didn't tell me any of this; but it's obvious now - he had become much more cautious about being on the street after dark and had stopped attending some of his usual meetings. He often talked to Father John in hushed tones. Maybe it was someone at the Mission who told him about your reputation -and that's why he decided we should start a new life in Singapore.'

Raffles put his hands together and considered this information. It was all beginning to fit into place, but there was nothing concrete enough to make a direct connection between the man called Pieter Steffens and the person he knew as Sidney Percy.

Chin Ming looked up and said, 'There is more. Papa says he received a letter from a friend in Malacca telling him about a mysterious man who had spent some time there. It was rumoured that the man arrived from Macao, and at first everyone thought he was Dutch because of the way he dressed. He was very secretive, and no one was able to find out anything about him, apart from his name. That's when they discovered he wasn't Dutch, after all; he had an English name.'

Raffles sat bolt upright and waited for Chin Ming to continue.

'It says that he didn't stay long in Malacca, but while he was there, he formed an alliance with a Chinese merchant. They moved to Singapore around the same time. Papa's friend sent a description of this mystery man, asking if Papa remembered him. Papa says the description resembled that of the person he knew, but he was puzzled because his friend in Malacca told him that the man's name was Sidney Percy.'

All the colour drained from her face. 'That's the man who came looking for Boon Peng; the man who has harmed Wing Yee!'

Raffles was now sure he had enough information to get the man taken for trial in Calcutta. He must find a way of getting Percy - or Steffens - to admit to his real name. He wanted to ask lots more questions, but the girl was exhausted and clearly shocked by the information she had just revealed. There was already enough information for the time being; he must insist that she get some rest.

'Thank you,' he said. 'Everything you have told me is extremely helpful, but you are very tired. I think you should rest; go to bed now, you've had quite a day. There will lots of time for us to talk again tomorrow.'

Chin Ming smiled gratefully. She was almost too tired to get to her feet and walk the short distance to the room she would share with Wing Yee. Sophia, who had quietly returned after settling Wing Yee for the night, took her arm, picked up a candle and guided her along the veranda.

*****

Raffles looked across at Dick. 'Time for you to retire too, I think,' he said.

'What about you?' he replied.

'Oh, I think I'll just spend a little time examining the papers that I collected from Sidney Percy's house,' he said.

'Then let me help,' Dick said. 'I'm not at all tired now and I want to know more about the man who has caused all the trouble.' Raffles thought the young man sounded very grown up all of a sudden. It was all too easy to forget that he was no longer the shy and frightened boy he'd rescued six years ago; he would soon be a man. He also had to admit that if hadn't been for Dick's tenacity then they might never have caught up with the so-called Sidney Percy. He too needed to find out all he could about the man, before he began the interrogation tomorrow. He looked across at Dick and smiled. 'I'd be glad of your company,' he said.

Together, they spent the next two hours painstakingly searching through every scrap of paper Raffles had collected from Percy's house. The bulk of the material consisted of notes from Boon Peng, containing nothing of any consequence. They were both beginning to tire when Raffles remembered the pouch. He put his hand into the pocket of his coat and handed the small package to Dick.

'I found that at the back of the bureau just before I left the house,' he said. 'I couldn't examine it properly because the light was beginning to dim, but it's always possible that it might contain something of interest.'

Dick carefully loosened the drawstring and pulled out two scraps of paper. He looked at them briefly before handing them straight to Raffles, who read first one, then the other. Then, he looked at them again, studying the content more carefully. Dick waited for what felt like an eternity before hearing Raffles' response.

'Yes!' he said, looking relieved, 'this is exactly the sort of evidence we need. The larger note specifically refers to young women coming from China at the beginning of November, and it states quite clearly the price Boon Peng asked Sidney Percy to pay for one of them.'

'What if he says they never arrived, or that he never went ahead with the purchase and Boon Peng kept all the women for himself?' Dick asked. 'Chin Ming and Wing Yee told us they'd been living in Boon Peng's house.'

'He might well say that Dick, but this smaller scrap is, in fact, a receipt. It simply reads, *'Copy. Received from Mr Sidney Percy the sum of Fifty Silver Dollars for one Chinese female.* It's dated 3rd November 1822.' He paused briefly to beam at Dick. 'And look,' he added, 'right next to the date is the red mark of a *Chinese chop*. I'm sure this particular seal can easily be identified as the one belonging to Towkay Boon Peng.'

'Excellent,' Raffles continued. 'This is probably Percy's own handwriting. I doubt whether Boon Peng's use of English was so sophisticated. It will be easy enough to obtain a sample of Percy's scrawl. The important point is, this piece of paper has Boon Peng's stamp on it - it confirms the fact that the transaction took place. This, together with the information Chin Ming has already given us is more than enough to convict the man of wrong-doing.'

Dick's initial grin gradually developed into an enormous yawn. 'Sorry, Uncle,' he said.

'Not at all,' Raffles replied, 'I think it's time we both turned in. We need to be fresh in the morning when we question him. We still have no proof that Sidney Percy is, in fact, the same person as Pieter Steffens. The very fact that he used the same initials - only in reverse, makes me think that it is extremely likely. It would be typical of a man as arrogant as our detainee. Let's put all these papers together now, then I'll take them into my room for safekeeping.'

They bade each other goodnight, neither of them quite believing that all the searching for the missing women was, at last, over.

CHAPTER 26

The following morning, Raffles asked Dick to accompany him to the barracks. He said it would be useful to have the interview captured with a few of Dick's sketches, but more importantly, he believed the young man deserved to be present during the interrogation. They walked in silence, both consumed with their own thoughts. Lieutenant Jackson had set aside a small room for the purpose, well away from the comings and goings of the sepoy lines. Raffles settled himself at the table and Dick sat quietly in the corner near the window. A few minutes later, the man they knew as Sidney Percy was escorted into the room and shown to the chair across the table from Raffles. Lieutenant Jackson said he would remain immediately outside the door. Percy sat, with his arms folded, glaring straight ahead; his tightly clenched fists revealing whitened knuckles.

'So, what am I to call you?' Raffles began.

'What do you mean?'

'You say you are not British, so presumably Sidney Percy is not your real name. Tell me WHO you really are and how you came to be in Singapore.'

*****

The Dutchman had not expected this. He'd assumed that the guard would leave him in an empty room and that his interrogator would enter later, demanding answers about the women. He hadn't imagined Raffles would be there already, awaiting his arrival. He'd spent the entire night trying to work out how much Raffles knew about him. In the end, he decided the authorities could not possibly have much to go on other than the complaints made by two worthless women. He might still be able to bluff his way out of this.

*****

Dick watched every move he made, every twitch of every muscle in his face. He noticed that once in a while his nostrils flared, and his pupils dilated. Dick picked up he pencil and began to sketch the outline of the square head. The short, black hair was combed forward; it was feathered all across his broad forehead and reached down to the lobes of his ears. Dick continued with the eyebrows, that arched above dark, pene-trating eyes. They turned now to look at him, but he refused to be intimidated by the man.

'I lead a nomadic life,' Percy said as he returned his focus towards Raffles. 'I consider myself to be an adventurer who goes where the mood takes me, and I no longer think of anywhere in particular as home.'

'And why is that? You must have been born somewhere. Where are your family?'

'Well sir, I've heard that your own birth took place on a ship just of the coast of Jamaica, what nationality does that make you?' Percy taunted.

'True,' Raffles replied. I was born on board a merchant ship, off Port Morant in Jamaica. My father was master of the *Ann,* but I was brought up in England.' He was just about to detail his early career in Leadenhall Street and his transfer to Penang, when he realised what the prisoner was up to. 'But this is not about me, Mr Percy, it's about you. I shall continue to address you by that name until you choose to tell me the truth. Now, once again, I am asking you to tell me, where were you born?'

*****

The evasive behaviour continued for another hour. Percy avoided giving a straight answer to anything Raffles asked. He was conceited and he was full of his own self-importance. Dick finished the full-face portrait and moved to the opposite corner, where the light was better. He could now see a dark shadow of stubble beginning to develop along Percy's top lip and around his chin; the rest of his face was remarkably pale. There was no hint of emotion and the expression on his face was full of disdain. Dick wondered how on earth Uncle was going to proceed and whether he intended to challenge Percy about the name revealed by Chin Ming's father.

*****

Raffles eventually pushed his chair back from the table. His head was beginning to throb and he knew he was getting nowhere.

At the beginning of the month, he had appointed three magistrates and together with them, a fledging constitution was being drawn up for the settlement, but it wasn't yet agreed upon. There was no system in Singapore for trying and sentencing people for crimes as grave as those Raffles believed Percy had committed. However, if he was going to ship him off to Calcutta, as he'd threatened to do, there needed to be evidence of his misdemeanours.

In the end, he decided to take a risk. During his years in Java, he'd picked up a sufficient understanding of the language spoken by the descendants of the original merchants who had settled there from Holland. He looked straight into the cold, defiant eyes of the man sitting across the table from him and addressed him in his native Dutch.

'Pieter Steffens, you have been posing as a British merchant and are therefore guilty of misrepresentation. I have reason to believe that you have paid for women to be brought from China for your pleasure; you have regarded these women as your slaves and have treated them badly. Slavery is a felony in Singapore. This, together with your other crimes, will not be tolerated in a British settlement. I shall return here tomorrow morning with the three men who have been appointed magistrates and you will be required to answer these accusations. You are entitled to have someone speak on your behalf; do you wish to name someone who might be willing to do this?'

'*Vervloekt zijt gij*, Raffles!' Pieter Steffens exploded in his mother tongue.

Raffles ignored this outburst, merely taking it as confirmation of what he already knew about the man. 'Take him away,' he said, returning to English. Then, he rose from his chair, leaving Lieutenant Jackson to deal with the Dutchman. Dick hastily gathered up his sketchpad and followed Raffles out of the room.

'I need to consult with Alexander Johnston and some of the other magistrates as quickly as possible,' Raffles said as they strode away from the barracks. 'Do you want to come with me, or would you rather be elsewhere?'

'If you don't mind,' Dick said, 'I'd like to find Baba Tan. There was no time yesterday to tell him that we'd found Chin Ming and Wing Yee. He was always suspicious about Boon Peng's business dealings with a European, but nothing could be proved. I'm sure he'll want to hear the latest news and I'd like it to be me who tells him what we've found out.'

'Yes, of course he should be told,' Raffles replied, 'but can you ask him to keep the information to himself for the time being. I think we need to discover a lot more about the Dutchman before the story is spread throughout the whole settlement.'

'I understand,' Dick said. They walked together in silence, along the track that led from the cantonment back towards town. Raffles turned into the Company office and Dick then broke into a trot as he headed in the direction of Baba Tan's warehouse. He couldn't wait to tell his friend about everything that had happened since they last met.

Raffles asked Johnston and two others, whom he'd appointed as magistrates, to join him for an urgent meeting. He chose David Napier and John Morgan, both of whom had, he knew, gained the respect of their fellow merchants. Abdullah was also included in the meeting as he would be required to take notes, during a more formal interview the following day.

The fledgling proclamation that Raffles had issued earlier in the month dealt initially with land registry and regulations about the free port. Its third component was longer and more complicated. In addition to addressing the need for magistrates and police in the settlement, it dealt with certain provisions for the administration of justice in cases of emergency.

'Excuse me, Sir Stamford,' David Napier said,' should we not be inviting Colonel Farquhar to join us?

'Unfortunately, Colonel Farquhar has had some business dealings with the man who is under suspicion,' Raffles replied. 'I fear that, if he was involved with the interrogation, he might feel compromised. Besides, a new Resident will be arriving from Calcutta very soon. In the meantime, all regulations under my signature will have the force of law as soon as they've been registered.'

Napier and Morgan looked at each other knowingly. They'd both heard rumours that Colonel Farquhar was due to be replaced and this latest piece of information simply verified the tales being circulated in the bazaar.

The five men focused their attention upon the process of dealing with criminals. They spent the entire afternoon - and some of the evening - considering the information they had to hand and the best way to proceed.

'We need to ascertain that the *chop* on that receipt is the one used by the towkay,' John Morgan said.

Raffles shocked the other four by jumping to his feet. 'The tailor!' he almost shouted. His compatriots continued to look puzzled.

'Boon Peng arranged for some garments to be made for Chin Ming and Wing Yee. The name of the tailor who did the sewing is Lim Chow; he might have some sort of paperwork that details the order and the work to be undertaken.'

'Who? What has this to do with ...?' Napier began.

'Chin Ming and Wing Yee are the two young women we rescued from Pieter Steffens' house - the man previously known as Sidney Percy. Before that, they had been in a house owned by Towkay Boon Peng. He was sending them out into the harbour whenever a new ship arrived - to attract crew members to visit the brothels.'

'Why haven't we heard about this before today?' Napier continued.

'That doesn't matter right now,' Raffles said, 'the point is - actually I've thought of someone even better than the tailor. The material used for the garments was purchased from Baba Tan. I'm sure he would have kept a record of the purchase - and hopefully, it will show the towkay's *chop*.'

Raffles scribbled a hasty note, asking whether such evidence was available. Johnston offered to hurry over to Baba Tan's warehouse whilst the others took a break. Whilst he was away, Raffles used the time to bring the other two gentlemen up to speed with everything that Chin Ming had been able to tell him.

*****

Lieutenant Jackson marched Steffens across the barracks and pushed him back into his cell. The room was tiny and airless. Steffens strode from one side to the other and back again. He beat his fists on the door, but no one took any notice. The guard, whom Jackson had left outside spoke neither English, Dutch nor any of the Chinese dialects - there was no way that he could be cajoled by the prisoner's powers of persuasion.

Steffen's eyes protruded from a face that was already a deep shade of red. His nostrils flared and he started to grind his teeth. He was furious with himself for falling into Raffles' trap; how on earth had the wretched man discovered his real name? It was true that the note the girl had stolen would not help his case, but it made no reference to his Dutch origins. He was positive that he'd destroyed anything that referred to his early life in Java. He continued to search his mind for any clue that would enable him to counter the accusations being made against him when Raffles and his magistrates returned the next day. After all, he hadn't actually admitted to his former identity. Yes, he'd cursed Raffles in Dutch, but anyone could pick up a basic understanding of the language - Raffles himself had obviously managed to do that.

*****

Dick and Johnston returned to the Company office together. They grinned from ear to ear as they placed a sheet of paper before Raffles. It was an order to supply fifteen *bu* of top-quality silk and thirty *bu* of less expensive, plain silk. It was issued by Baba Tan and addressed to Towkay Boon Peng; it was dated 12th November 1822. In the corner of the page was Baba Tan's signature and beside it there was a bright red mark.

Raffles pulled out the velvet pouch from the place where he had hidden it; his hands trembled as he loosened the knot and began to slacken the drawstring. He placed the receipt on the table beside the one issued by Baba Tan. It was a perfect match.

The lamps had already been lit when Raffles, Dick and the

three magistrates left the Company office. The usual hustle and bustle around the quay had quietened now and everyone was settling down to enjoy a fragrant bowl of soup or one of the many succulent dishes available from the hawker stalls. The enticing aromas filled their lungs as they shook hands, satisfied at last, that they had been able to come up with a reasonable plan and had sufficient evidence to back it up.

*****

Pieter Steffens had been offered no food for several hours now and water was no substitute for his usual intake of alcohol. As the light began to fade, so did his energy. He was still angry, but he was no further forward in coming up with a strategy to defeat the loathsome Raffles. He'd hated the man from the very moment he first heard his name. He still remembered the day the British arrived in Batavia; Raffles was appointed Lieutenant Governor, introducing his so-called liberal reforms which brought an abrupt end to the attitudes and practices that had been encouraged by the whole Steffens family for four generations. No longer able to live his parasitic life, he hadn't stayed to find out what life under the British administration would be like. Instead, he decided to seek his fortune elsewhere.

Right now, however, his wrath was aimed at Soong Heng's daughter. Who would have guessed it would be she who found the evidence that Raffles could use to incriminate him? He comforted himself with the knowledge that the only thing he'd left in that drawer was a bundle of receipts concerning his business deals with Boon Peng. There was no way that she could know he had anything to do with her father's abduction. He continued to pace about, searching for inspiration, but as it grew dark the walls closed in on him. He pulled at the neck of his shirt so that he could breathe more easily. He was no further forward in thinking of a story which might deceive the magistrates the following day. 'Damn them - Damn the lot of them!' he screamed.

CHAPTER 27
January 30th 1823

Dick was already washed and dressed when Raffles appeared the next morning. He carried a bowl of freshly prepared papaya and placed it before him, noting how tired and worn he looked. 'I've squeezed lime juice over the fruit, just the way you like,' Dick said. 'I'll ask cook to bring your coffee and eggs when you're ready.'

'That's kind of you Dick,' Raffles said, 'but I'm not sure I can face any food.'

'It's going to be a long day, and I'm sure Sophia would want you to eat. If the Dutchman continues to be obstinate, then you'll need all your strength - it might even help to prevent one of your headaches.'

Raffles couldn't help marvelling at how grown-up Dick sounded these days, almost as if they had changed roles. He picked up a spoon and slipped a slice of papaya into his mouth; its cool sweetness was refreshing, and the remainder soon disappeared. Dick sat opposite, chatting about nothing in particular, while Raffles consumed the rest of his breakfast. By the time he'd finished, he felt much more relaxed.

Dick accompanied him to the Company office, where they found the three magistrates waiting for them. The four men spent just under an hour going over the plan they'd drawn up the previous evening, before being joined by Abdullah. Then, they all walked the short distance to the barracks.

Raffles took the lead in laying the accusations before Pieter Steffens and each of the magistrates posed supplementary questions in turn. The Dutchman had chosen not to invite anyone to be with him during the proceedings. Over the course of the next few hours, they gradually extracted enough information from him to piece together a picture of his life. He reluctantly admitted to his Dutch name and origins, but would not disclose much else, until Raffles asked the question, 'What made you go to China in the first place?'

'You dare to ask me that,' he said, 'it's because of you sir, that I lost my home and my family. I was barely twenty when you and Lord Minto landed on the coast, just along from my home. You drove me away from everything that I had ever known! If anyone is to be blamed for my misdeeds, it's YOU!'

Raffles looked at the other men, unsure of how to react. Johnston now took the lead. 'Tell us what you mean,' he said.

'My family had been in Batavia since the seventeenth century,' he said. 'We mixed with Javanese princes and established a successful business. After the V.O.C collapsed, my father seized new opportunities in South Africa; he doubled his wealth.'

Raffles realised immediately what this meant. Steffens' family had gathered local people together and transported them to the new Dutch settlements. The whole family had acquired their wealth by buying and selling slaves, no wonder he had no conscience about his own behaviour. Raffles rarely lost his temper, but his patience was running thin. He banged his fist on the table. Pieter Steffens jumped, then glared at his interrogators.

'I never came across your family,' Raffles said, 'during the whole of my five years in Java - maybe they moved away. Whatever the truth is, you cannot blame me for your decision to flee, nor for the choices you made when you got to China.'

'I've no idea what you mean,' Steffens said. His voice now lacked the conviction of his earlier bravado, but it was obvious that he wouldn't freely admit to the charges Raffles had laid before him.

'Don't be an idiot, man,' Raffles said. 'I have in my possession three pieces of evidence that confirm, beyond any doubt, that the life you chose to lead during the last few years has been totally unsavoury ...'

'What do you mean, three pieces of evidence?' Steffens interrupted.

'I have here two notes, taken from your home. They prove that you paid money to Towkay Boon Peng for a woman to be brought into the settlement from China. I also have a witness, who tells me that she accompanied the said female on a junk that arrived here last November.'

'That trollop would say anything to save her own neck. Just because I paid for a woman to be brought here doesn't mean that I had anything to do with her thereafter! I certainly didn't profit from the transaction.'

Raffles placed the two notes before the magistrates for them to examine. He was beginning to feel exhausted by this Dutchman and his constant prevarication. 'My witness assures me that the woman she accompanied was handed over to the towkay and that you in turn took possession. Why would there be an acknowledgment of the money you paid if you changed your mind?'

Steffens' mind was racing. He was desperately trying to think of something that would contradict the accusations being laid before him. Boon Peng was dead so they couldn't summon him for interrogation. They may have his concubine hidden away somewhere, but at the end of the day she was just a common prostitute, her word would not count for much. 'The towkay had promised me something special,' he said. 'The money I paid certainly justified my expectations, but the transaction turned out to be unsatisfactory. I simply returned inferior goods. I have no idea what happened afterwards.'

'But you are admitting that money was handed over. You refer to this particular human being as if she was a mere commodity, just like the people your family bought and sold in Java, not to mention the people you exploited in Guangzhou.'

'I assure you, sir that I passed through Guangzhou only briefly! The Dutch factory was a boring place,' he scoffed. 'Everyone was very dour and totally lacking in imagination; they had neither a sense of humour and or a thirst for adventure. They bore no resemblance to any of the old families I had known in Batavia. It was a great disappointment.'

'I think you mean they showed no interest in the business proposition you put to them?' Raffles responded. At last, he thought his persistent probing was beginning to get somewhere. 'You set yourself up in Macao, I believe? Everyone knows that it's become a holding place for the ships bringing opium from India. The authorities in China are trying their best to curtail the trade, to prevent further spread of the addiction, but you didn't care about that, did you?'

'You, sir, can afford to have your high and mighty ideals, but the people I deal with are the scum of the earth. Most are devotees of the opium pipe, some have a gambling habit, none are capable of looking after themselves. I was simply providing them with an alternative existence.'

'And you also dealt with government officials, willing to take bribes?' Raffles continued. 'The same people who helped you escape when the going got tough. All you've ever been interested in is yourself and the money you can make. You've continued to exploit human frailty ever since you settled here in Singapore - gambling, prostitution and more slavery. Don't ask me to believe that altruism was ever a motive for your behaviour!'

'You cannot prove any of this!' Steffens shouted, banging his fist on the table and attempting to defy his interrogators yet again.

'I said earlier that I had in my possession three pieces of evidence,' Raffles said. Here is a letter, written to me by someone who knew all about your involvement with some of his own countrymen - men who had also become corrupted by greed.' Raffles placed Chin Ming's scroll before Johnston and indicated that this was the document to which he referred.

'Gentlemen', he said, 'the scroll is written in a formal Chinese script, but I have an English translation for you to examine.' He gave Chin Ming's interpretation to Napier who was sitting at the other end of the table from Johnston. 'I propose that we take a break, gentlemen,' he said, 'so that the magistrates can examine the papers that I've put before them and you Mr Steffens might want to reconsider what you have to say for yourself.'

*****

When they reconvened nearly an hour later, the bluster had gone out of the Dutchman. Raffles continued with his charges, this time focusing on those made against Steffens regarding his treatment of Wing Yee and Chin Ming. He made the occasional ribald remark about women who he so obviously despised, but after another hour or two he had become silent. Raffles had agreed with Johnston and the others, during their recess, that when the evidence had been exhausted and they had satisfied themselves that there was no point in prolonging the interview any further, a formal recommendation would be made. It was left to Alexander Johnston, as the senior magistrate to perform this duty.

'Pieter Steffens,' he said. 'On behalf of the people gathered here today, I am recommending that you be sent to Bengal for a more formal investigation of your crimes. This is in accordance with the code of law recently drawn up for this settlement. Have you anything you wish to say?'

The man in front of them glared in defiance. He tossed back his head and looked Raffles straight in the eye. 'A curse be upon you and this place,' he said. 'You think you are so superior. I tell you that the administration in Calcutta is just as corrupt as anything I've ever been involved with. Why do you think the fools in China are so hungry for opium, eh? It's because it takes their minds off the drudgery of their lives. Your precious East India Company created the market when they could no longer produce enough silver to pay for the tea they are so anxious to buy. They own the poppy farms that produce the opium in Bengal, then they process it and use it as a source of transaction in China. Send me to your precious court if you please, but they won't find it in their power to hold me for very long.'

Raffles refused to enter into any further conversation with Steffens. He summoned Lieutenant Jackson and gave the order for the prisoner to be returned to his cell. He needed to return to the Company office as soon as possible so that he could write a report and gather all the necessary paperwork. Then, he knew he would need to question both Chin Ming and Wing Yee again so that everything they had witnessed was well-recorded. Right now, he wanted to rid himself of this man as soon as possible, but there would be no ship leaving for Calcutta for another ten days. He needed to use the time wisely. If the charge against Pieter Steffens was to hold weight, the evidence must be absolutely watertight.

CHAPTER 28

Raffles spent the next few days talking to Chin Ming and, when she felt strong enough, Wing Yee. Besides being traumatised, the older woman lacked the confidence to speak in English in front of people she didn't know very well, so most of the exchange centred around Chin Ming.

In order to put her at ease, Raffles began by asking her about her early life and about her father. By the end of the first morning, she was chatting enthusiastically about her childhood and early teenage years, but he could see the pain behind her eyes whenever she mentioned the ordeal of being separated from her father and her concern about his whereabouts. Towards the end of that particular. afternoon, she was beginning to talk more openly about her journey to Singapore.

Abdullah joined them the following day, so that everything could be recorded accurately. It was just approaching lunchtime when Wing Yee emerged from the shadows. She still looked pale and fragile and she flinched as she tried to hobble towards them. Dick, who had been listening in on the conversation leapt to his feet and ran to her side.

'Why don't you lean on me?' he said, offering her his arm. She smiled gratefully and with his help, edged her way across the veranda to join the others.

'Chin Ming has been telling me all about your time on the junk,' Raffles said. 'It must have been very frightening - especially during the big storm.'

'I enjoy thunderstorms,' Wing Yee said, brightening up a little, 'I like light in sky - make me feel,' - she struggled to find the right word, then settled on, 'good.'

'Well, maybe there will be another storm soon, to help with your recovery,' Raffles laughed. 'In the meantime, do you feel up to joining us for some lunch?'

'My lip still - er - sore,' she replied, 'but much better - and quite ... hungry.' Her vocabulary had come on by leaps and bounds in the last few weeks, but she still missed out the occasional word or struggled to find the right meaning.

Wing Yee stayed with the little group after the soup bowls had been taken away. She listened intently to what Chin Ming had to say about her time in the rickety house and her eventual transfer to Boon Peng's abode. Most of what the girl said was familiar, but some of it she hadn't heard before and shivers went up and down her spine, as she was reminded of the way the girl had been treated.

Together, they told him about the arrangements within the towkay's house; the time they spent together and his daily visits. They recounted their journeys out to sea whenever a new ship arrived in the port and remembered the other storm, when Chin Ming had been so frightened. They described the day they had watched a gathering of Europeans down at the quay and their curiosity about what was happening.

'That must have been Christmas day,' said Dick. 'It's a Christian festival,' he added. A missionary, who was on his way to China, spoke to us. It was very hot and he spoke for a very long time. And that was the day that I told Uncle about seeing you on the bumboat.'

'It was Dick, you see, who first thought there was something wrong,' said Raffles. 'He told Baba Tan - one of the Peranakan merchants - what he'd seen when you arrived, and together they'd been looking for you for many weeks by the time I heard about his concerns.'

Chin Ming smiled briefly at Dick, but immediately felt awkward, just as she had done when he waved to from the shoreline. She lowered her gaze, blushing furiously.

'So, when was the first time you met the man who took you out to the house where we found you?' Raffles asked Wing Yee.

She looked at Chin Ming before answering. She was still concerned that she might be blamed for Boon Peng's death.

'If you've had enough questions for today, then we can continue tomorrow,' Raffles said, thinking that her hesitancy was a sign of fatigue.

'No, not that,' she said. 'It ...'

At this point, Chin Ming intervened. She went on to tell Raffles everything that had happened on the day of Boon Peng's death and the abrupt appearance of the *Ang Moh* when they tried to get out to find someone to help.

'Did he say why he was taking you away?' Raffles asked.

'He said better if we not in house when body moved,' Wing Yee responded. 'We say no, but he insist. He go away short time, but lock us inside and take keys. We cannot escape and - where we go? I worry about towkay, think people blame me; say I make him to die. We not like *Ang Moh*, but not know then he such bad man.'

Raffles sighed deeply. He knew that the trauma these two women had faced was not unique, but it appalled him all the same. 'Perhaps, we should all take a break,' he said. 'Talking about such upset is always exhausting, and I think we've all had enough for one day. Tomorrow is Sunday, so why don't we use that time to start thinking about your future, rather than looking backwards. I will need to talk to you further about your time in the *Ang Moh*'s house - but that can wait until Monday.'

The next day they woke up to torrential rain. Chin Ming had hoped to show Wing Yee the view of the town from the edge of the hill, but the usual brightly coloured vista had already disappeared into an uninviting misty shroud. From the veranda, there was nothing to be seen beyond the grey obscurity that had completely enveloped them. She heaved a sigh of relief; glad that there appeared to be no sign of thunder or lightning. She returned inside, to find found Wing Yee and Dick with Sophia. They spent the rest of the morning examining some of the drawings Dick had done when he'd visited the Botanical Gardens before Christmas. Wing Yee recognised many of the plants and was eager to tell the others about their medicinal qualities, but she had to ask Chin Ming to translate for her.

'Uncle sent some seeds and young nutmeg trees from Sumatra to be planted here quite a while ago,' Dick told them. 'When we returned to Singapore, he invited his friend, Nathaniel Wallich to come here to design an experimental garden. Mr Wallich is in charge of the Botanical Gardens in Calcutta, but he came for a short while and planted nutmeg, cloves, kaffir lime trees and a lot more besides. When you're feeling stronger, maybe I could take you to the gardens and you can tell me all about some of the other plants?'

'When feel better,' Wing Yee said, 'I like very much. It will be,' she paused momentarily, searching for the right words, 'something looking forward at.' Her muddled words made everyone smile, but it pleased them that she was beginning to feel more relaxed in her new surroundings.

The four of them spent the rest of day chatting idly. Raffles joined them in the late afternoon, by which time the rain had ceased. As dusk fell, the sky donned a scarlet cloak, streaked with shades of gold, before fading into a watery pink and disappearing into the night.

The following day was spent recording as much detail as Chin Ming and Wing Yee could remember from their time at Pieter Steffens house. Chin Ming's version of events was fairly straightforward, but Wing Yee found it difficult, at times, to put her ordeal into words.

She was embarrassed to talk about her life in Guangzhou, thinking that these Europeans might make harsh judgements about her and decide that she had deserved the vicious treatment she'd received from the Dutchman. It was Sophia who was the first to realise why Wing Yee might be feeling uncomfortable and suggested to her husband that she and the young woman might withdraw for a while.

After settling themselves down in the coolest part of the house, Sophia asked Wing Yee to tell her about her childhood. Slowly, and with prompts from Sophia, she recounted the time spent with her father, learning about plants and herbal cures. This, inevitably, led on to the story of her father's downfall and the unfortunate state of affairs the family then found themselves in. The language was faltering at times, but it made sufficient sense for Sophia to work out what was being said, and to empathise with the young woman sitting beside her.

'It must have been terrifying, the day your mother left you at the brothel,' Sophia said.

'At first, I am shocked. I not know about those places; my mother not warn me. Other girls arrive same day as me. Some very frightened, others not so much - accept what is happening; it their fate.'

'How long did it take you to realise what kind of establishment you'd been taken to?'

'Not long. At first, we only serve other women; those who there long time. They not like new girls - we are threat to them - they bully us very much. One girl so unhappy, she hang herself.'

'But you managed to survive?' Sophia said.

'I very lucky. Madam Sing find out I know about herbal medicine. Many times, I tell about salves and balms - help for monthly pain and headache. After little while, I help one older woman; she not so careful with men, she become pregnant.'

'So, you became invaluable to Madam Sing, I imagine?' said Sophia.

'Thing she like most,' said Wing Yee. 'when I tell about ways to mix herbs together - help keep women clean, no disease. That day, Madam Sing say she happy to find me. That when I know, must not be unhappy - about things cannot change, I decide will use what I know. But always, I look for better life.'

'And that's why you came to Singapore?'

Wing Yee went on to tell Sophia her story about the sea captain, his quest to find young girls for a client in Singapore and how she had become involved. She told her about the bargain they had struck, how - with Chin Ming's help - she'd made sure Shu Fang had overcome her opium addition. She recounted their arrival in Singapore, and her the move to Boon Peng's house.

After a little while, Sophia began to ask questions about the events that had taken place in the Dutchman's house. Wing Yee was anxious to explain that she would have done anything to protect Chin Ming, but when Sophia continued with her questions, she confessed that she had no idea he would behave towards her as he had done - like an animal. She went on to describe his barbaric behaviour when he discovered Chin Ming had escaped; how he'd threatened her, hit her and left her tied to a chair.

'I think you should go and rest now,' Sophia said. 'What I'd like to do, is re-tell your story to my husband. It can then be written down and you can read it afterwards. Is that alright?'

'I speak English only little bit,' said Wing Yee, 'cannot read.'

'Then perhaps Chin Ming can read the report to you once my husband has completed it?'

'No,' she said. 'I not want Chin Ming know things man did to me. Please - you read what written? Then, I sign.'

That evening, when all the paperwork was finally done with, Raffles and Sophia, Dick, Chin Ming and Wing Yee sat quietly on the veranda together. The efforts of the past few days had exhausted each of them, but there was a peace about the place this evening and each, in their own particular way, felt a sense of triumph. The moon was on the wane, but the sky was dotted with a trillion points of brilliant light and the cicadas began to embark upon their nightly overture.

*****

Dick woke early the following morning; he marvelled at the golden glow that hung in strands between the trees that surrounded the house. He felt as if he could tackle anything on a day like today. He put his hands over his eyes, to shield them from the bright glare, as he looked directly ahead. From this point on the edge of the hill, it dipped straight down, revealing all the comings and goings in the town below. After a moment or two, he realised that Chin Ming and Wing Yee stood nearby, admiring the panorama. He sauntered across to them.

'No rain to spoil your plans today,' he said to Chin Ming. 'The view is perfect.'

'Yes,' said Wing Yee. 'Good to wait two days before I see.'

'And how are you feeling now?' Dick asked.

'Better, thank you,' she replied. 'I not try walk downhill yet, but very soon I go. I walk little bit more every day.'

'I'm glad to hear that,' said Dick, 'because I really do want to show you the plants in the Botanical Gardens.'

'Soon,' she said, 'but today, you take Chin Ming for walk to town, can do? It long time since we do what we want, not what others say. She not wait for me, she see things and tell me.'

'I had been thinking about asking her to come with me today,' Dick replied. Then he turned towards Chin Ming and said, 'I'd like you to meet Baba Tan and I know he will be very keen to meet you.'

The girl looked flustered. For all her liberal upbringing she wasn't sure it was appropriate for her to be seen with a young man who wasn't a close family member. Wing Yee realised immediately what was going through her head.

'I'm sure you will be safe - with the son of the Tuan, he will take good care of you,' Wing Yee said, reverting back into Cantonese in order to explain the depth of what she felt. 'You told me that you used to run errands for Father John in Guangzhou, including your trips to the docks. If you came to no harm there, then a stroll down to the quay in Singapore will not be dangerous. Besides,' she added, 'the Dutchman is now safely locked up himself, you have nothing to fear.'

Chin Ming smiled, shyly. 'Thank you,' she said to Dick.

'We'll go after breakfast - before it gets too hot,' he said, 'and of course, I will tell Uncle where we're going.'

*****

They began the descent just before ten o'clock and soon fell into easy conversation with one another. Chin Ming asked him lots of questions about his own boyhood and how he came to be living with the Tuan. By the time he had told her about his liberation from servitude in Bali, they had reached Hill Street.

'It's just along here,' he said, pointing towards Monkey Bridge.

She hesitated when she reached the other side and looked nervous.

'Give me your arm while we hurry past Boon Peng's house,' Dick said as he realised why she had stopped. 'There's no one there now,' he said. 'Uncle told me that it's all been boarded up, you'll be alright.'

They hurried on together. When they reached Baba Tan's warehouse the whole place appeared deserted. Dick called out and then, out of the shadows, came a man who reminded Chin Ming of her father. His height was the same and his build very similar. The way he wore his *queue*, pulled over his left shoulder and tied with a red ribbon; the elegance and colour of his tunic; but most of all it was his smile, so warm and welcoming. She began to feel quite faint.

Baba Tan caught her just in time and eased her onto a chair. Dick rushed to her side.

'I'm so sorry, sir,' she said, 'it's just, that you remind me of someone ...'

'I apologise for startling you and causing distress,' the Peranakan merchant said. Then he did, what he always did when there was a crisis, he invited them both to take tea with him. The ritual gave everyone time to relax, and Chin Ming was able to recover from encountering someone whose appearance brought back memories of her missing father. It wasn't long before they all felt more comfortable and at ease.

Dick had brought Baba Tan up to speed with developments on the day that Pieter Steffens had been charged, and the Peranakan merchant had been delighted to offer the receipts he'd received from Boon Peng as a vital piece of evidence. He'd also asked his friend, Lim Chow, if he had any paperwork that might be helpful. Now, they talked about what had happened in the last few days and the extraordinary behaviour of the Dutchman. Baba Tan said that all his acquaintances had been shocked to learn that the man they had believed to be English was, in fact, a Dutchman. Learning about his unsavoury lifestyle, however, was less surprising and everyone was relieved to hear that he was being taken away to Calcutta.

Then, Baba Tan changed the subject. In just over a week's time, it would be Lunar New Year and he told them that both the Chinese community and the Peranakans had already embarked upon making their preparations.

'Oh, I'd forgotten,' Chin Ming said. Initially, the mention of the festival had alarmed her; it was yet another reminder of the trauma she'd experienced almost twelve months ago. When she was over the initial shock, she added, 'Wing Yee and I will need to get our hair cut. It is more important than ever this year to cut away anything old.'

She glanced at the rolls of material piled up on Baba Tan's

shelves and he realised she probably longed for a set of new clothes for the celebration too. He wondered whether she realised the material for the *pien fus* and *quipaos* given to them by Boon Peng had come from this warehouse. Dick had already told him that those garments had all been left behind in Pieter Steffens house and that neither Chin Ming nor Wing Yee had expressed any desire to be reunited with them.

To distract her, he simply said, 'I know someone who will trim your hair. I could send him up to the Tuan's bungalow. Would that be acceptable, young lady?'

'That would be wonderful,' Chin Ming replied. 'Everyone is so good to us, thank you, thank you.'

'Leave it with me,' Baba Tan said. 'I will send a note up to the house when the man I have in mind is free - but rest assured, it will be arranged in good time for the spring festival.

CHAPTER 29

After supper, Dick excused himself and went for a walk along the path that led to the spice garden. When he returned, sometime later, he could see the outline of a figure perched on the edge of a rattan chair at the far end of the veranda. It was indisputably Uncle, his body showing signs of tiredness and his face contorted with sadness. Part of him was loath to disturb the figure gazing out to sea, but this conversation needed to happen. He waited a few moments, indulging the man who had helped to shape his life, leaving him to linger a little longer with his thoughts and memories.

'Come and join me, Dick, I can see you hovering over there beside the heliconia.'

Dick padded across the rough grass that was already damp with dew and lowered himself into the nearest chair. They smiled at each other knowingly.

'Did you see the shooting star plummet over the harbour a few minutes ago?' Raffles said. 'It made the whole of the plain glow and when the light flashed across the bridge the river sparkled like shards of glass in sunlight.'

'I saw the last bit, just as it was disappearing in a pinkish blaze. I love nights like this, when the sky is inky, clear, and dense - with all those hundreds of stars shimmering. Even the cicadas stop their croaking to take it all in, but the part I like best is the smell of the frangipani. It just drifts on the warm air and engulfs the whole garden. Who wouldn't enjoy living here?'

'Well, it's certainly one of the things that I'll miss most

when we get back to England, especially during the dark and dreary winter days. What about you, Dick, what will you miss most about Singapore?'

'That's what I've come to talk to you about Uncle.' He took a deep breath before continuing. 'I've decided not to come back to England with you. I want to stay in Singapore.'

Raffles was taken aback, but he tried hard not to let his disappointment show. 'I see. Have I upset you - done something that's caused you to make this decision?'

'You've always treated me well - and since signing the adoption papers, like you own son, but now I think it's time for me to stand on my own two feet - to make my own way in the world.'

Raffles remained silent. His throat was scratchy and sore; his focus blurred.

'During the time we've spent together, you've lost three of your four children. When you get back to England, Ella will be waiting for you in Cheltenham. She was only a baby when you sent her back to England and Sophia tells me that another baby is now expected. You'll need time to get used to all that. I think you need to make room for your own children now.'

'That's quite a speech,' Raffles said trying to come to terms with Dick's news, which had come as such a shock. I hadn't realised how much I've come to rely on him in the last few months, he thought. But of course, he has his own life to lead. I mustn't be selfish. Still, I should make sure he's thought this through, that he knows how much I value him. He stood up again.

'I am longing to see my little girl again and to introduce her to a new sister or brother, but that doesn't mean there's no longer room for you in my heart. Sophia and I both see you as the son that Leopold might have been, had he lived. We've shared so many things together Dick - so much pain, but such joy as well. I've tried to include you in some of my work here - think of the way we worked together to rescue Chin Ming and Wing Yee.'

'Being with you and doing things together is incredible - but you have so many demands on your time and so many reports to write - you are always so busy.'

Raffles flopped into the nearest chair. Dick was right. He felt guilty about not paying more attention to the fact that he'd become a young man? I should have involved him more in my work, he understood that now.

'My headaches haven't helped, of course. But I'm sorry if you've felt left out. I suppose you're thinking of how long it took for you to find the right moment to tell me about Chin Ming,' Raffles said.

'I understand Uncle really, I do. It was marvellous when you asked me to make sketches of the town - it's helped me understand your proposals and see your dream for the settlement start to materialise - it's all been so exciting. But you see, it wouldn't be the same in England.'

'You'd still be part of the family and I could involve you more in my work - and there would be far fewer people demanding my time. I'm hoping to settle down on a farm somewhere in the West Country - wouldn't you like to be part of that?'

'Being with you and Sophia - and taking care of Ella and the new baby would be fine, but ...'

'But what?'

'Do you remember, when I travelled to England before - you introduced me to your friend, Mr Wilberforce?'

Raffles nodded.

'The British parliament had passed his anti-slavery bill but it didn't stop everyone assuming I was your slave.'

'I soon put them right though,' Raffles said, 'and I'd do the same again if it was necessary.'

'I know you would Uncle, but that's not the point. Mr Wilberforce's bill had been passed five years before we landed. Here in Singapore, there are many nationalities, many languages, many skin tones - no one has to explain where they're from or who they are. I fit in here.' Dick came to sit beside Raffles. He didn't want to upset him, but he needed to stand firm.

'There's no point in going back to Papua. My mother is dead and as far as I know I have no other relatives - I wouldn't fit in there either. This is where I belong, this is where I want to live.'

Raffles now looked resigned. 'What will you do out here on your own?' he asked, trying not to sound too concerned. He put his hand to his face and sat, in a characteristic stance, giving Dick time to think about it.

'What would you say if I asked Mr Johnston to give you a chance in his business? He might even offer you some accommodation - only until you get on your feet, of course.'

'I've always admired Mr Johnston,' Dick said. 'and I have considered asking if I could help him.'

'You seem to have it all worked out,' Raffles said. 'and I only want what's right for you. If you're sure that's what will make you happy, then so be it. We can sound out Johnston as soon as you like.'

'That would be helpful Uncle, I would like that,' Dick said. 'There is one more thing ...' he stood up, before continuing.

Raffles looked quizzical. He now stood too, waiting whilst Dick took another deep breath.

'Please hear me out before you say anything.' He paused, then continued, 'when you adopted me, I asked if I could call you Uncle - that is what I've always called you and it is how I will always think of you. BUT I'll be twenty next year; ready to make my own way in the world. I think it's time for a change, I would like to call you Raffles, just like everyone else does.'

For the first time, Raffles saw not a boy standing before him but a young man. Someone he was proud of, someone he loved like a son. It was time to let go; he smiled at Dick and nodded to show that he understood.

'Remember,' said Dick, grinning from ear to ear, 'with me staying here. I'll always be able to make sure that your name is never forgotten.'

*****

A few days after their excursion to Baba Tan's warehouse and Dick's talk with Raffles, Chin Ming found him sitting in their *talking place* - as it became known. It was just beyond the house and was a favourite spot with the younger members of Raffles' household, providing both privacy and a perfect vista. When they looked back in their later lives, it would hold a special affection in all of their hearts.

He was sitting there all alone, completely preoccupied as she approached.

'Is something wrong?' she asked, 'you look worried.'

Dick patted the ground beside him. 'Come and sit down,' he said. He waited until she was settled, but instead of addressing her directly, he turned his face towards the horizon. He seemed distracted. Whatever had unsettled him, it must be of major importance; it was a long time before he began to speak.

'Uncle told me a little while ago that he intends to return to England in a few months' time.'

'Will he be away long?' she asked.

Dick took a deep breath. 'He's going back for good. He says he may return for a visit in a few years' time, but his headaches are getting worse and the doctor has told him that the only thing he can recommend is to return to a cooler climate.'

This news rang alarm bells in Chin Ming's head. 'Perhaps Wing Yee could make him one of her special salves - that might help his headaches?

'It's a kind thought, but it's not just his health you see - Sophia is expecting another baby in September. Their three eldest children all died in Sumatra. Only the youngest, Ella, was saved and she was sent home to England - just six months before we came to Singapore. I think they want to protect this new baby - to make sure it has the best chance of survival.'

Chin Ming tensed, and for a brief moment held her breath. She tightened her grip on the book she was carrying. The old feeling of abandonment encompassed her, just as it had in the past. I thought I was getting better at this, she said to herself. First, I lost Mama, then Papa. I've only just begun to believe that Wing Yee is a permanent part of my life. I was hoping that Dick might become a friend too.

'So, you'll be leaving here too,' she said at last.

'No,' Dick said, shaking his head. 'England isn't for me.'

'Why not? Won't Sophia and the Tuan expect you to go with them?'

'They did,' Dick replied, 'that's what made my decision so difficult. They have both been good to me and I feel bad. Uncle and I had a long talk - he says he understands, but I suspect he hopes I will change my mind. When they arrive in England, they will have a new baby to care for. Then there's Ella; they haven't seen her for over a year and she's still very young - they will be busy with their real family.'

'You sound as if you are trying to convince yourself - and I'm sure they would still want to include you in their plans,' Chin Ming added. Secretly, she was pleased he was staying, but felt uncomfortable about saying so.

'It's not just that. I've been to England before - I didn't like it very much.

'Wing Yee - and I - would be glad if you decide to stay here, but you were just a boy then; it might be better now you're older,' she said. She hoped to offer some encouragement whilst making it clear that she and her friend would think themselves fortunate if he didn't return to England. Actually, she would be unhappy if he left.

'But that's not the point,' Dick said. He hesitated before

continuing. 'In England, everyone kept trying to touch my hair all the time, it made me feel like a freak. That has never happened here. I keep my hair cut short and most people think I'm Malay. I have my own friends here; my own dreams. I can be who I want to be.'

A smile crept slowly across Chin Ming's face. Then, all of a sudden, her mouth felt dry and her legs shaky. She turned away from him so that he wouldn't notice the tears behind her eyelids. She drew a deep breath and pointed to a ship of no particular consequence in the harbour. When she turned back towards him, her eyes lit up and she felt much relieved.

'Well, I'm delighted you've decided to stay,' she said, 'and I'm sure Wing Yee will be happy too.'

'You're not thinking of going back to China then?

'What would I do there? That man - Pieter Steffens - made me think about Papa being on board the *Tek Sing* - the junk that was shipwrecked, last February, off the coast of Cochin.

'You believe your father is still alive then - that there might have been some survivors?'

'I have to hope so, but anyway, I'm positive he is not in China. Those documents I found at the Dutchman's house imply that he and his friends knew my father. Whatever happened between them, I need to discover the truth. Until I know for certain what happened to Papa, I have no interest in leaving Singapore.'

'I'm sure Raffles will be able to help,' he said, feeling full of confidence. Dick was aware it was the first time he'd not referred to his guardian as uncle. They had a new relationship now, and it felt right.

'He won't be leaving here for a while yet and once he's seen the Dutchman on his way to Calcutta, he can begin to make some enquiries. Besides, if Steffens actually knows anything specific, then I'm sure Raffles and the magistrates will get it out of him.'

Before they could continue, the noise of a horse whinnying

caught their attention. It was followed by a series of slow crunching sounds, accompanied by clouds of dust rising from the foliage that fringed the track just below them. As far as Dick knew, neither Sophia nor Raffles was expecting a visitor today, so he was intrigued to discover what was happening.

It turned out to be Alexander Johnston's carriage, but the man himself was nowhere to be seen. As the horses came to a halt, the door of the carriage swung open and out stepped Baba Tan, followed by the man who Dick recognised as Lim Chow, the tailor.

'I've brought my friend to cut hair of young ladies,' he said, 'just as I promised. 'Is now a convenient time?'

'I didn't know ...' Dick began, but was interrupted before he could finish.

'You didn't know we planned to visit today, Master Dick. No, I'm sorry for not sending a note, but my friend Lim Chow came to see me this morning, and Mr Johnston kindly offered his transport so that we could do the hair-cutting straight away. Mr Johnston understands how important it is to do such things before the spring festival.' Baba Tan looked directly at Dick and put his index finger in front of his lips. Dick had no idea why his friend was being so secretive, but it was a harmless enough whim, so he said nothing further.

Chin Ming went to find Wing Yee. This morning, she looked much more like her old self and the thought of having her hair attended to filled her with pleasure. A stool was dragged onto the veranda and as she sat down, she indicated to the man wielding the scissors how much to cut off. As each lock of her glossy black hair fell to the ground, she breathed a sigh of relief. This symbolic act of cutting out all the bad things that had happened to her of late, liberated all her feelings of guilt and anxiety and laid down some seeds of hope. By the time the tailor had finished snipping away, she had regained some of her natural poise and looked much younger than the thirty summers she so often fretted about.

It was Chin Ming's turn next. Despite the memory of her dishevelled state in Pieter Steffens mirror, she decided to have only a small amount of hair trimmed off - just enough to satisfy the new year traditions. She told Dick later that she wanted to make it as easy as possible for Papa to recognise his daughter, should he ever come looking for her.

Both of the visitors accepted the invitation to lunch and enjoyed sharing the dishes prepared by cook - rojak, chicken rice, gado gado and other delicacies. Afterwards, Baba Tan showed them some lengths of red fabric that he'd brought along.

'I thought young ladies might like to make banners - to decorate house for the spring festival - and I thought you wouldn't mind,' he said, turning towards Sophia.

'Of course, I don't mind,' she said, 'just as long as I'm allowed to join in. You must tell me what we need to do and when we need to start? I'm looking forward to the celebration - the first in our new home.'

As they prepared to leave, Dick noticed Baba Tan having a quiet word with Sophia. He assumed a payment was being made for Lim Chow's services, but there was something furtive about their behaviour, which he couldn't quite put a finger on - maybe he was just imagining things.

Later that afternoon, the East Indiaman arrived from Calcutta. It was a magnificent craft and Dick wanted Wing Yee and Chin Ming to sit with him in their *talking place* to watch the cargo being unloaded. They both declined his invitation and walked back towards the house, where they could spend some time with Sophia and take tea. It wasn't until Dick had been watching the comings and goings in the harbour for some time that he realised his mistake - such a scene might bring back painful memories for both women. He hoped they would forgive his thoughtlessness.

*****

Alone in their room that evening, Chin Ming told Wing Yee about the conversation she'd had with Dick, prior to the arrival of Baba Tan and Lim Chow. They talked long into the night and then, the following morning, asked to speak to Raffles in private.

'Tuan, you have been very kind to us,' Chin Ming said formally, 'but we understand that you will be leaving Singapore shortly, that you will be returning to England? We know we cannot stay in this house after that time,' she added. 'We would like to stay in Singapore, but we need to find a place to live and to earn a living. Could you please give us some advice?'

'Whoa,' said Raffles, 'all this is much too fast. I presume it was Dick who told you about my plans?'

'When we sat in our *talking place*,' Chin Ming replied, 'yesterday morning.

'It is now only the beginning of February,' Raffles said, 'we won't be leaving Singapore for at least another three or four months. There is plenty of time to discuss such matters. The main thing right now is that you both get your strength back. The new Resident will be arriving next month, and he will eventually move into this house. It may surprise you, but I've already given some thought to where you might live - a place where you can feel safe.'

'We not have money,' said Wing Yee. 'Cannot pay?'

'Don't worry,' Raffles replied, 'I have an idea. From what I've learned about the two of you in the last week, I think what I have in mind will suit you very well indeed.'

The two women looked at each other, not sure of what to say or how to react. The Tuan had indeed been good to them, he had saved them from the despicable Dutchman and offered them his home, but at the back of their minds they both had the same thought. Neither of them wanted to believe that the plans the Tuan talked of had anything to do with the Madam Ho and the brothel, but what else could he have in mind?

CHAPTER 30
February 1823

Raffles looked at the two women sitting in front of him. Anyone meeting them for the first time would just see two attractive oriental women, surrounded by an air of serenity. No one would believe all that they had suffered since arriving in the settlement; thank goodness they were now well on the way to recovery.

'There is a good deal that I would like to accomplish before I leave this place,' Raffles said. 'Not everything is going to possible, but I have two burning desires that I really would like to fulfil,' he said, 'and each of you can play an important part in helping me to achieve them.'

Wing Yee and Chin Ming looked at each other, not knowing what to expect. They looked anxious, but remained silent. Then, they focused their attention on Raffles, eager to hear what he had to say.

'For a long time now,' he began, 'I've been wanting to establish an Educational Institution in Singapore, for cultivating languages and the culture of China, Siam and the Malayan Archipelago. Unfortunately, circumstances have been such that the founding of such an establishment here has been delayed, but I am now in the process of raising funds and gaining support for such a project.'

'But I don't understand, where do we come in?' Chin Ming asked.

'You, young lady, told me a great deal about your upbringing - the value your Papa placed on education. I'm aware that you speak several languages and it's obvious that you have an ability to teach. There will need to be a school for the younger children too; when they are old enough, they will be excellent candidates for the Singapore Institution, as I intend to call it. You would be perfect to work with the them - to teach them their letters, help them start to read, to write, to understand numbers ...'

'Do you really think I could do that?'

'She can,' Wing Yee said, 'Chin Ming teach me. When we leave Guangzhou, I know only few English words. Now, I understand many things - and getting better all time.'

'You see, Chin Ming, you already have an advocate. I need no further recommendation,' Raffles said.

'But not me,' Wing Yee said. 'I not teach.'

'No,' Raffles said, 'but Dick has told me all about your interest in the experimental garden.' 'He says that you know a great deal about the medicinal qualities of plants. My second ambition is that the Botanical Garden, should continue to grow.'

'Dick tell me about garden and man who plant it. But Tuan, me not gardener, cannot.' Wing Yee replied.

'Maybe not,' said Raffles, 'but when Dick takes you there, you'll see that Wallich produced an excellent design and did a great deal of planting before he returned to India. I intend to find someone who has similar knowledge and experience, and whose vison will enable him to create a garden similar to the famous one in London.'

Wing Yee began to fidget, this all sounded very ambitious and she wasn't sure where she fitted in.

'Once the experimental garden gets underway, there will be a ready supply of plants, many with medicinal qualities. You could begin with those, then think about using the herbs and spices that are brought from China and the Moluccas. I thought you might like to work as an apothecary?'

Wing Yee gasped. 'But I am woman. No one think woman

can make medicine and cure sickness. People not trust.'

'Unfortunately, that may be so. But I have another idea that would overcome such an obstacle. If you'd be prepared to work alongside someone who already has a well-established business and also has a particular interest in the health of the settlement, would you think again?'

Wing Yee nodded, but remained cautious.

'You've met Baba Tan. He is the kindliest of gentlemen. I don't expect you to make a decision based on one meeting, but he wants to help. He feels he knows a little about you through the conversations he's had with Dick and both he and his wife would like to get to know you both better. They have talked it over and have already offered to give the two of you a home, after I leave Singapore.'

'But why he do that?' She was already wondering whether this arrangement would be similar to the one she'd had with Boon Peng, but she was reluctant to ask.

'He is a very generous man and would like to help people who have not been as fortunate as himself. He is keen for you to help him set up a clinic. He couldn't start this enterprise without you; he needs your expertise. You would be solely responsible for making the medicine and he will make it available to those who need it.'

When he stopped talking, Raffles realised that he'd latterly become so absorbed in his own enthusiasm that he hadn't stopped to examine the reactions of either woman; not until now.

Wing Yee bit her lip and instantly winced because it was still sore. She glanced at Chin Ming to see if she could work out what she was thinking. The idea of being welcomed into a home and feeling safe was enticing, but she now had so little confidence in her own abilities and thought she might even struggle to remember the details of her father's medicinal remedies.

'This small school,' Chin Ming said, 'where would it be?

300

How many pupils would I have? Would I be there by myself?'

Raffles could understand their caution. The traumas both women had faced during the last six months were bound to have a lasting effect. His proposal for the fledgling school was still embryonic, no details had been finalised, but maybe that was a good thing. If she was involved in planning the project, it might help to increase her confidence and gain her commitment.

'There is a plot of land in Telok Ayer Street that would make an excellent base for a schoolroom. It is just a short walk from Baba Tan's home, so you would only have to go a short distance.'

'I would be happy to chaperone you, if that would help,' Dick said. 'I'll not be far away at Mr Johnston's.'

She smiled. Inwardly, she felt a little foolish. In Guangzhou, she'd roamed the streets without any thought of danger, she wanted to feel like that again. 'Thank you, Dick,' she said, 'that would be helpful - just until I find my way around.'

Raffles was pleased that she had not dismissed the idea out of hand and might even be considering it as a real possibility. 'Please remember, at present, these are only ideas buzzing around in my head, he said. 'I'd like to know what you think and listen to any suggestions you have to make,

'You haven't said how many children there might be and whether or not I'll be there alone.'

'Do you remember meeting Abdullah? He came here to take notes when I was asking you about the time you spent with the Dutchman.'

She nodded. 'He is your secretary?'

'He is that - and so much more. I first met Abdullah when I visited Malacca, years ago. He was still a young man. Abdullah's upbringing was very strict. His father insisted that he learned languages and many other things; as a result, he believes that everyone has a right to education. He is as keen as me to start an educational establishment here. He also

301

understands the need to start with the small children. I think the two of you should run the school as a joint enterprise.'

Chin Ming felt a strange mixture of calm and elation, all mixed up together. For the first time in months, she had something to look forward to, something worthwhile to do that would make Papa proud of her. Dare she begin to hope that her luck had changed?

She took Wing Yee's hands in her own and squeezed them reassuringly. When she let them go, she was humming to herself and dancing around in a circle. She was too excited to think straight, but her eyes shone with happy tears. An enormous grin spread right across her face, and her obvious gratitude could no longer be contained.

*****

When Monday morning dawned, Raffles left the house early. He chose to walk down the shady path that led to the town, instead of taking the carriage. At this hour, he always enjoyed filling his lungs with the renewed freshness of the foliage and the sweet scent of frangipani blossom. He'd arranged to meet the captain of the East Indiaman at the Company Office. Alexander Johnston, who would be travelling to Calcutta on business, joined them; he had agreed to be the official in charge of handing over Steffens to the authorities in Bengal. The three men spent the morning going over the paperwork and discussing the security arrangements on board the vessel.

Back at the house, Sophia and Dick managed to distract Chin Ming and Wing Yee for the entire morning with preparations for the Lunar Festival. They had acquired two red and gold paper lanterns - a present from another of the Chinese merchants - in addition to the swathes of red fabric provided by Baba Tan. Dick was given the job of climbing onto an old stool so that he could reach the wooden rafters that criss-crossed the edge of the veranda.

Sophia handed him the end of the first length of fabric and he tied it to the beam. Chin Ming and Wing Yee then gave directions about the way the fabric should be draped and where to hang the lanterns. They changed their minds several times. Poor Dick was beginning to despair when, finally, they all agreed that the everything was correctly placed. When the four of them stood back from the house to admire their handiwork, the transformation astonished them and they agreed that it was perfect.

*****

They had just finished eating lunch when a loud siren was heard in the area of the harbour. This was the signal that the East Indiaman would be leaving within the hour. They all looked at each other, knowing what this meant.

'Come,' said Dick to Chin Ming and Wing Yee, 'I think you should see this. It will be perfectly safe from this distance, but you need to know that the Dutchman has finally left Singapore.' He took each of them by the hand and guided them towards their *talking place*. Sophia stood quietly by their side.

The harbour was a hive of activity, with bumboats, sampans and other craft ploughing between the river and the larger ships anchored out in the bay. Fat sacks, stuffed with spices, and large rattan baskets carefully packed with fragile porcelain, waited to be loaded. It reminded Chin Ming of the day that she sneaked herself onto the junk back in Guangzhou - all so long ago now. They had been standing on the edge of the hillside for about ten minutes when they noticed something odd - the noise of the hawkers, the towkays and others milling around in the frenzied crowd on the quay below, faded into a mere buzz.

Out of their line of vision, a carriage had arrived. It was when they saw the sepoys marching towards the edge of the quay that they realised what was happening. The crowd parted as Pieter Steffens, with his hands tied firmly behind his back, was escorted from the carriage to awaiting bumboat. Lieutenant Jackson got in beside him, followed immediately by Alexander Johnston.

Chin Ming and Wing Yee tightened their grip on Dick's hands, as they watched the small craft edge its way along the river and out into the harbour. Dick wondered what had happened to Raffles - why he hadn't made his presence obvious for this final part of the Dutchman's story. Everyone watching the scenario from the hilltop now focused their gaze on the East Indiaman - the bumboat drew alongside and two of the soldiers hauled Steffens aboard. The four men who would take it in turn to act as his guards followed. Finally, Johnston climbed the rope ladder and took his place on the ship.

Chin Ming began to fidget and released her hand from Dick's grasp. She moved to stand closer to Wing Yee and slipped her arm around her friend's waist. Another siren from the ship focused their attention and they realised that slowly, it was beginning to move. It had already started the journey that would take Pieter Steffens to his trial in Calcutta - he was finally out of their lives.

All four of them stood completely still, not quite believing what they had witnessed. In fact, the events of the past hour had been so overwhelming that none of them had heard the sound of an approaching carriage. As the wheels came to a halt in front of the house and the horse let out a triumphant cry, they spun around to see Raffles leaping from the landau. Baba Tan remained seated on the leather-upholstered bench, grasping a large cardboard box; he looked very pleased with himself.

Dick was the first to respond. 'I looked for you at the quay,' he said to Raffles, 'we've all been watching the Indiaman depart - where have you been?'

'I handed over all the paperwork to the captain this

morning,' he said. 'Johnston has boarded, as you probably observed, so I decided to watch from the side-lines - I didn't want to give the Dutchman the opportunity to discharge another round of abuse.'

'That makes sense,' Dick said. 'But isn't this Mr Johnston's carriage? And why all the excitement?'

'It is indeed Johnston's landau. He's asked me to use it whilst he's away - but come, Baba Tan needs some help with that box he's holding.'

Raffles gestured for the women to join them on the veranda. Baba Tan, with Dick's help, negotiated the steps, keeping the box held aloft. He placed it in front of Chin Ming and Wing Yee. They looked, first at each other, then at the others.

'Open it,' Raffles said, 'it's for you.'

Chin Ming bent down and lifted out a bright red silk *pien fu*; it's cut was simple but the soft folds revealed a tiny motif cascading down one edge of the tunic. 'That one is for Wing Yee,' Baba Tan said, 'it has the sign of the Dragon woven into the fabric.'

Dick began to realise why Baba Tan had brought Lim Chow to cut the women's hair. He already had their measurements, of course, but it had provided an opportunity for him to see for himself, who would be the recipients of his handiwork and to design their garments accordingly.

Baba Tan nodded towards the box again, indicating that Chin Ming should investigate further. She lifted out another red garment, one that was embroidered throughout with fine golden thread. It caught the sunlight as she lifted it up and held it against her body.

'It's exquisite,' she said. 'I've never seen anything so lovely - see how it shimmers in the light.'

'We chose dragons for Wing Yee because of the stories she tells about dragons and we thought that particular fabric was appropriate for you,' Raffles said.

'Wing Yee told us that your name means *shining gold*,' Sophia added. 'As soon as Baba Tan lifted it down from the shelf, we decided it was exactly right for you.'

'It's beautiful,' Chin Ming said, a smile spreading slowly across her face. 'The very first thing I remember seeing when we arrived in Singapore was the glint of sunlight on the golden sand. The silk thread that held Papa's scroll together was also gold, and now I have a *pien fu* which is decorated with beautiful stands of gold. You couldn't have given me anything more perfect.'

'Something special to wear for the Spring Festival tomorrow,' Baba Tan said. 'You will both look wonderful,' he added, turning to include Wing Yee.

Sophia and Raffles clapped their hands together and Dick joined in to add his approval.

'I wish I could have given you back your father, Chin Ming. I'm truly sorry that I've so far failed to find out what happened to him,' Raffles said, 'but I will go on looking; I will do my best to find out what occurred after he was abducted by Steffens' cronies.'

'I appreciate everything you've done to help,' Chin Ming said, 'we both do. Wing Yee and I cannot thank you enough and I know you will continue to help for as long as you can. I came here wanting to find Papa; he may not have arrived here yet, but I am convinced he is still alive. I will never give up hope.'

'Tomorrow, is a new start; we begin the Year of the Goat,' Raffles said. 'Baba Tan tells me that a mythological goat assisted the God of Justice. We can but hope that it is a good omen for bringing Pieter Steffens to trial. I also understand that the Goat is a symbol of good fortune. So, let us enjoy our own good fortune and rejoice in the fact that spring brings new life and new hope for us all.'

EPILOGUE
Four months later

On 9th June 1823, Sir Stamford and Lady Raffles boarded a ship that would take them to Bencoolen, where they planned to pack up all their possessions before returning to England. So many people had wanted to say their goodbyes during those last few weeks and Dick wondered how they managed to keep smiling. Only four days ago, Mr Crawfurd, the new Resident, presented Uncle with a silver tube containing a statement signed by the leaders of all the merchant groups - Chinese, Malay and European. It extolled his virtues and acknowledged that something quite extraordinary had happened before their eyes.

Even today, they'd been accompanied to their boat in the harbour by people of all races, in a succession of bumboats and sampans. Dick was amongst them, of course, along with Abdullah. He looked up, Raffles was summoning him to come aboard; he climbed the only remaining ladder and stepped onto the deck. A lump hurt his throat as he followed his guardian to the cabin he would share with Sophia. Raffles' face was flushed and his cheeks looked damp. Dick said nothing.

'I want you to live a full and happy life,' Raffles said. 'Remember me sometimes, write to me often and enjoy every single moment.' He pulled Dick close to him in a bear-like embrace and just as suddenly let him go. He handed him a purse full of silver dollars, told him to return to the quay and not to worry.

Dick thought his heart would burst. Now the moment of

parting had finally arrived he couldn't imagine life without the man who had guided him and protected him for so long, but he knew he had to let him go. He'd told him that he wanted to stand on his own feet, and he'd meant it - the umbilical cord had to be cut.

'Maybe, one day, I will visit you in England,' he said. 'Goodbye, Raffles - and bon voyage.'

GLOSSARY

Ah Ku: a polite term of address in Cantonese for a Chinese prostitute.

Ang Moh: is a phrase used to refer to white people. It literally means "red-haired" and is used mainly in Malaysia and Singapore.
Other similar terms include *ang mo kow* [red-haired monkeys]; *ang mo kui* [red-haired devil]; *ang mo lang* [red-haired people].

Baju: a short jacket or shirt.

Bu: The weights & measures used by the Chinese businesses in Singapore were the same as those being used in China: Chi, Bu and Li. [1 chi = 0.3 metres; 1 bu = 1.6 metres; 1 li = 553 metres]

Buaian: a hammock or swing, traditionally hung at low level for keeping babies safe.

Chinese chop or seal is used in East and Southeast Asia in lieu of signatures in personal documents, office paperwork, contracts, art, or any item requiring acknowledgement or authorship. The Chinese chop is most commonly made from stone, but can also be made of ivory, or metal.

Daban: during the nineteenth century, a foreign agent was known as *supercargo* in English and as *daban* in Chinese. In Cantonese, it is pronounced *tai-pan*, but this term only came into common English use after the rise of private trading from 1834 onwards. A private captain was his own supercargo; a large East Indiamen might have five or more.

Gambier: a climbing shrub native to tropical Southeast Asia. Gambier production began as a traditional occupation in the Malay Archipelago. By the middle of the seventeenth century, it was established in Sumatra and in the western parts of Java and the Malay peninsula. It was initially used as medicine and chewed with betel nut. Local Chinese also began to use gambier to tan hides.

Lalang grass: a species grass native to tropical and subtropical Asia. It grows from 0.6 to 3 m (2 to 10feet) tall. The leaves are about 2cm wide near the base and narrows to a sharp point at the top. It can penetrate up to 1.2m (3.9ft) deep, but 0.4m (1.3ft) is typical in sandy soil.

Lily feet: feet altered by binding were called lily or lotus feet.

Munshi: A Persian word, originally used for a contractor, writer, or secretary, and later used in the Mughal Empire and British India for native language teachers, teachers of various subjects especially administrative principles, religious texts, science, and philosophy and were also secretaries and translators employed by Europeans.

Peranakan: a Malay word that means 'local-born'. The Peranakan community is unique to Southeast Asia. It has its origins in the interracial marriages that took place between immigrant Chinese men and non-Muslim women such as Bataks, Balinese and Chitty [descendants of old Hindu families] from Malacca, Penang, Trengganu, Burma and Indonesia in the sixteenth century.

Pien fu: consists of a tunic, usually silk or satin, extending to the knees. Under the tunic, women wear billowing trousers or a long skirt. The colour and the decoration are steeped in symbolism. It was traditionally worn only during formal occasions.

Qipao: evolved from a tubular-shaped garment that was originally worn by both men and women. During the Qing dynasty it had become a loosely-fitted garment and hung in an A-line. It covered most of the wearer's body, revealing only the head, hands and the tips of the toes. Most of them were made of silk, and embroidered, with thick laces trimmed at the collar, sleeves and edges.

Queue: a plait of hair, worn at the back.

Shenshi: *Shen* literally means a sash and implies the holder of a higher degree or an official; *shi* indicates a scholar] membership of which was acquired by either passing at least the lowest level of the Imperial examinations, or by purchasing an educational title. *Shenshi* were expected to perform a variety of functions. Because of their training they were prominent in the promotion of education and all matters connected with the dissemination of Confucian ideas.

Temenggong: an old Malay title of nobility, usually given to the chief of public security. The Temenggong is usually responsible for the safety of the raja or sultan, as well as overseeing law and order within his area of responsibility.

Towkay: the word is taken from the Hokkien, meaning the head of a family business. It is commonly used in Southeast Asia to refer to Chinese entrepreneurs or any successful self-employed Chinese man. In Mandarin, the word is *toujia*.

Tuan: [in Malay-speaking countries) sir or lord: a form of address used as a mark of respect.

V.O.C: [*Vereenigde Oostindische Compagnie*]: The **Dutch East India Company**, officially the **United East India Company** founded by an amalgamation of rival Dutch trading companies in the early 17th century. In 1603, the first permanent Dutch trading post in Indonesia was established in Banten, West Java, and in 1611, another was established at Jayakarta [later "Batavia" and then "Jakarta"]. The company has been criticised for its monopolistic policy, exploitation, colonialism, uses of violence, and slavery.

Vervloekt: the expletive used by the Dutchman means '*Damn you,* Raffles'. It is translated from old Dutch rather than from the modern from Wolters dictionary. The word *vervloekt* is the proper translation of 'damned'.

Xiau: a form of musical theatre that existed in ancient China, and evolved gradually over more than a thousand years, reaching its mature form in the 13th century. For centuries Chinese opera was the main form of entertainment in both urban and rural areas

ACKNOWLEDGEMENTS

This book was inspired by my love of Southeast Asia and its fascinating history. I am indebted to Jayne Woodhouse and Deborah Swift for their coaching skills, unflagging support and encouragement. I am enormously grateful to those who read the manuscript, offered constructive feedback and gave helpful suggestions, especially Sandra Horn and Tracy Burge; also, to Valerie Bird, Penny Langford, Debra Adamson and Jan Carr.

I am grateful to Nick Courtright and his team at Atmosphere Press for providing the opportunity to turn the manuscript into the novel, with special thanks to Asata Radcliffe, my Developmental Editor and Ronaldo Alves, my Graphic Designer.

My thanks to the British Library for access to the India Office Records and other archives, to the National Library of Singapore for additional material held there - especially Makeswary Periasamy, Senior Librarian and Kam Kit Geok in the Archive Reading Room. The official documents, diaries and letters were essential for my deeper understanding of the last nine months that Raffles spent in Singapore.

The bibliography for this book is too long to list, but I would particularly like to mention *An Anecdotal History of Old Times in Singapore 1819 -1867* by C. B. Buckley, *Raffles of the Eastern Isles* by C. E. Wurtzburg, *A History of Singapore 1819 - 1988* by C. M. Turnbull and *Raffles and the Golden Opportunity* by Victoria Glendinning.

This novel is a work of fiction. The protagonists and the antagonist are the product of the author's imagination and any resemblance to actual persons living or dead is entirely coincidental. The historical characters mentioned in the book form a backdrop to the story and the issues that are raised; some of their actions relate to historical records but those which connect specifically to the plot are also products of the author's imagination.

Last but not least, a special thank you goes to my husband who has travelled with me - sometimes physically and always spiritually - on my writing journey.

About Atmosphere Press

Atmosphere Press is an independent, full-service publisher for excellent books in all genres and for all audiences. Learn more about what we do at atmospherepress.com.

We encourage you to check out some of Atmosphere's latest releases, which are available at Amazon.com and via order from your local bookstore:

Here We Go Loop De Loop, a novel by William Jack Sibley

Abaddon Illusion, a novel by Lindsey Bakken

Twins Daze, a novel by Jerry Petersen

Queen of Crows, a novel by S.L. Wilton

The Jesus Nut, a novel by John Prather

The Embers of Tradition, a novel by Chukwudum Okeke

Saints and Martyrs: A Novel, by Aaron Roe

When I Am Ashes, a novel by Amber Rose

The Recoleta Stories, by Bryon Esmond Butler

Voodoo Hideaway, a novel by Vance Cariaga

Hart Street and Main, a novel by Tabitha Sprunger

The Weed Lady, a novel by Shea R. Embry

About the Author

Elisabeth Conway grew up in the Worcestershire countryside but fell in love with Southeast Asia when she went there as a student of social anthropology. She has lived and worked in the Malaysian archipelago and returns there as often as possible. Singapore has become her spiritual home.

Elisabeth has previously published non-fiction, and short stories. She has always enjoyed delving into the background of people and places. She loves to talk to Singaporeans on buses and at hawker centres, as well as undertaking considerable research in libraries and museums. Being aware that she is writing about a meeting of different cultures, she writes with sensitivity and perception.

Learn more at: elisabethconway.com

Lightning Source UK Ltd.
Milton Keynes UK
UKHW010701230721
387608UK00002B/190

9 781639 880089